PAEFALL: HONEY & IRON

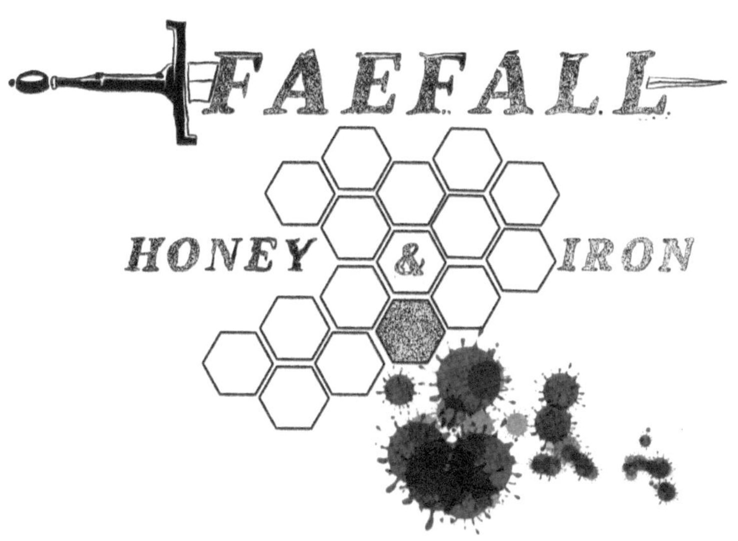

FAEFALL
HONEY & IRON

PRESTON NELSON

LAZY KNIGHTS PUBLISHING

For Michelle, You have never stopped.

…Ever.

The Grand United
Empire
of
Avalar
Gabler's Nest
Mere Pond
Squawtch on the Ice
Grey Pine
Port O' Plenty
The Wheel
Hollow Hill
Ivory Longhall
Rune River
Frostfast
Starflight Shore
Stormstrong
Korpiklaane
Deepsteal
Little Light Beacon
Jasperfell
The Dune March
Dunmarn
Brimstrongin
Black Pearl Bay
Calul Luta
Blackstone
Long Oar
Honeyvine Swamp
Harvest Hearth
Nutleigh
AVALAR
OZWYK
Bellit
Blossomvine Beach
Strixroost Hollow
Flytrap O' Blue
Ruby Beach
Leaper's Ledge
Sunset Rock
Tidefall
Perespring Deep
Three Troll Towers
Lordsport
Starling Crag
Steepvale
Skyroost
Perenstown
Old Still
Talon Isle
Daggerton
Wildcat Rest
Rogue's Rest
Honeystone
DANEAU
Beliel
Hope's Hill
Burtonfall
Savagescale Isle
The Wormwood
Brimspite
San Canair
Stonestall
Hammerdale
Codd Skine
Cobalt Bridge
Perenstone
The Witchwood
Harris's Hill
Oleheg
Candlespar Cape
Sweet Orchard
Frog Pond
Mistwatch
The Far Fort
Castle Town
Huga Clan Hall
One Dwispel
(20 miles)
Imperial Seat

ACT ONE:
PRINCES

TALOR I

"You misunderstand, control isn't vanity, Talor. It's simply what needs to be done. No matter the cost."

The silver sun broke on the black-blue waves of the Shining Strait, as the small ship sailed south. The light on the prince illuminated the dark circles and worry lines on his face; pale, but healthy. His dark hair fell in his eyes as he leaned against the railing, rocking and shushing the bundle in his arms quietly. The little girl opened her eyes, golden as a coin, burbled fussily. She burped and then quietly settled back into her father's arms. Salt spray and wind left the morning with a chill that penetrated wool like it was silk. With a slight shiver, he pulled the little girl to his chest and released a worn sigh.

The prince, still mostly a boy himself, carried the sleeping little girl across the fine wood of the deck. They came to his cabin door, where the watchful eyes of one of the Grey Guard, the big Shoreshrike knight, sat vigil. Though the prince didn't personally care for Jurgen Shoreshrike, he was grateful to have a guard with experience at sea watching over him and his. A curt exchange of nods led Crown Prince Talor Artus into the royal cabin of his personal schooner *Zeal*. Talor tiptoed, secreting the sleeping girl through the room, as a figure in bed snored softly.

The young father ever-so-slowly lowered the quiet bundle to the basket below. The creeping of the dawn light across the floor moved quicker than the Prince's steady hands leaving that baby's side. After long, long moments, he unfolded himself and stood, allowing himself a mostly silent sigh. Tension fell out of his shoulders as he slowly crept backward, the fine leather of the soles of his boot feather light on the woodgrain below. A smirk settled on his lips as he softly lowered himself on the bed, beside his sleeping wife below.

"She is finally quiet. I don't think this one cares for the rocking." His voice was low, but not so low that Kiara, his wife, could not hear.

Her long, plum-tinged tresses shifted and she moaned the very specific groan of a young mother in the dawn hours, "...It hardly counts as 'aiding me with the babe' if you wake me anyway when you're done." She lightly shoved a pillow in his direction in a feigned outrage. "You ought to be resting, pacing is poor preparation for the tourney." The lilt of her accent played musically with the vowels in her words. She turned toward him. Her emerald eyes shone from a face radiant with exotic beauty. Slim fingers traced a line over the knee of his rough wool breeches, tender and gentle.

"The tourney is the least of my worries, it's all a circus for Vernus. Mother got to speaking with that Saddler woman and it all went out of hand." He twisted a ribbon on the blanket restlessly, thumb and forefinger taking his anxiety out on the poor strip of cloth. "My brother is turning *sixteen*, I don't understand all the pomp."

"Well, if you end up across the field from *my brother*, you'll be a bit more concerned with the tourney." Her chuckle was quiet, but very earnest. She shifted amongst the bedding, resting her head in Talor's lap.

"The tourney is all a silly little dance, and the 'Debutante's Procession' doubly so." He frowned, suddenly more of a sullen teenager than a Crown Prince. She chuckled and she kissed him. She smelled like spice and grass and warm spring wind as she always did. Her lips had just a taste of mint, as they always did. She nuzzled into his stomach, her soft bronze cheek on the sky blue of his tunic.

"You're chilled." She pulled back.

"There is a cool breeze across the water this morning, Selora seemed to enjoy it on her face." He paused, "...Do you actually think your brother would *beat me?"*

She was more sheepish for a moment, before replying, "I'm sure it would be an excellent contest" in a not-entirely-unsincere tone. She sat up, turning toward the window, a leaded glass piece, depicting three eyes in golden yellow. It glowed with the light of the early dawn. "How far are we from port?"

The Prince turned to his wife, all too aware that she was choosing to change the subject, "We should arrive sometime shortly after mid-day, Father's ship should arrive a few moments before ours, and we can gather on the docks for the grand procession into the city." He sighed, clearly dreading the prospect of a 'grand procession'. "Then His Grace will take us to the castle to present the heirs..." He trailed off, eyes moving to a small trundle in the far corner of the room, blankets ruffled. The bed was used but empty, "Where is Hobar?"

Kiara nodded softly, hands pulling a soft down covering from the sleeping three-year-old boy curled around a stuffed doll of an owl. "He heard you leave with his sister, and felt left out. He declared a royal event and climbed into bed with me. Who was I to argue?"

The Prince brushed a lock of black hair from his boy's perfect ear. *This is all for him.* The boy's eyes shot open, gold as his sister's and his father's. They seemed to take up all of his tiny face as he shrieked, "DADDY!" with explosive joy. Though they had only been on *Zeal* for two days, the boy was quickly growing restless on the ship, with little to do other than stare at the sea and hassle sailors.

At her brother's yell, the infant Selora began to howl in harmony, causing their lady mother to collapse face first into the pillow with an enormous huff. Muffled by fabric and down, she mournfully commanded, "Take him somewhere or make him be quiet. I do not care which, Talor, but that baby needs to sleep."

The Prince was a brave young man, skilled at arms. He had faced raiders at Borrowhall and elven pirates at Coralspear. He had chased bandits through the Greatwood, and even taken an arrow to the calf in the process. He knew this was not a battle he would win, so he snatched up his son, summoning a calm fatherly joy, "Let's find something to break our fasts with, eh, Hobar?"

The boy squealed, "Yea! 'm hungry!" He squirmed, turning to sloppily plant a wet kiss on his mother's head, "Bye, Mama! We will bring you something!"

His mother grunted, before rising and making her way to the squalling infant. Talor rose, taking the boy and settling him to the floor. He helped the boy dress as the queen-to-be undid her bodice. As she set to feeding their daughter, the heir to the Empire took his heir down to the galley.

As they left the room, the big knight guarding the door stood to follow. The enameled white plate armor he wore squeaked.

"You'll never sneak up on anyone wearing that, Jurgen. You need an oilcan."

"I'll take it under advisement, my Prince."

"You can stay here and guard the princess and my daughter, sir. My son and I are quite capable of finding the galley of my boat ourselves."

Though Shoreshrike was less than forty, every hair on his head was white, and his eyes as grey as the frigid seas surrounding the islands of his heritage. He was a terse man, and Talor had a hard time reading him, without… *pushing,* which was something he preferred not to do with those he would rather trust. Reaching into the minds of your allies would oft times yield knowledge no man wants.

The only sound was the creak of wood and hempen rope, and those hard grey eyes were on him. "I'm sworn to protect the line. You and the boy, that's the line. I will be following."

Talor frowned, he could certainly try to force Shoreshrike to stay, but it would likely only end in verbal rebuff from his royal father. The other Grey Guard on the ship, Ser Darywn Tymm, was a much more genial, easy-going man. He was the sort whose company the prince would not have minded, but Shoreshrike was something else. "Fine, fine, but I will be allowing the young prince to question you relentlessly." He turned to the boy, "Hobar, did you know that Ser Jurgen is from a place with *snow?!*" The princeling squealed and began babbling at the huge knight, every third word unintelligible. While every burst of noise ended in a question, the little boy was too excited to wait for answers.

As the trio made their way down a set of carved stairs, winding tight, the Prince's mind wandered to what was to come. In the following days, in the high yellow walls of Honeyhome, the future of the empire would be shaped, and he intended to control what was to come. He had been exchanging letters with the Empire's young lords for years. Some heirs, some lords in their own right, but this next generation of young men would come to control the Empire of Avalar in the next decades, and without Father's influence, he would forge bonds of trust, if not friendship. He had been sending letters to six lords for years and now, for the first time, these men who would govern massive swaths of *his* kingdom would be gathered in a single place. Honeyhome would be full of lords-to-be of his kingdom.

His kingdom.

His.

He hated that.

It is not that Talor Artus resented responsibility, far from it. He was a man who took care with his children. He tended well to his lords and peasants. The young Prince had even taken the time to study both sword and sorcery to further his ability to do so. He resented the dance, the game, the masks, the politics. "Men will never say what they mean and only ask for half of what they crave" –a lesson his royal father had instilled in him early on. Talor was not only a man who said what he meant, but something in his royal blood allowed him some influence over men's hearts. It was a tempting thing, this gaze into mens' minds. But Talor feared to overuse it.

He had seen what reaching too far, too many times could do to a person, and it would not happen to him if he could help it. *But you were given this power to rule...*

He pushed a bit of a reddish sauce across his plate with a hearty crust of bread, using it to mix with a puddle of velvety yolk. His gaze miles away, he mindlessly munched as his son continued to prattle at Shoreshrike. The boy was asking now about the great black and white wolfwhale on his shield. To the shock of the Prince, Jurgen actually perked up at this, and managed to hush the boy long enough to actually speak, "We call them wolfwhales, because they hunt just like the packs of beasts in your woods." He laughed, "Great packs of them, they'll grab tuna and seals just like herds of deer, surrounding them…" He gave a sincere smile before clamping two big gloved hands down on the boy's shoulders, "and chomping them up!" Hobar made another delighted squeal. The Prince returned to his thoughts, amused.

Of the six young lords, Curr, Saddler, and Mirebreaker were all solid enough. Two of them would be in the tourney as well, and he would likely spar with at least one of them. Saddler had a brother who was widely regarded as something of a prodigy with a blade, dangerously so, but Talor liked his chances against the other two.

Ironarm of the Greatwood was another sort. Torvald, his first name, was a bookish, sickly man, almost a decade older than the other young lords. He had no children. His heir was his cousin, a knight of Clan Stagg. His participation in Talor's scheme was vital, but would need to be earned. The Greatwood was the home of the old kings and the Learners. Their support was powerful. Talor had no idea how to win Torvald Ironarm's support, but the Stagg boy might be more pliable.

The inheritance of the Western Fisher Kingdoms was even more chaotic. The High Lord, Ludo Fisher, was nearing ninety years old, and had lost his three oldest sons. Technically, his heir is his thirteen-year-old grandson, Leland. The boy was unimpressive, so Talor had been writing his older cousin, as well. There was also another son of the High Lord, an uncle to both of these boys, but he was only eight.

All three were figureheads of factions maneuvering to seize Lord Ludo's high seat upon his death, and all three boys could make a valid claim. *If the Lord is too weak to make a decision, it should fall to his liege, –name a new lord and let the old man retire.* The entire situation was a geyser waiting to burst and sink the peace of the most fractious of his father's realms.

His thoughts were of war in the west as father, son and the dour knight made their way back to his chambers. The sun had risen further, round as a silver coin in the blue sky. The salted scented wind had turned warm, and the seas calm.

The final young lord was Karas Reave, the older of his wife's two brothers. He had no doubt that his brother-by-law would consent to his plan and would even likely be his most fervent supporter once declared. However, the Prince also knew that Karas Reave loved nothing more than to watch him twist in the wind. He was unsure what dance steps he would need to make to please the High Lord of Ozwyk, but he was not looking forward to them.

His brother-by-law consumed his thoughts as Shoreshrike settled into his chair beside the door. The father and son passed the threshold to find Lady Kiara dozing in a padded chaise. Lady Kiara clutched baby Selora to her chest.

Before the distracted Prince could act, his son blasted excitedly, "We brought breakfast, Mama!" Talor didn't recall fetching anything for his wife.

"SCRAMBLES" the boy yelled, turning out his pockets. Two handfuls of scrambled eggs fell from the boy's pockets with a plop, as his less than impressed mother snapped back to consciousness.

Perhaps feeding his sister would have kept the Lord of Ozwyk happy. Shame.

VANDRE I

"If you don't get out of here right now, she's going to kill you. If she doesn't, I will. Now go. Don't you dare look back, you sonofabitch."

Walking hurt the hips. Most folk would talk about the pain in an ankle or a knee, but those would eventually toughen and fade. Distance would put pain in the hips, a deep, thorough sort of pain. He pulled his cloak tighter around him, more habit than need. Though the sun was low in the sky, the evening was warm, the Goldengrass was not a place often chilled.

He could have ridden the donkey, he reckoned. But he worried that climbing on her back would kill her. The old jenny was swollen-bellied, knock-kneed, cross-eyed and swaybacked. Its mismatched ears pointed to different directions, in a manner that didn't manage to offend every sense, but were certainly trying to. The creature only had three teeth left in its head, but that did not seem to prevent it from eating nearly anything it could fit in its mouth. The man in the cloak was reasonably sure it was blind. It was a foul-tempered, rank-smelling and it had earned the man's begrudging respect through its brainless, simple, stubborn refusal to just *die.* It was a hideous beast of burden, and it seemed to have little control where it shit, even for a donkey. The old man in the brown cloak had named her *Beauty,* and she was carrying his sword, armor and every other worldly possession.

He was called Vandre, he had passed his fifty-second year, and he had wanted a fucking horse. The pack horse he had acquired in Stonestall was a fine young thing, far too fine for a lifetime delinquent like himself. Likely why it had been lost while he'd slept in a roadside stand of cypress and willow.

The fire had been his biggest mistake. It was clear looking back, now. Too much from his wineskin and his fire had grown with his drunkenness. He had hidden most of his things high in the trees, as was his custom, but there was no hiding the handsome young gelding. Half drunk and all asleep, Vandre was snoring when four fat farmboys in kerchiefs woke him with a kick to the ribs. The biggest of the four had pressed a hayfork into his chest, not knowing that the sleeping man was in mail. Sleeping in his ringmail was uncomfortable, but this was precisely why he did it. At least, that was the way he deluded himself. *Mail was easier than companions.* Whenever he passed out without removing it, he could spew a crowd of justifications, and most of them would even bring friends. Drunk and bleary-eyed, the old sell-sword tried to focus on the boys in brown rags circled above him, but something about the way the firelight made their shadows jump made him feel sick so he focused on the hayfork instead. "...imnotstraw." He drunkenly mumbled, low and rumbling.

The fat boy leaned down, beads of sweat glinting on his great red skull, "The fuck did you say, man?" Vandre mumbled something unintelligible, his mouth more cotton than tongue. The farm boy ignored him, leaning on the fork harder. "They kill horse thieves, y'know. Where'd a poor old tosser like you get a fine lookin' animal like this?"

Vandre tightened his left hand, the other farmhands surrounded his plundered steed. They cut the horse's long lead. Vandre sighed and then used the dagger in his left hand to cut off three of the fat boy's toes. As filthy rags, flesh and bone yielded to honed, hard steel, the would-be horse thief crowed like a rooster at slaughter. The high shrill siren shriek sent chills down his spine and spooked the packhorse. Its back legs lashed out in a frenzy and caught one of the farmboys in the temple. The boy was limp and dead before his knees had finished buckling. A pool of blood rapidly grew from streams from his eyes, nose, ears and mouth, spreading dark into the soil under him.

"My foot!" The fork clattered to the dry dirt, dust rising up as more blood mingled with the thirsty silt.

Grunting, Vandre willed himself up. *Let's go, Old Man. You're old and fat and slow.* His right hand found the fork handle and with a practiced, wheeling whorl cracked it into the neck and jaw of the whimpering boy above him. *But they're fatter and slower...*

Vandre cursed under his breath as he watched the blonde mane of the young packhorse swirl off into the shadowy grass. *...and stupid.* As the horse receded into the dark, never to be seen again, murder entered the old man's heart.

The slow procession of folk trudging northward brought Vandre back to the present moment. The tourney was bringing folk of every sort to Honeyhome, and the roads had been full. Too full to *find* anything more useful than Beauty. The old farmer had been loath to part with her. Vandre's bloody scowl and a flash of his sword's hilt was enough to get the old man to part with her for less coin than even she was worth. Vandre grunted at her and jerked her lead as the cart ahead of them lurched to a stop. She stopped, blinking her eyes out of sync. Vandre called out, his voice coarse as the gravel the grand procession rumbled forward upon, "What's going on up there?" He fingered the tight roll in his pocket, eyes narrowing at the hoary-bearded dwarf in the cart in front of him.

"Delay at the city gates, the guards are searching everyone closely." His Commontongue was surprisingly good for a Jortmunn, the hirsute, broad-chested mountainfolk that occasionally made their way west to human lands in search of fortune, fame or peace. This man's fortune was a four fat oaken barrels of some foodstuff or another; a purple-red dribble slowly seeping and drying, sticky-sweet, from a seam in the barrel.

Something about the puddle of the red brine in the straw unnerved Vandre. He led the limping Beauty around the left side of the cart, so the old sellsword could come face to face with the dwarf. Two eyes sparkled gem-bright from a bushy tangle of beard and hair. Vandre assumed there was a mouth, nose and two ears somewhere in that mess as well. "What are you carrying, friend?" There was nothing in his tone to imply that he considered the solid little man a friend.

"Great big mushrooms soaked in fine dwarvish wine!" He bumbled, pride clear in his booming kettle drum voice, "I'm hopin' I put enough salt in that the Chalk-Chests let me through the gates. I fear if we have to go 'round the long way, we'll be too late for the tourney and the feast."

Chalk-Chests...

Vandre scrambled, trying to recall the roadway to Honeyhome in his memory. He had criss-crossed every kingdom in the empire in his travels, and even sailed south to Baruz, across the Trader's Strait once, but once you had seen one shining city with its tall walls and banners blowing free, you had mostly seen them all. After the decades, they all tended to blend into one, especially with the spirited application of wine, ale and spirits.

Chalk-Chests...

Every damn fort and castle and tower in the Empire kept its own sigil, a representation of the family that lorded over it and its associated lands and city surrounding it.

Chalk-Chests...

His heart sank, as the dwarf started prattling again, "Too little salt and they say it's not brine, it's still wine! And those bastards in Hope's Hill each got a stick up their arses so big you could burn that log all winter!" He laughed a rough, stony laugh. Thick but nimble fingers uncorked a wine-bladder and squeezed a thin stream of purple-red into the lower half of the beard. He snorted and chuckled once more before leaning down and offering the bladder to Vandre.

Vandre reached a leather-gloved hand up and took the bladder, firing a stream of his own into his mouth. He turned to see the shaggy beast attached to the cart unload its own bladder in a heavy stream of steaming urine. Covered in coarse grey hair, and the size of a horse, the great dwarvish goats were foul-tempered things, and intensely loyal to their owner. Vandre looked at the great curving horns of the goat, each longer than his arm and thicker than his wrist all the way through. Even if he'd wanted to take the beast, it would be more like to gore him to death than carry his bags. He took a second, longer draw of the wine, as the old dwarf eyed his swordbelt cautiously.

"Careful with that, you *grostub* don't like our wine so well. You ain't quite as..." He trailed off as Vandre took a third pull, this time never breaking eye contact with the farmer, despite the fire spreading through his chest. Eager to change the subject, he motioned to the shield slung over Beauty's scabies-ridden haunch, "You a knight?"

Vandre tossed the winebladder back to the dwarf, who snagged it without taking his eyes from the slim sellsword. The torch in his chest had reduced itself to a candle. He patted the standard with a broad hand. On a swamp-green field, a tan cat leapt, claws extended. "Ser Jemes Wyse, lordless knight off of the Brinegate Panhandle." He lied, extending a hand.

The shield and its standard *had* belonged to Ser Jemes Wyse; so had a stallion long dead, a helm that Vandre had lost down a gorge in The Greatwood, and the swordbelt that Vandre still carried. Ser Wyse had little need for his things, his body was weighed down with red-stone and moldering in some swampy pond in the Lowlands. Vandre preferred not to use the dead knight's name unless he had to. But it seemed that his only way to make Honeyhome in time was to use the dead knight's name, not just his clothing.

Thankfully, he and Wyse had been of a similar age and size, and Wyse was not a man of any sort of fame. It had been no matter to saddle up into the man's life, just as he took the man's horse. He pulled the cloak away from his chest, revealing a twin tan cat to the one on his shield. Vandre turned toward his ignoble steed and shrugged, "Lost my horse to thieves, bandits. Ten of 'em. I wasn't gonna carry my things, and the price was right." He showed a mouthful of yellow teeth in a broad grin. He shifted his weight, left foot to right, trying to ease the ache in his aging hips.

The dwarf nodded, eyes still on Vandre, "I suppose you can stand up now, Amber" Beside the old man, a solid-bodied dwarven girl –hair the same coffee-brown as her father– unfolded. In her shaking hands, she held a heavy oak and brass crossbow, cocked and aimed center mass at Vandre.

Every instinct told the old sellsword to pull his blade. He ignored them in turn as the bitter red wine began to soak its heat up the back of his neck. He raised his gloved hands to his shoulders, fingers spread wide, "No one needs to hurt anyone, girl." His gravelly voice shook with the same rhythm of her thick, white arms. He gestured to the leather pouch at his belt, "If the pair of you would allow, I would like to give you coin for the drink. Then, I'll take my Beauty here up the line, and see if an anointed knight can aid at the gates, huh? Out of your face, on my honor." He lied again.

The girl looked to her father, and they exchanged curt nods, "Go on, then!" She barked, without lowering the crossbow.

He bit his lip, hands lowering toward his belt as she trembled even more wildly. His heart was racing, but he took a long inhale of the warm grassy air. He exhaled and calmly requested, "Can you at least take your finger off of the trigger, Amber... Is it?"

She nodded curtly again, to the man in the cloak below the cart this time. Her father whispered something, too low for Vandre to hear. She removed her finger from the trigger, all the same. Vandre smiled, all yellow, once more and very deliberately reached into the pouch at his belt. He frowned, fingering a silver hunk of metal. He lifted a fine silver comb hair pin, inlaid with ivory, and stones of black jet. The young Learner he had lifted it from was miles away before he even began to miss it. It was the single most valuable thing that Vandre owned, beyond his sword and ringmail. He held it out, showing the fine metal, and the educated eyes of the dwarves recognized it for the fine work that it was. "How about this?" Vandre waved it cautiously, watching their eyes follow. "Do we like this?"

The father grunted affirmatively, "Aye, we like."

Vandre gave the dwarves one last yellow grin, almost sad. He flipped the pin open, and with every ounce of his considerable strength, drove the sharp needle deep into the haunch of the great foul goat attached to the cart. As predicted, the thing kicked back. And as predicted, it hurt. But Vandre managed to twist his body, and let the heavy ringmail on his ribs take the brunt of the blow, rather than his tender head or neck. It knocked him backward. The force sent him sprawling from the side of the cart, landing in the silt at the feet of the unbothered donkey. Vandre's third and final prediction came true when the goat reared, screaming in agony, its shriek all-too-human. The shaggy, horned animal surged forward sending horses and carts scattering in its enraged wake. Amber flipped backward over the bench seat of the cart, landing amongst the straw and briny wine behind them. The crossbow tumbled through the air. For an instant, Vandre was hopeful. Sure, he had likely lost the comb before he could pawn it, but a fine dwarven crossbow like this might be worth twice as much. The father tugged at the reins, his harried shouts blending with the screams of his goat. The whole cart surged forward as the crossbow crashed into the mud behind it.

Vandre scurried to grab the weapon, but heard a slosh. He barely stepped aside as the leaking barrel of mushrooms tottered off of the back of the cart and fell, crunching down onto the crossbow and bursting. Hundreds of pounds of palm-sized, pickled mushrooms, salt and wine slammed the weapon to bits and soaked Vandre's boots. Far off, the dwarves rolled across the golden hills of wheat and stone. The goat still shrieked and the cart bounced wildly as another barrel flew off and burst. Hungry peasants, unconcerned at the plight of the increasingly distant dwarven merchants, began scooping the mushrooms up. They devoured the cleanest ones they could find. Sulking at the shattered crossbow and lost silver comb, Vandre pulled himself from the dirt, the ache in his ribs just beginning to blur the edge of his awareness.

He stood, groaning and hacking, but he stood. He took the lead of Beauty, still oblivious to the goings-on around her, and the aged, injured pair limped forward. Vandre tried to stand as tall as he could, showing the sigil on his broad chest. As he approached the gates, he slid the shield from Beauty's haunch, and carried it high, alongside his other tan cat. Despite the increasing tightness in his ribs, he stood, shoulders back, head high and strode through the common folk like a knight.

Hope's Hill was not where Vandre had wanted to end up. In his haste to put Stonestall behind him, he neglected to remember what lie between Stonestall and Honeyhome:

Hope's Hill, the Crossroad of the Plains. The ancient city sat behind high granite walls, on a purewater spring the center of the vast dry plains. Five road gates and two river ones controlled traffic in and out of the city tightly, because Hope's Hill was not a place for sin. Clan Albin, the overly pious lords of the lands, were devoted to purity. As such, alcohol, pipeweed, coffee, sweets, spices, music, art and dance were all expressly forbidden in the walls, let alone of any sort of crime, like gambling or ladies of the night. It was exactly the kind of place that could get Vandre killed. But the sky was growing dark and he had almost been robbed twice in two days. His ribs hurt. His hips hurt. He wanted a bed, or at least a dry pile of straw.

The two Albin guardsmen stood vigil at the south gate, The Sun Gate. As Vandre and Beauty pressed through the gathered crowd, one of the guards, a slim, plain-faced man of middle age noted his shield and standard, waving him forward with a hearty yell, "Hail, Ser! Are you a knight anointed?"

With a rasp, Vandre lifted his head, "Aye, anointed and injured." He stepped forward, leaning harder on the old donkey than either one of them would have liked. She swayed unsteady and so did he. "Ser Jemes Wyse, off of the panhandle at Black Pearl Bay." Brinegate was too nearby to use with these men, so he let the further city serve his lie. He spit, blood in his phlegm, "I was jumped by horse thieves out along your road, must have been a dozen. They got my gelding, but I managed to pull this thing off of the cull line."

His eyes met those of the guard –bright blue under his silver peaked helm. Vandre had eyes of a muddy brown, no particular beauty in them, but they were sharp. When he noted the slim guard glance toward his superior, the younger man to his left, he knew he had them. "Commander, this one is a knight anointed needing aid, we ought to let him see the Learner, yeah?"

The commander, a man ten years younger and six inches taller than the first guard, turned his attention toward Vandre, hushing the red-haired woman squalling about her children at his side. "A knight?!"

Vandre nodded, rather than lie again, and the excited first guard finished for him, "He's Jemes Wyse from up north, headed to the tourney he said. Got jumped by them horse bandits I keep telling you about!"

In his own peaked silver helm, the commander, barely more than a big blonde boy, looked Vandre up and down. "A lordless sword…"

Vandre grinned again, "Well, be that as it may…"

The smaller guard chirped in, "A lordless sword is still a knight, commander."

The big blonde bull of a boy bored into the bent old bladesman, "Who took your vows, Wyse?"

Inside his salt-and-pepper head, wheels were turning. Naming another lordless sword of no regard would leave him in the same lamentable position as he was now. But naming a known knight or lord ran the risk of this bulbous blonde bastard knowing them. He sighed, stern, looking the boy over. "Lord Lucius Cutfrey himself, lad. A personal friend." He held his gaze on the big lad's. He would be gambling in Hope's Hill after all.

After a moment longer than some weeks Vandre had lived, the blonde lad relented, stepping aside, "Just… clean up after that thing. We try to keep the *filth* out of our city, ser."

Despite the fact that he could feel the swelling bruise under his ringmail, he smiled, leading Beauty through the gates, "Of course, of course. What sort of knight couldn't be trusted within your lovely walls?"

LILAH I

"Lilah, I have such wonderful news! You're going to marry a knight, and the heir to the Greatwood. Ser Mandel Stagg has made us such an offer!"

Trees were better than walls. Lilah wasn't much of an outdoorswoman, but she was fairly sure of this. After a long sail across the Great Bay, Lilah had decided that sailing was worse than trees. She'd endured the journey with her two sisters, her mother-by-law, and two small children. Nuttley, where Lilah and her sisters had been raised, was a small city in a great forest. While it did have wooden walls, most of the city's defense was handled by archers and spearmen high in the trees. The walls of Honeyhome were the largest Lilah had ever seen, a massive stony edifice covered in creeping ivy and the most adorable little purple and white flowers.

Her husband, Reuben, leaned to his father and pointed to the battlements above. "That's where the Bloodsinger died innit?"

"'Isn't it?'" Ser Mandel Stagg corrected. Lilah's father-by-law was a somber man in his mid-fifties. Balding, clean-shaven and impeccably dressed, the old knight carried himself with the grace of a man much more significant in the world. "Enunciate. Open your mouth and use your tongue, or I will find someone to shorten it for you. It is clearly too long."

Rather than using his tongue, Reuben held it; his jaw set and eyes rolling.

In an attempt to make peace, Lilah spoke, "The Bloodsinger, I love that song about him! How does it go again?" She stumbled, trying to remember the tune, *"I sailed far north and there's nothing to fear/for once I came ashore, my...* uh, *my knife took your ear..."*

Deeply annoyed, Ser Mandel pinched the bony bridge of his nose between thumb and forefinger, "Reuben. Don't the children need attending, or perhaps there is literally any other purpose you can set your lady wife to?"

Lilah frowned. Ser Mandel often spoke like she wasn't present. Reuben simply nodded, taking his Lady wife by the arm more roughly than she would have liked, and led her off with a slight jerk, roiling under his breath. She faced him, confused. "Did I misspeak?"

Reuben spat on the ground bitterly, "Yes."

Lilah searched the face of her husband, trying to find his emotion and coming up empty, "Oh. That was not my intention, my lord. I am sorry. I-I… I don't even know what I did?"

For all his notions of chivalry, Reuben was rarely gentle when he had been upset. She had done it twice in ten minutes. He placed a hand on her chin, strong fingers gripping her bottom jaw, squeezing pain through her mandible and teeth. He jolted her face to meet his, pulling her roughly to the right, leaving her inches from him. His breath was hot and sickly sweet with Malbes mead. "Of course you don't."

She could see thin slivers of white on the edges of his big green eyes. Though reddened from drink or pipeweed, his eyes were wide-awake and clear. A thin bead of sweat was running from a soaked spike of brown hair, down his cheek. The drop finally soaked into the light shirt he wore, emblazoned with the bronze stag and green sun of Clan Stagg. He pulled her, face to face, literally nose to nose. His clammy skin pressed to hers. "I don't think you understand much of anything, Lilah. I do not want you to speak unless spoken to, especially around my father. This tournament, this engagement, this is all far too important for you to ruin."

She pulled back, trying to break the iron arm of her spouse, but struggling in vain, "Reuben. You're hurting me. Stop."

Horrified, the knight let go, settling back into composure. He stumbled back against a greenery-blanketed wall. He took a moment. Trembling, he cupped his own face with those strong hands. Oily tears welled at the corner of his eyes, "That was unknightly of me. You are my lady wife. You are the mother of my children, You should be afforded with more respect. I will not fail in my responsibilities again."

You will. Lilah knew she wasn't a particularly smart girl. She had been pretty and her father controlled an important river port and that was enough reason for her to be given to Reuben. *You say this every time you lay hands on me... or other parts with other women.* She let neither thought pass her lips. Lilah wasn't particularly smart, but she was no fool either.

She placed a rosy hand on Reuben's cheek, now came her battle. "My lord, pay it no mind. It will be no problem whatsoever." If Lilah had a knife, she would have opened her husband's throat; a mace and she would have battered his skull to shards. "You are under such immense pressures, I cannot even fathom them, my love. I shall learn my place, of course." In her dreams, he screamed, but today, she would play the dutiful wife once more. She pressed a handkerchief to her sore jaw, wiping his sweat from her face.

Reuben straightened in validation, taking the lace kerchief from his bride without asking. He dabbed the corners of his eyes and cleared his nose with a long honk. Another spit to the fine cobbled stone below. He pressed the fabric back into Lilah's hand without a word. The pair emerged from the sheltered garden path as the picture of young parents.

As they crossed the yard, arms linked, the young couple in the moonlight caught a glance of other nobles. But Reuben ignored whatever shouted greetings may have come up. They had only arrived two days ago, and a few of the nobles had gathered in the shadow of the walls, in Hivehall's famous Gateside Garden to see the flowers this evening. The night had grown into one of wine and pipeweed and mead and music and laughter. Reuben had even pulled her into his lap, as they all breathlessly laughed around a bonfire swapping stories. She and Reuben were one of many couples. The quiet little spider-lord from Ozwyk, Purvon Webb, smiled broadly. With his slim spider's fingers, he opened a small wooden box and produced colors and quantities of pipeweed the likes of which Lilah had never seen. His bounty was enjoyed by all. Their laughter had carried high into the night and across the yard. Lady Lenore Vellen, who always seemed so stern and serious, sang for the gathered and intoxicated masses; her eyes glinting an eerie green in the moonlight as she whirled and sang. She wept when she sang the song of a young Tallman Knight dying on the halberd of a Coralspear man, at a tourney, centuries ago, *Winter Ends at Springs Blade.* Thick-bodied Joelle Bridge told jokes and stories so bawdy that even Reuben blushed at the Southern Lady's crass hilarity.

The noise attracted more bodies of course, and as it was her duty, as the wife of a man who might someday be a lord, she knew every name for every face; handsome Marten Mirebreaker, Lord of the whole Lowlands, followed closely by disgusted-looking little lordling who could only have been his brother, Slade. Lord Darwyn Tymm of the Grey Guard, whose older brother had married Reuben's younger sister some years back. Even Carelin Marle, who sat the King's Council as Grand Admiral, poked her head through the greenery carrying a cask of black rum she'd 'been saving for this sort of debauched moment.'

Most interestingly, however, was the contingent of the Wyldefolk who arrived: Hullen and Ellari Curr, who Lilah knew as Ellari was family to Reuben –a cousin of middle distance. They were followed by Curr's own three sworn swords; tall, grim Torchbearer, dashing, cocky Goldenlocke and burly, bombastic Hornblower. After watching them for a moment, passing the pipes and papers and chalices, Lilah knew that Ellari Curr was sleeping with one of her husband's men. After another moment, she was sure she knew which. Lilah smirked as Ellari took the smoking glass from her lover's hand. Lilah leaned over to her husband's ear, as her head was swimming from the smoke and the very fine Mables mead, still sweeter than honey. "I think she's fucking him." She whispered with a lazy toss of her hand.

At the prospect of scandal, Reuben's attention returned to his lady wife, "What?" His brows were furrowed in confusion and a hint of annoyance, but interest rang true in his tone, "Who's fucking who?"

Reuben's voice was fine and clear at the best of times–a commander's voice. Tonight with the added valor of drink, he must have been even clearer and louder, because the Curr girl's round, pale face swung toward them both, eyes wide. She placed the smoking glass in the waiting hand of her lord husband, and across the bonfire, she stared at Lilah. Lilah was shocked that no one else saw it: It wasn't just the way Ellari laughed at something her lover said, a laugh that was far more real than the shy smile she offered to Hullen. There was a jealous glint to her eye when Joelle Bridge whispered something salacious to the sworn sword, a blush that turned her pale cheeks pink when her hand brushed his, passing the smoking glass. Curr had no right to be angry, it was clear to anyone who bothered to look.

Reuben shook her shoulder lazily, "I said, who's fucking who, love?"

Lilah pressed her plump lips together and didn't part them. Ellari's pale face went paler, as she whispered something to her husband and deliberately rose. Lilah's heart pounded against her ribs as Reuben's breath hit her ear, "Did you want to sneak off to the bushes? Is that it?" He gave her a gentle shove to her feet, before rising to his own and adjusting himself. "I've had a bit, but I think I might manage to rally." His firm hand slapped her on the rear and she felt her face grow rosy, mortified. The prospect of the bushes with her drunken husband sent her insides to knots of anxiety, but she would take a heated buck over an angry bitch.

As they left the crowd behind, Lilah breathed a sigh of relief, only checking over her shoulder once, to see Lady Ellari settled back next to her handsome husband, eyes of moonlight following the receding backs of Lilah and Reuben. Of course, now she had a lust-filled Stagg boy on her hands. Reuben, for all his faults, had never been a cruel or unskilled lover–the conceptions of both Neal and Theasa had been rather *enjoyable* enterprises–but it was late. And she was tired and drunk. And they were in public. Hopefully, he was as drunk as he seemed, unable to perform in his "duties". A pink hand went to his chest, and she turned, stopping him.

"My lord, I'm afraid I'll get a frightful chill out here." She was feeling slightly desperate. "And I fear someone will see."

He groaned, turning back to the fire and the wine and the Curr girl, before she grasped his collar and kissed him, mead and smoke mingling as their tongues did. After a moment, she broke the kiss and met his gaze intensely, "No, my lord, I still need you. Just... not here." She gripped his collar, and started pulling him back toward the castle and after a moment's slightest resistance, he followed. As they followed the fine cobbled path along the high wall, his knightly father had happened upon them, and the night had gone to shit, frankly.

They now stood at the base of the tower that the Malbeses had offered for guests' use, she with her sore jaw, he, his bruised ego. He nodded, pressing his lips to her hand without passion, "I will return when the rest of the young lords and I have finished preparations, tend to the children, and I will be back in due time."

"Reuben, the sun set six hours ago. The children are asleep, as should you be. Drinking all night will leave you in no condition to fight tomorrow. And that's to say nothing of that Webb boy and his demon weed." She didn't know exactly what steps the Curr girl might take, but she knew she cared little for this dance. Lilah had every intention of avoiding the Curr girl for the next two days, after which point, they could all sail home and she'd need never look at a homely Curr face ever again. She sighed, giving her shoulders an uncharacteristically masculine shrug, "Do whatever you will. That's all you do anyway." She broke away from him, as he started to say something, but she had no time to hear it.

He would be upset, she was sure, but here in the tower, there were enough strange bodies that he'd be unlikely to lay hand on her. Two Malbes guardsmen in gilded scale stood at the stair, joking between themselves as she rapidly left her angry husband behind. Apparently, the one with the boil on his nose was upset that he had drawn duty both tonight and tomorrow night, during the Debutante's Procession. His partner, a thin broomstick of a man, had only drawn tonight, and Boil thought that was unfair. Upon seeing her, Broomstick nudged his shorter friend and both men straightened, allowing her to pass unbothered.

She made her way up the stairs, gripping tight the fine railing of brown-gold brass. As she made her way back into the fine guest quarters, everything was gold and yellow and white. The sickening sweet of honey dripped from everything here and Lilah had just about had enough of it. *The Rasks don't go 'round wearing squirrelskin cloaks, and Curr oughta be the one wearing antlers, not Reuben...*

She settled into the overlarge chambers the young family had been given, first checking that the children were nestled tight and safe. She left their room, taking care to close the door quietly. Silent steps led her across the fine Durdan rug, thick purple and gold thread cushioning every step.

"It's about time you came back, it's hardly proper to leave your children in the hands of the servants in a strange place for bedtime. You're lucky I was here; the children were in want of a mother." Tall and straight as the hemlock tree on the Ironarm shield, her High Lord Brother's shield, Lady Grete, her mother-by-law, filled the doorframe of the chamber next to the children.

Lilah rankled, but there was little else to be done, "Of course, my lady." She attempted to push past and end her night, but after a pair of steps, her mother-by-law cleared her throat. Lilah stopped in her tracks, and without turning her head, she spoke, "Thank you, my lady. My children are blessed to have a grandmother such as you."

Satisfied, Lady Stagg turned back toward her doorway, before calling back once more, "Did you lose Reuben, Lilah? Where is my son?"

Lilah's big buck teeth pressed into her soft bottom lip as she inhaled sharply. "Ser Reuben had pressing business with the other young lords, and thought it would be best I returned to attend to the children." She still refused to face Lady Grete.

"Hm, I suppose so..." There was little warmth in her tone. There never was. "You know, Lilah. It might be best if you find some way to start... *providing value* to the household. I mean, I have Reuben. We have little Neal and Theasa. But, darling, remind me..." She let the hurt about to come build, "If you don't make my son happy, why do we need *you?*"

Lilah could have snapped. Lilah was good; she wasn't smart, but she tried and she was *loyal.* And this mean old woman with her awful haircut and dead eyes was just so *mean.* It wasn't that Lilah was alone, she wasn't. She liked Reuben's sister well enough, and the High Lord and his wife were always very kind, though they were so very odd. But, whenever anything important happened, she was shunted to the side. The whole house refused to give her any chances, any responsibility. Lilah crumpled inside, "I don't know, my lady." Lilah still refused to face Lady Grete, she would not give that vicious old crone the satisfaction.

"What a *wretched thing* you are." Lady Grete wheeled away, muttering words like "stupid" and "useless" loud enough that Lilah could hear them when the heavy oaken door clicked shut.

Lilah put one foot down, feeling the thick rug bear her slight weight under the shifting sole of her soft silken slippers. She strode, sullen, finally finding her chambers. As she finally slumped into her pillow face first, the sobs came, great juddering things that sent quakes through her body. She cried so hard, she thought she'd be sick again, like she had after dinner. It was so hard to even eat, let alone keep food down. Everything just felt so big, all the time, and she couldn't breathe. She couldn't eat. Her skin hurt. It hurt to be.

But no matter what, Lady Grete Stagg would never see her tears. Never again.

DRAKE I

"My boy, it's not only Clan Canar and myself that you would do the dearest honor, but Lord Ludo and all of the Fisher Kingdom and Scattered Isles. Drake, we hurt for honor. You are overfull. Please!"

Making smoke was a secret that the Ducks had kept to themselves for four thousand years. It took a certain blend of yellow brimstone from the far island of the same name; lime and salt crushed to fine powder; mixed with the piss you took after a long night drinking wine, and some hunks of charcoal. There was more to it, magic and prayer and a gift to the Golden Boy. Drake had barely finished shaking the last few drops from the end of himself, preparing that specific ingredient, when he was rudely interrupted by an enormous figure, red and horned.

Birse. The thought was not a pleasant one. Ser Drake Canar wheeled a grey-leathered heel on the bare stone floor of the borrowed barracks, barely getting his manhood put away in time. The enormous *ifre'croi* filled the entire doorway with his broad frame. Calling the big hellheart "ugly" wouldn't be inaccurate, thought Canar, but tact didn't make looking him face-to-face any less unpleasant. It was a face that the fell souls of Hell had decided to mark, for whatever reason. Drake Canar was not a small man. He stood of average height and maybe a trifle slim of build, but Birse dwarfed him entirely. Had they been face-to-face, they would have been face-to-sternum. Thick cords of muscle moved under the skin of the huge hellheart, apparent in his neck and bulging, bare arms. The Hellheart was dressed richly, as was afforded the personal guard of the prince. A prince. There were two, Drake reminded himself. He ran long fingers over the Shield of the Six he held–hundreds of years old and freshly repainted.

Six months ago, Ser Dulles Bleake held this shield. Where a handsome plum and white duck sigil had been rendered, a skull hanging from a long chain had been painted. Men of Grey Guard were allowed vices, just not women. Bleake had taken to them all once he'd arrived in the Shining Isles of Avalar. Food, wine, pipeweed, Bleake had indulged in it all. In less than a decade, he'd gone from the solid-bodied knight who had earned a spot protecting the sovereign and his line, to a flabby bloated joke, the punchline of the Grey Guard.

Worse, he lacked the grace to get himself killed. He hung on for forty more years, this massive brown stain on both the Grey Guard and the Fisher Kingdoms. The man served since the current king –now a grandfather himself– was a toddler. And never once had he distinguished himself in combat, tourney or deed. Finally, in his eighties, his eyes began to fade, his steps grew slower. One morning, he did not rise. This wasn't especially uncommon, but when Ser Jurgen went to rouse him, he found him breathing shallowly with a purple-red sputum framing his mouth. In three days, the old man was dead, and the Crown began the search for the next Grey Guard on the fourth.

What came next had been a whirlwind, letters sent from every corner of Fisher, islands, rivers, mountains and fields. Lord Ludo Fisher –the high lord of the Western kingdom named for him and his kin– had been inundated with every young knight and sellsword that could claim even a cousin in the western lands. Thankfully, Lord Ludo's legendary cleverness had only grown with his age; Fisher's representative of the Grey Guard would be the finest of their own sons, and Lord Ludo would find him himself.

It was only when the high orange sail of the High Lord's *Masked Bandit* appeared far in the eastern horizon, bound for the port at San Canar, did Drake begin to worry. Drake was the third son of five in his house, and had become known as a tourney knight of great renown, even though he was but two-and-twenty. That, however, was not likely why Fisher was sailing west. Canar and his brothers, one older and one younger, had gone south last year. Not as raiders like many men of the Scattered Isles, but to aid the isolated islands of the Far Fort against ghoulish pirates from the Dead Shore. The Smokescreen had been his brother Donal's idea. Donal had been serving as his squire and brought up the ancient method of burning braziers of The Smoke on the stern of the vessel. Fires burning, the ship sailed into the wind to create huge curtains of black clouds to blind and choke rival boats. Donal had been the one to execute it, too, shouting orders to the men on the ship, commanding fire and sails and steerage. Someday, Donal would captain a ship of his own, and he would outshine them all.

Drake had started high in the ducksnest, harrying anything that got close enough to hit with a bow. His older brother, Piken, was a better archer. When he placed an arrow through the throat of a far-off helmsman, Drake decided his own talents were best used elsewhere. He gave his brother a firm slap on the shoulder, "I believe this ranged stuff is for a different sort than me." He gave a wild grin and kissed his big brother on the forehead, "But, perhaps a change of venue might help me rally." He stepped from the wooden planks beneath his feet, almost weightless for a moment. He was sky and sea, wind and water, wild and free.

He dove.

The drop from the mast into the smoke wasn't quite twenty feet, but when Donal would later tell the story to others lisping and spitting in the throes of excitement, the drop became nearly fifty. Tales grow in the telling and Donal would not shut up about it. Ten, twenty, fifty or a mile, Drake dove from the ducksnest, and slipped into the water shrouded by smoke and silent as sin. Grey-green saltwater filled his world before he righted himself. With a spray Drake swam for the nearest ship he could see.

He could not have said he had a plan when he dove. Perhaps the spirit of the Wildcat had overtaken him, he could not be sure. But when his climbing spikes sank into the soaking, salty, black wood of the devil ship, his chest and shoulders and arms burned with effort and he laughed. He pulled himself up the side of the ship, drunk with ecstasy and bloodlust. His cleated boots slipped only once, on the iron joist holding two beams together. He did not fall, but he would not repeat that mistake.

In the smoke, they did not see him. Over the waves, they could not hear him. Drake was a suitable enough knight, but on this day Undus himself turned Drake into a phantom, through the smoke and hell, he stalked these men. Dagger and sword sent eight men to their unending rest before the pirates could even manage to find him. He managed three more even after they had, before slipping back into the sea over their stern. Drake had not known whose ship it was, even when he had left it. He was surprised as anyone else when those eerie ships turned and sailed back to the Dead Shore. But when stories started coming north of a ghost in the smoke who slew a Pirate King, Piken and Donal had immediately helped the legend grow into something even bigger.

The stories had beaten the boys back to San Canar, borne on the wings of messengers. A hero's welcome awaited all three and the men who had followed them, but it was Drake that everyone cheered for the loudest. He didn't think himself a hero, he had just been lucky. The rest had disagreed, and it was out of his hands. Ser Drake Canar was the greatest knight in the west. Then Dulles Bleake died and Ludo Fisher sailed to ask him to bring back the honor to the rivers and seas. It meant giving up more than Drake could ever have wanted, but he had little other option.

And now the Devil was in his doorway.

"The Prince wants you." Birse was never a man to use two words when one would do. *Matter of fact, I reckon that big one would rather just use no words at all and haul me down the hallway by the scruff of my neck.* Canar did not like the look of Birse, not because he was helltouched, but just because Birse made every Grey Guard feel nervous. The Grey Guard were an ancient and respected order of men who gave up their claims to hearth and wife and home, in order to suffer for the rest of us. Service for these men was meant to be total. They were sworn to vows and anointed in the name of the gods; as such, only a knight may become a Grey Guard.

Birse made a mockery of all that, said the Old Goat. Ser Cole Canden was the oldest member of the Guard now that Dulles was dead; he was nearing fifty, and had held his shield for over twenty years. "That thing gets afforded the same honors as our order, but only a knight should protect the line. That thing is not a knight, it's not even a man. It profanes our order, just by existing." Ser Canden rarely hid his feelings and even more seldom changed his mind, but Canar did admit his notion had merit, even if it seemed somewhat *orthodox*. The Guard had been created in response to a series of evils committed by a personal army of the first King Stauton, some six hundred years ago. The younger prince possessing a personal guard as such, was a direct rebuttal by the Crown as to the effectiveness of the Guard in its current state. Drake laid the blame directly at the fault of his predecessor, but there was little to be done about that now, since he was dead.

The Dashing Duck rose, and after a trio of dancer-quick and dancer-light steps, he snatched up his dagger and sword and his belt of small glass capsules, each loaded with the Smoke. Birse snorted at them, "Tricks and toys aren't as good as a good man with a good blade, little grey duck."

Drake arched an eyebrow. He wasn't an arrogant young man, but freshness in the Guard left him in need of identity. Drake Canar would not embarrass Fisher further, so he bit, "Luckily for the Line, I'm an incredible man."

Birse snorted again, but said nothing.

The big devil led Drake down a narrow corridor with high, six-sided windows, which let just a taste of silver sun in—just enough to send every gilded surface to be seen to glitter and Clan Malbes loved to gild. Door handles, hinges, railings, locks were all golden. The swords on the wall shone with gold, the armor of the commanders of their guard was gilded. Clan Malbes had gotten rich trading golden honey for dwarven gold and intended that no one ever forgot. It was a desperate and cloying sort of display, in Drake's opinion. The Lord was making sure every person that walked down every hallway in the keep knew exactly how rich the Malbes swarm was. It was just verging on this side of pathetic. Birse swung his arm-thick red tail back and forth as they walked, and the young knight had to deliberately deny the urge to "accidentally" step on it.

As Birse led him into the chamber, he found himself face to face with Prince Vernus Artus, his small sister, the Princess Bara, and their Queen and mother, Natasha Harlock. Though the crown prince and the heir were not present, one of Drake's brothers, Ser Darwyn Tymm, was. Standing guard with his great bladed shield and heavy mace, he was not wearing his helm, topped with its jester's cap crest, but the Grey Jester looked no less deadly without it. He flashed a broad grin to Canar, who returned it in kind. There was no time to tarry with his brother, the royal family had summoned him and he went to a knee, as both Birse and Tymm did as well.

The Prince spoke first; most referred to his voice as a fine thing, a trumpet call, but secretly, Canar found it nasal, "You three may rise, Birse, I have no further need of you at this moment. Take your leave, but do not go far, I may require you shortly in the yard. Prepare my training mail and mace; I'll be battering my cousin at sparring once we've finished here."

The big Hellheart stood, dipped his golden-horned head to his charge and gave Canar a wicked, knowing grin before making his exit. Canar and Tymm rose, exchanging glances. Tymm's broad grin had reduced itself to a sheepish smirk, as if he too knew what was coming.

The Prince continued as his eight-year-old sister stood and tried to speak with their lady mother, who immediately shushed the girl. Under her breath, Bara muttered ".... listens... ... dead clown... ...war." The Princess was an odd little thing, admittedly, prone to bits of thievery and lies, but otherwise a fairly sweet and good-hearted little girl. It irked Drake to see her ignored, but there were bigger giants to slay.

"Ser Drake, welcome. I hope the castle of Honeyhome is to your liking, good ser. Are you enjoying the hospitality of our hosts?" Vernus smirked.

Something was afoot here. The prince rarely smiled and when he did, it usually meant some prank or cruelty. Drake gave a cautious nod, meeting the golden-eyed prince, then his mother, then the prince again. "I am, Your Grace. Hivehall is wonderful, second only to the Crownkeep itself. Our hosts have been gracious, the food–"

"Good, good." He said in a manner that implied he could not possibly have cared less about the food or any other part of the answer that he was being given, only that it was being given. "Now, as you well know, we're all here in honor of mine manhood."

His mother gave him a glare that nearly melted the crown on his head, "Your *ascension to* manhood."

"My manhood!" He scratched himself, "That's what I said, mother. And in honor of mine manhood, I have decided that all six of the Grey Guard shall be entered into this tournament!"

Drake's guts went to stone. *All six of us?!? Madness.*

"And then, I decided that both my brother and father should enter as well."

The King?! Gallus Artus had participated in tourneys in his youth and quickly found a large distaste for martial pursuits. And even that was closer to thirty years ago than twenty.

The boy prince crumpled into himself, "But then my royal father declared me a dullard, and said I may have one Grey Guard and my Brother."

His stomach and intestines resumed their normal duties, but Canar was no more sure of the Prince's meaning than he was previously, "Your Graces, I am sorry, I do not follow your meaning; surely you don't mean that you chose me to represent you?"

Tymm's chuckle broke an awkward, hanging silence. "He was not given a choice, Ducky. The five of us voted to let the new knight deal with this *noble task.*" Though his words were kind, his tone was not. And the unkindness was not being pointed at Drake.

If Ser Darwyn Tymm had expected the Prince to notice the disrespect, he was an expert at feigning surprise when the boy did, "Hm. Amusing." Every soul in the room could feel thoughts crashing into one another, forceful as continental drift in the Prince's spinning mind. "Ser Tymm, your brother has entered the tourney, has he not? The Lord of Leaper's Ledge?"

Tymm arched a thin orange eyebrow, nodding.

"Wonderful!" Vernus' smile was pointed, "Your brother can contend with mine in the first round! The Laughing Lord of Leaper's Ledge against the Crown Prince, fantastic." His gaze turned on Canar. "Of course, you have another sort of brother in the tourney…"

Canar stood, setting his jaw, trying to look older, wiser and fierce than he felt. He carefully fingered one of the capsules at his belt, trying to gauge the reaction of the older knight beside him. His emerald eyes were locked on the young prince, and Canar must have been the only person close enough to notice the ever-so-slight quavering of his strong jaw.

"Well, since I'm being so vicious to your blood brother, I think it may be best to be gentler with your sworn. Perhaps… one of the women in the tourney." Vernus smirked at his mother, whose eyes were daggers, ultimately impotent here, among those who must defend the line. The young prince was flipping through a stack of parchments, looking at names and numbers and figures, "Duck, I'll let you have the Haymaker woman."

"Your grace, there's no honor in that! She's twice my age and a woman!" Canar's plaintive yelp made him feel half a boy and all an idiot. *Better to lean into it, I seemed to have fucked myself. Let's fuck my way out of this,* "There's no show there, either, my prince. What do the commons get from me battering a woman? What do you?"

"I get to see you fight the winner of my brother versus *his*." Vernus pointed a finger at Tymm, "And if you don't defeat the woman, Canar, or if you decide to attempt some chivalric show of forfeiture, I promise you, I will make you an even bigger laughing stock than Bleake ever was. I will make hurting you my hobby. *Beat the woman, then you can fight my brother."*

It was all Drake could to not vomit. Queen Natasha cursed under her breath, taking the princess with her in a huff. Their fine silken dresses, trailed behind them, shining. Darywn broke into a laughter that was completely devoid of humor.

"You can't expect me to fight my charge." Drake was considering removing this attitude from the Prince with his short sword, but decided better of it.

"If he consents to it, which Talor will, we both know he will, you have no option." He smirked. "I was going to let you fight Moorbjorn, Duck. You're our newest Grey Guard. I wanted you to look good. Now, you're going to be my whipping boy." He laughed, shrill, before lifting a small silver goblet to his lips and swallowing a long draw of golden Malbes Mead. "You can thank that idiot clown of yours, you are both dismissed."

Both young knights were watching the other. It would only take a moment… but they left. Drake honestly could not say why. But they strode in silence from the chamber, back to the yard. In front of the high trees and hedges Canar placed a hand on Tymm's shoulder, and they broke into laughter, deep and racking, before Tymm settled, wiping tears from his eyes, "We are *absolutely fucked."*

Together, they were the two youngest men on the Guard. Tymm was two years older and had been serving for four, and was the easiest of his brothers to bond with. Drake liked his easy manner, and though Ozwyk was far, Tymm made it seem like Leaper's Ledge and San Canar were sister cities. "Forget that pisswater black rum you raiders drink." he had said one night with a careless toss of his long ginger locks, "We'll tour the Ledge and drink sparkling wine made from fey grapes." His smile made the rest of the world blur at the edges. Drake wasn't… well… he hadn't, but, well, if he was going to…

The Grey Guard were forbidden to have women.

And Ser Darywn Tymm was certainly not a woman.

HARTWIN I

"A wealthy lord with hungry peasants is no more a Lord than a monster, Hart. Take care of the smallfolk, they're what makes us lords, and we'd be them but for Lumen writing us a different tale. Take care of the commons, Hartwin."

The four dead farmboys had ended poorly. His sister smelled them first, she had been riding out ahead of the carriage that held Mother. The rest of the Saddlers, including beastly, hunched, gouty Father, had taken to riding the road. *What sort of horse-lord would arrive in a wagon?* had been the cry of his Lord Father, and for once, Hartwin completely agreed. Except for mother's carriage of honeyed gold, and a scant few supply wagons, every member of the Household was ahorse. A great line proceeded back for miles, the finest horses bred on the finest road in the nation; a grand procession from Stonestall to the Goldengrass. Even the humorless Hartwin found some pride in such a display, power, wealth, grandeur, he may be born of horse farmers, but Hartwin Saddler was born of the richest horse farmers to ever walk the globe, and he would be damned if any of the lesser lords forgot that. He was heir to the Goldengrass and he would not allow insult.

Harlow rode out from a thicket of cypress and willow that surrounded a low, dry hollow some yards from the road. She was a wild thing, and containing her was a chore in and of itself, Hartwin found it best to let his triplet sister explore at her own pace. Her attention was fleeting at the best of times, and she would return to the line faster than not. However, her horse came loping from the hollow at a rapid canter, with a pale girl on its back. Her face was bloodless-pale when she slid from her horse and rushed to her Lord Father on back of his old warhorse, Agro. Lord Byrony reached a massive calloused paw of a hand down, and swung his grown daughter onto the back of the old black horse as if she weighed nothing at all.

Dressed in silk and riding leather, the young Saddler lady was the picture of grace shattered. Great roiling tears streamed down Harlow's face as the Lord tried to calm his daughter, attempting to make out her words between the terrified sobs. "I-I-I went looking for flowers in the thicket, papa. Someone butchered them like hogs!"

Hartwin watched as the great oaf fixed his gaze on the trees rising from the low hollow, "Who, girl? Who's butchered? Hogs?" He brushed her tears away with one carrot-thick finger, not ungently. Lord Byrony Saddler had a reputation for care, caution and kindness among both his lords and peasants, but Hartwin marked it as weakness. Why tarry with Harlow when the butchery was dead ahead? Hartwin put his heels into his horse and motioned for two of his guard and for his triplet brother, Hugo. The quartet set down the hillside, riding down the grassy hollow toward the thicket.

Ser Hugo Saddler was a knight anointed and far more gifted with sword, axe, knife, bow, polearm and hammer than his brother could ever have hoped to be. He was a good three inches shorter than his brother, who was older by minutes, but outweighed him by thirty pounds of rock-hard muscle. If there was a more dangerous swordsman in three hundred days' rides, Hartwin did not care to meet him. Each of the triplets had their purpose in Honeyhome this summer: Hartwin would be meeting with the crown prince and the other heirs and young lords in a show of friendship and brotherhood for the future. Hartwin found that notion inane, but the opportunity to interact with the other men that would rule the six nations of the empire was too sweet a plum not to pluck.

Hugo was simply attending for the opportunity to hit someone. He was a simple creature, more like his father than either of the other triplets. He was more than happy to follow the direction of his siblings or their mother. Hartwin had always kept Hugo safe from the dangers he was not quite bright enough to see and explained the insults he was too slow to grasp. In turn, Hugo was a shield of muscle and martial skill that kept the promises made by Hartwin's quick wit and grand vision.

Harlow was being brought for a different purpose. She was being offered up like livestock to a weak-armed and weak-willed prince four years her junior. Their mother had attempted to arrange her wedding to the older Prince, Talor, but had lost out to that purple-haired tart from Ozwyk. The slight had not been forgotten by Lady Kalistah Malbes-Saddler, and the rumor that she had talked her own lord father into holding this tourney for her own purposes held a little more stink of truth to it.

As the quartet parted the trees, the smell hit them first—that specific odor of rotted flesh. As the four young men entered the rounded clearing, they found the horror. The four boys had not been dead long, no more than two days, but the stench of rot in the early summer humidity clung to the inside of Hartwin's nostrils in a greasy, sticky way. He felt in need of a wash just from being in the presence of such filth. Corpses did not unnerve him, but corruption, rot, and disease certainly did. Hartwin distrusted anything filthy or foul, he kept himself well bathed and perfumed. And he expected the same of those around him. As such, his personal guard, "The Young Stallions" were the shining standard of the entire Goldengrass.

Hugo pulled his sword from his belt, wheeling his horse in a tight circle, his sober green eyes meeting Hartwin's, "They died rough,

Hart." Hugo had a gift for stating which anyone could see: One of the boys was facedown in a massive red-brown stain in the dust, and when one of the Stallions prodded his skull with a boot, shattered skull shards shifted beneath the skin sickeningly. Across the thicket, one of the boys was pinned to the ground– a hayfork through his gut, inches into the dry ground beneath him. Animals had been at him, his face, hands and right foot were gone, blood stumps and a clean skull's grin.

Hartwin pulled a kerchief from his coat, as the smell began to overtake him. His mouth went dry, sticky strings of saliva across a sandpaper tongue. Cold sweat began to seep from his clammy pores, and he shouted out to Hugo, his voice muddy and heavy in his throat, "Is that a head?" He motioned with a shaking right hand as Victory, his roan courser, began to back away, responding to the tension in his master's voice. Hartwin steadied his oldest friend, and shakily dismounted, rather than be sick on horseback.

Hugo dismounted his own horse, a big black stallion born of their father's warhorse and approached the remaining two bodies. One of them, more a bundle of rags than a person, was covered in a murder of black carrion eaters. Hugo scattered them with a toss of a stone, sending them into the sky with a chattering cacophony of screeches and black feathers, "Flyin' black rats!" He turned his head when he heard his older brother call out, "Probably, lemme look." He took two heavy steps, boots sending clouds of dust in the dry. Hugo poked at the fourth body, and the head rolled away freely at a light touch. "Yeah, it's a head."

Hartwin felt the bile rise in the back of his throat as the surprised farm boy's face, rubbed with dust, became visible. Though no animals had been at this corpse, the boy had taken a severe beating before he had been decapitated. His plain face had been mashed, beaten across his skull. His lips were swollen and bloody, his front teeth shattered to bits. Hartwin's breakfast, salt bacon and black beer filled the back of his mouth, bitter and acid burning. He spit, trying not to gag further.

Behind him, the clop of hooves approached, though Hartwin was too busy being ill to care who it was. He spit again, bread and bacon and beer and bile. Two more Stallions had arrived, escorting his cousin, Ser Doyle. Doyle was born to his aunt and was a Selach by name, but Aunt Euana had refused to live in the crumbling ancestral keep of Brinegate, so they remained in the Saddler Household. Doyle was a young knight of some small renown and was hoping to win one of the places in the tourney being held for the last three men standing in the melee. *Even if he earned his way into the tourney,* Hartwin thought to himself bitterly, still holding back vomit. *He wouldn't be able to best Uncle Hinric, let alone Hugo.*

Doyle and Hugo had taken a small huddle with the highest-ranked Stallion present, when Hartwin had managed to pull himself together, wrapping the kerchief around his nose and mouth to best handle the odor.

"A circle of wetland trees in a dry spot and they've all been savaged?" Doyle's seafoam eyes were too big for his head, and made him look like some kind of salamander, as far as Hartwin was concerned, but they were huge and searching, while he watched Hartwin sidle up.

"Tales from the sewing circle." Hugo snarled. *At least he's retaining sense.*

"What tales are these?" Hartwin interrupted and Hugo broke into laughter as the other two straightened up sheepishly.

"Doyle says the men are calling this here a fey ring. Sayin' the unseelie killed these boys." As always, Hugo's bluntness left little room for discussion. The unseelie did occasionally make their way from the Shadowed Hells that the old Owl Kings had managed to drive them back to, but that stuff was rare. When they did, though, violence followed. The air in the clearing seemed heavier than it should have been, suddenly colder and eerie still. Hartwin spun, surveying the scene with the practiced eye of brilliance he afforded himself. One of the Young Stallions was examining something in the dust beside the corpse with the shattered skull, so Hartwin approached his man.

"Hail, what do we see?" Hartwin made a point to be polite but firm with the help–remain approachable, but still of higher status. It allowed for better trust to be built with the commons.

"Horseshoes, m'lord. But ain't none of the dead boys got a horse." The stallion, clad in gilded mail and horsehair-braided helm, waved a trio of long fingers in a sweeping motion toward the cracked ground, where, unmistakably, shod hoof prints had pounded the ground. The Stallion turned toward a thin tree at the edge of the thicket, some twenty feet away. A half dozen feet of rough hempen cord were frayed on one end and tied tight around the base of the tree on the other. "Somebody made off with a horse, m'lord."

Hartwin agreed, and called out to his brother and cousin, "Hey, boys, look what I found. Horse thieves! …Must have been twenty of them!"

Doyle nodded, "Aye, not twenty, but at least one. I got boot prints over here, and all of our dead boys have feet wrapped in rags." He called back from a squatting position, examining the ground.

Hugo called to the Young Stallion commander, "Have your men bring the head to my mother's witch. Maybe she can pull some secrets out of it." The gleeful look on his face was a sadistic one; Hugo often commanded the underlings to do disgusting or humiliating tasks and frequently seemed to enjoy their discomfort. Whether the head or the witch was the prospect more feared, Hartwin was unsure. He reached a hand into a pocket and seized on a small parchment-wrapped parcel, no bigger than a pack of cards. Hartwin carefully unfolded it, producing a pinch of dried and shredded leaf. He placed the small wad in his mouth and chewed, allowing the mint leaves to spread their cooling oils across his tongue and down his throat into his swirling gut. He drew a deep breath, blinding himself to the horror around him, searching for his center. Cold sweat.

A great, heavy hand came down on his shoulder, and without thinking, Hartwin called out, "No, it's quite alright, Father. I'm—"

"You're swaying, Hart." The fine, clear voice was not Father's, nor was the heavy hand. Hartwin opened his eyes to meet his cousin, attempting to steady him. Doyle's broad, mindless mushmouth was making more pointless words, but Hartwin couldn't make them out, however the ground was coming up very fast and suddenly all was dark and silent.

He was bare-chested and on horseback, though Victory wore no saddle. Though he was no warrior, his uncle's sword hung from a scabbard at his waist and his brother's heavy thundering shield sat low on his back slung on a leather strap.

He squeezed Victory between his legs, no that wasn't right, Victory was his legs. Or he was Victory. He and the horse were one and he was running, free and bare chested through the Goldengrass.

Other figures ran with him, he did not know their faces but he knew they were the other young lords. A boy, who was a great, shaggy black hound as well, loped through the grass like a cur hunting a squirrel. Great spreading branches like antlers swirled in the corner of Hartwin's eye, attached to a grim, stony facade. A slim, robed figure, haloed in light sat on back a great turtle, moving slowly, great earthquakes erupting where it trod. Flashes of fire showed a man who was fire and man and Dead, all three at once. This Burning Boy. This Chimera. Beside him, a child clad in furs crowned himself with refuse. Even when he was still, things beneath his skin squirmed.

Above it all, it shone: like the face of the gods itself, the Prince flared. Without wings it flew, this Prince. The two man-eyes saw, but when its third eye opened and shone bright and gold in the center of its head, it became terrible to behold.

They ran through the grass, these beasts, these boys. Hartwin's heart thumped in his chest. The silver sun hung high and shone low on the Goldengrass. The gentle heat hung on his skin like the softest kiss. There were no sharks in the grass. No fins, no gnashing teeth. A cloud crossed the sun, and chill took hold.

Clouds of swirling grey and brown smoke filled the sky, bloated and sickly to bursting. These clouds stirred with constant churning—a strange segmented fluttering to their motion. As soon as they appeared, they grew, swelling thick and dense, becoming twisted, full things of smoke and sparking light. In the sky, the Prince burst its terrible third eye open, radiant light of the heavens tore at the black smoke, but it quickly began to drink the light, and then it drank up The Prince itself.

As the dark drank up the Prince and the silver sun and the sky itself, it began to snow, which the horsewhowasHartwin found odd. As they began to settle around him in little drifts among the stalks of grass, he saw that it wasn't snow at all.

Feathers, countless thousands. Grey, brown and black.

The horsewhowasHartwin remarked to itself how very odd this was as it mindlessly mawed a munch of gold grass. It thought it heard a screech as it noticed how very dry the grass tasted today.

The talons were upon the horse before it could swallow its grass.

"Well, you've earned yourself a terrible little fate, haven't you..?"

Lights swirled above his head as something bitter and chalky flooded Hartwin's mouth, as a pair of strong fingers viced his nostrils shut. By reflex, he swallowed and was amazed at something tasting so chalky, yet burning his throat and chest so much. He sputtered, sitting up as the fingers released and the world shifted back into focus. He had been laid out on a horse blanket, in the shade of the fattest willow in the thicket. The low, sagging branches thatched into one another, giving him a verdant umbrella, hiding him from the mid-day's heat. He pushed some locks of his red-brown mane from his eyes, and was greeted with his mother's witch.

They called her Hellendre, and she had arrived in a crate when Hartwin was four. She had been shipped from some coldwater city in the continent. She was an orphan, and when Uncle Hinric had laid eyes on her performing magic in the alleys for coin, he had her secreted into Stonestall, as Mother would love her. As usual, Hinric was wise to the ways of the heart, and Lady Kalistah had fallen head over heels for the awful little thing.

Were she not touched by the demonic realm, she might have been attractive enough. She was tall and shapely and of an age with Hartwin. Her face, other than her pointed canine teeth and pupil-less brassy eyes, was well sculpted with full lips and a dainty nose. Her hair was thick and voluminous, of a healthy auburn, despite the pair of horns that curled through it. And though her skin shone as verdant as the spring grass of the plain, it was free of both scar and blemish.

Groggily, he questioned her, "W-what did you say?"

"I said you've earned yourself a terrible little fate, Hart." She smiled, her pointed teeth a perfect ivory. She pressed a soft hand to his forehead, and frowned, "You don't have a fever, but you are disgustingly sweaty."

Had she seen my nightmare? Hartwin shuddered, Hellendre had eerie powers over man, beast and mind, seeing into his heart was well within her purview. "What do you mean?"

"Riding off into the wood like that, you are lucky all you got was dizzy." The heavy-lidded brassy eyes searched over his face, watching his pupils, "Foolishness like that is expected from Hugo and Doyle, but you are supposedly wiser than that, Hart."

He groaned, rolling over, "I will not be lectured by *the help*." His skull felt like it was two sizes too small and shrinking, "What happened? Some sort of spell or the unseelie?"

She poured water from a skin into a small pewter cup, and pressed it into his hand. He drank it, clear and icy. He drained the cup, and passed it back. "It would be most wise to let the Learner have a look at you, but I think, Hartwin, you may have fainted."

The tall heir was incensed, "I did not faint! I'm sure there's some poison or unseelie trap you are unaware of, where is Learner Powell?"

Hellendre had refilled the cup with more water, and was offering it to Hartwin as he gracelessly stumbled to his feet on legs that were both too long and too stiff. He stumbled forward, and she suppressed a giggle. "He was attending Harlow. She was having one of her hysterical incidents, that's why your Lady Mother had me sent in his stead."

Harlow has an 'incident' every few days, it's why Mother keeps changing her staff; Hartwin thought to himself, a slight tightening of his jaw the only betrayal of his annoyance. He steadied himself on a tree, noting that the bodies in the clearing had been removed. "What happened to the dead boys?"

"Your father insisted they were buried and blessed." She gave a sheepish smirk, "Shame we never found the last boy's head..." She practically scampered to a low bush, once laden with early summer raspberries, but picked clean. The three-foot green tail swinging from the base of her spine brushed the dust, and Hartwin sighed. She bent low and produced a burlap sack, maybe a bushel. Something inside was leaking red-brown into the burlap. It was roughly the size and weight of a medium pumpkin, and hung heavy as Hellendre lazily swung it back and forth, skipping lightly. She was humming along with the songbirds in the trees like the bloody sack in her hand was a basket of sunflowers. Behind them, Victory rankled at the smell of blood, but the little witch looked at him and spoke without words, and the roan calmed. The hellheart then peered at Hartwin with those big liquid-metal eyes, framed by long, delicate lashes. "Don't worry, I won't make you look."

Hartwin ran a shaking hand through his red-brown hair and calmed. He shuffled backward, an uneasy hand finding purchase on Victory's mane. He watched aghast, as Hellendre settled cross-legged on the same worn green blanket he had just been stretched out upon, "It's not the blood, I don't mind blood..."

She nodded, for a moment, she saw through him and he felt naked. Hartwin was never sure in moments like this whether she was using her gifts on him, and even more fearfully, he didn't think

Hellendre was either. Despite her *disfigurement,* Hartwin rather liked this little monster his mother kept leashed, and that was saying something, because appearances meant everything to both of them. Hellendre gave an easy answer, "It's the rot, I know. It could be moldy grain and you go green. But red never bothers you."

He tried to say something, but she shushed him, placing a small silver trinket on the blanket beside her. She then produced a bit of charcoal and a small hunk of rock salt. She broke a small chip from the charcoal before tossing the rock salt to Hartwin, in want of a knife. The only blade Hartwin carried was a small thing for cutting twine and rope, but after a few minutes of struggle, he worked loose a pair of penny-sized scraps of salt, which Hellendre deemed sufficient, thanking him once more with her big doe eyes and gentle smile. She tossed the charcoal and the salt in a small clay jar, no bigger than a fist. Runes in redwine had been smeared across the surface. She opened her satchel, sniffing a fine pink powder, and adding a couple pinches to the pot. Two drops of a thick, yellow-green oil from a droppered bottle followed, then finally, Hellendre removed the crystal pendant from her neck, a long blood-emerald in sparkling crimson, she twisted the crystal free, revealing its secret nature as a glass vial. Hellendre added a quartet of drops, a clear liquid that caused everything within to melt together, congealing into one iron-red, clotted mass. The red bothered him as she placed the sack in the center of her crossed legs, it bothered him more when, despite her best efforts, Hartwin could tell she was pouring it into the mouth of the decapitated farm boy.

"You still might want to look away for this part, Hart." Hellendre's face was not commanding or stern; for an instant, Hartwin thought she may have been pleading. The Heir to the Goldengrass did not look away; he set his jaw and he watched as his mother's witch spoke with the dead.

ELLARI I

"He's not made to rule, Ellari, not like you. It's wrong, but it's the way of law. Do your best to temper him, teach him. Do not let him stray far from you."

The bone corset made her ribs ache, thick fingers of antler squeezing her narrow frame into some semblance of curves. She tensed her abdomen, pressing the sore muscles against the sore bones. She pressed her own thin fingers against the indigo silk on her tummy and stuck her tongue out. She wrapped the tan belt around her waist, letting the black-blue metal rings clink together, almost musically. All of the Curr nobles wore the rings of the Elder Iron somewhere on their clothes, one of the few signs of their high birth. She fingered the rings, she liked the elder iron, always cold and shining.

It supposedly brought luck to those who wore it, but Ellari didn't feel especially lucky today. She stood, rising from the borrowed bed, in this fine borrowed room, in the manse being lent to her Lord Uncle and his court. She crossed the warm rug on the floor, yellow and honey-brown. The Lady pulled a pair of sensible black boots over her silk socks. She was more accustomed to fur and wool, but here where the breezes blew warm from the sea, she was told to wear silk and satin. Her bare shoulders were also disconcerting, and she reminded herself to wear a shawl to keep the high silver sun from cooking her pale skin pink.

The slim girl moved to the low table in her chamber, brushing aside his wine bottles with a sigh. The letters were undamaged, thankfully. She gathered them, bundling, folding precisely and sliding the small stack into the sad, brown satchel that always hung from her shoulder. She gathered herself, five quick steps from the desk to the door. She looked herself over in the small silvered mirror hanging beside the door. Each corner held a carving of one celestial of the family. She tried to see herself in the mother, Caeliach, but her eye kept wandering to that wild daughter, Mazka. She forced herself to meet her own gaze. Though she came by the last name Curr, twice as it happened, her look was all Ironarm. She had her mother's blood and her mother's look, save the single streak of white in her hair, which was a common Curr trait. Her mother had been gone thirteen years now, and her face was only seen in dreams and mirrors as of late. She straightened her strand of white, a heavy silver bead hanging from it to her cheek. It was not a beautiful face –stern and sad, her cheeks were still holding more baby fat than she would have liked, and unless she kept it plucked, a few nasty red-brown hairs would sprout from above the corners of her mouth. The hairs did not bother her, per se, but no one took too ugly a woman seriously. Few took too beautiful a woman seriously, as well, and Ellari admitted herself some fortune in that.

Ellari Curr took one more deep breath, and put on her armor, stepping through the door clad in her face of the High Lord's Lady Executor. Her day here in Honeyhome was full, but first, she would need to find her husband.

She made her way down the sun-soaked hallway, grand windows of tall, clear glass, wrought in the honeyed-brown gold that Clan Malbes seemed so fond of. Every window was framed with the green ivy and fragrant little purple and white flowers that attract bees to every corner of this city. She heard chattering from the sitting area the Curr family had been afforded and found her mother-by-law tending to Masha, her husband's sister. Lady Gail Curr had been born Lady Gail Woodbjorn and was wed to Lord Hullen Curr III, the High Lord of the

Wylde, one of the most powerful men in the empire, Ellari's Uncle… and the father to her husband, Hullen Curr IV.

Marriage to your first cousin was once fairly common in the Empire, and while it was not frowned upon, it was not exactly ideal. Ellari had been betrothed to Hullen shortly after the death of her parents. Her father, heir to the Wylde, and his wife were slain in their carriage during an ice storm. The cabin was emptied of gold and jewels. Burgess Curr had been found with a crossbow bolt in his throat and one in his eye, his sword still in his right hand. Lady Alla, born an Ironarm and died a Curr, had been struck with only a single bolt. It had pierced her heart.

Ellari put away that memory, folded and bundled like the letters in her satchel, and rounded on her mother-by-law. Gail Curr was a large, burly woman, thick of shoulder and thicker of waist. The tall redhead had born, raised and nursed four children, and had a body that reflected that. Gail Curr was womanly, not in a girlish way, but as a mother born of fisherwoman and spearwives–strong and solid. The Lady of the Wylde was braiding her daughter's thin brown-grey hair, three tight braids, braided into one another. A very elaborate, traditional Wylde fashion, a style meant to impress and dazzle, a style singularly ill-suited to the little Lady Masha's big, round head.

"What do we think, dearheart?" Gail swung her hips a half-blink before the rest of her– a practiced motion of a graceful woman. She smiled at Ellari, matching her smiling eyes with her stern daughter-by-law.

Ellari gave a practiced motion of her own— a tight, professional smile. "It looks lovely, my lady." She crossed the room, giving a glance to the misery-prone Masha. She looked especially unhappy today. She had been loaded in a carriage with the rest of her family and spent the better part of a month riding and sailing to the tournament. Worse still, for Masha at least, the girl was being presented as a potential bride for the king's skinny second son. Ellari had agreed with her Lord Uncle that the matter was at least worth investigating, but after laying eyes on Vernus, both Ellari and Masha objected to the match. After they had arrived in Lord Malbes' castle: Hivehall, the two younger ladies of the court had stolen away from their escort, giggling wickedly down the hallway.

Ellari and Masha were oftentimes closer than cousins and shared more than sisters. And though they were both incredibly well-behaved young women, marked for their intelligence, piousness, humor and manners, Hivehall was *boring*. They had been among a herd of nearly thirty young ladies being herded down another stuffy hallway to look at tapestries or paintings of dead nobles or dead animals or some such dreariness and the temptation to sneak away and do anything else was too overwhelming. They had managed to escape Miss Maeve, their tall, strong-armed stewardess, and quickly moved down a side hallway, and out a tall doorway. Bumbling from the dim, stuffy hallway into the clear, sweet sunshine was a shock to be sure. The smoking woman standing beside the door was an even larger one.

She had been old, past forty to be sure. And she held a long wooden pipe, carved with lilies inlaid with something green and shiny. Ellari was very good with her jewels, but she wasn't sure. The woman only came to Ellari's shoulders, and the stink of pipeweed hung close to her. She was dressed in plain riding leathers, not like a lady at all. The only feminine items on her person were a light smear of pink on her lips and a white lily flower tucked behind her ear. She drew a deep pull from her pipe and hoarsely shouted at the two figures sparring in the yard.

"Get your shield up, boy, for cryin' out loud! You don't let your form slip!"

"No matter how poor the duelist you are facin'." A squat, mustachioed man grunted beside her. Though he seemed confident in his words, he still kept his voice low.

She passed the pipe to the man, somehow shorter than her, before noticing the two girls. Masha had immediately begun to fumble for the door handle. The leathery woman gave the girls a warm look and beckoned them closer with one hand, waving at her compatriot to scatter the smoke around the pair of them. "Well, lovely afternoon, my Ladies, I don't believe I've had the pleasure." The shift in the woman was instant, practiced manners despite the skunky odor and red eyes. The man with her did the same; the scarred face and mustache shifting to a chivalric mask of reserved geniality.

Ellari remembered her courtesies, practiced as a dance at a ball, "Lady Ellari Curr of Rime River," she gave a shallow curtsey before introducing her companion, "And this is Lady Masha, daughter of Lord Hullen Curr, High Lord of The Wylde." Masha gave a small bow of her own, mumbling a hello under her breath.

The woman in the riding leathers pulled a glove from her left hand and reached out, gently brushing the hair that Masha had artfully "allowed" to fall in her face. "Well, Lady Masha, if you're going to try and impress the prince, he needs to see your face, little one." Her hair cleared, Masha's face was plain to see.

Calling a fourteen-year-old girl "ugly" is not something that Ellari would readily do, especially one that Ellari loved as much as she loved Masha. That said, more than one servant had been punished severely for referring to her as "Little Lady Bulldog." Clan Curr's sigil being a dog had not helped the comparison, nor had the fact that a round head and strong jaw gave it a certain accuracy. *If her face matched her heart, she'd be the envy of every woman here and have every man chasing her,* Ellari thought to herself. In the end, it mattered little. Masha would be wed to some high lord or another, just as she had. Marry; secure the line.

"The Prince?!" Masha's shout was almost a squeal. On the field, two young knights were locked in combat. The taller of the two prowled athletically around the smaller, ringing his sword on the smaller knight's shield after every few practiced dance steps. Both knights were clad in plain practice mail, saving their finery for the upcoming days –grey mail, plain full-face helms, plain wooden shields. Save for the size difference and the choice of weapons, they were two fresh, plain twin soldiers. The smaller knight swung a blunted mace wildly toward the midsection of the taller, who caught it with his shield and sent the mace and the arm holding it bouncing backward. A shock of reverberation ran up the arm of the smaller knight, causing him to yelp loudly under his visor.

The taller knight spun, using the haft of his sword to ring the smaller knight's helm like a bell, which sent him spinning. The taller knight took a moment here, clanging his sword on his scuffed oaken shield. He gave a deep hoot of his own, echoed by a few of the young knights on the sidelines. The old squat knight with his blonde mustache near Ellari called out, an edge of annoyance overtaking his chivalric tone, "Quit showin' off!"

The tall knight spun his head toward the sound and began arguing back with the old squat knight. His helm made it difficult to hear his words, but Ellari certainly heard a few phrases she was reasonably sure were not meant for mixed company. She politely ignored them. She had, on occasion, spent a long night drinking with her husband and his sworn swords. Ellari Curr was no shrinking violet. She whispered to the woman next to her, "I'm so sorry, I don't mean to be rude. I do not know who *any* of you people are!"

The lady cackled, "Oh, sweetling! With the exception of the young Prince out there, well…" She turned and slapped a turtle in bronze against beryl, sewn in fine thread on the chest of her short companion. Ellari instantly recognized the sigil of Clan Mirebreaker, the lords of the Lowlands. They were the high lords of the southernmost nation in the Empire–a Clan equal to her own. Ellari's mind spun, searching for what she knew about the squat swampmen. She gasped, "You're the Bloody Lily! And that makes him…"

Lady Carmine Lily-Mirebreaker interrupted her, "He hates that nickname."

The Bloody Lily was one of the most famous tourney knights of their age, and she had married one of her greatest rivals, the squat, powerful Ser Tullus Mirebreaker, brother to the Lord of Okoboji.

The Snapping Turtle.

Surely she should have known. The squat frame, the flowing blonde waterfall of hair, the curved horseshoe of a blonde mustache; who else but The Snapping Turtle? Ser Tullus had finished shouting at the tall knight in the arena, and without a spare second, as the smaller knight had regained his feet.

More recognition came tumbling out, "Your daughter! Jasmine, she came down with us! She married my uncle! She's inside!"

Lady Carmine placed a gentle hand on Ellari's shoulder, "Oh, we know, girl. We broke our fast with her this morning, don't worry. Even got to visit our grandson. But right now, we're here for Lord Marten." She nodded back to the field, where the smaller knight was charging the larger.

"Lord Marten?" Masha's unsteady voice warbled forward. Strangers were not a strong suit for the young lady.

"He's the Lord of the Lowlands." Ellari answered, "He's my age, a bit older than you. He and his brothers are orphans."

"Ser Tullus is advising his nephew, helping Marten learn to rule with grace and dignity." Lady Carmine's gentle tone almost made one forget that she was dressed like a man and reeked of pipeweed.

"Kiss my fuckin' ass!" yelled the graceful, chivalric knight, as he turned away from the field. "I would knock his fuckin' head in myself if I wouldn't get executed for it."

The taller knight was laughing, his voice booming in his helm, as the smaller knight lunged forward, swinging his mace wildly. The taller knight leapt away once, laughing; twice, still laughing; but then, on the third strike, something incredible happened: the smaller knight put every last ounce into a wild upward arc, and it caught the larger knight right under the chin.

The leather strap under the taller knight's chin stretched and snapped, and the plain grey bucket helm was sent spinning, twirling through the air and crashing to the dust. The tall knight tossed his head of long black hair and planted a boot, smashing his shield into the visor of the smaller knight. A grimace crossed the face of the taller, unhelmed knight. He cracked the shield into the front of the smaller knight again, a dazed stagger taking hold. A third shield bash, this one even harder, knocked the smaller knight on his rear end, and a swift kick to the chest knocked him sprawling.

The taller knight spat, cursing under his breath, before turning away, rounding back on Ser Tullus. The Snapping Turtle flew to his feet and found himself in the yard, in the dust, nose to nose with the tall young knight. Now that he was closer, with his helm off, Ellari could get a much closer look at his face. He was handsome enough of, an age with Ellari, definitely noble-bred, with dark skin and striking blue eyes, having a bit of scruff of a goatee and even a few thin whiskers of a mustache poking above his lips.

The taller knight was everything a man should be, though it seems he had a bit of a hot temper. Masha had not taken her eyes off of him since the helm had come off. Currently, he was face to face with the Snapping Turtle, both of them screaming spittle at one another.

Ellari gasped. *Wait. That's Mirebreaker.*

If that's Mirebreaker, then...

The screams were replaced by a strange, hollow sound, like the ringing of a tea kettle but a few notes lower. Both men paused, as did Lady Carmine, and every other person in the yard. Every set of eyes turned to the smaller knight, Prince Vernus Artus, who had begun to wail. The noise wasn't a shriek of pain or panic, but a high howl of frustration. The brown leather boots on the knight's feet began to stomp as the wail broke into sobs. "Heeeeeeee ch-ch-chchCHEATED!" The smaller knight sat up and began to fumble at the leather strap on his helm. The voice rang out again, wobbling through sobs as gloved fingers failed to work the buckles on the helm. "He u-u-used his shield to h-h-hit me! He cheated! Someone get this thing off of me!" He stumbled to the far sideline where a squire took a smack before removing the helm and replacing it with a circlet of gold as thick as Ellari's thumb.

Terror took hold of Ellari as the situation became dangerously clear. The Lord of the Lowlands had just embarrassed the High Prince of the Realm. Afraid as she'd ever been, she pulled Masha back through the door. Lady Carmine was far too distracted to even attempt to stop them. Finding the slow-moving herd of ladies grazing their way mindlessly through the building was a simple matter, and their absence had thankfully gone unnoticed. It was some hours later, and neither Ellari nor Masha had heard what had become of Lord Marten, though the frenzied wails of Prince Vernus had not filled them with confidence.

Still, tomorrow was a new day and Masha's mournful voice broke Ellari from her memory, "What does father expect of us today, Ellari?"

Ellari looked over the spread presented, with which to break their fasts, the bounty of Clan Malbes was laid in front of them, and it was indeed a bounty. A basket of brown boiled eggs was nestled into a twin in wicker, stuffed with great hunks of cheese, every hue of ivory and gold. Fruit of every tree was stacked on platters–apples, grapes, melons, and berries that Ellari could not recognize, all of them absolutely fecund with juice. Salt ham and rashers of bacon lazed in honeyed sauces, both sweet and savory. Loaves of thick, crusty wheat bread had been sliced and laid beside creamy mountains of butter in daffodil. Clan Malbes did not skimp on luxury.

Ellari availed herself of the fruit and a bit of the bread and butter and settled in beside her cousin. The two of them chatted for a few minutes, never breaching the subject of the crying prince, at least not in front of Lady Gail. After breakfast, Ellari politely excused herself, and made her way to the yard in search of her husband. After a short walk, she would find him with his three best friends, two men that would do anything for their lord, and the man he did not know had taken his wife to lover.

Hullen Curr the Fourth turned from his three sworn swords when he saw Ellari and said something to them. Ellari could not hear it, but the three of them chuckled and dispersed. Ellari watched the back of the man she desired recede, but turned to the young lord she had been wed to– the cousin she had been wed to.

The younger Hullen was wolfish, good-looking and bombastic– another young lord perfectly groomed to rule. His eyes met Ellari's and he gave her the easy smile that won the hearts of soldiers and servants alike. "M'lady, to what do I owe the pleasure this early?" If he had overheard Lilah Stagg's foolishness last night, he did not react.

He was sweating lightly, just enough to cause the roughspun cotton fabric of his tunic to cling to his tightly muscled frame. He had been sparring with his companions, there was no doubt, but that would need to wait for later, even if the four of them had all been allowed to enter the tourney. She bowed her head politely, "My lord." She reached into her satchel, producing her stack of letters. She extended them, the top piece of parchment ringed with the purple-red of the base of a wine bottle. "I had hoped you'd be able to read the correspondence that 'you've' been making with Prince Talor. On account of the fact that you're meeting with the rest of the young lords tomorrow night..." His icy eyes met hers; neither spouse budging. "Midnight. Very secret." she reiterated. "My lord."

"I had been busying myself with... preparations for Prince Vernus's tourney. I may have skimped on preparation for Prince Talor's council." For a moment, he was not a young lord-to-be, but a sheepish teenager who had been caught failing in his duties. Ellari had excused herself shortly after the Staggs had absconded. She had searched for them, but after seeing them with Ser Mandel Stagg, she had been unable to approach, or call out or do anything shy of fret for the remainder of her restless night.

"These preparations involved wine?" Again, she held the stained letter inches from her husband's face.

"I was fraternizing with the other young lords and knights, building bonds of friendship and all that." He pawed at the ground with his left foot, nervous energy readily apparent to Ellari's practiced gaze.

"Hullen, I cannot attend this council in your stead." She folded the letter with a huff, "Which knights were you bonding with?"

"Well, I believe that Stagg knight was there, Ronald?"

"Reuben." Ellari's heart sank. *He came back.*

"Reuben! Yes! Lovely fellow, the picture of chivalry, my love. He's got a bandit lord up there in the Greatwood –"

She stopped him, "Who else?" *If the Stagg girl had spoken to him...*

'Well, Chad and Esben and Hale, of course." She smirked inside, never loosening the mask. "And Maesh brought over that Learner you like; the one with the book, we talked to him for a minute, great big beard on him, like one of those mountainmen!"

This was too much, "Learner Vaughn? He's *here?!*" She grabbed Hullen, all manners lost, "What did you talk to him about, what did he say, Hullen? I need you to be very specific."

"Well, the cider was flowing, I do not rightly recall the manner of the discussion, but I did mention you, and he promised to introduce himself if he saw us together." Ellari's stomach dropped out. Learner Vaughn had seen more of the world than any man in the last three hundred years. He had written essays and tomes that Ellari had studied by rote. She was, in short, overwhelmed at the idea of any discussion with the Sojourned Learner.

"You are not forgiven for not doing the reading, Hullen." She shoved the letters into his arms roughly, causing him to stumble backward, "But let's see if I can keep you from embarrassing the entire Wylde."

And perhaps, I can too.

SLADE 1

"There's my brave boy, don't be so stern, Slade. Laugh, smile. Sh... I know you're afraid. When... you and... Marten and Jamen. You must take care of one another for me, boy. Tullus and his wife will help... but they're wild... Slade, you're the only one left who knows how to act noble.."

"You're going to get caught immediately." He placed his good hand on his younger brother's shoulder.

Jamen dangled his tortoise over the chest of clothes they were packing, "You think?"

"If you don't, you'll kill him. Being in a dark, hot trunk that long, with no food or water? Yes, Jamen, you will kill your turtle." Slade nodded in a rhythm with his dire warning.

Jamen wailed so loudly that behind them, Gar, the huge blonde smithee, dropped the large canvas duffle with a clangorous crash that could have only been rivaled if he had shoved his household's cookwagon and every last pan, knife and iron in it off a cliff. "Aw, fuck!" He saw the teenage lordling and his wailing brother and realized he had cursed loudly. His face blushed rosy-pink, and he stumbled, "Sorry, apologies, m'lords, just... didn't wanna damage the ..enamel... Never you mind." Noticing the wailing six-year-old, he shoved the duffel to the side, hearing it clatter and clang, wincing slightly as it did. Once the duffel was sufficiently in the hall, Gar bounded over.

Garland, Gar for short, was about thirty. The top of his curly crown of golden hair brushed most of the doorframes in The Moss Mont, the ancestral keep here in Okoboji. He was thick-chested, and brawny, but held onto a stubborn layer of babyfat that made him seem less threatening than a three-hundred-fifty pound ironworker ought to be.

His Uncle Tullus thought that no one knew that Garland was his bastard, sired on a woman of Clan Tallman, a couple of years before he'd wed Aunt Carmine. Uncle Tullus had gone to great lengths to hide his shame from everyone, but still to do right by Gar. He had covered his tracks remarkably well, but Slade was a remarkably bright boy. He had noticed the discrepancy in the bookkeeping a few years ago, doing some reading when he was nine. Chasing one rabbit hole down another led to the realization that his Uncle had secretly been paying for not only the smith's lodging and food, but martial training with blade and shield for some reason.

Rather than confront his knightly Uncle, Slade did what Slade always did. He set his mind to find answers. It had been obvious in retrospect, Gar and Tullus shared the same big blue puppy-dog eyes, and those eyes had been shared with their Lord Father. Slade and his brothers had eyes of that same blue, though they favored their mother in almost every other way. When a ten-year-old Slade had presented his evidence to Father–audits of spending and maps detailing the knightly journeys of his uncle, opposed to women who may have fathered Gar, an essay by a Learner of the Goldengrass on patterns of appearances in breeding pairs of horses and several very provocative illustrations–Lord Gellen had laughed so deeply, Slade had feared him choking. The High Lord, like his brother, a stout keg of a man, had pulled Slade in close, kissing his forehead and laughing at his brilliant boy. *He had known, of course. That was Father: room enough for everyone at his table and behind his walls.* He had died three years ago, alongside mother, choking on the swamp fever that had killed so many that hot summer.

They had died three years past, and Slade Mirebreaker still had not remembered how to smile.

Slade watched his secret-bastard-cousin comfort his screaming baby brother."Lord Jamen, what's wrong?" The big man was far more gentle than his size would ever begin to hint. His tone and softness put Slade in mind of a great stuffed pillowman– something that could only bring comfort, despite hands that could bend steel.

"Slade says I can't bring the Captain!" Jamen roughly shoved an ancient, placid-natured tortoise in Gar's face.

"The Ca–Captain?" Gar was confused, but Gar was often confused.

"The Tortoise." Slade finished, "Though, his name is Umi."

Gar held out two tremendous hands as hard as the iron they worked, but gentle and deft. He motioned for Jamen to hand him the tortoise, which the small boy did. He lifted the ancient thing, so it faced him, eye to eye. "Seems to me, about ten years ago, your Lord brother called him 'Little Uncle', making fun of Ser Tullus."

The big turtle reached out for Gar, clawed feet digging through soil and finding only air.

"And, five years or so before *that,* Lady Jasmine named him Oliver and led him through the gardens on a pink ribbon. Hand to the Golden Boy, that's a truth."

Jamen's crying had stopped, and he was focused on the big smith and the turtle.

"And before that Ser Tullus and your Late Lord Father, bless him, named it Shelldon and tried to get it to race a sloth from Assora for a pile of cabbage and carrots."

"Wait, who won?" Slade was genuinely curious.

"That's not the point, boys. The point is, this turtle here was old when Lord Gellen, bless him, was a boy. He'll still be here when you have boys to play with him."

He handed the turtle back to Jamen, who hugged it to his chest tightly.

"You can leave him here, Jamen. He'll be here when you return." The boy began to lower the tortoise back to the ground, gently releasing him when his claws brushed the floor. With his lower lip wobbling, the boy nodded to Garland. The big-hearted smith wheeled back to the hallway, lifting his clanging duffel, "And no matter what you call that big turtle, that miserable bastard will still be a miserable bastard." He marched down the hallway, calling back to the boys, "Now, hurry up, your Lord Brother wants to be on the ship by mid-day!"

The Emperor had been a cousin to their Lord Father, their grandmother Artus herself, and their Great-Grandfather a king. By right, Marten was fourth or fifth in line to the high throne, depending how you counted the girls. Slade saw little point in paying such things any mind; the Lowlands were plump with her own issues, and unless the Crown intended to intervene, they were all but useless to him. The divide between the wealthy inner houses and the poorer ones, stretched thin by elven pirates, spring squalls and a galling lack of sailing vessels, was growing larger. Old resentments were starting to flare once more. Clans Bridge and Plover, both younger than most of the great clans, had lucked into massive amounts of wealth from land, sea and field, while many older, prouder houses struggled. The Lords of Brimstone and Coralspear, proud men both, were now sending letters on the fortnight, begging for men or ships or at least leave to cross the Trader's Strait and burn out these ruffians in their caves and hovels.

Marten could not give them men or ships, because he had neither to spare. Marten could not give them permission to go attack the continent. Relationships between the Empire and the Kingdoms of the continent fell to the King, not an eighteen-year-old High Lord.

Still, letters that Marten had been receiving from the Crown Prince and sharing with Slade had been interesting. Marten valued Slade's critical eye and vast swathes of knowledge– little bits and pieces picked up here and there that seemed to become part of his way of thinking. Leading men came as naturally to Marten as the swing of a sword, he was tall and handsome and strong; in every way the perfect lord.

Slade stroked his own face with his good left hand. He took after their mother, they all three did. Dark skin, dark hair, thin, fine Haymaker features, but the big pools of peacock blue were shared by all the Mirebreakers, even cousin Jasmine, widowed with her baby far away in frigid Rime River. He wasn't vain enough to care if he was handsome. He was smart, and that was enough.

Marten had laid it out best: there was no need for rivalry between the brothers; they were better together. Marten had the martial skill and could make men love him. Slade had strength of character, knowledge and wisdom. Marten wasn't the perfect lord; they were made to rule together, and when the time came, they could even find a place and duties for little Jamen. Three brothers, one kingdom.

Still.

He raised his right hand. His malformed hand. When he was born, the cord that joined him by his belly to their lady mother had bound itself around the fourth and fifth fingers of his right hand– the two smallest. The labor had been difficult and had taken many, many hours, and by the time that Slade had been unbreeched and brought into the world, the two smallest of his fingers were as black as the moss in the deepest parts of the swamp. They never grew, and by the time he was five, he had demanded that the visiting Learner, a great bear of a man called Vaughn, remove the hideous, twisted little black mouse–bones from his hand. The result was half of a hand that served well enough holding a quill or a paintbrush, even a scalpel. But Slade Mirebreaker would never hold a sword or axe in his dominant hand, and that was that.

The first leg of the trip had been slow going, as his brother was making a point to visit many of the keeps of their Lowland Kingdoms that he had yet to visit since his ascension to high lord. They had been fed like they were being fattened and given gifts of every stripe to curry favor. Lord Lukas Axe, the somber one-handed Lord of Brimstone, joined them once they had left his smoking island keep. His heavy cog of red and black wood kept pace with the smaller, lighter Mirebreaker ships, with their sails of viridian silk, shockingly well. At Brinegate, portly old Lord Selach paraded his twin daughters in front of Marten and Slade, speaking of their beauty, intelligence and chastity, and the bonds that twins have. Deeper and more profound than simple sisters, he said. One heart, mind and soul in two bodies, you see. As Slade watched the girls move in perfect unison, he was inclined to believe the old lord, pale and blubbery and disquieting as he was.

The next morning, Uncle Tullus had pulled them both– he and Marten–aside once they had raised anchor once more, he grumbled under his thick blonde horseshoe mustache. "That, boys, was a *bottom-feeder*, and I don't care if he is your sworn man, Marten, do not trust him."

The deck shifted uneasily beneath their feet as Marten looked over Tullus's face, looking for the joke, "Why not, ser? He offered us fine food and fine wine and fine beds."

"Aye, and flesh, too, I'll trust you were smart enough not to partake?" Uncle Tullus didn't even have to look at Slade, but Marten only smiled sheepishly.

"...Both of them."

Uncle Tullus had only struck Marten on one occasion since he'd taken the Austral Seat, but this became the second. Though the Young Lord had a good four inches on his uncle, it mattered little, as the old knight swung a cupped hand vigorously into his nephew's ear. A thunderclap sent Marten to the deck, groaning as Slade sniggered, furious, Uncle Tullus turned to him too, "If you think it's funny, or if you feel like bein' that bleedin' dumb, I swear to the Gods, I got plenty fer you too, Slade." He brandished the black of a green-gloved hand like a war-axe, and Slade raised his hands in protest.

"You'll not have to tell me, I'm not so stupid as to leave a bastar–"

Crack.

In his Uncle's defense, Slade had earned that one.

A month after setting north, sailing the black-blue waters of the Shining Strait, they had arrived in Honeyhome. The entire city was full to bursting, to say nothing of the keep of Hivehall itself. White walls buzzed with swarms of activity, and Slade felt excitement creep into his chest. Tonight, Marten would take him around the yard. There were no official gatherings, but the young and rich and beautiful would always find a place and cause to celebrate. Honeyhome was warm and filled with gardens and fountains in the green spaces. Slade had little interest in interacting with the gathered nobility, but what was important was that he would prove that he *could.*

Careful, awkward, cautious, quiet Slade would show Marten that they could rule together in truth –that he did not have to simply be the power behind the throne– and Marten could use his friendship with the Prince to get Slade into his clandestine meeting of the Young Lords tomorrow night, after the first day of the Grand Tourney.

The door to their borrowed chambers swung open hard, smashing against the plaster wall, sending a thunderous reverberation through the door, the wall and Slade's chest. Rage and bluster and teenage frustration preceded Lord Marten Mirebreaker into the room, like a herald's call. Behind him, he could hear both the thunder of his Uncle and Aunt. Marten shouldered his way through the door, before he looked at Slade, and shook his head, mouth open but jaw set at a frustrated angle. "Fuck the Prince, we're leaving."

WHAT?

His heart hit the back of his throat as he rose to his feet, scattering the papers in front of him. "Marten, we cannot–the tourney…" He lowered his voice, hissing through his teeth before his Uncle and Aunt could hear. "The *meeting!?!*"

"I don't care." Marten was fuming.

If Marten had been a tornado of rage and bluster, The Snapping Turtle was a monsoon. He came through the door, spit flying from every word, splattering itself across the plain practice mail that the Lord of the Lowlands was garbed in. "You could have *killed him*, you— DULLARD."

The flats of his big palms thumped the boy lord in the chest, and he stumbled backward onto a low, flat reclining sofa of yellows and browns, left to sprawl across in the sunlight of this solar, no doubt. The old knight wheeled on his young lord, "I can't trust you in a sparring match with the Prince! You almost beat the king's son to death. Why?" He paused, letting the question hang in the room, Lady Carmine filed in behind him, quiet, but no less choleric. "Because you *let him knock your helmet off?"*

From his chair, Marten slouched back, raising his chin, defiant. The few sparse whiskers he called his "beard" spiked skyward. Finally, the High Lord of one of the six greatest kingdoms in the world spoke, "The little fucker had no business in the yard."

Slade swore he saw Uncle Tullus dismiss the urge to hit Marten again. "If you leave, you're layin' even more insult at the feet of the king, and I will not let you do it–not to me and not to your brothers." He turned to Slade, his usually jovial face somber. "Where's Jamen?"

"He's asleep in our chambers. They had a cheese with bacon hunks in it at the midday meal. He ate too much of it and has a stomach ache now. I gave him some lime and mint." Slade was ashamed, but didn't understand why.

Tullus looked at Slade and then Marten. He took a long, sad breath and looked back to Slade, "You're a good boy. You're just like your father, and I mean that with all the good I got in me." He collapsed into himself, turning to Marten, "Gods save us all, you're just like *me."*

Uncle Tullus stepped back into the hall, the chamber door clicking softly behind him. Aunt Carmine hung there, silent for a moment, "Don't leave the chambers until we come back, Marten. We're going to speak with the King and Lord Malbes."

As she placed a hand on the brown-gold doorknob, Slade asked her the question that had been bothering them since they'd left the apartments this morning, "How was your breakfast with your daughter?'

Lady Carmine Lily looked at Slade with her weathered brown skin and weathered brown hair, and she smiled, "It was lovely, Slade. Thank you." She slipped through the door to find her knightly husband, with a final "Do not leave, either of you."

An hour later, Lord Marten had kept one of his promises. At least, he had found a place for them to socialize. A few folks had gathered in the Great Gate Garden, and the sound of their revels had drifted high to the window of the tower where the boys had been sequestered. Escape was simply a matter of telling the servants to attend to Jamen when he rose and walking out the door. The two Malbes guardsmen at the bottom of the spiral stairs were more than happy to trade their silence for a pair of shiny silver suns. The tall one, thin as a spear, was far more educated in matters of nobility, whereas his shorter friend with the pimple on his nose, had no such airs. But Spearshaft and Pimple were paid, and would remain silent.

The Silver Sun was setting as the brothers hurried across the dusky yard, shadows long as they slipped between the hedges into the Great Gate Garden. As the pair parted the trees, the smell hit them first– that specific odor of bonfire and pipeweed and roasting sausages. As the two young men entered the six-sided garden, they found the revels. The party had not been on long, no more than two hours, but the stench of smoke in the early summer humidity clung to the inside of Slade's nostrils in a sharp, acrid way. He felt in need of a wash just from being in the presence of such debauchery.

Smoke and song and skin and spirits and snowdrops seemed to spiral circling Slade Suffice to say, the second son of the Southern swamps was stunned speechless. A dozen lordlings or more were lazed around a bonfire, drinking Malbes Mead, and Madapple Cider, and some awful blackstrap rum.

Marten pressed a horn of something pale and frothing into Slade's good hand, before giving him a wink, "It's just a beer they make here, kids' stuff." He leaned close, taking care not to embarrass Slade, using the din to hide his advice. "Try not to drink it too fast, and I'll get you some more if you need."

Overwhelmed, all Slade could do was nod. As his brother led him through the tall sentinel trees, low hedges and those odd little purple and white flowers that Slade could not quite place. He took his first pull of the beer and instantly disliked it–sweet and sour and bitter. It stunk on his tongue, and he decided the closest thing he could imagine to it was moldy pickle juice. It was awful, but he would be damned if he would be rude, so he carried it along and sipped it whenever it seemed appropriate. Names he knew escaped him–and those were rare enough, a grinning red-haired knight, a tall and pale-blonde girl, with a heavy northern accent. A handsome young man in the Goldenlocke colors was kissing an older maid in the blues and greys of one of the two Jytte Clans. He tried not to stare, but Marten had to grab him by the collar and pull him along their way.

The brothers settled in near the fire as Slade decided to hurry down his thin yellow beer. It was not improving with warmth. They sat together for a good while, really. After he had finished his first horn of beer, he was looking for a servant to hand the thing off to. When he extended it to a passing girl in Malbes yellows, browns and purples, she lifted a pitcher and sloshed something burgundy into it, filling it full. By the time Slade had worked up the courage to try it, a pretty, pale girl was singing. She wore wings on her headdress, and her left eye glinted like a cat in the dark. The first cup of beer had set Slade's cheeks to buzzing, not unpleasantly. He tasted this purple stuff and found it not entirely repugnant… on the first drink.

Slade kept sipping to be polite, and Slade was very polite.

Slade had been occasionally allowed a glass of sweet white cider or would be given a jigger of corn whiskey on wet cold nights, when the fogs grew thick on the swamps, the ghosts of his dead fingers danced and pricked him, but he never drank to excess, ever, before tonight. He watched as the singer whorled. The songs of dead heroes and beautiful tragedies gave way to a bawdy girl shaped like a kettle, and when Slade blinked away the haze provided by a fourth horn of drink, he recognized the usually businesslike Lady Joelle Bridge. Her pink cheeks were flushed to plump red apples, as she guffawed her punchline, *"It's awfully small, you can't pick up branches with it, and you can't even breathe through it! Put your breeches back on, son; it's nothing special!"* She puffed air between red lips to make a trumpeting elephant sound, as if to drive her joke home. She noticed Slade and smiled at him broadly, "Glad to see you out of the library, little lord."

If there was insult there, Slade didn't sense it. He politely nodded, raising his horn, slurring slightly, "Sthanks you, My Lady. S'very good joke, about elephant trunks and…" the words he turned over in his head were examined carefully. Anything too clinical, and they'd think him some sort of– intellectual, which he was, but that sort of reputation stunted the sort of respect Slade was hunting. "Penish… Pensisesis… Penii?"

She chortled, as she stepped toward him, smirking at the bronze dragon-turtle stitched onto his jerkin, "Well, an elephant trunk is a damn sight finer than a *turtle head."*

The laughter returned again, this time with a crueler edge to it. Lady Joelle, for her part, was horrified at the words she had said, and clearly regretted them instantly. As the young lord and ladies and the sons and daughters of the older ones began to laugh Slade down, Lady Joelle made a breathless apology, lost in the scores of laughter.

Someone yelled out, "He's tiny, crippled *and* slow on the draw!" And that was too much. Slade, drunk, overwhelmed and far from home broke into a run, away from the crowd, into the bushes, into any place safe. As he pushed into the greenery, he heard the sound of his brother tackling Ser Rolof Deepreach, the tall raider knight who had so loudly mocked him. Marten was raining practiced elbows down on Deepreach's face. A slender Grey Guard in purple managed to pull Marten off Deepreach, aided by three men of Clan Malbes. Blood ran down Marten's chin as he spat a red mouthful on Deepreach's boots, laughing filthy curses.

This was all well behind Slade; he was running, racing. All that mattered was putting all the distance he could find between himself and anyone in that garden. As he hurried toward a circle of arched vine and those little purple flowers that were everywhere, he raised his right hand to shield his face from a few loose hanging strands of green. The world turned to mist, and he remembered what flowers they were.

Nightshade.

He ran. How long he was running, he could not say. He was not a speedy creature, but not for lack of trying. He was running through chest-high mist that felt more like mud. He was still in Honeyhome, in the gardens at Hivehall... was he? It had suddenly grown overcast, heavy, clouds in the sky obscuring the final flares of silver sunset. Sunsets. Twin flares of light piercing the cloudy twilight. One east-of-northeast, one almost straight northwest. Every sailor knows his skies, and every Mirebreaker is a sailor. Something was strange. The shadows in the trees had gone blacker, impossible to tell where gloam ended and blackwood began. Something thrummed, too. Something impossibly huge and nearer than Slade would have liked . And for all his knowledge and logic, the boy was terrified.

Though shrouded scourges swirled in the silvered mists around the boy, he found sense. He reached his left hand down and pulled the light Lutinese dagger that Uncle Tullus made him carry. His good hand gripped it gracelessly, but it was better than nothing, he supposed. He pressed through the fog, holding the dagger in front of him. The longer he held the dirk ahead of him, the more confident he felt. As his confidence grew, he found that the fog grew thinner. Though it was still slowing him, after a few moments, it was more akin to walking into a breeze than slogging through mud.

Though the mists' innumerable invisible fingers had released their grip on Slade's clothes, the thrumming was growing ever greater. This great burring drone penetrated the sky and its clouds; it echoed through the black trees with their twisted bony fingers. It shook the ground, grey ash and dust shifting with its rhythm. It pounded into the boy's chest, aching him, as he pressed deeper. As he moved through these awful, black, misty gardens, it occurred to Slade that he may have left Honeyhome somewhere in his tracks.

Though he could still see the high wall to his right, it was not whitestone. Slade pressed himself through the thick air and grew close enough to examine the facade. It was a yellow-sort of brownish. Almost brass in the right light. He pressed his dagger into it, and found it yielding. Perhaps it was the residual wine in his rapidly sobering blood, but Slade grew the courage to touch the wall and found it waxy.

He peeled a long sliver and pressed it into a ball the size of a lemon before sliding the strange substance into a hidden pocket on his jerkin.

Though the thrumming had begun to grow, forcing Slade to bite down on his bottom lip. He continued. The wall on his right, and the high-domed crown of Hivehall silhouetted in black against the sky on his left. Slender Slade continued, with his thin dirk extended. Voices snaked over the gloom and through the drone. Slade lowered himself into the mist and snuck forward, each step slower and more deliberate than the last. He listened, creeping ever closer.

The first voice was like a man's, though lower, and echoing. "--pens to that half, mirrors this side, Tellaoma. And tides are rising on both sides, that only feeds into itself." He couldn't see the source from his hiding spot, nor even how many figures there were. Danger be damned, Slade crept nearer.

Whatever answered was not a man, too much air wheezed when it spoke, too much flesh rattled and warbled, and deep within the source the voice, something chimed along a dull ting. "Weeeelllllll zzzzzztheennn, peeeerrrrrrrhahaaaapzzzz, iiiiiiitttt haaazzz beeeecomeee time forafloooddd-d-d-d, to purge both zzzzsssshoooreeeszz."

"There are reports of the blight on our side out east. Here." The man-voice was pleading, but stern, "Do not act as if you are blind to it, even here. The eastern beacon dims."

Slade looked to the sky again. The eastern "sunset" did seem to be a lesser one.

"ZZZZThe balancezzz wiiiillll reeezzzsszstore itsssseeelf." Whatever it was made a sagging, sucking sound, and Slade soon surmised it was inhaling. Something like a bubbling burp burst forth,

following more of the awful voice, "Zzzthe aaaaragonite deeeep haaaszzz madddee thiiiszz beddd, leeett–tt ittt-tt zzsleeep in itttt."

"The Argonite is not maintaining the bulwark, Tellaoma." Slade finally pressed close enough to see the figures in the yard, speaking low in the shadow of Hivehall's high dome. "'Man and beast, seelie and fell,' or are the old oaths so quickly lost here, too?"

"Man and beast, seelie and fell..." Slade turned the words over in his head. They held the scent of familiarity, but they meant nothing at the moment. He lowered himself to his belly and had gripped his dagger in his teeth. The leather tasted oily and he felt entirely foolish, but he needed both hands to creep along the low fog, in this strange dust and ash. Even the least fertile grounds, rare as they were, at Honeyhome were gorgeous golden sands, and here... silt and smoke. Finally, he was near enough to see, though he wished he had not.

The man-voice was coming from a bird-man-thing. Feathers of black, brown and grey cascaded from its shoulders– a wing-like mantle. Set into its black face were two huge, pitiless aurelion eyes. The bird-thing was unattended, save a storm of feathers that moved in his wake.

Whatever a Telloama was, Slade wished it had stayed a mystery. It had the face of a woman– a mask of iron wrought in celestial beauty. From its strange, fleshy tone, Slade had not expected a creature so lean. Pale perfect feet hung six inches from the dust below it, it simply hovered. Up shapely legs, porcelain white, hips, and a sexless womanly shape. It was a woman, though paler than the palest corpse and devoid of her... Slade stumbled over his own thoughts. ...Genitals.

Its nude body was flesh, wreathed in an eerie lightless glow. Her flesh seemed to scuttle and shift– jewels tumbling over one another.

It was hairless, even its head, though it wore an iron mask, hiding its face. The mask seemed to be bolted or nailed directly to the nude woman's head. Only her chin and lower mandible remained visible–black lips and a maw of pointed teeth. When it spoke, it rattled with the thrum of...

Of...

The... castle...

The High Dome of Hivehall rose against the slate-colored clouds. Mounds of albumen churned where Slade had expected to see brass. Something massive and pallid and fleshy and segmented rose fecund into the sky, pregnant with dark shapes stirring against sinuous tissues. The whole thing thrummed and shook within great chitinous trunks gripping it in claw-tight fingers. The great larval white firmament was set into more of the brass-gold substance, as the wall behind him.

The source of the thrumming was before him, it filled him, it shook him, it horrified him. As he felt it inside, churning with his heartbeat, he had to flee. Away from the bird-thing, away from the high thrumming, away from the naked woman. He scrambled to his feet, a long-legged fawn on ice, graceless and frantic. If the Bird-Thing or Telloama or the horrible, high dome noticed his expeditious retreat, they did not care. His feet beat the silt and dust, small clouds rising, mingling into the fog.

His heartbeat was doubling the thrum now, pounding like a cicada against the finger-thin bones of his chest. Black branches and hanging vines clawed at his cerulean eyes and inky tresses, but he would not slow; he ran; as far and as fast as he could.

South. To the ocean. To the swamps. To safety.

To water. Always water. Water was home.

There were wings behind him. Then nothing.

He woke the next morning, the morning of the tourney. He was in his borrowed bed, high in the tower. Jamen and the silver sun beamed brightly over him, filling his vision. His head felt as if it had been removed, dunked in tar and hastily reattached, but he was otherwise fine… until he sat up and his stomach shifted and so did the world. Fighting off wave after wave of nausea, he steadied himself and rose.

"You got back late." Jamen stared at him, deathly serious, "You are in so much trouble"

Slade shook off the morning cobwebs and intense hangover, ignoring the taunt, "Is Marten back?"

"He has a black eye that no one will talk about. I think his sword hand is broken. He's got it wrapped in gauze, but he won't tell anyone what happened."

That noble moron. If Slade had more thoughts on the matter, they melted away when he reached in his pocket and removed a perfectly round dab of beeswax, the size of a lemon.

ILLYSTRE I

"Lordsport is a viper's nest, Illystre. It's a den of villains and rot, topped by a navel-gazing old fool. You should not place yourself there. Search for your secrets, boy, but do not let it corrupt you."

"I think this entire ordeal is a farce and a wasteful one at that," bleated the old Lord of Defense, his thin lips flecked with dried spittle. Just watching this shriveled little sheep in his horned chair made Illystre parched. He lifted the wine chalice to his own lips and found its contents sweeter than he generally enjoyed, but let it have a chance to play on his tastebuds before dismissing it entirely. "The Empire has emptied our reserves too deeply in our reconstruction of the… Eastern provinces."

He won't even dignify Ozwyk with a name. That's charming.

"The Prince doesn't require such extravagances, I agree." The cords of sinew in Learner Franz's neck showed tension as the old monk spoke. He turned to the king, seated at the head of the table, in his high seat of honor. "The boy, Your Grace, to be frank, if I may…" Illystre generally liked Franz; he was intelligent and compassionate, with a good sense of humor, like everyone's favorite grandfather. But one could never accuse the old pedagogue in his bisected robes of black and white, of being brave.

"Speak freely, Franz; yours is the counsel of a learned friend." Wreathed in shadow, the king, crown and throne were one shade of spike and black bent iron. Emperor-King Gallus Artus III spoke in a way that made men listen. Even without the sorcery in his blood, his voice carried the weight of royalty.

"As a younger man, I had the pleasure of leading your education and instruction in many of the finer practices of my College, as you well recall, Your Grace." The smile on Franz's face was tinged with a wistful sadness, but it was genuine.

"I recall mathematics and figures being a devil I shall never slay." The king's laugh was rich from the dark, and the assembled Eight laughed with him.

From his plush, stallion-crested chair, the Lord of Finance laughed loudest, "Thus ensuring my continued service ever on." Under his spanning mustache, Lord Hinric Saddler grinned. Not yet thirty, the baby brother of the Goldengrass's High Lord had become something of a spitfire in his rapid rise to the Council of Lords Ascendant. Illystre watched Saddler closely, tasting the wine again, tasting the sweet grapes, plump in the sun. At first it had been mildly pleasant, but it was fast growing cloying and syrup-thick on his tongue– much too sugary. "And I am ever grateful for the opportunity, Your Grace." Saddler's chip-of-emerald eyes noticed Illystre's smoke-and-ice gaze on him, and they met. *No warmth when he laughs.*

From the end of the table opposite the King, the red-faced Lord Executor huffed back at Franz. "Continue, please, Learner." The words rode puffs of hot air as Ser Grigori Bridge tried to return the table to task.

"Thank you, my lord. As I was saying, I have instructed both yourself and the Crown Prince Talor. And in my many years as a teacher and student, I found you both remarkable in both intelligence and ethic, Your Grace. To be blunt, both you and the Crown Prince were enjoyable and rewarding pupils." He paused, waiting for the King to affirm him, but finally continuing on when the King did not. "And I currently oversee the instruction of both Prince Vernus and wee Princess Bara. And... while I find Bara to be a student much like you and Prince Talor." He paused again, trying to find the words to remain polite but honest, "Prince Vernus is no such student, Your Grace. On the rare occasions that he makes any sort of effort, well, the results are... unencouraging."

The noise that King Gallus made was not one of surprise. *At least he knows.*

"I think rewarding such behaviors in the Prince is ill-advised, Your Grace. Let his betrothal be some small thing, If he must have a tourney, have an afternoon of jousts on the island. This *endeavor* at Honeyhome seems too huge. Too costly" His calloused hands worked the parchment in front of him nervously, folding one brown corner over itself back and forth.

"Damn the cost! Why are we letting a sixteen-year-old boy pick his own wife?" Clifton Torchbearer's directness was downright impressive. The Lord of Judgment was a tower of a man missing his left leg; he had bid himself to stand too rapidly, slipping, kicking his tower-topped seat backward and banging a fist on the table. "Apologies, Your Grace, but the boy needs a firm hand, but he is being allowed to run rampant acr–"

"ENOUGH."

The chill in the air was palpable. Where there had been laughter moments before, silence hung like a shroud. The King's voice was no longer a genial thing. Illystre tensed, sitting up. He fingered the light Lutinese throwing knife on his thigh, but a glint of gold from the shadows betrayed his thoughts, and his fingers stopped without his command. "I am not devoid of humor, councilors. Am I not a merry man? But I will not be told how to raise my children. I am wise enough to ask you for counsel on matters where I require it."

He rose from the shadows and stepped into the light, his fury clear. He was a handsome man worn thin by time and the crown he bore. Golden eyes set deep above dark, sleepless circles, the Emperor of Kings looked less like the shrewd politician he was known as and more a phantom. "This is not a place I require it." His tone made argument impossible, "My wife has already made commitments to Clan Malbes, who is looking to fund much of the proceedings, isn't that correct, Lord Hinric?"

The Lord of Finance gave an affirmative nod, "I believe so; my sister-by-law is handling many of the arrangements with her father, Lord Dobson Malbes."

A thin cackle escaped the one-eyed blonde woman to his left, but it was quickly stifled. Illystre looked to Lady Carelin Marle and furrowed his brow, curious to understand what she found so funny, but unable to ask. *Likely she knows, as well we all, that the mere proposal of a Tourney in Honeyhome is to serve the Saddler girl up to the prince.* The young Lord Spymaster chuckled to himself. *A honeypot hanging above a bear-pit.*

"Then it is a settled matter, a proposal to be voted on. Make your decision, but know that if Queen Natasha is displeased, you may all bear the brunt of her displeasure. I leave it in your hands, Lord Executor. I grow weary." He leaned hard on the table, the golden shimmer in his eyes fading a moment, leaving them but muddy brown-grey pits, as the King drew a sharp inhale of breath. The Grey Guard in the corner, Ser Auberon Sozen, rushed up, but the king steadied, his eyes shining once more. He raised a hand, staying Ser Auberon, "Do not– I am fine, good Ser." He took a pair of carefully measured steps toward the exit, meeting a second of the Grey Brothers at the doorway– the still wet-behind-the-ears Drake Canar. "Do as you will, Lords and Lady." The Canar boy followed the king out, duckling in file.

Once King Gallus had retired, plump Ser Grigori took over. Bridge had served as Gallus Artus' Lord Executor for the last nine of the King's thirteen-year reign. The rotund man in pink took the position, after the previous Lord Executor, Lord Morsk Selach, had been dismissed and summarily sent to the Far Fort to live out his days in hard labor. If sentenced to the same fate, Lord Bridge would likely burst like a dropped winebladder.

The little, pink, round man was inhaling small buttery pastries layered with chocolate. They came from Sienne, or at least the style of them did, Illystre knew. Bridge was notorious for not just his appetite, but his sweet tooth. Despite the flakes in his prodigious moustache, he spoke gracefully, "Well, my lords, the king has made his wishes quite clear, unless someone has an objection." His eyes moved from Torchbearer to Clearcall to the old Learner, "Perhaps simply moving to a vote is the most elegant solution."

"Here, here," chuffed Lord Hinric in agreement.

Bridge offered his own vote first, as his wont to lead, "I, personally, am in favor of the grand tourney for our Prince's coming of age. Lady Carelin?"

The Lord (*or Lady?*) Admiral grinned wickedly, the lilting tones of her island accent playing musically, "Aye, I'm in favor; who am I to upset our fine lady Queen?" She reclined lazily in her own high seat, headed with a handsome Marlin wrought in cedarwood. She was young and beautiful in the way that only a wild blonde woman can be. She and Illystre had *flirtations*, but they were not like to seriously pair. Still, she was dangerous and pretty and commanded more tall ships than any other clan on any shore.

Bridge chomped another pastry, "Lord Varyon?"

Clearcall frowned, but he constantly frowned. The puckered Lord of Defense only offered two words in vote, "Absolutely not."

"Hmph" was the reply from the Lord Executor as he settled back into his green and silver chair, clawed feet and chitinous finish. Bridge gave his own frown, looking to the Lord of Judgment next. "Lord Clifton, you must at least see the reason here."

The tall, grim Torchbearer spoke through gritted teeth, "I do not. I will not support this stupidity. No. I vote 'no'."

Principled old fools, but one has to respect the dedication to their philosophy. Illystre lifted his wine cup again, pressing his lips to it but drinking none, despite appearances. *Still, those two hold no surprises...* He turned his attention past the empty throne to the Learner's Seat of Honor on the left. A place beside the king, as he may offer his constant knowledge– a plain wooden stool. Oak, three legs, no back. Looking at it, Illystre was not entirely sure the wood was even sanded. Franz was a very well-regarded man, even in the remarkable lineage of the High Learners. *This one though...*

"Learner Franz, please!" Bridge may have been Lord Executor, but without the consent of the council, funding the tourney would be impossible. The plump little crawfish was growing anxious, it was written plain on his cherry-red face. "Do you consent, at least?"

Carefully, Franz continued to fuss with the browned parchment in front of him, working his little corner of it back and forth tensely. "My lord..." His practiced fingers continued as his mind raced, looking for reason, justification, anything and coming up bare. "I–"

The parchment corner tore.

"I cannot, Lord Bridge." Franz's face was heavy-lined with a morose frown, "I'm sorry, old friend. I cannot spend gold on a party for a spoiled boy while good men starve in the wilds of Ozwyk, just for a chance to work life back into their grandfather's farmland."

Shit. He's good. Three no-votes put Bridge and his tourney in jeopardy. And worse with the next vote going to...

"Lord Hinric? How do you think we should best proceed?" Bridge knew the answer, as did every person in the room– it was only a formality.

Hinric smirked, setting down his own empty winecup, "I wouldn't miss such an occasion for all the gold under Durdan. Yes, absolutely."

Three yes-votes. Three no-votes. And only one Lord Ascendant left to vote. The Lord of Spies. Illystre smirked, he spun his plots, and he voted yes.

That had been months ago, and he had put much in motion since then. He and his sister and her sickly Lord Husband, Torvald Ironarm, the High Lord of the Greatwood, had stumbled on some... strangeness in the histories, regarding the fall of the Old Forest Kings. The Owl Kings, the legendary and extinct Clan Mertens; from Ferren the Uniter to The Sea Owl to Good King Finn, the Owls had ruled Daneau for five hundred years. After forty years, known as the Decades of Disgrace, they had fallen. Illystre's family had been their stewards, Clan Coldhearth was as much a part of the history of Daneau and her royalty as the castle of Three Tall Towers itself. Though the castle was no longer the seat of the empire –with the extinction of the owls– it had been given to Clan Coldhearth, Illystre had to know why. Eager to aid, Isolde, his sullen sister, and Torvald had made the necessary arrangements, using divination and threats.

And now? He was hours away from getting his hands on a genuine Starheart crown, and instead of studying and preparing– He ducked the swing of a sword, gilded-sheen. Ser Hugo Saddler was, without a doubt, the finest sword Illystre had ever seen. Illystre was a fine combatant in his environment, of course. He was the Lord of Spies, after all, but that environment was one of shadow and subterfuge and pinpoint strikes taken at the perfect moment. Coldhearth men wielded shadow, secrets and stealth, rarely swords.

Hugo Saddler wielded a sword and he was fucking *fantastic* with it. Ten years younger than Illystre Coldhearth, the Second Son of the Goldengrass shone like golden starlight on the field. He wore green silks and gold pauldrons, his leathers and mail dyed and gilded to match. On his head, he wore an open-faced helm, the nasal and crown wrought in verdant enamel, with horsehair pluming from the peak.

Sweat ran down Illystre's forehead; his padded hood was lined with mail. Hopefully, that would be enough to keep Ser Hugo from accidentally decapitating him. He stepped, placing a practiced kick to the midsection of Saddler, who doubled over with a grunt. The Lord of Spies wheeled the short baton he was carrying in lieu of his dagger over the back of Saddler's helm, ringing the golden armor like a bell. With a roar of rage, Saddler swung his heavy family shield into Illystre's gut, and the thunder took him.

He had liked Purvon Webb. The two had much in common, creeping in the shadows, valuing knowledge, stealth and espionage. When it had been announced that the little Spider lord would be facing a woman in the first round, Coldhearth saw it for the slight it was intended to be, but Webb did not. He knew the Vellen woman by reputation. She was a witch, from a long line of witches, and they held an ancient keep in the very northernmost tip of the Goldengrass. Lusher and greener than most of the plains, Spring O' Blue was a place of magic and mystery, even for someone as practiced in finding secrets as

Illystre Coldhearth. The spring where the city got its name was regarded for its healing waters, and mysterious ancient roads nearby went straight off of sea cliffs, as if headed into the sky itself.

But Lady Lenore Vellen was not the regent of that fiefdom. Her brother, the bedbound Lord Poe, was. Rumor was that she kept him in such a state with fell magic and poisons. Personally, Illystre was suspicious. Vellen men had a reputation for being sickly– only the sons, never the daughters. Lord Poe was the latest in a long line of men who ruled Spring O' Blue and Witchpine Hall in name only, as their mothers, sisters, wives, cousins and daughters did the real work.

So, the second match of the first round of Prince Vernus Artus' birthday tourney had been set: the Little Spider Lord against the rumored poisoner of Witchpine Hall. Illystre wondered if there had been a reason the gamesmaster had set the two so early in the festivities when he'd first seen the lists, or if the timing had been purely accidental.

He had, of course, carefully arranged his own pairing with Hugo Saddler. The usual combination of threats, bribes and good old-fashioned midnight knee bashings had granted Illystre a contest with the most dangerous man in the entire Empire. Most would consider such a contest suicide, but Illystre needed an alibi. Saddler wouldn't kill him, and losing a contest against the most skilled knight in the kingdom was to be expected. So what if he may have let Ser Hugo win a little more quickly to save himself the pain of what would surely be an inevitable beating? What mattered was that he was in Honeyhome for the tourney.

If the pairing of Webb and Vellen in the second match had not been a pure accident, the way it finished was. Webb, like Coldhearth himself, was an athletic, acrobatic sort. The smaller men simply had to be in these contests of martial skill and sorcerous gifts. Illystre had been among the throngs of folk preparing near the arena's western gate. His squire, a cousin to the Marianos lords called Homer, had been helping him get his cloak over his leathers when they heard the gasp go out from the stands. Webb had leapt onto the railing and attempted a daring, flipping vault over Vellen.

What happened next depended on who told you the tale. To hear the Lord of Judgment tell it, the witchwoman summoned an unseelie shadow to bind his leg to the rail as her evil eye went green. The Lady Admiral Marle would later tell Illystre that the boy slipped.

Whatever the reason, Lord Purvon Webb's daring vault became Lord Purvon Webb's tragic impalement as he drove the blade of the halberd into his own chest and the haft of it into the dust. The only scream louder than that of Lady Vellen was that of the Lord's younger half-brother, Miles.

A recess was taken. Three Priests of Eresh drifted in from a low tunnel, in their faceplates of blank, featureless metal– elves from continental Alista, knife-sharp ears protruding from their slitted hoods. *Alvari.* They were alien creatures here– strange beings both heavenly and unseelie. Respectfully, reverently, fearfully, the crowd held their silence as the somber elves removed what was left of the boy from Vellen's halberd.

Lady Lenore Vellen had been anointed in what looked like gallons of the boy's blood. She sat on the edge of the arena, pressed against a golden wall of painted wood, shaking and sobbing to herself, "I… saw…"

Healers from the house– women in robes and leathers and feathers collected her– singing prayers of mercy for both Vellen and the dear lost Webb. They lifted her, and when she was unable to find the way to walk, they carried her, dragging her feet in the dust.

One of the Malbes' men, thin as a rail, turned to Homer, "If the Silver Sun has any mercy, Madapple will kill that girl in the next round. Gods."

The boy was grim in the way only a ten-year-old boy could be at the best of times, but the sight of the blood-covered Vellen had shaken him deeply, "What-what, why m'lord?"

"Because some people just weren't made to handle that much red, Homer..."

He had come to awareness roughly: a ringing in his ears, his skull and everything in that general vicinity. His mouth was full of something chalky, foul and burning, but it was not blood. Something closed his nose, and he swallowed. As light returned to the edges of the world, the grey rogue of the Three Tall Towers saw an angel.

"He's okay! Get the Learner!" Brassy eyes and horns to match swirled down to him, "Yer going to be okay, m'lord. I promise." Her skin was green as the sentinel pine on The Still Waters. He heard the voice of the Saddler's Learner call out, blending with the familiar drone of High Learner Franz, "Thank you, Hellendre..."

Who was the Saddler's Learner again? You're supposed to know this, Illystre.

...Lord of Spies. You know this. Powell.

But who is she...? Hellendre. Such a strange name.

Before he slipped back into blackness, he managed a ghost of a whisper, "Hello, Hellendre."

ROLOF I

"Men are but flesh, even the kings and godly men, and flesh will tear. Given enough time, flesh rots and flesh dies, but your line– that goes on forever, boy."

Sailing a fortnight would have been preferable to five days ahorse, but no one had asked his opinion. As a rule, Rolof disliked horses. They were panicky animals, skittish around blood and noise, and those were two of the things Rolof liked best.

As he sat in the stands watching the spirited matchup between a big mystery knight in tortoise shell and some big, bearded lout of a northman, he snorted. This wouldn't be much of a contest, not for longer. The Big Turtle and Ser Esben Hornblower were of a size, sure. But for some reason, the huge mystery knight was wearing nearly new, well-built, castle-forged plate and carrying a greatsword of equal youth and quality. Hornblower was clearly not used to combat with someone he couldn't just outmuscle. He was all but unarmored, leather and a few foraged pieces of ill-fitting armor. The Turtle stood a head over Hornblower, but the big northman likely outweighed him by fifty pounds, and that included the armor. Hornblower crunched a buckler into the turtle's mailed arm to little effect. The Turtle, face hidden behind his beaked visor, returned the favor, smashing a mailed fist into Hornblower's unprotected face. Two streams of blood erupted from Hornblower's broad buttony nose.

"Serves him right, who's he think he's gonna beat like that, half-naked?" Rolof grumbled to his companion, the only man in this crowd Rolof considered his equal in martial matters.

"Hnnh." Ser Sancho Madapple was a man of sparse speech. But he did make a sharp inhale of amusement when a bloody

Hornblower stumbled forward in an attempt to tackle the Big Turtle, who only needed to double-step backward quickly. Hornblower fell face-first into the dust. *This one doesn't strike unless he has to. Softhearted. Good to know.*

The Turtle swung on him, speedier than one would have expected from a three hundred and fifty-pound man in full plate and chain. His voice boomed under the helm, "Yield!" and Hornblower did.

Sancho spit, "Needed more oomph. Big, meaty boys bumpin' meat shouldn't be bloodless."

"Hornblower is bleedin'. And there's been plenty today." Rolof's mind went back to the witchgirl killing that flippy little bug, and the horror that occurred in the Prince's match.

"A nosebleed and a coupla fairy-lords out of Ozwyk dying ain't hardly a tourney." He pressed a horn of strong Dwarven beer to his scarred lips. He grunted a burp through his mustache.

He's drinking more these days. Must be for the pain. Something green glinted among the scar tissue tight on Madapple's jaw, then faded.

Back in the arena, the thin Master of Games lifted the Mystery Turtle's gauntleted glove and Rolof harrumphed. "I hope he keeps winning, he's big, but he's soft. I'll cave that stupid visor in, and he will flee weeping." Deepreach would need to win three times to end up facing the Turtle, that deep in the semi-finals, and so would the Turtle. Deepreach's quarter of the bracket was full of green boys, old men and disgustingly enough, a woman. Even one as celebrated as The Bloody Lily had no place here, as far as Rolof was concerned. As if summoned, his woman appeared.

Larissa was lean, sharp and hungry. Larissa was not his woman, in truth, but they shared a son, and had been together for almost ten years. Her husband would likely be as furious as she was right now. Rolof did not mind, she was always beautiful in her fury. As she pressed next to him in the bleachers, Ser Sancho nodded, "My lady." with barely more than grunt, it was nearly a burp.

She glanced over at him, practiced, predatory eyes searching the massive knight. Ser Sancho Madapple was not the biggest man in the tourney, that was likely Red Ronnie Tallman–a massive northern noble, bald as an egg, with a beard that reached his waist. If Madapple was not the largest, he was certainly second or third. And he was by far the cruelest, fiercest and most feared knight in the realm. He stood half a head over Rolof, and Rolof was a big man. "Ser Sancho, you seem well."

He grunted, "Knocked the Tember boy across the yard. My next match left the arena cryin', screamin' covered in blood, so I'm feeling mighty good about my tomorrow too." Thankfully, Ser Sancho was in the other half of the bracket, and they would only need to face each other in the finals. Rolof had a hundred ways he could beat Madapple and half a hundred more that were solid bets. Given the likelihood that they would eventually need to fight each other in earnest, he preferred to keep his secrets to himself. He rose, the bench groaning in relief as his weight left it, "My horn seems to have drained itself, be well, Ser Rolof. Lady Fisher." He nodded politely, pressing his lips tightly and moving through a crowd that was wise enough to part for him.

Lady Larissa Fisher was married to the High Lord Ludo Fisher, and Rolof had been her sworn sword since he was nineteen years old. He had won the honor in a melee, knocking a tooth from Lord Ferrer Bleake (then only Ser Ferrer Bleake) in the process. This had amused Lord Ludo to the point that he had not only given the boy the sword of protection for his wife, but had a fine bronze and iron helm commissioned for him. As gifts of service over the last decade, he had gifted pauldrons, a breastplate, gauntlets and Rolof's pride and joy; in lieu of a shield, Deepreach wore a chain-half cloak. He had grown up fishing with nets in the surf, and this felt much the same. It flowed over his back and arm like water, and not only could he block and parry, he could often grapple the weapon straight from his opponent's arm…

"We need to speak, Ser." Her words brought him back from his equipment, his slight smile fading. Her eyes, huge blue things of sky, sea and steel, had turned on him.

"Of course, Lady Fisher." He managed to keep his annoyance in check, as he followed the rushing young High Lady through the crowd. Though the gathered smallfolk did a poor job parting for Lady Larissa, Rolof managed to part them with a shouted threat. He hoarsely bellowed, "Move, I've got leave to kill threats to the high Lady, and if you stand in her way, I name you threat!"

The crowd split, most folk scurrying to the sides of the path as Rolof yanked his falchion from its sheath. Three feet long, bronzed, and wickedly sharp, the single-edged sword was made to slash and chop. Rolof had taken many a limb with it on both raid and field. Most of the little fish had parted for the knight and lady, but a brave boy with a nose that had been broken at least once stood in the path. He could not have been more than twelve. He was caked in mud and dirt, likely a ragged orphan from the streets of the city bubbling around the castle. *Barely more than a hungry mutt acting out for scraps.* Rolof shook the falchion at the boy, who only stuck his skinny little bird chest out defiantly. *If you want to act like a cur…*

Rather than cut the boy down, Deepreach backhanded him, hard. The ragged child shouted breathlessly as the back of Rolof's right hand took all the air from him. The boy fell to the ground, finally wheezing after a moment, then crying, sobbing and choking all at once, as air re-entered his lungs. Rolof chuckled to himself as he stepped over the boy. He extended a hand, helping his Lady step over the prone child as if he were a puddle or pile of horse leavings. She gave him a satisfied little noise, and once over him she leaned low, "Oh, you poor dear." Rolof flicked a copper at the sobbing boy's face; it caught him in the forehead. The solid little thunk it made harmonized with the boy's sobs like music, and Rolof led his lady away, both of them beaming.

The Turtle and Hornblower had ended the third set of matches on the day. Four sets of four combatants would exchange their blows, winners would be determined and a break of an hour would be taken to allow the next set to don their armor and the spectators to piss, drink and feast. It was as big, gaudy, time-consuming tourney format as there and though Rolof had been very interested in watching some of the finest knights in the Empire, the tournament had been extremely underwhelming.

Other than the ugliness with the Vellen girl and the Prince killing those Ozwyk lords, many of the so-called grandest warriors on land and sea had shown to be more song than reality. The pious Lord Mabon Albin of Hope's Hill, where vice was banned, had shown up for his match so stinking drunk with Hinric Saddler that he had fallen ass-over-wine goblet from the raised dais and broken his arm. Sleek young Ser Chaddar Goldenlocke, sworn to Rime River, had looked a fool against the strange bird-woman from the Scorching Sands of Hro'Catis, thousands of daegrids south. Even Prince Kyne Reave of Ozwyk –known for his skill, speed and sorcery– had fallen when he tried to use magic on the tower-tall Torchbearer boy, and the black steel of the northern boy's ancient family sword drank it up like water swirling a drain. The Canar Boy, the new Grey Guard, had quickly dispatched some southern woman from House Haymaker, which irked Rolof on a level he wasn't proud of. The loss of that ancient position to some unbearded boy had been a point of contention between Rolof and his own Lord Father, back on their own waters, the island city of Ryleth. *No matter.*

He put that particular frustration aside and smirked at the most satisfying result he had seen today. Lord Marten Mirebreaker had been gloriously shamed. Rolof prodded the angry, purple bruise under his scarred right eye. The scar had come from some stupid Crowe on a raid; the bruise had been Mirebreaker's doing. The Lord of Okoboji had taken offense when Rolof had shouted a joke at his dull, little pervert of a brother. The skinny little boy never made eye contact with anyone, ranted and mumbled and, worst of all, the second Mirebreaker couldn't even hold a blade, for he was a cripple. Of course the little worm needed his Lord Brother to fight his battles for him.

Mirebreaker had punched Rolof with a closed fist, in the face, repeatedly. Granted, Rolof himself looked nearly as bad as Ser Sancho, but the Bronze Kraken had *heard* Mirebreaker's hand shatter something on his forehead, before the reckless boy Lord began using his elbow instead. And sure enough, today, the stupid little turtle had arrived with his sword wrapped to his hand in silks and leathers. He had even managed to defend himself admirably against Lord Mortimer Osprey. Osprey was the much-loved Lord of Talon Bay, a mustachioed archer who hunted with some strange sea hawk. A useful man to have in a war or on a ship, but a poor tourney knight. Before he had broken his hand,

Mirebreaker's victory was a foregone conclusion, but injured, he had fallen in shame. It almost made the sore face worth it.

They had whorled through stands selling pies and silks and banners, past silk pavilions with shields and banners for knights and high houses, painted in every flashing hue of the rainbow. Deepreach sped past the catspaw of Swyft as Lady Larissa snorted at the Fox of the Witchwood. "Warrior women and green druids, bah."

As they snuck behind an ale tent, Larissa finally stopped him, as they were surrounded by silk on three sides in this narrow little alley. Once there, the hardness fell from her face as she lay her head on his chest and sighed deeply. "My Lord, I need you."

Normally, those words were tied to a very specific purpose. Rolof was no master to the ways of women, but both her manner and their location made him rather sure that was not her implication today. His broad paddle of a hand gently stroked the bare olive skin of her shoulder, "M'lady." He was unsure of what else was needed from him.

"My Lord Brother demands satisfaction, Rolof." Her tone was resigned and annoyed in matching parts.

"Your Lord Brother drank fermented fish guts and shit himself in front of the whole kingdom, love. I am unsure of how swords might set this right." She glared up at him, her fury rousing his passions further. He pulled her closer, pressing himself into her through his breeches, "Though, you may find this sword somewhat more useful."

With a groan, she shoved him away, spinning a few angry steps. "He claims he was drugged! And I heard much the same from Lord Albin's camp."

Sluggish currents of thought in the tall knight's mind began rerouting themselves. It *was* strange that both Lord Albin and Lord Gorge had acted so oddly, to be true. "You mean someone is steering the lists in their own directions?" He froze. "I had just been drinking ale from the…"

"Quit being a child, I'm sure you are unmolested… For now." She was right, he knew. He drew a big breath, searching over his body, feeling for any sign of injury, illness or intoxication and felt none. "You're facing a sworn sword of those Saddlers, that Selach boy, yes?"

The Bronze Kraken rankled; this Selach boy was unfamiliar to him. He had ridden along with the stupidly huge horse breeder's household. The knight, alongside the Big Turtle and the bird-woman had been the last three standing in the melee, and thus granted entry into the tourney. "Yes, saw him in the melee. Uses a spear and a net." He found the second part especially egregious; *No matter.*

She grinned, her long nose sharp against her face. "We know who would do such a thing, don't we? Who would dare lay hands on the Carrion King?"

The Scarecrow Lord.

On the Scattered Isles, life was difficult. Most of the islands were cold, rocky jags in cold, salty seas. Some of the larger islands did have fertile soil or plains or mountains and mines, but most folk lived and died by the bounty of the Coldwater Seas. Ryleth, his home island, was the largest, but was also among the poorest. Little grew in its rocky soil, its high mountains only held stone and bronze. The cold waters around the island teemed with kelp and cod and octopi. The Krakenmen had grown strong and wise on the things they dragged from the deep. That strength and wisdom granted there led to hungry eyes from Clan Deepreach and their axes. Raids on the fertile farmlands on the mainland became common.

Fisher and the Scattered Isles would war against one another for centuries, until the Old Owl Kings would bring the Scattered Isles under heel… in theory. In practice, the raids continued, just under black banners. Clan Crowe had taken exception to this and had traditionally crucified the captured raiders, nailing the men to trees and then wooden trusses and then set them on the high cliffs overlooking the sea. The current Lord of their Clan, Lord Liam Crowe, was known as The Lord of Scarecrows, because he had taken a special interest in renewing the practice. The young Lord would capture, try and sentence raiders, executing them, all under the Empire's law. Embarrassing Gorge would certainly be something the pretty-boy lord would enjoy. *On the other hand...*

"Your brother drank rotten fish guts and shit himself." Rolof repeated his theory. The men of Clan Gorge worshipped some awful black crow demon, Gargol. To honor him, they slammed back shots of alcohol made from fermented fish, rotting kelp and poison from the urchins that clung to the rock of their black cliffs at low tide. "That vile shit is enough to make anyone ill." He pulled away, "I'm not going to jump like some attack dog, wench. Prove it, and I'll scalp the boy and bring you a cord made of his locks."

A pair of forceful steps put a few feet between Rolof and his lover, but he did eventually turn back, "I live and die at your service m'lady, but I'll not kill an innocent man, with no cause."

She surged at him, all fury and grasping hands, "My word should be cause, Rolof! I know it was Crowe!" Her hands found his shoulders and spun him around, "Ser, you must confront him! When Karl takes the Pilfered Throne, Crowe needs to fear us!"

I have a better chance of taking that stupid hunk of metal than that boy does. He couldn't say as such, of course. That would send her into a rage, and that would likely inflame his passions further.

"Fine. I will speak with Crowe after my match with the Saddler boy."

"You will speak with Crowe, now, Ser Rolof."

He sighed to himself, through his nose, tensing his jaw feeling the bruised flesh ache. Here, in this alley, among the flapping silks and smokey smells of roasting meat and root vegetables, all of his strength meant nothing. He could deny her nothing. He should be preparing–preparing himself for Ser Doyle Selach. Instead, he would wile away his hour finding this blonde Scarecrow and make sure he would never play his smart little tricks again.

"Yes, m'lady, I'll find Crowe." *And cave his fucking smug little head in.*

END ACT ONE

SOMEWHERE OUTSIDE OF GYENT:

A Bridge Between Acts

The bird-man-thing whipped its head toward the noise, great yellow eyes searching the underbrush and fog for whatever was rushing away. Telloama tried to speak, but the man-bird-thing stopped her with a raised finger, talon-sharp and leather-tough. He looked to his left shoulder; tidbits of feather and motes of smoke clung together and slowly coalesced into some little winged thing, which hopped and snapped its beaked jaw. The bird-man-thing turned his gaze to his right, and another little bird snapped. "Go. Follow the footsteps. Whatever you find, bring it to me." The pair of black birds flew off, silent as the fog beneath them.

The man-bird-thing turned back to Telloama and it spoke again. Though its beak did not open, its voice boomed hollow. "The anchors have all gathered here, in your hive, Tellaoma. I do not believe they even understand why."

The hovering woman, all cloudy white and eerie glow, turned on him, "ZZZzzIiiiif zzzzthey do notzzz zzknow." She buzzed and the high dome of larval flesh and chitin thrummed with her, "ZZThey have forgottenzzz."

"The Fox remembers!" The thing-man-bird quorked angrily. "The witchwood is deep and she is part of it!"

"One… isszzz not four, my Prinzzzzzzzz." Through the strangeness, her voice took on a warmth, almost tender. "We musssszzzt draw zzzthe zzzcirclezzz cloooozzsee, gather who remainszzzzz -kk- here. We lozzzst thiszzz battle centuriezzsz agzo, you know this more than anyone."

The man-thing-bird swooped its great feathered mantle around itself in a defiant huff, huge yellow eyes unmoving over his stub of a beak. "You are the Queen here, Tellaoma; this bird is only a humble vagabond. All the same, I don't intend to die."

As he spoke, his two little black birds flew to him, tumbling from the black underbrush. The first returned to smoke and feather, before settling among the feathers in his mantle once more. The second, light as a memory, swift as thought, swooped onto his left shoulder before pressing its own stubby little beak toward his ear.

Even the great thrum of the horrible fleshy dome dulled a touch as both Telloama and the thing-man-bird silenced themselves to listen. When it was done, the little flapping black shadow settled into the mantle like its partner had.

"One of them crossed the Nightshade Gate, Tellaoma. The Hive is endangered." He looked to the throbbing dome above them. "How many innocents sleep in there, waiting to be born?"

The light within Telloama seemed to flicker slightly like a candle flame in a light breeze. Like a firefly, "I.. -…zzztoo many." She descended, this angel lowering herself to the dirt and ash, and she took a pair of dainty steps. She placed her lily-white hand on the bird's shoulder in the dirt. "Whatzz would you have meee do -kk-?"

"The Nightshade Gate. Let me use it. Let me cross." His tone was pleading, but booming and clear– a commanders' voice.

"The riiizzzsskszzz –"

"I can move among them. I will gather the anchors. I can bring them here. If they don't come of their own volition, I will drag them. If the Aragonite cannot maintain his hond of the bargain, neither will we. None of it." His voice had gone iron-hard, black and pitiless. "We close the gates and the blight can take them, they have earned it."

Telloama, still mingled in the dust with this bird, "I– I grant you my leave. Use my gate."

The bird dipped his head with respect before swirling through the fog in the same direction that the boy had fled.

To their side.

ACT TWO:

KILLERS

TALOR II

"Wha-what have you done, boy?"

He wasn't sure who was screaming anymore. At first, when the foul green ooze in its thin glass jar shattered against his shield, the scream was his own– a deep grunt from his diaphragm as his boot slid in the dust, chalk and gravel. *A glint of gold and then the jar.*

When he smashed upward, bashing forward with the heavy tower shield, sending glass and foul bilious acid upward, it was a scream in his muscles, every fibre straining to lift the heavy wood and iron.

Push.

He reached out, gold and light and warmth that was his alone, that only he could sense, that flowed from him. He felt it spread from the center of his forehead, and suddenly the heavy tower shield seemed to weigh nothing at all. *A glint of gold in the stands, and then the jar.*

Glass and acid flooded the grinning harlequin mask of Lord Jack Tymm's helm, and the sizzle only came an instant before the scream, as carved wood melted away like candlewax. The high howling shriek that faded into a burble belonged to Smilin' Jack. *A glint of a golden eye and a bone-white smile.*

In the end, Talor couldn't say why he reached out, but as the Celestial Prince stood above the dying jester, smile burnt bare for all to see, he opened his third eye into the mind of the dying man. The scream that followed was his own, high and mocking and merciless. He barely recognized his own wails as he felt the light in the mind of the Lord of Leaper's Ledge go out. *A glint of a Golden Eye in the Royal Box, and Tymm became a puppet on a string. Father tried to kill you.*

Blue. He went unconscious as the shrieks blended around him and the dust rose to meet him. All he could feel was blue.

Swimming in the shallow waters around The Isle of Avalar was the first place that felt like home to Talor. His earliest memories were smiling in the surf of the Shining Strait. He was back there. He was small... no Bara. No Vernus. He was toddling in the sand, warm in the light of the Silver Sun. The green-blue surf filled the air with crashing spray and the scent of salt. Above them, sea birds harassed and harrumphed, cawing and cackling as they dove, dining on the scraps they could gather.

Here he was safe, here he was with... Father. Father was young again, too. Not nearly so gaunt, and through his black stubble he smiled. Ahead, he saw mother waiting, arms holding her swollen belly. She beamed at the pair of them, father and son. His father was tall and strong, and his golden eyes were clear and bright again. Father's long, strong fingers gripped the boy Prince's tiny hand firmly, warming, lovingly. Carefree and boyish once more, the boy he used to be skipped with his father.

...There was something else too. Something red... orange... he wasn't just in the surf with his father. He was somewhere else too, someone else. He was tall and broad, standing in his smallclothes on top of high redstone cliffs. He could feel strong muscles move under unfamiliar pale skin, spotted with brown freckles. A hundred feet below him, he could see the gentle blue waters of a bay below, shining under the silver sun. Somewhere behind him, among the sparse seagrass and thin soil on the clifftop, a voice called out. A boy of eight or so, pale and red-haired stood in his own small-clothes, freckled and slowly cooking pink in the silver sun, "Jack... It's so high."

He felt himself grin, and a voice he had only heard in grunts and screams answered, "Darwyn, come here." The boy, Darwyn, took a cautious step, and Talor knew his face– Ser Darwyn Tymm, but only a babe.

His own Grey Guard, and the brother of the recently deceased Lord Smilin' Jack...

Jack...

...

Jack...

...

"Jack!" A third voice rang out, another pale, freckled red-head– this one a bleak teen, some middle brother thin and frowning. "You alright?"

"Y-yeah." He felt himself answer. Stumbling at first, confidence building to a crescendo of manic joy, "Brain was someplace far, far away, boys!"

He looked at the stolen memory of the man he killed, and he felt himself grow nauseous inside. Jack Tymm bounced backward a few yards, strong, young and very, very alive. "Leaper's Ledge is simple, boys. It's our birthright and our burden." This man never stopped moving, Talor was only along for the ride, and this man's body felt like crackling lightning. Static and sparks crept under his skin, stillness was an uncomfortable thing that would only grow into actual pain in a few moments. "A hundred-an-twenny foot drop, straight down into the sweet blue water of the bay."

Tymm's face broke into a grin so wide the back of his neck began to ache, "As long as you sprint and don't slow, at all, you're fine." He bounced back and forth, jogging from foot to foot, all youth and electricity. "But, if you stop, hesitate for a second..."

Tymm dropped low into an athletic stance and rushed forward, breathlessly laughing the last sentence, "You'll end up a red stain on the ROOOOOOOOOOOOOCKS." His voice carried into a laugh riding the warm sea breeze updrafting around him. With a shift and a twist, he slipped between the waves with hardly a splish.

Blue. Safe. Blue.

He swirled among the blue-green salt. Long ribbons of gold and warmth caressed him, filled him and consumed him. Here in the womb of the sea he was safe. He was Talor once more. Adult Talor. Himself.

He broke the surface of the water, snatching a deep breath of warm, salty air. Talor's dark bangs hung sodden on his forehead as a shadow blocked the warmth of the Silver Sun. He was in the shallows of the Isle of Avalar once more, though with the new cloud cover, the air grew dense with a chill that came from someplace beyond the water. Talor pushed against the ivory sands, under the surf, feeling them squish and spread between his toes. The sea birds above had begun to bicker, angry and shrill.

The cold wind grew colder and the shadow on the Silver Sun grew thicker. Talor raised his own eyes of gold to the darkening sky and saw the cloud churn. It was no flock of seagulls, the birds were vicious predatory things, black and grey and brown.

Water, back to water. He had to get back to the water. The ribbons of warm gold.

An iron grip pulled him out of the water. His Father towered above him. The king's face– a gaunt frowning mask. Gallus's eyes had lost their gold and gone to smoke and mud. This corpse of a man croaked at him, "Not there. Not the water."

Bits of him crumbled away, dry and shaking as he spoke. Flesh turned to wisps of smoke, his eyes grew dark and black, pits of night and fear. "Never the water." King Gallus's face became a grinning skull, The skull cackled in Jack Tymm's high howl, "Now, you gotta leap, boy!"

With the strength of a God, the dead king threw his prince into the sky.

Clouds of swirling grey and brown smoke filled the sky, bloated and sickly to bursting. These clouds stirred with constant churning, a strange segmented fluttering to their motion. As soon as they appeared, they grew, swelling thick and dense, becoming twisted full things of smoke and sparking light. In the sky, the Prince burst its terrible third eye open, radiant light of the heavens tore at the black smoke, but it quickly began to drink the light, and then it drank up The Prince itself.

As the dark drank up the Prince and the silver sun and the sky itself, it began to snow—feathers, countless thousands. Grey, brown and black.

They tore him to shreds. Drank me up.

You killed Jack because Daddy tried to kill you.

Jack's voice echoed in his own mind, fresh, alive, no mere memory. "You killed me, because the King used me to try an' kill you."

Talor woke, sweat and sheets clinging to him. He and Kiara slept in the third finest bed in the castle. As he watched his bride dream beside him, the prince reckoned he would not sleep further this night.

VANDRE II

"Hk... 'Course this is how it ends, kill't by a boy. ...No. You look. You watch me die, Vandre."

Honeyhome smelled like flowers and mead. It was full of pretty young highborn girls wearing silks, which clung to them in the summer heat. This was a marked improvement, after his time in the bare oak and stone of Hope's Hill. He was watching a chesty little thing with buck-teeth scurry through the tourney grounds when his companion called out, "Jemes!"

Vandre did not respond.

"Wyse! Hey!"

Oh shit, right.

Vandre turned his attention to the willowy wood-elf beside him. He was a tall, skittish thing–a deer with thumbs. "Clovis" he had introduced himself. Vandre wasn't sure it was his real name, but if it was, the kid was painfully naive. "Yeah? Sorry, I was..." he watched the girl with the plump lips and squirrel-skin mantle turn a corner toward the pavilions, "Looking for people of interest..."

The elf groaned, underwhelmed, "Well, if you're quite done, I believe we're supposed to be in the stands, though."

Vandre grunted back, "Yeah... I know, but I needed something to sip on. It's hot, elf. Not that you'd notice." The early summer had broken into an unseasonable blaze on the second day of the tourney. Sweat wasn't just sticking to the pretty young highborn girls, Vandre was soaked. The roughspun wool of his tunic chafed wetly against him, sawing into his tired flesh. And of course, the elf was perfect. If there was any sweat on the boy at all, it was dewdrops. *It's not enough to live five hundred fucking years, but you need to be perfect and beautiful for all of it, too?*

Vandre struck off, as Clovis called after him, "Wyse! I don't think this is… uh.. Wise? What about our companions? We're supposed to be… y'know..?"

Vandre stopped and rounded on the elf, stomping back, his brown eyes blazing, "We're supposed to be what…" He growled, leaning close and spitting the last word, stretching it into a slur, "…Elf?"

He whispered, "Y'know… *interfering?* Like how we drugged the Carrion King and Lord Mabo–"

Vandre clamped a brown leather glove over the wild eyed elf's mouth, "Shut. The. Fuck. Up."

Clovis nodded, an understanding filling his eyes, and Vandre slowly released his fingers from the Elf's mouth. "The other two can hold the bench down for fifteen minutes while I find a sausage and take a piss, I swear. C'mon, kid, I'll buy you an ale."

The elf was incredibly useful, but good lord was he naive. *…Fucking 'Clovis?'*

When he had arrived in Hope's Hill, two weeks ago, he had been hurt, victim of a couple of beatings. Seeking out an actual Learner, a healer, meant making his way to the castle; that was a risk he had been unwilling to take. He had settled behind a stable behind an inn, which was packed, though it sold only milk and boiled water. The donkey had begun rooting through the refuse at the end of her lead, but Vandre was too busted up to care. His ribs were worse than he had thought, and the longer he lay here, the worse they felt. Shortly after midnight, his coughs went red, and Vandre had been waiting to die.

Sometime before dawn, he had woken. To his shock, he was not dead. As a matter of fact, when he sat up, his shattered ribs did not pain him. He ran his hands over his chest, his wounds had been knitted. And the alley he had passed out in was gone, he and Beauty… were in a field. Firelight was flickering against high, beautiful trees. *I'm back in the thicket. Any minute, four fat farmboys in kerchiefs are gonna jump you. You're in Hell, old man, you've earned it.*

Rather than a red-skulled farm boy, the elf he would later learn was Clovis popped his head into view; genial, "H-hello!"

Though Vandre's initial reflex was, as always, violence, he stifled it. He said nothing, blinking at the face above him. Despite his somewhat wild eyes, the elf seemed safe enough. A long nose, high cheekbones, fine, dainty elvish features, all things to be expected.

"I'm sorry, I went through your things." The elf was young. Vandre sat up in a rage, but found himself somewhat queasy when he did. Gently, the elvish boy steadied the old man, "I didn't take anything, but I think we may have a mutual friend."

The elf pressed the tightly rolled scroll Vandre had been hiding back into the old sellsword's hand. "I-I-I didn't read it!" Shaking, he held up a twin, the same grey parchment rimmed in red, "I have my own…"

"Hnh." Vandre didn't like this, someone, somewhere was using him. He shifted again, painlessly, "You do this?" He nodded at his healed ribs, and the elf boy nodded back.

"I did." He turned toward Beauty, "I am sorry I couldn't do anything for your donkey, she's… a specimen."

Vandre slowly rose, the pain in his hips from the extended march wasn't gone, but it certainly had dimmed. He smirked a tick, "Well, you do good work." Vandre didn't ask how. The boy was an elf, they had their ways, sure. He was also practiced, courtly and polite, which reeked of education, maybe even nobility.

And that had been that, the pair made their way northward to Honeyhome. The trek had become even more crowded, as knights and lordlings began to overtake them the next day. Flapping banners of green, gold and black announced the arrival of the household of Clan Saddler. Two hundred men and at least twice as many retainers all mounted on some of the finest horses either Vandre or Clovis had ever seen. The jests and sneers from the lordlings at Beauty and the old knight had rankled him, but when something hit him in the back of the head, he wheeled around dagger in hand. All he found was the laughing heir to the Goldengrass, who had hurled a bar of soap.

Hart fuckin' Saddler.

Vandre sheathed his blade without a second's delay. Between his personal guard, his brother, and whatever freeriders and sworn swords that would be attending this procession, stabbing was sadly not an option. "Apologies, m'lord. I didn't hear you call out." From high on his fine roan horse the lanky young lordling sneered.

"I didn't."

The cold stiffness in his tone left no questions. He lifted a linen over his nose, and Vandre took his measure. Hartwin Saddler was tall, maybe even as tall as the elf. He was built like a rider– light and lean and upright– all corners and angles. Whatever little fat on the thin rider was a slight softness around the belly, but even that was minimal. Saddler had sharp, cruelly intelligent eyes, green chips of moss and juniper made glass. His face was long, a few sparse roan hairs poking from his chin in a boy's attempt at a goatee. A mane of thin red-brown hair had been pushed back from his forehead in a swoop that ended shortly below his ears. He was young, handsome and highborn. Vandre wished he could stab him. "More apologies, then, m'lord." He poked the soap bar with his booted foot. Ahead of him, the Elf had stopped, turning his big pale eyes back toward Vandre and the young Lordling. He moved to speak, but Vandre hushed him with a glance. "Ser Jemes Wyse, Knight of the Panhandle." Vandre turned back to Saddler, leading with his lie. "My…" he looked to Clovis, "*charge* and I are headed to Honeyhome, for the tournament." He extended a gloved hand palm down, a traditional show of submission of a knight to a lord. It showed he wasn't holding his sword.

"An old man on a broken donkey? Sure to win the whole thing." Saddler laughed, his voice a cruel bray of mockery. "She stinks like shit."

"…Yup." Horde of herded horsemen or not, Vandre had near reached his limit. The old man wasn't proud, but this level of disrespect sent all his violent tendencies to lighting up his brain like fire.

"That's what the soap is for."

"I figured as much, m'lord." What came next would be absolutely crucial for the future of not only Vandre, but the whole kingdom, but no one present knew that. Vandre looked the heir to the Goldengrass over. One leap, one tackle, one struggle, one dagger stroke. It would be over, but the story of the robber knight killing the golden colt over soap would be a song for the ages.

Vandre sighed into himself, and bent low, picking up the soap. "…Thank you, m'lord. I'll get her cleaned up."

Too big a meal ticket to pass up. Fuck.

"The soap is for you." He sneered at Beauty, "Personally, I'd put that *animal* out of my misery, but you make a handsome pair." She grunted, huffing, and dropping a half dozen "road apples" amongst the dust of the road, "I wouldn't waste the soap on the donkey."

By now, Clovis had sidled up silently. His big silver sun eyes were saucer-wide as he looked over Saddler, taking in the boy, the horse and the banners. Vandre begged the boy not to speak with a frown and furrowed brow, but something shimmered behind Clovis's eyes.

…The elf's eyes had gone the same vibrant green as Saddler's. And the boy elf in the long cloak produced a handsome leather satchel. Vandre had immediately noticed it, it was finer than anything else that either of them had been carrying. He had considered stealing it back on the first night, slitting the elf's throat and leaving him in the ditch, but considering that Clovis might've saved his life, he sheathed that option for a possible future fray.

Clovis opened his little satchel and sweet smells suffused the area. Dozens of tiny vials of sweet oils and fragrant powders sparkled in the silver sunlight. Blocks of paraffin and incense, perfume and soap, bundles of twiggy little sprigs and dried leaves. Vandre was instantly glad he hadn't robbed The Elf. If this stuff had any value, the old sellsword didn't know where to sell it. Clovis began speaking to the Lordling, who seemed lost in his words, "My Lord! Apologies for my bodyguard, he's a common-born thing, but an effective blunt object."

Eyes of green remained locked on eyes of green, as the Saddler boy dreamily replied, "Oh… Yes, can't hardly blame you for the… help…"

"Exactly, My lord!" Clovis gave Vandre a smirk and light waggle of an eyebrow, "Now, if you are who I think you are, which is the heir to all we see, I know you are a man who enjoys his perfumes and powder. Your reputation and the reputation of your Young Stallions well precede you, my lord."

Who the fuck is this man? What's the mask? The timid healer or this...

The elf cracked open a vial of something glass, and a smoky-sweet scent flooded Vandre's senses, but a swat on the shoulder from the Elf brought him back to reality. "Now, my lord, isn't this just the finest cologne you've ever had the pleasure to imbibe?" Saddler nodded, eyes glazed. "I've got a whole bottle, just for you, m'lord..."

Something in the elf's voice had changed, almost musical. If Vandre listened too closely, he swore he could feel his brain sparkling between the cracks. He decided not to listen too closely.

"I would be more than happy to make a gift of it, m'lord. And in return..."

What the hell is the Elf up to?

The boy rounded for the masterstroke, "We might be able to mount a couple of your spare animals. We've gone far on foot and the tourney is still mighty far."

Saddler smiled, "Oh, yes, that's... of course." Clovis pressed a pear-shaped glass bottle into the stunned lordling's hand, who then called for one of his men, a tall knight with a crowned green shark on a golden field of waves. Upon hearing the command of his lord, the knight looked confused but nodded, and led Clovis and Vandre away to the small herd of animals Clan Saddler kept along the train.

Once they had been mounted on a pair of fine young fillies, with Beauty's lead secure to his saddle, the old sellsword finally spoke, "You are just full of surprises, aren't you?"

The elf turned his silver sun eyes toward Vandre and smiled sheepishly, all doe-eyed humility once more. "Y-you're too kind."

Kindness has nothing to do with it. Vandre would be watching this one more closely.

The rest of the ride north had been uneventful. Among the hundreds of men, women, children, horses and dogs, Vandre, Clovis and Beauty were just three more souls passing through those high yellow walls. Further veiled correspondence had put them in contact with two more degenerates, a pair of young women. Another elf– this one an Alvari from the tribes in Ozwyk– and a scowling little gnome carrying most of an armory in her various pouches and pockets had been waiting in the clearing where Vandre had been instructed to put up his pavilion.

After sniffing around one another, the quartet had eventually come to the conclusion that they had all been contacted by the same shadowy architect, and had resolved to wait for further instructions. They had spent the first day of the tourney lazing in the sun, on occasion using the sneaky little gnome and the satchel of Clovis's herbs and poisons to… make a little money on the matches. Who cares if Lord Mabon Albin breaks his arm and looks like a drunk? As far as Vandre was concerned, the high Lord of Hope's Hill needed a little humbling anyway. The gold he'd gained betting on Albin's opponent clinked in his coin purse, a music that was sweeter to the grizzled old man than most others. He had a fat, greasy pork and venison sausage on a stick. His horn was full of ale and even though this mysterious Architect had somehow found out about Wyse, he could not help but feel hopeful. And, perhaps, he mused, he could pay to keep this Clovis around for a bit. He generally mistrusted elves, but this one seemed… especially useful.

Vandre paused and caught himself. *Do I actually enjoy this boy, or is he using his magick on me?* After a tense feeling in his gut turned into a stone one, Vandre's resolution was to split from this party when their mutual interest was done. Even the useful ones.

The gnome girl, who called herself Scarlet, was a slight thing, all elbows and knees, but she moved as quiet as frost over the grass, and had eyes of ice that missed nothing. When she had drugged Albin and Vulton, she had been an artist, blending herself into the environment and the crowds like a swirling phantom in crimson. As Vandre and Clovis returned to their seats in the high bench stands, Scarlet extended a piece of parchment, "Someone just tossed this at me feet from under the bleachers, I tried to track 'im, but he was too quick." She was forced to shout over the sounds of the final match where the young knight with crowned shark on his shield was battering some knight in a bronze helm that looked like an octopus.

Scrawled in the same hand as the rolled letter that had come to him a month ago, the same hand that threatened to tell the world where the *real* Jemes Wyse's body lay in a swamp– were three simple words.

Tournament Grounds. Midnight.

ROLOF II

"There is no shame in enjoying a clean kill, boy. A sense of accomplishment in slaying without suffering is earned. Unless, of course, suffering was your intention, and that has its uses too, son."

When the dust had flooded into his helm's eyeholes and breath slits, he had gagged. Rolof vainly struggled in a rage against the woven brass wire of the laughing idiot shark's net, but the Bronze Kraken was stuck fast. He grunted, muscles straining iron and bronze fighting against themselves. Rolof grunted as something in his knee slipped, cartilage on bone. He flexed, scanning his whole body with a flash of thought.

The chain, Rolof realized, his gut squirming, *my cape is caught in the net.* The more he struggled, the tighter Ser Doyle Selach bound him. The lanky Selach bounded around him, as the crowd laughed and screamed in delight. The rabble chanted *"Shark! Shark! Shark!"* in rhythm, and Selach brought the hard, blunt back end of his trident down onto Rolof's bruised body in time.

The Falchion, if I can just grab the sword. His right arm was more free than not, pinned by the binding net somewhere around his tricep. Between his chain cape and the strands of wire held tight, his left arm was lost to him for the moment. *My sword can change that, I just need my sword.* His fingers gripped the bloodstained dust, tentacles grasping for a hold that was not there.

His sword was eight feet away.

His right hand gripped; his toes and ankles pushed. Ser Doyle Selach cracked him in the ribs. Rolof could feel bruises and welts raising in his skin and a copper taste flooded his mouth.

His sword was seven feet away.

More dust shoving itself under Rolof's bleeding fingernails, more desperate crawling. The lump of cartilage in his knee stretched itself further, searing Rolof's entire leg from within. Selach brought the hardwood down again, as the commons in the stands erupted. This time, he found purchase on the less-armored leather gorget on the back of Rolof's neck. The Kraken Knight felt his backbone crack, as waves of greens and purples invaded the corners of his eyes. His hand refused to make a fist.

His sword was six feet away.

His legs kicked, toes piling the dust in gouged ruts. He ground the helm, breastplate and knees through the dry choking dust. He strained against the net again. This time, Selach brought the end of the trident down on Rolof's unarmored sword hand, predator-quick. Rolof felt bones shatter, splinters of blazing white pain crawling up his arm, full on to the shoulder.

His sword was five and a half feet away.

The hand would no longer grip, the toes and feet swum impotently in the dust. He thrashed, no longer a proud kraken, but a common minnow, thrashing and gasping for air in a net. Selach slammed a booted heel into his ribs, rolling him onto his back. Rolof reached still, his broken fingers trembling without command. The crowd was frenzied, loving this handsome young knight, hating Rolof.

His sword was five and a half feet away.

"Yield, Ser!" Selach called down to him, smiling from under a gilded helm peaked in horsehair, 'You fought a fine match, there's no need for bloodshed." The Shark of the Goldengrass had turned the points of his trident downward. Three brazen spearpoints met the boiled leather of Rolof's right armpit, the arm he could not stop reaching with.

His sword was five and a half feet away.

"Fuck you, boy." Rolof's breath was tinged with a mist of blood, he could taste it condensing inside his helm, "You will need kill me." Rolof was more than happy to be the third fatality of the day, rather than submit to this loudmouth boy.

Selach went a bit pale, leaning low, pushing his forked spear into Rolof's ribs, "Ser, I am not going to murder you in a friendly contest."

"I do not submit." Rolof wriggled, starting to feel every blow he had taken, as adrenaline slowed. Tension began to lock cold muscles in place.

Selach raised his gaze to the royal box, calling out to the Prince seated above. Rolof had only looked at Prince Vernus Artus for a few scant moments, but he had been impressed by the boy's directness and boldness of command. The boy was barely paying the contest any sort of attention, in truth. He was seated next to an enthralled-looking young girl in orange and brown silk. His arm was around the young lady's waist, with one hand up her shift. "Your Grace!"

Artus jolted with a yelp, attention back to the field. Behind him, Birse snorted with laughter. Vernus restored his hands to himself and answered, "Good Ser, what would you have of me?"

Selach kept the trident pressed to Rolof, but there was no malice in it. The crowd's hurricane of noise had fallen to a dull murmur. Ser Doyle Selach gave a respectful request, "This man refuses to submit, Your Grace. He warred with honor today, but I wish to do him no further harm. I ask you to declare a victor."

More annoyed than stately, the King's second son rolled his eyes. "Oh, sure. You, Ser Doyle Selach. You certainly won. What say you, Ser Rolof?"

Ser Rolof Deepreach decided he would feign unconsciousness. He was more than lightly surprised when he actually fell unconscious. His rest was black. His rest was always back. If Ser Rolof Deepreach dreamt at all, he had never recalled one.

Though his defeat at the hands of Ser Doyle Selach had been the most public, it was not the most frustrating of his failures that day. At the request of his lover, his woman, Lady Larissa Fisher, Rolof had made a mission of hunting down the smug little Scarecrow Lord of Maze Hall. Deepreach located Lord Liam Crowe's pavilion easily enough.

He had settled among the other older, honored clans. Clans that cared for honor and reputation before gold. These old, proud Clans had set their tents and wagons and pavilions further from the high walls of Hivehall. Clans like Woodbjorn, who were the fierce Warbears of the Starlight Shore, in their furs and Elder Iron Scale. The domes of woven pine boughs and leaves housed Clan Ludna and their wild wanderers. The green and orange canvas tent of old Clan Greeneye, those forest oracles, butted up against the dyed sunset silks of Clan Sage, the dragonflies of Mistwater Watch. Dozens of other older clans hung their standards; The Lioness of Lavica, The Swirling red and green koi of Sozen, and the tall hagstone of Clan Blackcart mingled with a forest of lesser standards, clans fallen or dishonored, and upjumped sellswords.

The tall tent of Clan Crowe was striped in orange and blue, and where most lords would set their armor and standard, Lord Liam Crowe had hung three effigies. All three were child-sized dolls stuffed with straw and chaff, made of undyed roughspun. The first, a low one on the left, was dressed in the striped black and red jerkin of Clan Cork. The helm of the dummy had been splint and a hatchet had pierced this rag and strawman clear through to the wooden pole that held the whole thing upright.

The center had a mantle of gull feathers and a drinking horn tied to its face– a rough approximation of the vulture of Clan Gorge. This dummy had been pin-cushioned with iron stakes. The final scarecrow had a head with braided rope dyed purple, a mockery of his own kraken. *The boy thinks he's funny. A scarecrow mocking raiders. Sheep mockin' the wolf.*

Rolof marched up to the tent, but two of Crowe's men stood sentinel. Tall, thin, grim men– men of fighting fishers and farmers. They wore mail and patchwork, the style of the Reaper Knights of Strawman's Hollow. Rather than helms, each man wore a padded hood, and in lieu of spears, the Reapers carried a scythe of silver, set into the black wood of the Moorbjorn swamps.

As Rolof approached, clad in his own colors– seaweed, violet and bronze. The tall Kraken knight nodded curtly, he had no issue with these men. Loyal men served a lord, and it's hardly their choice where they're born. "Hail, allow me pass, I have business with your lord."

The scythes crossed with a clack, a violent rebuttal. The guard on the right grunted, "M'lord is in council and not to be disturbed."

Rolof shouldered forward, "I am a knight anointed, and on business from the wife of the High Lord."

The guard on the left chuckled lightly through his nose, "Don't you mean your *Patroness...*"

Rolof cocked his head, misliking the man's tone, his face, his posture, his *implication.* His first impulse was to help this man die screaming, as was his second, third and fourth. Thankfully, before he could act on them, a commotion had erupted somewhere in the middle distance. Screams pierced a few tents down, under the banner of a Rask

Squirrel. Both men shifted toward the scream, and their instant instinct to protect was all Rolof needed. He shoved past the distracted guards and toward the pavilion.

The tent was two feet away.

He grunted, as the two guards responded– two thin untrained men against mighty Rolof. They grabbed, he planted his knee and felt something twist, but paid it no mind. He extended his right hand,

The tent was a foot away.

Rolof turned his face toward the guard who had mocked him and snapped forward, forehead striking forehead. The younger man hadn't expected that, and tottered backward, dazed and gurning. In a man-to-man contest of strength, few could best Ser Rolof Deepreach, and this common-born guard was not remarkable. Rolof bowled him over, sending him to the soft grass below.

His hand opened the tent flap, and he slipped inside.

Immediately, he was greeted with a haze of grey smoke– a heat unnatural. The tall canvas of orange and blue towered high, higher than it seemed from outside. The afternoon sun seemed to dim, and he knew Crowe had not been alone.

Three of them sat at the brazier, though their faces did not match their shadows. The first man was on the right, massive and muscular. His mane of shaggy brown hair fell to his shoulders, though his beard was trimmed neatly. He was dressed in bearskin and scalemail of ancient blue Elder Iron. Instead of a man, he cast the shadow of a great bear, mouth wide, terrible.

Next to him was Crowe, the young lord sat with his feet up. His bare chin rested in his hands as his long blonde tresses fell around his face. Great blue eyes stared into the brazier. The boy was dressed in black chain and blue wool, his leathers dyed orange. He leaned on his great silver scythe, lost in thought. His shadow was too thin, its angles too sharp. It smiled and danced on the wall, even though the Crowe was still.

And finally, another Lordling, maybe in his twenties. Not as big as the bear, but not as small as the Scarecrow. He was pale, like a shut-in or a man who had lived in a deep, lightless cell. His hair was dark, pulled and tied in a small knot on the back of his head. He was dressed simply, brown roughspun and undyed leather. His armor was a black chain vest and little else. Around his shoulders was draped a great mantle of feathers, brown, grey and black, wreathing him in clouds of down. An old grey sword hung from his belt, and he carried no helm that Rolof could see. He was speaking, though he stopped when Rolof entered. His great hunched shadow was some twisted blend of bird and man, flapping and snapping. A bird-man-thi–

The final Lordling, the bird, saw him. This Bird locked pitiless yellow eyes on Rolof. There was a rush of feathers, wings and shadow and then nothing.

Rolof woke later, limping on the winding footpaths between the many, many tents. The further from Crowe's pavilion he strode, the less he remembered of how he'd gotten there. By the time he'd reached his pavilion to retrieve his armor for his tourney match with Selach, he only recalled something about a bear.

By the time he had been carted off of the field and untangled from Selach's net, he had forgotten entirely about the Scarecrow Lord. In the low medical tent, Lady Larissa Fisher would appear over him, with Karl. While he was slowly cut out of the net, the Lady he could not wed and the son he could not claim watched him writhe and grunt.

They stayed mostly silent, only giving a gasp when his mail was removed, and the full landscape of his wounds bloomed to view.

His ribs weren't broken, though it may have hurt less if they were. His entire torso was covered in red, purple and even blue, as each hit from Selach's trident had left its mark. As he thought, the Learner Lizan confirmed that his right hand had been broken. *No matter, he'd lost.*

Karl Fisher, the "son of the High Lord", fixed his dark-greys on Rolof's own dark-grey eyes. The boy was dark haired and lanky and eight. Lord Ludo was near ninety, stout, and had been blonde-haired in his youth.

"Are you unharmed, Ser?" The boy's little round face lit up when Rolof smiled at him.

"I am perfectly well, m'lord." Rolof lied.

"You lost bad."

Rolof's smile melted into a grimace, "I did, Karl, I was there."

Lady Larissa smiled down to him, her nose especially beak-like. She kissed his lips, the brush of her teeth on his bottom lip a seductive promise. She broke the kiss and whispered, "I've found a way for you to make up for so many embarrassing failures today, Rolof."

He rolled onto his side, grunting in pain, "Of course, My lady"

"Apparently, the prince is gathering the young lords tonight, Rolof." Her voice was warm and sweet, but Rolof knew her well enough to know this was meant to be mocking, "And he seems to not know that Karl here is the next High Lord of Fisher. He forgot to invite him."

Rolof knew enough to know where this was going. "I will escort him and make him known."

Larissa smiled, "Perfect. The meeting is seven hours away."

Karl squeezed his unbroken hand, warmly.

Rolof sighed.

The meeting was seven hours away.

ELLARI II

"It is not a pretty thing, but the fact remains, to live, you need to eat, child. And to eat, you need to kill, baby."

When she had first seen the lists, she had cursed so loudly that Masha had buried her face in a pillow, absolutely sure that the door would burst open and not only her Lord Father would be there, scowling and white-haired, with a retinue of guards to drag her to the dungeons immediately. When he hadn't, Masha had raised her big round head to ask, "I didn't think Ser Reuben was especially dangerous, why are you afraid for Hullen to face him?"

Masha, sweet, good Masha.

Masha had no idea that Ellari had been carrying on for years with one of Hullen's sworn swords: secret meetings, secret embraces, secret kisses, secret *other things*. Ellari, for all her notions of maturity, professionalism and capability, was still a teenage girl that had been betrothed at four years old. To her cousin. Because someone killed her mom and dad.

Blaming her for a dalliance here was foolish, especially, when such things were downright expected of the sons of noble lords, Ellari wouldn't let guilt tie her down. So she and her paramour would continue their clandestine meetings in secret, unable to so much as touch outside the closed curtains and doors of her chambers or his.

And now... Hale was facing Kyne fucking Reave. Her tall, grim champion had been set against the deadly, one-eyed warlock Prince from Ozwyk and her husband was facing a man who likely knows of her affair. She regretted not tackling Lilah Stagg when she left the garden party. The arrival of the lists had been a difficult morning.

Ellari needed her tower, her Lighthouse, and after dismissing Masha to spend time with Ellari's aunts Jasmine and Gail, Ellari returned to her own borrowed chambers. She hurried to the largest chest of clothes she'd packed, hurriedly flinging the lid open and pulling a small rolled bundle she'd secreted in the bottom, just along the back right corner.

When in a sea of silk and satin, her hand hit roughspun muslin, and it was no more satisfying than if she had made land in a real stormy sea. She pulled on the rough, scratchy shift– little more than a burlap sack with holes for your head and arm– and tied a belt made of hempen cord around her waist. She kept her sensible black flats on.

She unrolled the final bundle, deep, hunter-green and softer than sin. The cloak had been a gift from Hale, who said he purchased it from a strange old elf in Korpiklaani on a winter's day. Hale, who was generally quite humorless (which Ellari found charming), was entirely serious about his story of the wuldelv who sold him this fine cloak. She wrapped herself in greens and browns, hunched her shoulders and shoved her hair in her face. Where a sullen teenage-noble girl had been standing moments ago, most would now see another scrawny common boy, wandering from pavilion to pavilion, waiting for the morning's contests to begin between Breaking Fast and The Robin's Hour. She wrapped herself in the cloak; the scent of oil and leather and wood and smoke filled her nostrils, memories of a night shared together with only the stars and this cloak and Hale Torchbearer.

She counted her five quick steps from the desk to the door once she had packed her sad brown satchel under her arm. She pulled a small knife from one of the trays of dishes that her husband had left on the desk. She wiped a smear of some yellow, crusted mustard on

Hullen's breeches which he'd left half-slung over the chair, cleaning the knife before she pocketed it. She would need some kind of way to keep safe among the commons, but Hullen was more likely to notice a dagger missing from his collection before he noticed his wife was missing.

She drew the oversized cloak around her with a flutter, wings of moss and summer keeping her hidden as she swooped out the door of her borrowed bedroom and down the long staircase. When she finally reached the ground floor, the two Malbes guardsmen there, called after this strange common boy hurrying in front the noble's quarters, but Ellari was swift, and the big one with the big nasty carbuncle on the side of his nose wasn't. His skeletal friend was too busy laughing at the big man's failure to grab the slight little commoner who slid between his legs, giggling. Ellari would need to get past Carbuncle and Skeleton to get back upstairs, but that was a problem for later.

She crossed the yard, a ghost in green. The yard was full of young lordlings and knights, all abuzz about the results of the previous day's Dawn Melee; three fresh faces had emerged as contenders, but Ellari had little time to listen. She was on a mission. Across the yard, she heard her husband's staccato drumbeat of a laugh, and pulled her cloak tighter as she pressed toward the walls and out of the gate.

Winding through the dusty horsepaths and flapping banners, Ellari Curr pushed through the masses, breathing in smoke, perfume, sweat and sun. After tense moments, she spotted the red and yellow sunburst pavilion of Ser Hale Torchbearer. Hale had, like most other knights, driven a post into the soft ground, and on it, he had mounted the shield of his house– a red lighthouse on a yellow sunset, The Lake Light Beacon.

Ellari slid between the canvas sheets of the doorway and into the little tent.

Inside, light from the open flap above danced over the neatly organized barrack. It was suffused and scattered by treebranches above; chaos of glittered silver over the perfect order that defined Ser Hale Torchbearer. He was preparing for the tourney, bare-chested, bare-shouldered– a tower of pale flesh, muscles lean and taut. His strong back was to her. If he was surprised at her presence, he did not show it.

"Not now, I am sorry." His voice was low, tense and restrained, as it always was. Of all the men in Rime River Keep, Hale Torchbearer was singular. Ellari had known him since childhood, one of the three fostered boys who grew to swear swords to Hullen. Where Chaddar Goldenlocke was a charming rogue and Esben Hornblower was as solid and loyal a friend as ever walked the earth, Hale was hers. They were two of a kind, even in their early teens. Hale was a moody orphan boy, a ward of his Lord Uncle. When Lord Clifton had been summoned to serve on the Isle of Avalar to become Lord of Judgment, he shipped Hale to Rime River. Lord Hullen Curr III was a cousin to Lord Clifton, and had a household of children– what was one more?

Sullen, tall and pale, Hale had kept to himself for months, a lonely boy who no one wanted. No one but Ellari. They had been thirteen, and she had been watching him over the tops of her books and lessons, hoping to catch a glimpse of those eyes, so blue they were almost black. Learner Maesh had sent them to the castle library to do research on the Sons of Good King Finn, but in the stacks she shoved this sad, beautiful boy against the shelves of histories, and for the first time in her life, shy little Ellari was bold and she kissed him.

She had already been promised to Hullen, of course. But he was a boisterous, loud dirty little boy, and Ellari liked Hale. Hullen preferred his hounds. Over the next four seasons, tall skinny Hale had grown taller, broader, and taken to martial pursuits like a tinder to flame. He had taken his Clan's ancient tower sword of elder iron, and made it a part of his body.

Wayfinder.

It was in his hands now, back in the tent. The Elder Iron, normally smoky-grey, was black diamond against his marble shoulders. He turned his blue eyes on her, always searching, always sad. She placed a hand on his sternum, pink on white. She smiled up to him, purpose lost for a moment, but when the world came tumbling back, her smile faded.

He had been sharpening the sword. Wayfinder was a big, two-handed brute of a claymore. To wield it required power, and most men would only be able to hack and chop with such a blade, but Hale *danced.* This was the first tourney he had entered, but when Hullen and the men rode out to harry bandits or put down rebels and raids, Hale would always return to her clean and unbloodied. He was no coward, he fought bravely and slew those who needed slaying, but he would let no man wound him. No man would take him from Ellari.

He had raised his tent around a stump of oak; a simple brown cloth had been set with his meager provisions, –dried venison (from the wood around Rime River), a hard white cheese, some crusty bread and boiled eggs (lifted from the kitchens here, no doubt) and a few small under-ripe looking pears. They had been carefully arranged. Hale Torchbearer was a man who was deliberate in each moment, each movement.

He frowned, tall and fierce and grim, "You should not be in here, my lady."

"How could I not come?" She wanted to embrace him, throw herself at him and scream until her throat bled, but she held back, tensing her hands into balls of oak, "We are utterly beset on all sides, chimera and stags and even the damn squirrels in the trees, Hale."

"If you are concerned about my match with Reave." He paused, his always-quiet voice low even by his standards. "Hullen took all of us after the lists were announced, and had us meet our opponents. Well, everyone save Esben. That's the problem with fighting a mystery knight, I suppose; when he takes his helm off, he's just another man." His eyes searched the soft grass that made the most of the tent's floor, save a mat under his bedroll and another under the crate where he kept his steel. His voice wavered, just a moment, "Reave seems like a good man, a fierce combatant."

"They say his sword drinks the blood of those it cuts."

Hale snorted. "Cookfire tales from old sellswords" His straight posture somehow went ever straighter.

Ellari implored, "What if it does?" She glared at him, "Stranger magics exist."

Hale shrugged, "I'll just not let him cut me." There was no humor, no jest. He made it sound simple, as if it were simply a matter of willing it enough. *Maybe for him it is.* The tension dropped from him. "You did not disguise yourself as a common boy in broad daylight and sneak into my tent to talk to me about Kyne Reave. We could have spoken about this anywhere."

She went sheepish; Hale had been there last night. He had seen her wander after the Stagg girl and unlike Hullen, he noticed that she had hurriedly left the party in disarray. Ellari knew he'd been waiting for her to come to him, she always did when she needed peace. He was her beacon, her tower, Ser Hale Torchbearer was her lighthouse.

"Lilah Stagg knows."

"She knows about us?" Hale frowned, but that was hardly new. "How?" He had swung Wayfinder from his shoulder, the point black in green grass. Strong hands gripped the hilt tightly, red and yellow leathers twining the handle. Set into the end, a hunk of yellow topaz seemed to glitter with a light all its own.

"I don't know. I heard her say something to her husband at the party last night" Her voice was low. She took two short steps toward him. After a moment, he chose to lay the sword on his bedroll and embrace her.

She laid her head on his bare chest, and felt the throaty rumble of his voice. "What did she say?"

"I-I'm not entirely sure." Her own voice was a soft thing, at least here it was. She pressed her roughspun shift into his bare skin. He showed no sign of discomfort, so neither did she.

A big broad hand palmed the back of her head gently, holding her to his chest, as the other drifted to the small of her back. "You don't know what she knows, or what she said, then she left, and nothing else has occurred since?"

Ellari nodded, deathly serious.

"I do not mean to downplay your concerns, but might it be possible that you are making assumptions based on incomplete evidence, Ellari?" He slid that hand from the back of her head and placed a pair of thin fingers under her chin, lifting her gaze to meet his.

He kissed her, stubble rough like fine sandpaper, lips soft as whispers of their secrets. At this moment, there was no Lilah Stagg.

There was no Hullen, or tourney, or Kyne the warlock. There was a boy and a girl and a kiss, and she loved him.

Who would tell her this was wrong? She would simply have to find this Stagg girl and settle matters, if she knew anything at all. "You're right. I should just… speak with her. I did try, last night, you know."

He nodded, "I saw. Very daring behavior." His smile was only in his blue-black eyes, and she had to kiss him again. More kisses followed, more embraces and more love. Some time later, when the afterglow had faded, she'd straightened her dress and hidden her hair, when she had wrapped herself back in the green, soft cloak, it was time for them to part.

As she made for the tent's door, Hale called to her. He was holding the sword, extended out, flat in both of his hands, "My lady, I only ask for your blessing now because outside these silken battlements, such a thing means both our lives."

She turned, a wry smile crossing her lips. She pressed her thin, soft lips to the cold steel, a gentle kiss, "My blessing is yours, along with my heart, good Ser." Their gazes hung on one another a final, touchless embrace as Ellari weaved herself through the tent flaps. She would return to the castle without delay and even managed to avoid Carbuncle and Skeleton by slipping a kitchen girl a couple of copper pieces for her to distract them with some light flirting so she might slip by unnoticed.

She passed up the stairs, through the silent chambers, nothing but a cloak and two swiftly shuffling feet. She rounded into the bedroom she shared with Hullen, and was shocked to find him standing above the wash basin, cleaning his face and hair with the soapy, steaming water.

He heard her, but he did not look up. "S'at you, 'Lari?"

Her heart was somewhere in her throat as she immediately shrugged the cloak from her shoulders and, shuffling her feet, she managed to wedge it under a small shelf of curios near the door. A porcelain bee in a jester's cap shook perilously for a half-second, but even as it rocked ever so close to the edge, it did not fall. She finally answered, shoving down any tone that may have been suspicious, at least, she tried to, "Oh, yes, m'lord. I'm just back from the–"

Hullen looked up, fixed his gaze on his wife and took her measure. She was pink and sweaty, covered in grey dust and green grass. Her hair was askew, and oddest of all, she was dressed in filthy rags, with a cord instead of a belt. He took a sharp inhale through his nostrils, paused, and then exhaled deeply, "What in the name of the Mother are you wearing, 'Lari?"

Her head was spinning, her ribs had become two skeletal claws squeezing the blood from her heart and the air from her lungs. She steadied herself on the doorway, and took a moment to find her center. *Talk about something he won't care about.*

"Mushrooms!" she blurted, loudly. Hullen hated mushrooms, he called them "dwarf fodder" and refused them, no matter the preparation. Ellari didn't have a special taste for them, but it was the first thing she'd thought of that he hated.

"Mushrooms?" His voice was more hesitant, confused, maybe, not suspicious. She was onto something.

"T-truffles, yes! There's a very specific truffle." She started, watching Hullen's thoughts already begin to drift, "I read about it in Learner Vaughn's book. It only grows here, only during this specific time of year." She was lying, but by now she had made the prospect so boring that Hullen wouldn't dare ask such questions again. She droned on about truffles, just to be sure. "It's actually due to the high concentration of bees here, their, uh, feces, is really good for the uh…" She trailed off as soon as she was sure he was no longer listening, "Hullen!" He jerked his head back up from *Snowsnarl,* his shortsword, always thrumming softly with a hum of icy-cold energy.

"Oh, I'm sorry, 'Lari." He sighed, "I'm sure it is incredibly interesting, I'm just so focused on all of this." He waved his hand over sheets of parchment, "Have you seen the lists?" Inside, she smirked. *He is so very simple sometimes.*

She feigned ignorance, "No, my lord, I was down in the grass all morning."

"Some truly interesting matchups, darling! Hugo Saddler has the Lord of Spies, he'll beat him in a second if he can pin him down." He rattled his sword into its scabbard before tossing the sword, scabbard and belt halfway across the room to the bed that they two shared. He dug through the parchment sheets before him.

The letters. Gods above, he was reading the letters from the Prince. Her heart broke to see him trying, knowing what she was doing to him. Hullen had never spoken to her cruelly. He'd never raised a hand in anger. He did his duties as a husband and together they had tried, in vain, to make an heir for a year now. Hullen was a good man, she knew this. He simply was not *her* man. From the bottom of the stack, he pulled the lists, the matchups of the tourney, and slid it into her hands.

"I've got that Stagg." He smirked, his joy palpable, "I like my odds, I'm ten years younger and much, much better." He gave a wolfish grin, filled with teeth and charm, in the way only a handsome young nobleman could. For a second, she wished she loved him.

"Chad has that bird woman from Asorra, Allie Shar? Allis Ar? I can't say it–"

"Al Eh Syar of Hro'Cratis, the City of Birds" Ellari corrected.

"Yes, uh, her." He nodded, "Have you seen her bird? She rides it like a horse! Like a big blue chicken! And a beak like a cleaver! I'd hate to end up jousting that thing." He ran another finger down the lists, "Esben has some mystery knight in Turtle armor, wearing the Mirebreaker symbol, but with the colors swapped. Huge lad, even taller than Hale. I reckon it's Jurgen Shoreshrike."

Though she had matters of greater import on her mind, her natural curiosity couldn't resist. Hullen wasn't stupid, in many things, he was wiser than she was, and his insight in this might be interesting, the Curr bit, "How do you figure?"

"He's fighting with a two-handed greatsword, not many men do that. Wearing freshly forged plate, which ain't cheap–"

"*Isn't* cheap." She corrected.

"Yeah, *isn't.*" *H*e rolled his eyes, but he continued, "But a Grey Guard, he could afford it."

"Sure…" Ellari narrowed her eyes a little, taking stock of Hullen as he spoke.

"And like I said, he's real big, like Shoreshrike." Hullen paused, suddenly bashful, "And, I know this bit sounds silly, but, he's wearing the colors of House Mirebreaker, but swapped, right?"

More than a little amused, Ellari encouraged him.

"Well, Shoreshrike is from Galder's Net, you know? And that's as north as north gets. Like the opposite of the Lowlands, so he's wearing the Mirebreaker turtle, just…"

"…Swapped." Ellari was *stunned.*

"I mean, I might be wrong, but I don't *think* I am." He shrugged, "Gets another Grey Guard in the tourney to keep the Prince safe." He looked her over, in her scratchy shift and cord, and he smirked, before rising and kissing her on the top of the head, "Truffles. That is very cute, really." He sauntered toward the bed, and picked up his sword, strapping the belt around his slim waist, "You'll be down in time? Chad's up first, but I want us all there supporting everyone, y'know? Bring Mash', too. She won't go if you don't drag her, but it'll be good for her."

Ellari nodded, still standing in front of the shelf where she had stuffed her and Hale's beloved green cloak, trying to spread her narrow little feet as wide as possible, obscuring everything behind her. "Of course, my lord. I'll be there in something much more." She glanced downward, "appropriate."

He smirked, "I know you will." He crossed the room swiftly, long legs and excitement hurrying his stride. He placed a hand on the door, gathering himself with a little shake. He turned back, deadly serious. "I almost forgot!" He drew his sword, and held it flat in his palms, and lifted it to her. Elder Iron remembered, Elder Iron held on to things. Snowsnarl had been forged with the blood of the last snowdragon seen in Daneau, nearly three-hundred years ago, and it had been one of Clan Curr's most famed treasures. And because it was Elder Iron and blood of ice, it was special.

"My lady, I only ask for your blessing now, because I want it to be mine alone, I want no outside eyes to profane it."

Her stomach hurt. If she could have hated herself to death, she would be ashes. She blessed it with a loveless kiss, a lie. "You have my blessing, my lord, and my love."

Elder Iron remembers. And though Ellari Curr was not superstitious, no one cheered louder when Ser Hale Torchbearer's sword Wayfinder drank the sorcerous flame of Kyne Reave and an unknown knight from Lake Light Beacon defeated the Warlock Prince of Ozwyk.

Elder Iron remembers. And when Hullen Curr's sword failed to freeze Ser Reuben Stagg, Ellari knew it remembered lies, too.

LILAH II

"They will try and tell you that your soft heart makes you weak, but there is nothing fiercer than a mother fighting for her child."

"I am positively *wilting"* Lilah's older sister, Lady Donla Rask, likely did not need to be out and about in the summer heat. She was late in her seventh month with child, and the humidity and sun left her red-faced and huffing. She leaned hard on her husband, Ser Sabbat of The Acorn Clutch. As was fairly common in the Empire, the Lady of the Clan had married a man of honor, but not a man of name. Ser Sabbat had distinguished himself fighting bandits and even a troll-spawn bandit lord in the greatwood, but he had no name nor lands. As many knights in his position did, he married the Lady of a landed Clan, and their sons would take *her* name. As such, the line endures.

Ser Sabbat was a broad-chested knight of forty, thirteen years Donla's senior. He was bald-headed, and had a great coil of braided black beard growing from his chin, down a ropy braid to his chest. He wrapped it three times into his belt. Donla was constantly threatening to 'cut the damn thing off', but Lilah found it endearing. She found Lady Rask playfully bickering with her husband even more endearing.

Their son, Irwin, bounded behind. He held hands with Lilah's own son, little Neal. Irwin was six, two years older than Neal, but barely an inch taller. Neal was a tall, strong boy. *So much like his father.* He was also patient, kind and sensitive. *Blessings in those differences from Reuben, blessings.* Neal was all Stagg, graceful, thin and light of foot. Irwin, though goodhearted in his own way, was a nervous, skittish little black-haired thing. He rarely sat still and seemed to blink too much, but he loved his little cousins dearly.

Lilah followed behind, making sure neither boy wandered too far. Beside Lilah, sauntered Doreen. The youngest Rask sister carried Lilah's own baby daughter. Doreen was twenty, and Theasa was two. Though she had spent precious little time with her baby niece, she had practically been sewn to the bairn's side for the entire trip. Theasa snored softly, brown-red curls gently catching in the breeze as she drooled onto her auntie's bare sunburned shoulder. Doreen was a skittish, nervous girl. As the last unmarried daughter of the Late Lord Daryn Rask, Doreen had been pulled into a web of machinations beyond her and was being presented to Prince Vernus Artus as a possible suitor.

Doreen was pretty enough when she smiled, though she possessed the big buck teeth of the Rasks. She smiled around children and trees. She smiled over a good cup of mint tea, or a whispered secret between sisters. Doreen didn't smile at the clash of swords, or drunken garden parties or dances with strange princes with cruel eyes. Lilah did not know how, but as she watched her baby sister cradle her own baby, she vowed an oath of protection. Doreen Rask would not be given to a cruel boy. Her sister would not wed a "Reuben."

Being among her family was a balm, and Lilah would do anything for them.

Though Ser Sabbat led, four of Donla's clan guards kept pace in boiled leather and forest-green capes. The tips of their spears and the tops of their quivers were tied with red, grey and brown squirrel tails—puffs of fluffy heraldry. The Rask Squirrel was not mighty nor fierce, but he was quick and he was cunning.

The boys, Irwin and Neal, followed Sabbat to a tree near Doreen's tent. With some protest, Doreen even handed over Theasa. Some of Doreen's maids had laid out a fine woven blanket, reds and oranges and browns. Ser Sabbat grabbed his Irwin by the waist, with one arm and held Theasa tight in the other, followed closely by little Neal. The quartet fell giggling to the blanket to prepare for a shaded rest. The ladies would enter the pavilion to refresh themselves.

As soon as the ladies entered the tent, her sisters started screaming. Like idiots. Lilah knew she wasn't brave or smart, but she knew whatever the little ragged creature in the corner of the room was, it meant no harm. Her sisters were being silly. It was half-starved, and unwashed dressed in rags, but Lilah immediately recognized it as a *kobold.* They were called lizard-rats, vermin drakes, or, rather rudely: shit dragons. The little beasts called themselves *mioldrekki,* and they weren't exactly uncommon in the Daneau, but to see one, unexpectedly, put her two sisters into a frenzy.

Donla screamed for the guard, waddling behind Doreen. The younger sister had snatched a stoke iron from the cold brazier and started swinging it like a broadsword, keeping it between herself and the intruder.

The creature was little bigger than a tom turkey. It wore a stained, little jerkin, black wool. The creature was, for all intents and purposes, a wingless little dragon-man. This is to say, it was not a mighty or beautiful drake, but a scrawny, mangy thing. It had broken open the small chest of dry goods in the far corner of the pavilion. The two little clawed hands were shoveling anything they could grab into its snappy little mouth: nuts, biscuits, crackers, dried meat, hard cheese, raisins, dates, prunes and the parchment and cheese cloth it was all wrapped in. There was a great Empire of Dragon-folk far to the south. Beautiful people, with tails and scales and horns, made in the image of their dragongods. Tall, powerful and magical, they were sometimes seen here, far in Daneau. But those were merchants, priests, princes, mercenaries, *men*. A different sort of man, but men all the same. This thing was clearly not that.

Upon hearing the screams of the women, the little kobold screamed something in a language that not one of them knew, clacks and hisses and chirps, *"Zjeer! Drekki vaq! Vaq!"* Crumbs sprayed from its mouth. It took another huge, exaggerated bite, *"Vaq!"* Bits of cracker flew wildly.

Donla screamed again, "What a wretched thing!"

Wretched thing.

Lady Grete filled a doorway in Lilah's memory, and words echoed, each one an arrow into her gentle heart.

Wretched thing.

Lilah took a step toward the little thing, hand extended, bending low. She moved slowly, gently. Her sisters objected, but a quick spin of the head from the middle sister sent them both to silence.

The little rusty thing rankled, hissing under its breath. Its eyes seem to grow, giant silver-green pools of patina and mercury. It bared sharp little sewing-needle teeth, and raised its little haunches, in an attempted show of ferocity. Lilah stifled a snigger, the little thing was a scared kitten, not a dragon.

The tone she used was gentle, motherly, "Are... you're hungry?" She raised a hand to her mouth, miming a bite of food.

"Vaq!" It chomped a date in half, swallowing the pit and meat in one fell go.

She smiled, slowly, softly. Her gentle nod followed even gentler words, "Do you speak *common?* Man-words?"

The silver eyes met hers and there was knowing, "Verm knows... some... word. *Vaq.* Eat. Starved." It trembled when it spoke, and along skin stretched taut with hunger, its little back and ribs were bruised and scabbed. Someone had beaten this poor little thing badly.

Sunlight flooded the tent, silver fire spreading through the dim tentlight. Ser Sabbat thundered in, followed by two low Rask guards, slick and powerful as hunting hounds. Ser Sabbat hurried to his pregnant wife. Donla shrieked again, pointing toward the little drake in the corner.

Without thinking, Lilah rushed to the edge of the tent. She slid manicured fingers under the canvas, through the grass and soil and yanked. Three wooden stakes popped free from the soft sod, and a foot-high gap of sunlight and fresh air opened. Lilah looked down at the little wretched thing, "Run. Get free. Don't let them hurt you."

The kobold just stared at her for a moment, taking a moment to translate and comprehend.

"Go!" Lilah nodded, waving a hand at the gap she'd created.

The little red thing nodded, and scrambled out into the grasses. Ser Sabbat and the guards groaned, and the old knight sulked toward her, "If'n you let those things out, they just get back in!"

Donla nodded in agreement, "I know it's cute, but it's a wild creature, Lilah. It is kinder to put it out of its misery than let it starve."

What a wretched thing.

"I was unaware that stabbing and starvation were the only options for a hungry creature." Lilah wasn't usually cruel, but she found her sister's words both callous and stupid, "Perhaps we could try feeding it. If not, I'm beginning to worry for the smallfolk of your lands… My lady."

Lilah– Loyal, quiet, simple, kind, docile, placid, *stupid, useless, wretched Lilah*– Lilah had never stood up for herself before, not to her family who she did, most deeply, love. And she would certainly not say such to the Staggs, her husband's kin, though she did not love them.

All the same, every Rask and Rask man in the pavilion was shocked. Donla, the Lady, ever the conciliator, spoke first, breaking the silence. "Well, it's back outside, no matter!" She shooed the guards back outside, and stuffed Ser Sabbat's arms with bits of food and snacks for the children outside, and bid him leave as well.

Once the women were alone, poor pregnant Donla waddled to her middle sister, her Lilah, and gently placed a hand on her cheek, eyes gently tracing a finger-shaped bruise along Lilah's jawline. The heat of the day had displaced just enough powder to leave it visible. Donla saw, and her eyes held understanding, "It is a fine person who shows unblinking mercy in the face of unrelenting horror, Lilah." Donla pressed two plump red lips exactly on the bruise.

Lilah made sure to reapply her powder.

Their rest was restful and their food filling, and their break shorter than they'd have liked. As the afternoon had grown even warmer, more stifling, Donla elected to stay back, patting her fecund stomach, "He's had his fill of sport today. I'll have a book and a nap, and perhaps he'll be wise instead of fierce." All the same, Ser Sabbat had arranged for a small covered palanquin to bear the gathered party back. Inside the carried little carriage, the shade and open breezes kept everyone cool and relaxed until they had managed to return to the tourney grounds.

During the break, she had been Lilah Rask again. A middle sister of three, a mother, a sister-by-law. She was loved for her gentle heart and her sweet tooth. She was appreciated because she reminded her family, her clan to care about everyone. In Nuttley, she had a purpose.

To the Staggs, she existed to hold Reuben's attention and produce heirs. To the Staggs, she was Lady Lilah Stagg, wife to Reuben, mother to Neal and the girl. She was nothing. Back at the tourney grounds, she was expected to be Lady Lilah Stagg once more.

As they stepped down from the palanquin, her mother-by-law greeted them without warmth or a smile. Lady Grete took Theasa from Lilah and handed her to the veiled nursemaid at her side. She commanded Neal to take the nurse-maid by the end. The little boy immediately stood straight as a sugar maple, doing as he was told. The thick-waisted nursemaid shuffled the children toward their seats as Lady Grete took measure of Lilah and Doreen.

Lady Grete's eyes lingered on Lilah's midsection, surely noticing some imperfection Lilah had not, but she said nothing. The smell of flowers and smoke and mead and sweat filled the breeze, a welcome taste of the day. Lady Grete looked over Doreen and, impossibly, her hateful face spread into an enormous smile.

Lilah recognized the smile. It had come frequently in the early days of her betrothal and courtship and marriage to Reuben. Compliments and smiles for her looks and her manners and her practiced graces. *Compliments for the way Reuben stared down her dress and watched her walk away with hungry eyes. Compliments for the port at Nuttley and the port under my skirts.*

Once Neal had been born, an heir, the smiles ceased. Every smile, every compliment went to Neal. You see, Neal was going to be High Lord of the Greatwood someday, Lady Grete had decided. Lady Grete was, herself, the older sister to the Greatwood's high lord. Lord Torvald had no children of his own, which meant that the ancient bloodline of Clan Ironarm had reduced itself to a trickle. Lady Grete's son, Lilah's husband, was heir to the Greatwood, and baby Neal was his heir. When Lord Torvald died, those two boys would make Clan Stagg the High Lords of one of the six great nations of the empire. Lilah spent most of her youth in a treehouse, the idea of being a High Lady made her stomach flutter. Granted, if Lord Torvald ever did have a son, Reuben would inherit nothing. Reuben's father was second son, uncle and great-uncle to a slew of a dozen Stagg men set to take his family home before he dared press a claim.

Lilah had been her path to the Metal Mount, but Lady Grete saw the whole empire through Doreen. *Controlling me was easy enough, why not use my baby sister too?* Doreen had no interest in participating in this "Debutante's Procession." Lady Grete had been *most insistent.* A chance at Prince Vernus and a throne had been something she dreamed of, even if she would simply be the power behind it.

As such, she had taken a keen interest in Doreen and had put the full coffers and force behind the pretty little squirrel's campaign for a crown. Doreen's interest was not strong to start, and now that they'd seen the Prince, it had wavered further. Lady Grete only spoke songs of the prince, speaking to his wealth, good looks and fine breeding. Lilah watched him leer and drink and knew she couldn't let this boy have her sister.

Lady Grete met Doreen warmly, embracing her, then Lilah more quickly, "Wonderful, simply wonderful!" Lady Grete produced a small amethyst tinged vial, and gently clouded it around the three women. The natural scents of smoke, flowers and meat disappeared beneath alcohol and ambergris and lilac. Lilah sneezed and Lady Grete glared at her, "There, we must be fresh as flowers, loves. We've a prince to catch and Reuben needs our cheers."

Lilah could feel eyes on her as she followed Lady Grete in tow. The Lady had dressed herself in a sweeping floral silk, and was carrying a lace parasol of Stagg green. Dappled sunlight spotted the old doe as she started off. Two retainers, skinny little daughters to one of her brother's knights, carried her bustle behind her. The Rask girls exchanged a knowing, tired look before following.

As they re-entered the arena, passing through a low tunnel, sounds from the bleachers above could be heard–laughing, singing, talking, footsteps and cheering, the sounds of sport and joy. They crossed back into the sunlight, and in the dust and two men were battling.

In truth, the contest was nearly over. Lord Reinhart Goddar was on his knees in the dirt. Above him, the famous tourney Knight, Ser Tullus Mirebreaker was scowling. Mirebreaker had sent the two short handled axes flying from Goddar's hands. The stout knight in the turtle armor drove an armored elbow into Goddar's forehead. A gout of blood sprayed from Goddar's forehead, as the blow split his skin. Goddar's head snapped back, then forward in a rage. Unarmed, Lord Reinhart elected to bite the Snapping Turtle. Or at least he tried to clamp his teeth onto one Mirebreaker's fingers, but he was met with a fist instead. The crowd erupted as the Lord of the Whorl tumbled backward in the dust.

"Who tries to *bite?*" Mirebreaker's rattling voice echoed from beneath his helm. The Master of Games had already taken the field to end the contest, in Mirebreaker's favor. Lilah heard scuttering beneath the stands, as they reached their seats. The breeze of their skirts sent a bit of feather and a scrap of cloth flying from the bench, with other grit and debris.

"Is Ser Reuben ready for his contest?" Doreen inquired to Lilah, a smile in her green-grey eyes and sunlight dancing on her pink cheeks.

Gods help us if Vernus gets a look at her, she's too pretty.

"The Curr boy, I do hear he's fierce, but my husband strikes like no knight." She shifted her bruised jaw.

Lady Grete took over, leaning over Lilah, "Ser Reuben will put down that barbarian boy, without issue." She reeked of the perfume and of her lunch-hour white wine.

Lilah leaned back, out of her mother-by-law's alcoholic haze, into the lap of an annoyed-looking older man with a gold coin sigil stitched into his fine black silk jerkin. Lilah grinned a nervous apology and pulled herself forward. She had avoided thinking about Hullen Curr IV and his wife Ellari since the party. *It is no business of mine. It's that simple.* Still, she refused to be caught off guard, her eyes scanned the crowd constantly.

"I do hear that Hullen Curr has a sword with dragon-ice." Lilah admitted, her voice tinged with concern, "My husband is more than a little worried about that Elder Iron bandit-stabber." Beneath them, down in the stands, someone dropped something heavy, and the whole bleacher rattled and shook.

The women settled in for the next contest, though calling it a contest was something of a jest. The young Lord of Sweetvine Swamp was brought out first. Lord Sharga Moorbjorn was barely past twenty, bulky and somehow both bearded and baby-faced. Some of the men in the tourney were heavyset; some, even could be called chubby. Lord Sharga was just fat. He was not athletic, he was not powerful. He was just overfed and timid. He wore a gilded little half-helm with wrought little bear's ears and a spear to match. A layman could tell he possessed little experience in combat through his tense stance and nervous smile.

A fanfare of horns blared from the opposite side of the arena, heralding the entrance of the formidable Bloody Lily, Lady Carmine Lily. The common folk adored her for her unrefined manner and swift swordsmanship, while the nobility respected her for her wise counsel and strategic brilliance. Women of Lady Carmine's caliber were a rarity, appearing perhaps once in a generation.

Her physique was compact and powerful, belying the strength within. She was a diminutive, middle-aged woman, yet she possessed the aura of a seasoned warrior, ready to face Moorbjorn. The contrast between them was stark: youth versus experience, brute strength versus honed skill. From the sidelines, the Mirebreaker clan cheered and hooted wildly, chief among them, the winner of the last match: Ser Tullus Mirebreaker, her husband. You could not see her smile under her frog-helm, but one only had to watch her to feel it.

Lilah clapped loudly for the Bloody Lily, as did Doreen. Lady Grete remained sour-faced, frowning at a woman only a few years her junior doing such a foolish thing. The combat wasn't. Lady Carmine had elected to leave her usual curved sickle behind today, choosing a blunted war-hammer, increasing her reach substantially. It only took one spinning thwack to the shoulder. Moorbjorn threw himself to the dust, sobbing.

The rabble and lords alike burst into laughter at the Lord of the Swampbears, echoing and cruel. However, this ceased when Lady Carmine offered the young lord a hand, and bid him rise. When he did, she raised his arm, with hers. Even dour Lady Grete managed a cheer at that, smiling at the display of sportsmanship and brotherhood.

Lady Carmine then bowed once, on her own, before turning back to her family. She yanked her helm off, before pointing at her husband, "You're next, Snapping Turtle! You've been ducking me for twenty years!" The crowd roared in approval, as Lord Tullus went red-faced with laughter.

"I guess I've run out of excuses!" The old knight called back to his wife, and one of most anticipated matches of the second round had taken shape: though past their primes, two of the most celebrated tourney knights of the age would cross blades for the first time, and they were wed. Lilah could not wait to hear the songs written about that forthcoming clash.

The Battle of the Knightly Spouses would need to wait, however, because what came next turned Lilah's guts to stone. Lilah's Husband, Ser Reuben Stagg entered from the northeast tunnel. He wore his green and bronze plate, shining in the daylight. Set into the center of the green Stagg sun on his breastplate was a saucer-sized mirror. Every night in the tourney had his tricks. Some had magic armor or weapons of elemental fury. Some just used unique weapons like the Canar Grey Guard and his smoke bombs. Reuben didn't own a magic sword, and though he was heir to it, he never took to the Ironarm family's ancient warpick. His only heirloom was the great green antlered helm he'd been given by his grandfather.

Given Reuben's vanity, the mirror seemed obvious in retrospect. Though not everyone was as distracted by their own reflections as Reuben was, the mirror drew attention to the center of Reuben's chest. The center of Reuben's chest was the most protected part of his body. Lilah was also keenly aware that her husband would often use the mirror to blind his opponents with reflected light, but he didn't care to admit to such underhanded tactics.

From the northwest tunnel, Hullen Curr IV strode in, surrounded by his three sworn swords... and his lady wife. Lilah slouched into her seat as not to be seen, and heard the bench and bleacher shift under her. All of the Curr retinue was dressed in the colors of Rime River Keep, blacks and indigo and creams, and Lady Ellari Curr stood directly between her lord husband and the man she was having an affair with.

Lady Ellari had begun to make Lilah furious. It simply was unjust. Lilah was a good, loyal wife. She protected the children, she stayed loyal to Reuben despite his own dalliances and his capacity for cruelty, she had the bruises to prove it. And here comes Lady Ellari Curr, *the power behind the Wylde.* Curr served as her Lord Uncle's Chief of Staff and, as such, helped with the rule of the most northern of the six Nations in a very real way. Lilah only dreamed of such respect. Even more infuriating was the reputation of Lady Ellari's husband: Hullen Curr IV was young, dashing and all things a knight should be. Reuben had spoken highly of him several times. They were becoming fast friends at this great gathering, which was something Lilah had desperately wanted to avoid.

Hullen Curr was dressed in ring mail of the black Elder Iron and wore a great shaggy brown mantle on his shoulders. The lithe lad looked little more than a wild animal, as he allowed one of his sworn swords, the blonde one, to strap him into a simple black bucket helm. Ser Hale Torchbearer approached, and with hands that had known his lord's wife, handed him his ancient sword. It was called *Snowsnarl* and was even known in the Greatwood. It was a true short sword, a simple one-handed thing. Though it had little reach, it was lighter than a whisper and thrummed with the elemental power of a vanquished ice dragon.

At least, that's what the stories said, but when Hullen Curr pulled his magic sword, there was no magic thrum. The blade was fine and a singular shade of blue chrome, but otherwise, it seemed entirely mundane to Lilah.

When the horns blew, both young men were mirrors to one another: Hullen in black, Reuben horned in green and bronze. Both men swung a shortsword in their right hand and carried a kite shield in their left. Reuben usually used a smaller buckler shield, no bigger than a dinner plate. Today, facing the wild northern ice magic, he'd opted to trade speed for safety.

It was Curr who struck first, the impetuousness of youth outweighing any sense of learned caution. Curr swung the sword, and Reuben shifted, letting the shield take the blow. The Green Knight didn't riposte. He didn't parry. He didn't even try to dodge, he simply let Curr strike his shield full on with the magic sword. Reuben grunted, but he set his stance and did not allow the younger knight to stagger him. Curr struck again, this time, striking forward, whippet-quick, stabbing with the point of *Snowsnarl*.

Ser Reuben caught it again, full on the shield. No attempt to dodge or counterstrike, but even from her seat in the Noble's bleacher, Lilah saw her husband's eyes and she saw his strategy plain as day.

He's testing them both– boy and sword. The boy is impulsive and battle-lusted. She mused to herself as another chop of the sword sent oak splinters flying from Ser Reuben's shield. There was not as much as a breath of frost on the wood.

After the third strike failed to freeze and shatter his shield as the stories said, Ser Reuben got off of his heels and put the fear of the Greatwood into the younger knight. Reuben was a good twenty-five pounds heavier than Curr, so the green knight started by simply muscling into the black. A low jab with the edge of the kite shield sent Curr stumbling as he prepared for his fourth slash of his decidedly-not-quite-magic sword.

Finally, as Curr growled under his breath, the two men crossed swords, and they danced. For all his initial fury, Curr seemed to have calmed himself after the shot from Reuben, and settled into a more skilled martial rhythm.

Slash. Riposte. Parry. Counter. Chop. Stab. Counterstab.

If the sword wasn't magic, the boy wielding it had earned its reputation through skill, it seemed. *He is very good, but if there was one thing Reuben excels at...*

The swords clanged again. Both men had long since cast their shields aside, and Reuben smirked as the heir to the Wylde swung his blade directly for the mirror at his chest. Reuben double-stepped backward, just enough to let his breastplate take the sword. As the sword clattered off of the thick metal, Reuben grabbed the silver-blue blade in his mailed hand, and with a groan, wrenched it free of Curr's grasp. A derisive snort followed as the green knight tossed the young knight's sword to the corner of the arena, into the dust and sweepings.

Reuben grappled the smaller man and began to drive armored knees into Curr's face. *...It is hurting people* Curr collapsed, as the arena erupted for the handsome Stagg knight. From across the bleachers, over her own hollow cheers, Lilah could feel Lady Ellari Curr's big silver-sun eyes gaping at her.

If I never see a Curr again, it will be much, much too soon.

Scant hours later, she, Doreen, and Lady Grete would be led into Honeyhome's Queen's Hall. They had all changed into their finest gowns, jewels and furs and set loose among the Highborn. Lilah's heart was in her throat, but when she saw that the three of them had been seated at the same table as Ellari, Masha and Lady Gail Curr at the "Debutante's Procession." The gods had been especially cruel, because Ellari and Lilah had somehow been given the seats right beside each other. There would be no avoiding Lady Ellari. Not only could they not ignore one another if they did not interact it would be noted.

Lilah's eyes met Lady Curr's, brown on silver. The silver showed a flicker of recognition, followed fear, then the ice of resolve. A tight professional smile crossed Ellari Curr's face, "Lady Lilah, I've been meaning to get to know you."

Lilah returned the courtesy, even though her heart threatened to hammer her ribs to pieces from the inside, "My husband speaks wonderfully of yours." This was true; Reuben rather liked the Northern Lord, and after the contest, they had spent the afternoon drinking with his sworn swords.

Lilah had spent the afternoon wanting to anxiously vomit or explode into dust, depending on the moment. With a practiced flourish, she introduced Lady Grete, "My mother-by-law, Lady Grete Stagg. She tells such wonderful tales of a youth spent beside your late Lady Mother." Lady Grete exploded into chatter, fawning over this 'niece who looked so much like her lost sister.'

Lilah hated them both.

Later, she could not say what the meal they had served was. It had tasted very fine, to be sure, but it sat in Lilah's stomach heavy and still for hours. There had been honey in it. After days in Honeyhome, Lilah was beginning to loathe the sticky-sweet drizzle that cloyed to everything: meat, vegetable or dessert, everything was brushed in it.

The Debutantes had been presented, and a dozen young, beautiful women had settled around a dais, where a small table of cheeses and fruits had been piled high, but remained untouched. Artus had shifted his focus almost entirely to the beautiful Saddler girl. Lilah was glad to see that Doreen was almost entirely ignored. She was heartened to see that Masha, the sweet little Curr girl who had been escorted by Ellari, was also safe from the prince's squeezing hands.

Lady Gail Curr had made her way to the middle of the ballroom, where she was breathlessly chuckling at something one of a half-dozen gathered noble ladies had observed. Lady Grete Stagg was beside her, unsmiling into her glass of red wine.

Lilah and Ellari had been sitting in silence for five of the longest minutes of Lilah's life. Lilah had counted the fifty-six embroidered purple and white flowers on the tablecloth four times, and the seventy-two little golden beaded bees three. She was on bee number twenty-six when Ellari Curr finally broke the silence.

"Your husband fought very well today, Lilah." She smiled weakly.

Lilah looked up and nodded a thank you, but could not find her voice.

The Curr girl stared into her eyes, two big silver suns imploring, "He is a good man, as is my Hullen."

The words came before Lilah could stop them, "If Hullen were the same sort as Reuben, he might deserve what you've done." Her mouth, which had been watery to the point of gagging moments before, was now dry as kindling.

Ellari Curr was a pale girl normally, but Lilah watched her go whiter than silk. Her hands crept across flowers fifty-four and five before finding Lilah's, white and cold and pale and stiff; a dead woman's fingers gripping Lilah's warm soft, pink palms. Her thin lips trembled, and parted, as she barely whispered, "Lilah, I-I don't know what you think you know."

Lilah's voice whispered, words came from her mouth, but she was no more in control of them than she was her oddly placid heartbeat. "You are *fucking* Hale Torchbearer." Her voice was small and passionless. Lilah had put herself somewhere very far away.

Ellari's inhale of breath was sharp and the squeeze of her fingers on Lilah's was sharper. The northern girl leaned in closer, Lilah could feel the heat of Curr's breath. "Please, you don't understand–"

Lilah was done being told she didn't understand. Lilah was done being told she was stupid, useless and *wretched*. Ellari Curr may have expected Lilah to be a squirrel, but she was about to find a raging, wounded beast. Lilah snapped, whispering under her breath, years of rage and frustration boiling free in a geyser eruption of fury, "Do not presume what I understand, Lady Curr. I understand you are wed to a good man, a man of honor and duty. And I understand that you and one of his *sworn-goddamned-swords* are breaking so many vows that I do not even understand where to begin. Which would be fine, if you were a fish-wife or a barmaid, but you are about to become the High Lady of an entire nation." She drew a sharp inhale of breath of her own, before jerking her hands free and continuing, "You only need to look to the Greatwood or Fisher to see what an unstable inheritance looks like, Lady Ellari. So, before you play 'hide the lighthouse' with your Hale again, understand that your duties and your decisions have effects that reach beyond your chambers. Gods help you if you mother a bastard, My Lady."

Lilah rose, shoving her chair back, "Loyalty may not be clever and it may not even be useful, but it is who I am."

Curr stared up at her.

"You may tell Lady Grete that the surroundings have left me feeling ill, if she inquires." Lilah checked the dais, and found Doreen chattering excitedly with a barely-bruised Lord Sharga Moorbjorn. Satisfied, Lilah wheeled away. She left the ballroom, the guards and the Curr girl and Doreen and the Prince and her awful bitch mother-by-law behind her in a mad, skittering dash, laughing to herself. *I must look mad to anyone looking, but Gods, do I feel free.*

She calmed eventually, her strides shortening once more to a confident canter. Lilah would make her way back to the tower, giving the guard at the base of the steps, the one with the boil on his nose, a polite smile. She would return to her borrowed chambers, dismissing the night nurse once she had seen to her sun-exhausted and sun-kissed babes. Both Neal and Theasa dozed peacefully, dreaming of tourneys and sunshine and pastries, to be sure. Satisfied, Lilah returned to the grand bedroom that had been granted to her. Quietly drunk on catharsis, she opened the curtains wide, allowing blue moonlight to pour over her and the chamber. Long shadows crept over the room, black on blue, a starless sea.

She drew a deep, cleansing breath, smelling flowers and sea-salt and tasting the cool, clean air. Tomorrow might be hell, but tonight she was free–

Something behind her scuttled across the floor loudly, and she froze.

It clacked closer, and she could not force herself to turn. Tapping steps slowed as they neared, and a small voice behind her rasped, "Lilah... You are Lady... Lilah."

Today had been all about bravery, so Lilah made herself turn, and was greeted with the familiar sight of two silver-sun and patina-green eyes staring up at her. The little rusty kobold was in her chambers. "Please... No shouting.." It held up two empty clawed hands, three fingers on each. It stepped forward, black talons clacking on a brown floor gone silver in the moonlight. "Lady Lilah saved Verm."

"How did you get past the guard? Have you been following me since the tent? This morning?" She puffed herself up, trying to make herself seem larger and fiercer than she felt. She slowly rounded away from the window, maintaining her distance, but trying to get nearer the door.

"Verm is... sly." It bowed its little horned head in deference, "Verm has been watching Lady Lilah and her... people." It reached into the rags that served as its jerkin, and produced something sharp. Something about four inches long, hooked and razor-sharp.

Lilah lunged for the nearest approximate weapon she could find; a lace parasol in Stagg green. With a swiftness that rivaled her husband's quickest riposte, she snatched it, snapping it open with a grunt.

Verm loudly squawked, dropping the sharp thing to the floor and cowering, "Verm protect Lady Lilah! Verm try to help Lady Lilah!" It fell clattering and skidded into a beam of blue moonlight, and Lilah saw it.

Four inches long. Bone white. Capped in black Elder Iron and blue diamonds. A dragon's tooth.

"Lady Lilah said... man would use dragon magic on mate in fightgame. Verm stopped him." The rusty little thing smiled up to her, folding its hands over one another, "Verm protect Lilah."

Gods be good, this is the heart of Hullen Curr's sword.

HARTWIN II

"Viciousness isn't cruelty, Hartwin. It is just survival, little love. Strike first, leave no survivors, sleep peacefully."

Though the tournament's first round had gone incredibly well for Clan Saddler, Hartwin's mood could not have been more dour. His Lord Uncle's victory over that pompous, puffed-chest Lord Mabon Albin had been a surprise, but a welcome one. Uncle Hinric was a fair fencer, but few had expected Albin to show up piss-drunk, embarrass himself and break his arm falling in the dust. Albin was the pious lord of Hope's Hill, a city that utterly banned vice, so the hypocrisy was not lost on Hartwin.

And Doyle's defeat of Ser Rolof Deepreach was even more shocking. His cousin had defeated one of the most feared knights in the west in fairly short order, battering the big knight in the Kraken helm with his trident, tossing him in a net to take Deepreach to the dust, and holding the pointed fork to the seam Bronze Kraken's right armpit, one of the few unarmored portions on Deepreach's body. Hartwin was not overly fond of his cousin, Ser Doyle Selach, but even Hartwin had a swagger of pride in his cousin's skill.

Hugo's defeat of Lord Illystre Coldhearth was the notion that was bothering Hartwin the most. Not the nature of it, Hugo was likely to win the whole tourney, defeating Coldhearth was a simple formality on the way to victory. No, what made Hartwin grind his teeth was what happened afterward. The gathered masses had surely been a little sensitive after the tragic events with Webb and Vellen, and Hartwin couldn't blame them.

But when Hugo used Hoofbeat, the family shield to give Coldhearth back every thump he had struck into it, the Lord of Spies was sent flying across the arena and passed out. Hartwin chortled to himself. *Fainting like a woman, how shameful.* But then Hellendre, his mother's witch, had sprung up from the bench beside Hartwin, and with a few energetic bounds forward, cleared the fence with a leap. The verdant Hellheart healer and sorceress rifled through the myriad pockets in her silks and sashes, pulling a vial of this and a chunk of that, sliding on a hip into the dust above the unconscious Coldhearth. As she parted his lips with a green finger topped with a perfect pink fingernail, Hartwin felt something that disgusted him to his core.

Jealousy.

She pressed a few drops of a chalky substance into Coldhearth's mouth, and then the grey-robed Lord of Spies sputtered awake. She cradled Illystre's head, muttering about the "Poor man", while Learners Franz and Powell checked him for injuries, finding nothing.

The mere idea that he was feeling possessive of Hellendre… disturbed him. Hartwin had been exchanging letters with four young ladies his father and mother had deemed acceptable for the heir to the Goldengrass to wed. Doreen Rask of Nutley was an idiot, but it seemed more likely than not that she would end up sister-by-law to the new High Lord of the Greatwood when sickly lord Torvald died without issue. Ser Reuben Stagg would become Lord Reuben of Clan Stagg, Regent of the Greatwood, and he was married to Rask's sister, a buck-toothed dullard named Lilah. Ficke Hornblower was a widow with a six-year-old in the frozen north. Though she controlled the key bay to the Wylde, Hartwin would much prefer to raise his own sons to rule. He had very little interest in either girl.

Still, the other two girls were more intriguing. Thana Fisher was clever, with a sharp tongue and bright eyes, more than a little pretty and of all things, a smith and tinkerer. Most men would find such pursuits off-putting, but Hartwin wasn't most men. Hartwin loved a clever woman. The sort of cleverness mattered little. In the end, it was intelligence and passion that attracted Hartwin. Thana's knowledge and skill was something Hartwin enjoyed dearly, even if he rarely comprehended craft and metallurgy.

However, the inheritance of the Fisher Kingdoms was little more than a midden heap full of vermin fighting over scraps, by far the most fractious of the six realms of the empire. Though he liked the Fisher maid enough, and her grandfather was one of his father's oldest and dearest friends, committing to her meant choosing a side in the conflict to come... and Thana's faction held few cards that left them likely to win. Hartwin fingered the golden horseshoe pendant that hung on a thin leather cord around his neck. It was a gift Thana had sent in response to a particularly *salaciously romantic* letter Hartwin had composed with some light collaboration from Harlow.

And then there was Lady Joelle.

Joelle Bridge was his age, soft and warm. She had been a frequent visitor to Stonestall in her youth. Her Lord Father had a deep need for fine horse, and the Saddlers bred the finest. He remembered the first time he'd seen her, a little plump and shy, but more clever by half with numbers and figures than anyone Hartwin had ever seen. When they had been seventeen, they had made love, each other's first –to this day Hartwin's only– lover. All awkward enthusiasm, salted sweat and breathless kisses, the pair had spent the afternoon in the high golden grasses near the lakeside, and had fleetingly considered never returning.

They had continued their tryst when they could, but her Lord Father would die short months later, his heart unable to bear the strain of his prodigious appetites for food and wine. Joelle would take his seat, and her visits would decrease as her duties grew. The business-like Lady of Rain Tower Hall would pass through the doors of her private chambers, the weight of the world would fall away and his plump, pink Joelle would fall into his lanky arms. They would tumble into her bed, and the weight of both their duties would fade like smoke in the breeze for a few hours.

As youth had faded into the beginnings of adulthood, the pair had been forced to spend time apart, as Stonestall and Cobalt Bridge were a week's ride apart. A fortnight is too long a time for a Lord or Heir to set aside their duties, so Hartwin and his Joelle had not seen one another in nearly a year. Tonight, at the "cattle call", he would see her. He would hear her filthy jokes and her rumbling laugh, and he would be able to touch her.

Her Uncle, Ser Grigori Bridge, sat in the chair Hartwin wanted more than anything on Earth. He would never be king. But Lord Executor was closer than any horse farmer would ever be. He loved Joelle, he did. But would he love her half so well if she wasn't so close to Hartwin's throne? The prospect of an honest answer made Hartwin hate himself a bit. A stampede of tension trampled his nerves to dust.

Even more tension rose in his shoulders and neck as his thoughts turned to Hellendre and Illystre once more. Hartwin couldn't have Hellendre for a million reasons; he was not even sure he wanted her. Still the sway of her hips when she walked away lingered like her perfume and the places where she touched him tingled with blush for moments afterward.

As if summoned by thought alone, the green and gold Hellheart filled his threshold, smiling. "My lord, your Lady Mother sent me to see how you are coming along." She looked him over, brassy eyes under green lids. He was dressed in verdant silk and golden chain, as befit a lordling. She was wearing silks of her own, swishing things of purple and grey smoke, a small gold chain running from the piercing in her nose to one in her right ear. Her eyes were lidded in a swoosh of something purple-blue. The had wound soft velvet ribbons around her brassy straight horns. She was a vision, a work of art, a treasure.

Hartwin inhaled. Hellendre smirked, "If you don't close your mouth, a bird is like to build a nest in there."

The mention of birds put Hartwin in mind of a half-remembered nightmare in the grass, and a terrible prince, a corona of stars. Light and shadow and feather and death. Talons. He shuddered and exhaled sharply through his nose. Nightmares would have to wait; tonight he sparred with both Princes.

He took his devil by the arm, and strode into the hallway.

An hour later, an entirely different devil was digging her nails into his arm, "Haaart, I-I don't like that boy. I don't like his look." Harlow begged into his ear. Her voice was a plaintive cry, childlike and worried.

Hartwin Saddler was finally getting to take the measure of Prince Vernus Artus, and he was not especially impressed. "Remember your breathing." His tone was measured, controlled, a show of comfort. His attention returned to the Prince and he knew at once this was not the shining three-eyed angel from his nightmare.

Vernus was terrible, to be sure, but there was no beauty or power in him. He leaned on a high table, sloshing a silver wine goblet back and forth. He idly chatted with two identical girls, one in indigo, one in silver. His downward glances followed their necklines, not their eyes.

The king's skinny second son didn't have the sterling reputation of his older brother Talor. Vernus Artus was thin-armed, with a pot belly and eyes that were closer to green than the famed Imperial Gold. Hartwin had heard rumors that Marten Mirebreaker had left the boy weeping in the yard the other day, but at best they were whispers of maids and squires. However, there was a bruise under the prince's eye, a mark on his perfect porcelain skin that no one would mention.

Before Hartwin could react, the Artus boy noticed them. A slow little smile crawled across his thin lips as he looked over Harlow. The prince drained his goblet, set it down and left the Selach twins without dismissing himself. He straightened his doublet, set with the three-eyed crest of Artus, hand-stitched a hundred and a half times. It was an ostentatious garment, and if you looked too long at it, it seemed to shimmer and quake queasily. The jacket was a sea of gold eyes on blue, and Hartwin hated it.

As the prince got closer, Hartwin could feel Hugo rankle a quarter-step behind. Both brothers were deeply protective of their baby sister, but Hugo was the one who might stab you. Harlow tried to take a step back toward her brutish defender of a triplet, but Hartwin held her fast. "We can not show weakness, Harley-girl." He was gentle but firm, "Chin up, we know this dance. Deep breath." She breathed. "Put on your mask, Harlow." She listened, she nodded. Opening her eyes, she smiled.

And when Lady Harlow Saddler smiled, she *dazzled*.

Another hour later, Harlow and the Selach twins were all three seated at the table beside the ugly little prince. They were not the only ones, of course. This was the Maiden's Procession, or at least that's what mother called it. He, Hugo and Doyle had taken to calling the event "The Cattle Call", because, well, all the little fresh heifers were being lined up for the new bull on pasture.

Maids of every shape and size from every corner of the empire (and a few of the far kingdoms outside of it) had congregated here in Honeyhome for a chance to be a princess. It was a women's tournament. A contest of beauty and competition of subtler manipulations, jockeying for favor and position with their own merits or their rivals' flaws, each of them clawing for a Starheart crown.

Little Lady Bulldog from the Wylde looked terrified in silks of midnight blue and cream, surrounded by a smattering of more serious northern women. The Bird Woman from Hro'Cratis grinned in her cloak of feathers and headdress of great bronze disks. A Madapple, a Rask… a Fisher..?

Thana?

He was more disappointed than angry. They had made no vows, and Vernus Artus was a prince. Thana Fisher was clever, and a clever girl would chase the prince. Hart blamed himself, having squandered good opportunities to commit. Thana had given him plenty, and he had been uncharacteristically indecisive.

Hartwin hoped no one saw him snap the little chainlinks on the pendant with a sharp tug. Though it was cold in his sweaty palm, a tantrum of a toss sent the thing into a potted plant nearby. Across the hall, Hugo and some of the other young knights had pushed some tables together, drinking sullen toasts to the memory of Purvon Webb and Jack Tymm, casualties of today's games. Reuben Stagg and Hullen Curr spoke in breathless whispers hidden from the rest. Hale Torchbearer and Kyne Reave chatted politely, no sign of their brawl earlier in the lists, new brothers, bonded in respect. Hugo, cousin Doyle and Uncle Hinric were cloistered together, sharing a roast capon and a big potted jug of red wine from back in Stonestall. He could have joined, he supposed, he lacked the mood for it. Instead, Hartwin Saddler, heir to the richest kingdom in the empire, sulked into his whiskey and watched the people he loved best in all the world shine.

He reminded himself of tonight's midnight council and resolved to make this glass of whiskey his last. He flexed his right knee, a tall boy stuck under tables too short. He stood and stretched, suddenly finding Hivehall's Queen's Hall too stifling. He quickly knocked back the remainder of his drink, returning the little horn cup to the table in front of him. Hartwin blotted the final drops from the corner of his mouth with a green square handkerchief. He turned through a set of open pillars onto a high balcony looking over the sea below, greeted with salt breeze and cool air.

He stood, watching out over the calm Bay of Bees, sweet, gentle waters that fed into the far-off Shining Strait. Out there, among the waves, lay the rocky jags and crags that made up the Shining Isles of Avalar. From the keep at Lordsport, Clan Artus had ruled since the last Owl King disappeared from Three Tall Towers in a stormy battle of smoke and sorcery. Dead or missing, it made no matter; King Rast Mertens was last seen nearly four hundred years ago. His cousin, Gallus Goldeneye, became King Gallus Artus I, and began a new dynasty from a new castle, promising peace and unity after the Decades of Disgrace.

Hartwin wanted to be on that island. His want had grown into an ache under his ribs. He would rule the Goldengrass, and he would rule it well. Five more kingdoms called out for his guidance, and from the Lord Executor's seat, his would be the voice that reached them all. And to be on those islands, to be at the table, Hartwin would be willing to slay a dragon, or run headlong through a wall. Blood was not a sacrifice that he feared, his nor anyone else's.

Ruminations of grandeur were whirling through his mind when a gentle hand found the small of his back. Shortly thereafter, a second played at the auburn fringe at the back of his neck– gentle lover's fingers. Plump pink lips purred in his ear, "No one broods like my Red."

His skin went prickly.

Joelle.

He wanted to be suave, he wanted to be clever. He wanted to say something romantic and set her to fluttering. Like a dullard, nothing at all came. That brain that had been whorling wild had suddenly gone stone. Devoid of other options, he did the thing he'd wanted to do most of all. Hartwin spun on a heel, and pressed his lips to hers.

She made the same surprised little squeak she always did when he kissed her suddenly, or a wandering hand found her backside and unexpectedly squeezed. Thankfully, Hart avoided that temptation for now. She leaned into him with a light moan and a giggle, plush and soft and completely his. When the embrace had finally broken, she raised a soft finger, tipped in purple, to the corner of his mouth and traced a rare smile. "Well, that fixed you right up."

Ten months of distance evaporated like fog in silver dawn's light, as he clasped her hands in his. Though they both often would sneer at mushy declarations of love and devotion, when it came to one another, Hart and Joelle were powerless. Before the hour was out, they had found a quiet corner of the veranda, and settled on a long bench. Her head rested in his crossed legs, her raven-black tresses spread over his lean thighs. She blinked lilac lids over murky aquamarine eyes stared up from her round cheeks, almost always tinged to blush. They talked out the tourney, she was convinced the Torchbearer boy might beat Hugo as he had shocked Reave. The castle was abuzz with discussion, a welcome distraction from the fates of Webb and Tymm.

"He's tall and moody and just a touch aloof, reminds me of someone." She teased up at him.

Hartwin smiled, but he shook her accusation away, "I watched that match beside my brother. Torchbearer didn't win, Reave lost. Sorcery is no substitute for pure skill. We shouldn't even allow that unnatural shit in the contests."

A slow finger slid up his ginger stubble and pinned his bottom lip down. "*Shit?* Such crass language, now where might you have picked that up, Red?"

"Well, a few of your letters have been educational in the finer arts of profanity, just the other day, Hug–"

Harlow screamed. It cut the night, ringing from pillar to ceiling and crashed out over the lovers' peace. Their eyes met, and in unison they flew from the bench, her stubby legs keeping pace with his long, through sheer grit and determination. Harlow, fragile, brittle Harlow, had long been a sister to Joelle, and her love for the girl was fierce as any. There was a clang of shield on steel, echoing deep. Rounding into the ballroom, the lovers found chaos. Ser Hugo Saddler had his fine brown boot leather pressed onto the red flesh of Birse's neck. Two Grey Guard, Sozen and Canar, were between Hugo's sword point and a sniveling Prince on the dais.

Beside him, Harlow was trembling, great heaving quakes of panic through her tiny frame. Juddering sobs and deep racking wails came from between perfect white teeth. In her left hand she still clutched the crystal stem of a shattered wine glass. All of the other girls cowered away from her. The table that had been before them had been flipped, wine and nibbles of food lay across the swirling marble floor.

Hartwin took command, all iron. "Hugo?"

His brute of a brother ground his heel into the struggling Hellheart's throat, "She screamed. Said the boy touched her. Didn't take kindly to it myself, Hart."

Canar, the younger of the Grey Guard, held a short dagger in one hand, and one of his smoke capsules in the other. He was bent, lean, low, ready to strike. Sozen, beside him, wielded a long staff, tipped in the Elder Iron. He was slack, water and motion made flesh.

"No one needs to die today, son, just a disagreement." Ser Auberon Sozen's voice flowed languid, cool and gentle.

Joelle shouldered past the two guards, blazing up the dais. She took Harlow in her arms and all the tension melted from the girl. Harlow went boneless, and Joelle pillowed her to the floor softly. "Get the Learner or the witch!" she called up from the floor, "Fucking *now!*" she barked at a man-at-arms, when no one moved.

Hartwin galloped to his brother, setting a firm hand on his shoulder and giving a gentle squeeze. "Sheathe it, Hugo."

"Hart, I don–" His voice trembled, a rare thing for the Brute of Stonestall. "They might ki–"

Hartwin cut him off, "Sheathe the *fucking steel,* Hugo."

As always, Hugo obeyed. Steel into sheath, but the boot stayed on Birse's throat. Hugo slowly turned his face on Hartwin, and Hart saw that his brother's right eye was rapidly swelling shut. He had been battered. "Okay, Hart."

Hartwin looked over his brother's bruised countenance. He bit his bottom lip, and looked over at the bodyguard under Hugo's heel, "He do that?" Hugo's only response was a silent nod.

Hartwin wasn't a strong man, he wasn't a violent man. He kicked the big hellheart in the ribs as hard as he could. It hurt Hartwin near as bad as it hurt Birse. He did it again. The big man sputtered and shook, and Hartwin leaned low, his voice a gentleman's calm "I don't care who you work for. You lay another hand on my brother, and I will bleed the Goldengrass dry, hiring men to cut your black heart out."

Hartwin straightened, folding his arms behind his back, and strode genially toward the pair of Grey Guard, all polite pleasantries, "Off him, Hugo." Hugo grunted an affirmation behind.

The older Grey Guard, Ser Auberon Sozen, maintained a reputation of poise, wisdom and careful confidence. Hartwin did not know the new boy, this Canar. Sozen lowered his stave, and with his eyes bid his younger compatriot do the same. Canar sheathed his steel, but kept his little glass marble in-between the knuckle joints of his third and fourth purple-gloved fingers. There was threat in the duck's grey eyes and his grey cloak; Hartwin was not in the clear yet.

Harlow murmured, and thrashed weakly in Joelle's arms. Bridge pressed the back of a gentle hand to the prone maiden's forehead and shushed comforts to her. Hartwin called out to Joelle, "What does she need, my lady?"

"The Learner, for fuck's sake. That'd be a start!" Her face was pale with worry, though her brows furrowed in righteous frustration.

"She'll be fine, no one hurt her." Canar locked his beady little grey eyes on Hartwin and Hartwin filed away this noble idiot for a later dissection.

"If you had the head to treat a disease, you'd be a Learner, not a bodyguard." He shouldered past Canar. Well, he tried to. Canar wrapped his leather-gloved fist around the silks, and chains of Hartwin's collar, and yanked him close.

"Not near my charge."

Hugo surged forward. Hugo had few principles, but 'No one touches Hart,' was sacred. Steel flashed as his gilded sword swung. The heavy oaken thunk of Ser Auberon Sozen's stave clacked clear through the hall as the monk-knight kept his own principles– 'Defend the line.'

Thankfully, the sniveling Vernus was not the line. 'The line' strode in, sword in his belt, golden eyes flashing. He was everything Vernus was not. Tall, strong, handsome. He wore dark wool and leathers, no better than any man who rode in his name. Beautiful and terrible.

Flanked by two more Grey Guard, Crown Prince Talor Artus entered and the world stilled.

"What is the meaning of this?" His voice was gold and starlight, and none could deny him, not even his brother. Beautiful. Terrible.

Canar was the first to speak, his hands loosening his grip on Hartwin's collar, "Your brother grabbed the girl. *Unchivalrously.*" He gave Hartwin a gentle shove back, but allowed him to pass. Hart scrambled up the dais to Joelle and Harlow as the Duck explained further, "She reacted loudly, Ser Hugo took offense–"

"I was gonna choke 'im, but the Hellheart and the Grey Guards got in my way." There was no lying in Hugo, at least.

To his credit, Talor Artus laughed. But it was a chilling, humorless thing, "Though I share the impulse myself, it's likely best that you did not manage to lay your hands on Vernus." He placed a hand on Hugo's shoulder, "Ser, you were simply defending your charges." His eyes met Sozen's, "This man has committed no crime, don't you agree?"

"The prince is untouched, Your Grace."

The crown prince looked over Harlow, and crossed to Joelle and Hartwin. His stride up the dais was effortless. "For now. At least until Father, or Gods-be-grand, the Queen hears of this." He turned to his brother, "Make your apologies and return to your chambers, Vernus. If you cannot do this, Mother and Father will be the smallest of your concerns." Beautiful and terrible.

The prince continued, all command, "Ser Auberon, Ser Drake, see my brother and his… pet." He spat the word at Birse, "Back to the castle. Ser Jurgen, Ser Gnash, you may remain with me."

Prince Talor had not been seen since the incident in the tourney this afternoon, but if the death of Lord Jack Tymm had rattled him, there was no sign. He divided his guards, and after he gave polite concern to the slowly-waking Harlow, the crown prince rounded on his brother.

Vernus had stopped crying the instant his brother had entered the hall. Presently, he'd risen and was brushing food from his jerkin, an impotent attempt at restoring his royal authority. As his brother approached, he stiffened, defiantly. "Yes, what?" He grunted as comprehension dawned on him, "Oh, *that,* yes, yes." He bowed low, mocking Harlow, "My apologies to my lady of horses for making her stampede." He turned off, "She's a bit of a nag, anyway…"

From the ground, the big crimson-skinned Birse gingerly pulled himself to his feet. The hellheart lowered his lips to Hugo's ear, "This is not settled."

"Seemed fairly settled with my boot on your throat." Hugo gave his sadist's grin, "but I will gladly knock you in the dirt again, demonseed." Birse chuckled and limped after his charge. The prince and his bodyguard disappeared through a small secret door reserved for the royals and their attendants, Sozen and Canar in tow. At this point, most of the gathered nobility had scattered, and even the drunkest dregs had found the exit. On the Saddlers, Joelle and Prince Talor and his greys remained.

With the sharp clop of heeled boots, Hellendre had finally appeared at the far entrance of the hall, a small outcry of shock escaping her lips. She hurried across the ballroom and up the blue-and-gold carpeted dais stairs, settling in between Hartwin and Joelle with her satchel. Hartwin felt himself rankle and lash out, "Where in the hell were you?"

Mixing a restorative elixir without looking, she spoke, "I was just enjoyin' the evenin', Hart."

Joelle raised an eyebrow, perfectly shaped in black, "'*My lord,* you mean.'" The look on her face was a suspicious one. Hartwin immediately felt a guilty pang, but he was unsure of its source.

Hartwin folded the guilt on itself until it was a burning diamond of anger, which he turned on the reason for his guilt, Hellendre. "You are not here to *enjoy* the *evening,* Hellendre." His tone had turned instructional, formal, master to servant, not the playful banter of two childhood friends. "Your duty is to Harlow. She is your *purpose.*" He was angry, he knew he was, still he regretted the next words as soon as they left his lips, "If you are not protecting her, why do *we* need *you?*"

If Joelle had heard the insult, she ignored it. But she was too busy shushing the disordered Harlow. Hellendre's gaze went wide, rolling over Hartwin. If she had tears, they did not fall from her brassy eyes. She stiffened, and gave a curt, professional nod, "Yes, sir, Ha– *My Lord.*"

Hartwin pushed the bile back down his throat. He offered his Lady a hand, and Lady Joelle Bridge took it. He helped her to her feet, and led her away. The help could attend to Harlow. He led his Lady by the arm to the crown prince and greeted him warmly.

Beautiful and terrible.

DRAKE II

"Only beasts kill for fun, and only monsters maim and wait for you to die."

Once Prince Vernus and his pet devil had safely been sent to bed without supper, Drake Canar followed the bald, brown, bouncing head of the cautious, careful Ser Auberon Sozen down the spiral stairs of the central keep, which had been granted to the royals. He was too outstandingly angry to focus on anything but the lines of the skull under his sword brother's shorn scalp. Once the pair had reached the empty veranda below, Sozen shook his head and spit on the ground bitterly, a rare show of emotion from the usually controlled knight. Exhausted, Drake was beginning to wonder if it was temptation or torment that turned his predecessor to vice after all.

The night had become a welcome respite from the heat of the summer silver sun, the humidity settling into a low fog in the valleys and wet places– the beaches and the bays. The stars sang in the sky, ten million-million silver candles floating atop waves of black smoke. The slow steady rush of the waves of the Bay of Bees far in the distances thrummed in rhythm with the twinkling starlight. The sickening-sweet smell of those damn purple and white little flowers had soaked into Drake enough that he feared a headache. Both men, the old monk and the young duck, paced the cobbled patio, each looking more like a caged jungle cat than a tired knight.

Finally, deliberately, calmly, Sozen broke the silence, trying for wisdom, "Service isn't supposed to be like this."

Angry, the youth rounded on him, "Whatever it's supposed to be, it is certainly not." Drake was an inch or two taller than Sozen, but The Iron Pearl of Black Pearl Bay was not a man to be intimidated. A little past forty, Sozen was unlike any of the other knights on the Guard, and given their eclectic natures, that was a strong statement. He was trim, but not thin. Muscular, but not bulky. He armored himself only in leather and padded cloth, and even his boots had soft soles. He carried no blade, no bow. Only a staff made of a heavy blackened wood, tipped with grommets of the Elder Iron on each end. When he fought, he was the whorling rush of the storm. He was wind and water and the hellish crack of thunder. Legs, elbows and staff could bring even a knight in plate off balance, and then all belonged to the Monk Knight.

Canar stopped himself, faced with the placid and intelligent Sozen, he felt like a child tossing his toys from the basket. Instead, he followed the older knight's lead and acted like a Grey Guard. *We cannot change the duty.*

"How do you do it?" Drake asked, tentative but earnest.

"Well, if we don't, they execute us." Frequently, Sozen's eyes glimmered with the chaos of a trickster all grown. They shone with that same sparkle tonight, two candles in a sea of black smoke. "Service for life tends to go that way."

Canar had given the same look he now wore in response to hundreds of his own Lord Father's prodigious plays of punnery– stone. "Do you have anything better than japes?"

Sozen leaned on his staff, eyes of night matching the sky above him. Though he was still, Canar still sensed the same whorls and whips of motion, but only in thought. Sozen was building his point with the same care he would face the most deadly hired knife. "Vernus is sixteen. And he's not the heir."

Canar nodded. "True enough."

"Vernus isn't even the heir's heir. King Gallus, Prince Talor, Prince Hobar." He snorted, "You could even push the babe, Selora, if you wanted, before the brat." He frowned, "Shame Saddler didn't gut Birse, though."

Canar smirked at that, despite himself. "Might have been able to, I've never seen a man move so quick." Sozen's silence was pregnant with past battles. At once, Drake knew that the older knight *had* once seen someone that quick, and it was *not* a friend.

The tension returned, its retreat only a fleeting beam of sunlight in this chill. Since the tournament, a dour pallor had hung over the six knights of the Grey. The day had started with enough promise, though the accidental slaying of Lord Webb had certainly been something of a trial. But, once the mid-day break had been taken, foodstuffs devoured and ales quaffed, the flapping banners in the silver sun had begun to raise the spirits one and all.

All six Greys walked the Elder Prince Talor to the ring, all six armored. The prince himself wore chainmail and a fine, padded blue jerkin. His helm was the same wrought, twisting gold as his pauldrons, with an eye of topaz set into the center of the forehead. Ser Gnash Selach had drawn the commander's lot that morning, so it was he at the prince's right hand. Selach wore scale and a bowl helm, so as not to obscure his vision. His great whalebone bow was slung over his back, beside his quiver. Selach was an archer, but no petty hunter or ranger, he was a sniper of no equal

At the Prince's left was Ser Cole Canden, enameled in blue and grey, his great warpick on his shoulder. The old goat scowled under his ram-horned helm. Behind him clanked Ser Jurgen in his white and black plate, his grand claymore *Wolfwhale* strapped to his back. Drake was behind him, sword, dagger and capsules. Drake preferred a light leather helm, rounded, bleached and dyed Canar violet. Sozen was behind Ser Gnash, and next to Drake was Ser Darwyn Tyrmm. Drake had been beside him when it happened.

When the Prince killed Darwyn's brother, Drake had been the one to take his arm and pull him back. Drake had stopped him, right then and there. And why?

Later on, even Darwyn couldn't explain why Jack had pulled the jar of the acidic ooze. Much like Clan Canar, the Court of Tymm maintained a strong interest in alchemy, and the acid ooze was one of their finer inventions. It was sold across the kingdom in little glass vials, a solvent so potent it was usually thinned in water.

Why did your brother have enough acid to eat a hole in a castle wall for a friendly tourney?

And Prince Talor…

If the Crown Prince's skill as a knight was something Drake would never question again. The boy prince had blocked the shattering glass with a great tower shield, near as big as he was. Tymm cackled like a demon, pulled his great green jar of death, and the Prince heaved shield, Tymm and jar halfway across the circle. The acid and glass hit Lord Smiling Jack Tymm right in those famous grinning gums. He was melting away like candlewax before his knees hit the ground.

Darywn's scream unnerved Drake's heart. With an athlete's quickness, Drake managed to grab the other knight by the arm. Ser Darwyn struggled against his fingers for a half-second, before watching his brother's corpse slump in the dirt and then collapsing himself.

In the arena, Sers Cole, Jurgen and Auberon had surrounded the Crown Prince who had collapsed himself, fits of maniacally sobbing laughter leaving him twisting in the dirt. The prince writhed, hands at his temples. His helm was forgotten in the dust beside him. Tears and sweat and dust and screams mingled as Ser Auberon tried to bring his prince balm, to little avail. Drake tried to rise, but Selach stopped him, already drawing the great whalebone bow. Selach was a soft, fleshy man, but his arms, shoulders and chest were powerful, and his voice rumbled like a rushing wave on jagged rock, "No, stay here."

Drake did as he was bid.

Selach looked over Tymm, who had fallen, inconsolable, on the ground. "Get his ass up, we need him. Something is wrong, I can smell it." Drake weakly tugged at Tymm's arm, trying to not rouse the knight too sharply.

Drake shook his head motioning at what was left of Lord Jack, "That's his brother. He's not going anywhere right now."

Selach cursed, "Shit. You're gonna be my spare eyes, okay Drake?"

"What?"

"Just keep an eye on this close up, I'm gonna focus on the far. Just watch everyone. Pull your dagger and that fog–"

"Smoke. The Smoke is sacred."

"That smoke you use, sorry. Pull your dagger and the Smoke and be ready, okay?" Selach hefted the weighty bow into position, nocked an indigo-feathered arrow, and Drake watched as his fellow knight's eyes seemed to lose focus, though he was clearly scanning the crowd and the high places.

Drake pulled his dagger, and thankfully, some glass capsules, before leaning low to the sobbing Tymm. "Stay low, you might be the next target."

Tymm's grief-reddened eyes turned to fury, "The Prince was the target, Ducky." He managed, before his eyes went back to pleading and his words shattered back into sobs. Canar gave him a firm squeeze on the shoulder before turning his attention to the crowd. He scanned the ground, the arena, the royal box above him.

Whatever grim assassin of the Iron Knife or hateful fae spectre Ser Gnash was expecting, it never materialized. The Priests of Eresh were the only spectres on the field, in their unsettling blank faceplates and robes of woven starlight. Gently, they tended to Lord Jack, but even they seemed unsettled. Only hours past, the silent elves had done their grim duty, removing poor lost Webb, and helping his spirit cross into the stars. They had been slow, gentle and calm in their motions, respectful and gentle. They had behaved much the same, until the tallest of the Priests, an elven woman who wore four thick braids of rope at her waist, examined the body of Tymm.

Drake was unsure if those tall alien priests from the continent could feel fear, at least like man does, but it certainly seemed like they were taking extra caution with the body. Sozen whispered to the tallest one, and was struck with a look of shock and tension that hung dense on him for minutes.

This realization struck Drake back to the present moment, back to the veranda, back to Ser Auberon Sozen.

"Tal– The Crown Prince killed the blood brother of one of our Sworn Brothers, Ser." Drake shuffled sullenly to a bench, gilded in that honey-brown gold Clan Malbes loved so well. The young knight finally collapsed onto the bench, the clatter of his scabbard on the wood hardly bothering him. "Accident or not, I am fairly sure there are no laws of chivalry granting council on this matter."

Sozen gave his wise smirk, "While chivalry has never been chief among my concerns, I am reasonably sure you are on the mark there, yes. We have a simple code, Drake. *'Preserve the line.'* I generally find answers in simplicity. Talor is not the line, not entirely, no more than Vernus is.*"*

Drake looked him over, and after a moment he saw it. Under the wise and grim mask, there was that chaotic twinkle, "You're not implying we... remove unworthy heirs?"

Sozen stayed silent, those big, black eyes unblinking, his lips unmoving.

Gods. It has happened before. The realization sat in his stomach like a stone, pulling him even lower on the bench.

"Do all the Guard know this?" The speed and tone of his question betrayed his newfound anxiety.

"Eventually." Sozen was no less placid than he had been moments before. He sensed this young knight's increasing discomfort. "Neither boy, Talor nor Vernus, are in any real danger. Not yet."

"Unless Ser Darwyn decides the Crown Prince is unworthy." Drake fixed his gaze on Sozen, gauging his reaction. Tymm had been sequestered to a locked chamber for his own good following the incident in the tourney.

"No. That's not how it works." Sozen's voice was firm, fatherly and warm, "Ser Darwyn does not get to decide. Nor you or I. The six vote. If there is no consensus, a member of the Line makes the final decision."

"...Oh."

"We are not black or white; we are no mere servants to the liege, we serve the line. The Empire's health depends on the Line, son." Sozen placed a steady hand on Canar's shoulder. "We are not farmers, we do not reap. We are gardeners. We trim the malformed and diseased buds before they can bring ill health or diseased fruit.'

The world was spinning, Drake's breath came in ragged rips. *I am sworn to this darkness. Sworn and bound until my dying day.* His gloved hands gripped each other, searching for the sense that left the world today and finding only fingers. "Men call you the greatest knight alive. 'The Iron Pearl' is such a stranger to fear that he does not even need to carry a blade." Drake lifted a hand, waving at the stave and its tips of the Elder Iron. "How do you live with the burden?"

Sozen pulled the stave and extended it, offering it to Canar. It was about six feet of some ancient hardwood that grew among the hardscrabble rocks and pools of Black Pearl Bay. Lighter than it ought to have been, every inch of the wood had been inscribed with scrawling runes of an origin unfamiliar to Drake's eye. The ends were tipped in the ancient iron of the Wylde and the northern climes of the Greatwood, Elder Iron. Its secrets were as guarded as those of Clan Canar and The Smoke. As such, Drake respected the stuff, even if he did not understand it.

"I don't, Drake. I avoid the burden in my way, I am only a man." His hand went to the boy's shoulder, and the old knight squatted down to view Canar face-to-face. "I do not carry a blade, because if I did, I would use it."

"What do you mean?"

"Tonight, when Saddler swung on you, I stopped his sword and no one bled." Sozen's star-gaze was fixed on Canar.

"No one but Birse." Canar cracked.

"Fuck Birse." Sozen smirked, but continued, "My point is, if I had a blade in my sheath, I would have used it. I would have taken Saddler's hand or more like, his head."

"You'd have been right to." Drake didn't follow, "He was going to attack the prince."

"If he kills his way through a Hellheart and two Grey Guard, he should be the one protecting the Prince, not me." Sozen's tone was grim, "As good as Saddler is, there was no way he was killing his way through the two of us, let alone the dozen other knights in the room. But all the same, I would have killed him."

"Ser, I would much prefer if you stopped talking in riddles." Canar was reaching his limit with Sozen's opaque metaphors, "Tell it plain."

"You have a sword and a dagger on your belt, and you stopped Hartwin Saddler with your hands. No man alive would blame you for striking him down with steel, you bid him halt and he did not." Sozen's tone held a weariness that had not been there moments past, "Who is the better knight, the man who doesn't trust himself with a blade, or the man who knows when to draw it?"

Drake's mouth went to ash, "I-" He pressed the staff back into Sozen's hand. "I am just trying to do right, Ser." He stood, stumbling forward. "If our duties are complete, I think I need some air, Ser."

Sozen's grip turned to iron on Canar's shoulder, halting his motion. "We all saw you best the woman in the first round, Drake."

Drake's stomach somehow turned even sour. With a judicious use of The Smoke, Drake had shrouded the field. With skill and stealth, he had managed to get himself behind her. And with a sweep of Lady Prym Haymaker's leg and a pressed dagger, he had earned her forfeit. It was the most elegant solution to the trap he had been laid in by Vernus that the rookie Grey Guard could devise, and it had landed him in deeper, darker waters.

"You face Prince Talor on the morrow, Drake." Forcefully, he turned the boy's shoulders toward him. "The second round."

Drake could not meet his gaze.

"Look at me!" Desperation had begun to cloud the edges of Sozen's voice, "I know Tymm is our brother, but the Prince is our charge. Talor Artus is a good man, son."

Canar finally broke Sozen's grip and dashed into the black darkness beyond the castle lights, though the older Guard still called after him. His heart pounded against his ribs, more ragged rips of breath tearing at his lungs. He forced each stride, loping anxiously toward a tree line near the edge of the yard. An owl's high, hateful shriek broke the metronome of Ser Drake's breath. He pressed himself against a black-barked tree as the cool fogs began their nightly surge from the bay, a welcome relief from the day's blazing heat.

I do not want glory. I do not wish to be the greatest knight, not even a great one. I just want to know which liege to protect, when to raise my shield. I just want to do my duty. I do not want to be the greatest knight, Lord Lumen, I just want to be a good man.

He could not say how long he rested there, but the fogs were still thick when he waded through them, moving toward the borrowed barrack where the Grey Guard were quartered. He rounded the corner, and he instantly knew he was no longer alone.

Hollow as the wind, the voice echoed, "Ducky… I heard that you and I need to have a conversation about the tourney and about *gardenin"*

There was no way of knowing how, but it mattered little. Ser Darywn Tymm was out of his locked chambers, and he had some radical ideas about all the fruit in the orchard. Gaunt of face, and pale Tymm shuffled forward, like a wounded animal, his left hand extended in an unsettling talon. His eyes were wild, and his hair a mess, "Seems that you have an opportunity to *prune."*

<u>SLADE II</u>

"Death is just another part of life, kid. There are worlds way beyond what we can even begin to imagine, even you."

The unusually cute girl with the round head and strong jaw had been watching Slade at work for most of the morning, though she thought he hadn't noticed yet. The library at Honeyhome was vast, certainly larger than what he'd become accustomed to at The Moss Mont. The library took the first three floors of one of the larger towers in the castle. A honeycomb of winding shelves and low desks, the stacks here were among the most extensive in the Empire. Only the Didactic College and the Crownkeep herself held more books, and that may have only been by reputation.

He had demanded entry at daylight. The sleepy-eyed old Learner that maintained the tomes was skeptical of his purposes, but eventually acquiesced, once Slade had shown he was aware of what he needed and what libraries were for. Adults frequently underestimated Slade, which he found incredibly frustrating. He spent the first hours reading on bees, wax, honey, flowers, nightshade, which were all subjects that the great library had in multitudes. He settled on a chair of yellow and brown, with cushions worn thin by thousands of research-driven backsides.

Lost in the dusty, sunny, wonderful scent of those ancient pages, Slade found a sense of tranquility, but little that could explain his recent... experience. He nervously fingered the great ball of beeswax in his pocket. He trembled slightly, recalling the dim twilight with its piercing beacons, swirling fog and horrible creatures. Slade had not been able to cast his gaze upward and look at Hivehall's great dome all morning.

Rattled beyond logic, Slade had wanted to speak to his Lord Brother, Marten about such matters, but after they had gotten back late, drunk and Marten with a broken hand, Uncle Tullus had forbidden them speak alone until he decided otherwise. This threatened to throw the Young Lord's Council into chaos for Slade; Marten was his only way in, and now he was forced to avoid his older brother. He dealt with the anxiety the way he knew how, he worked.

Once he had made himself relatively certain that the tomes on apiculture and floriculture were of little value to him, he was forced to attack his problem from a different angle. The naked woman creature had been *named*. Though Slade had been fairly drunk and extremely terrified, he had replayed the memory a half a hundred times in his head and had come back clutching the same name each time: *Tellaoma.*

He spent the next few hours looking through books or poetry and history and the far-flung cultures of Ajaua and Asorra. There was even a scroll of black vellum from Almythria, the land of the Beast-men, but it was locked away. No amount of protest, rage and attempted bribery would budge tired old Learner Halidon on the matter.

He had scribbled "Tellaoma" half a hundred times in half a hundred ways on his parchment. He had underlined it, exed it out, circled it, and even worn his coal to a nub rubbing it out to a black as dark as his mood. He was pouting as he thumbed through a book of old poems from before Ozwyk had fallen, when the girl with the round head and strong jaw appeared behind him.

"Is Tellaoma your betrothed or something?" She had a thick Wyldeman accent, harsh on her consonants.

Slade sighed, he took stock of this girl. She was pale, with a rope of braided blue Elder Iron rings around her waist. She was roughly his age, fifteen or so, and held herself with a sort of nervous energy.

The colors: indigo, cream and silver were actually remarkably flattering on her skin tone. She had blossomed, her shape more than a girl, but less than a woman. Her hair was a flat brown-grey. She kept her bangs in her face, a single stripe of white confirming her identity as much as the great black hound sigil stitched to the shawl over her shoulders.

Little Lady Bulldog.

Though, upon seeing her, he didn't see the resemblance. She was... *cute.*

Slade was rarely a person who enjoyed interactions with strangers, late night's issue at the party had been more than enough proof of that. But, here, one on one, in the library, he could do this. He could be *charming.*

"No, it's research." He was trying to cut her off from his work, without cutting her off entirely. "You're Masha Curr." He blurted. Slade was quickly recalling that he was devoid of charm on some base level and wanted to collapse into the thin yellow and brown cushion beneath him.

"I am." She gave the most miniscule of curtseys, a polite gesture, practiced but hollow, "And unless I'm mistaken, and I am soundly sure that I am not, you are Slade Mirebreaker." She gave a little smirk, though her eyes were mostly hidden behind a veil of hair.

He gave a wave of his crippled hand, more dismissive than he truly meant to be, "Well yes, but I stand out." He nudged a chair away from the table with a skinny foot and nodded toward it, "You can sit, if you'd like, I suppose."

"I'd like." And she sat.

She tugged at one of the books, and though he sighed, she eventually extracted the tome from the pile. It was one of the books on the Empires of Asorra, an incredibly ancient binding of legends and tales of wars and peace between dragons and men. She flipped through it, wide eyes lingering on a few of the more detailed drawings of battles and dragons. Masha made an impressed little noise under her breath, before turning her attention back to Slade, "What are you researching?"

He couldn't tell her about the monsters in the yard, he'd sound crazy, or worse, *childish.* But if he didn't say anything, she'd know Slade was somewhat strange and unusual, and that was simply an unacceptable situation. *Gods. I should not have even come to this stupid... tournament.*

Of course. He could simply change the subject.

"I could tell you, but it's pretty secret stuff, a personal project of the utmost importance." He paused, letting the silence hang pregnant, "But, if you told me why you're not outside watching the tournament, I suppose I could share some things..."

"It's hot. I got hot." She smirked, just a touch of wickedness crowning the corner of her mouth, "Who's Tellaoma?"

Crud.

"That's what I'm trying to determine." He blurted, before wishing he hadn't. It was only a lie by omission, but he assumed the young lady would think his description of a "buzzing naked angel woman" that "lived in the shadows and twilight" madness. She twisted her head quizzically, but decided that answer was close enough, and nodded. "Shouldn't you be watching your brother's sworn swords?"

Her face twisted to sour, a clear distaste in her manner, "I don't care for tournaments, really." She was oddly tense. Her easy confidence had shifted to rigid tension. She leaned over Slade's notes and his disparate book selection, "Okay, my lord, it's time to pay your debt, what in the world are you working on?"

Slade took a sharp inhale of breath. He *had promised.* "Fair enough, but it stays between you and I." He unfolded the parchment with all of the information he'd collected, scant as it was, and the rough sketches he'd made of Tellaoma, the thing-man-bird, and the High Dome of Hivehall. He then reached into his right pocket, and gripped the ball of wax with his three remaining fingers. He gripped it, anxiously, but he did not produce it. He would gauge her reactions.

"I know how completely broke-brained this sounds, but I need you to trust me, Lady Masha." He sat up straight, and without judgment, she smoothed the parchment with her hands, checking over the crude charcoal scratchings.

"...If you are trying to understand the birds and the bees, perhaps, you have a trusted adult you can speak with. I'm sure the Snapping Turtle–" She was being playful, but after the incident last night, Slade was taking no chances.

"It's not about... *intercourse,* okay?" Slade's words were peevish, but his tone held less anger than caution. "I did not see you at the gathering in the Great Gate Garden last evening, correct?"

"This counts as your next question." She hooked some of her long bangs on her left ear, exposing her forehead and her left eye– a perfect deep, cold, blue rimmed by long, dark lashes.

"It absolutely does not!" Again, his voice was higher and more petulant than he would have liked. He settled himself, trying to smooth out his voice, "Allow me to rephrase, 'I did not see you at the party last night.'"

"Correct." She confirmed.

"Good, then I can leave out the details that don't matter." He chuckled to himself, but then facing the prospect of giving her the actual events, he tensed his body. "Well, when I left the party, I experienced something, and I do not think it was just an effect of drink. I saw what I believe is a portion of the Unseelie Hells."

She did not laugh outright, so, small victories are appreciated, and Slade continued, "I saw two creatures in some… strange twisted mirror of the yard, one of which was referred to by the other as 'Tellaoma.'"

Masha was still silent, but she was studying his face, scrutinizing every word he said and the manner in which he spoke it.

"And I thought I was drunk or dreaming, until I found *this*." He plucked the lemon-sized hunk of beeswax from his pocket and placed it on the table between them, "In the Hells, the walls of the castle were different, they were made of this waxy substance, and I managed to collect a sample for proof."

Masha prodded the ball curiously with an extended finger. The flippant look that crossed her face showed neither fear or disgust. She picked it up in her delicate little hands and rolled it around, "Beeswax…"

Slade smirked, "And though it's none of yours, that's what I'm working on." Feeling clever, Slade managed a wink. The slightest pink crossed her cheeks, so Slade went in for the kill, "I shared my secrets. Why are you *really* avoiding the tourney?"

"No, my lord, that is none of your concern." She bowed her head.

"That's not fair!" His voice had gone full petulant, the warmth of red embarrassment spread through his cheeks.

Masha gently placed the ball of wax in the center of the table and gave him a sad smile, "I know. I don't really care, Slade."

Slade Mirebreaker was not one to leave well enough alone at the best of times, and here he was on a back foot and unwilling to give an inch, he pounced, "It's your brother's sworn swords, isn't it?"

The deep blue eyes of Lady Masha Curr betrayed the slightest glimmer of fear, but they soon showed only a bored annoyance, "Fine, but this counts as your next five questions."

Five?!?

Slade exhaled, "Fine, but if I don't think your information is worth it, you have to help me with my research."

"I had planned on offering anyway, you seem hopeless, but sure." She folded her hands over one another. Slade straightened his papers in front of him, eye contact made him uncomfortable.

She sighed, "My cousin is carrying on a tryst with Ser Hale and they think no one has noticed and it is becoming increasingly difficult to pretend I don't see her cuckolding my brother."

Memories of similar lies from his uncle in his youth flooded back to him, and Slade simply nodded. "I am truly sorry. Sex makes people idiots."

She snorted an adorable laugh, "I think they're in love, that's worse. They are even more foolish in love.

She brushed the rest of her bangs from her face and Slade finally saw Masha's full face at once, and all at once, he understood why men did foolish things for women. The red warmth in his cheeks began to redden like a swamp sunset, burning like fever. His mouth went dry, and he lost his words. "Y-y-yes. Well." He shook the cobwebs from his head, attempting a return to reason, "I don't know if court gossip is worth *five* quest–"

The next thing he knew, she was kissing him. Slade was sixteen, bookish, a little bad tempered and *odd,* but all the same, he had the same wants and desires as any boy his age. Even if he was much more measured and controlled than most. Though he was, technically, the Heir to the Lowlands, he had not been betrothed or even spent that much time courting girls. It's not that he was disinterested; just that other people were a puzzle Slade Mirebreaker had not quite mastered yet, women doubly so.

That is to say, this was Slade's first kiss.

When their lips broke, he tingled from chin to cheek to forehead. His heart pounded in his chest, "What was that for?"

"If my gossip isn't worth five, I hoped *that* might be worth something." She smirked, "I don't usually kiss boys I just met. I promise. You are just uniquely infuriating and I had to find a way to get you to stop talking."

"I had heard that you were *shy." S*lade smiled, most times it felt like he'd forgotten how, but in this moment, he remembered.

"I am not shy, I just only choose to talk to people that I know are engaged, my breath is far too precious to be wasted. You only get so much breath, why use any of it on folk too dim or distracted to appreciate it. Most people don't listen, why should I talk?"

Are all the girls in the north so wild? For the second time in as many days, Slade's head had been left spinning.

The sounds of padded footsteps approaching pulled the two apart to opposite sides of the table. Learner Halidon shuffled up, his bisected robes of black and white breezing behind, along with strands of his swept-back silver hair, "My lady!" His voice was nearly as withered as the rest of him, he leaned on a long, twisted wooden staff, wheezing as he approached, "The Lady Executor has been looking for you!"

Ellari Curr rounded the corner, almost on cue. The older girl gave cousin Masha a wide smile, then turned her attention to Slade. Ellari looked him over, noting his sigil and age. Calculations crossed her mind rapidly, and she plucked his identity from the air. "Lord Mirebreaker, a pleasure."

Slade frowned, "My brother is the lord, but you knew that, Lady Curr."

Masha turned, bangs back in place, those perfect blue eyes hidden once more. "Lady Ellari, what do I owe the courtesy?"

Ellari searched the table before answering, eyes lingering on the beeswax and the scribbled madness at Slade's eight fingertips. "We're on to the final quarter soon, my lord husband wanted to make sure you were in attendance for his match with Ser Reuben."

The final quarter?!

Slade vaulted to his feet, "Apologies, the final quarter? What time is it?"

Ellari looked at him, curiosity in her pale eyes. "Last Labors."

No. No. Nononononononononononono.

It was late afternoon, verging on dinner. Slade had intended to leave the bookvaults sometime shortly before mid-morning. His plan had been to make his way to the tourney grounds, hopefully watch Marten trounce Lord Osprey, and then have some lunch, before making his way back here, further research of course. Slade had envisioned leaving once more about this time, to make his way for his aunt and uncle's matches.

It seemed he had lost track of time among the books. Again.

"Apologies. Ladies, I need to be off, I missed–" He rose and began gathering up sheets of parchments and stacks of books..

"Your brother lost hours ago, Slade. I'm sorry, I thought you knew." Masha's face was tinged with regret. "I am so sorry. His hand—"

"He broke it last night, yes." Slade's tone had become as flat as his mood. "He broke it on Ser Rolof Deepreach's face on my account."

Ellari was the first to comfort him, 'Deepreach is an ass. Someone was bound to break a hand on his face eventually." She gave a kind, sad smile, "Though I am sorry it was your brother. He seems very chivalrous."

As Slade watched Ellari, she was not the succubus he had pictured when Masha told her tale. Ellari had a kind, sad smile, because she was kind and sad. She was no evil-looking spider-woman.

Slade snatched up his ball of beeswax with his good hand before tossing it to his mangled one. "He is most certainly that." He turned his gaze back to Lady Masha, "A few extra minutes in the face of the hours I am already late will be nothing. If you're heading back to the grounds, might I accompany you two ladies?" She bit her bottom lip, and he felt a little lightheaded, "If I'm not imposing."

Masha's own cheeks picked up a blush of red, as Ellari sighed deeply, "You absolutely are, but I am not like to get her to come without you." She chittered, annoyed. Before spitting the next phrase like a curse, "Children, Gods be good."

The walk to the tourney grounds was mostly pleasant, though Ellari pulled them out of the way of an approaching palanquin more roughly than she needed to at one point, and after that, had insisted they use only narrow footpaths with less traffic. With her cousin there, Masha and Slade would have no opportunity for discussion, let alone a second kiss. But, for one moment, when Ellari ducked around a corner, Masha grabbed his hand in hers and held it. Only for a moment, but she reached her perfect pink fingers around his mangled hand, and she did not recoil.

Even Uncle Tullus' later rage couldn't quell his high mood after that. And his Uncle Snapping Turtle had been furious. Slade had missed Marten's match and most of the first round of the tourney. For his part, Marten did not seem to mind, especially when he had noticed that Slade had been parting ways with a *girl* when he had arrived. Masha had held his hand, both of them, in parting, promising to meet him in the library tomorrow at dawn. Slade had completely given up on charm. He had thanked her and he had dully nodded, and wandered back to his family, barely able to remember why he was worried in the first matter, anyway.

"Where the hell have you been?" Uncle Tullus had a way of bringing a person back to reality. "Gar has been out looking for you since lunch!"

Slade felt a twinge of guilt at wasting Gar's time, "I am truly sorry, I was doing some research in the castle's bookvault and I lost track of time... ...as I can be wont to do." Slade gave a weak, nervous grin to his Uncle.

"With that one? She was in the book vault?" He bobbed his head at Masha, as Lady Carmine, his wife, helped attach the straps to his breastplate.

"Lady Masha, yes, ser." Slade affirmed, trying to remain respectful.

Ser Tullus frowned, "Cryin' sakes, Slade, I thought you were wiser than that. Girls are trouble, you're too young for such–"

From her husband's waist, Lady Carmine cinched a belt extra tight, cutting off Ser Tullus, "He's sixteen." She rose, as her knightly husband sputtered, "I don't see any harm in *talking* to girls. Hell, he might even be able to *hold a hand* or, gods forbid, *steal a kiss*."

She finally loosened the belt crushing her husband with a chuckle, "Slade is a good boy, he'll stay out of trouble. And besides, that Curr girl is okay. We met her, remember? She's *shy.*"

Slade kept his laughter to himself, even as Masha's words echoed to him, "I am not *shy*..."

The rest of the afternoon had been a blur, Uncle Tullus and Lady Carmine each easily won their first round matches, which set them against one another in the second. Long years ago, before they had been wed, both the Snapping Turtle and The Bloody Lily were among the most celebrated tourney knights of their era. Circumstances had prevented them ever from crossing blades, one would be ill and miss one tourney. One would be called away for duty and miss the next, and so on. But, they had grown to know one another, traveling in the same circles, keeping the same company, and eventually love would blossom between the pair.

Both Lady Carmine and Ser Tullus were proud, though, and though they never would reveal the result, the pair had a single sparring match. Lady Carmine had made it the single condition of her acceptance of his betrothal. The result had never been revealed to anyone save Slade and Marten's Late Lord Father, who served as the contest's sole judge and witness. He had taken the secret to his grave and Lady Carmine and Ser Tullus were no more likely to share it.

Slade had hounded their daughter, Lady Jasmine about the result, before she left to marry some years ago, but even she claimed ignorance. It then occurred to Slade that his cousin, having spent the last few years in the Wylde, would know Lady Masha well. Slade nodded to himself, resolving to speak with his cousin about Masha Curr.

Once the tourney had been dismissed and dinner devoured, Slade had finally managed to corner Marten. Slade had padded into Marten's chamber, silent and slow. His lord brother's chambers stank in the rank manner that only an eighteen-year-old boy could stink, and they had only been in Honeyhome a few days. Marten wasn't a particularly foul teenage boy, just an active one who preferred swims and rainstorms to baths. When he entered, Marten was seated near, at the desk. A significant little heap of gauze was piled beside him. There was a small dish of some poultice uncovered beside him, filling the air in the chamber with the stinging scent of herbs. It mingled with the scent of boy in a way that only made your eyes water if you breathed through your nose.

Marten had smeared some of the stinky grey lotion over his wounded hand, but the angry purple bruises had not even begun to go yellow yet. Each of his knuckles was a dimple in a swollen mess of flesh. His fingers seemed less terrible, thin brown spearshafts sticking from the wounded hand. There were scrapes on both hands, deep red gouges on both sets of knuckles, memories of his scrap with Deepreach. When Marten saw his little brother enter, it was all he could do to hide his self satisfaction. "Pretty damn nasty work, eh?"

Slade held up his own mangled hand, missing its third and fourth fingers, "Once these grow back, I will field your complaints." Marten laughed, and Slade shook his head, "Until then I will be thankful that my brother is so brave, and just a bit fearful that he is so bold."

"It was nothing. You'd have done the same for me." Marten gave Slade the same big blue knowing eyes that he always used when he was right. "So, Little Lady Bulldo—"

"Do *not* call her that. That is ridiculous. She is no common…"

Marten couldn't help himself, "Cur?"

"Fuck you." Slade smacked his older brother on the back, hard, which only slowed his laughter slightly.

Marten raised his left arm in mock defense, still laughing, "I yield, I yield. Do not be so vicious. Uncle Tullus will stick a boot between your buttcheeks if he finds you in here. He's still furious we snuck out last night."

Slade nodded dismissively, "Yes, yes, he's very angry about last night. How are we sneaking out tonight?"

"When did The Wildcat take you over?" Marten started wrapping the gauze around his wounded hand, winding white on purple. The lines of bandage were crooked and loose, hanging and bunched in odd places.

Slade snatched the bandages from his brother, perhaps a little careless. "You need to wrap the hand firmly, or it will heal crooked and crippled." He was suddenly extremely aware of his missing fingers. Deftly, Slade tightened the bandages firm and Marten grunted.

"Ow."

Slade smirked, "I thought you were supposed to be tough."

Marten flexed his hand in the bandage, "This is good work. …You ever think about becoming a Learner?"

Slade shook his head, "I'd never deprive the world of my brilliant political schemes… Speaking of… How are we getting out of the castle tonight?"

Marten grinned, "Leave it to me."

As it would turn out, "Leave it to me" meant "I will snatch you from your room in the dark of night, and lead you out very quietly", which in truth, is not much of a plan. But as Ser Tullus is no great jailer, it served just fine. The boys would be among the first to slip into the Great Gate Garden undetected. They were not the first, however. Marten rankled when he saw a tall, chestnut-haired figure. Once he saw the fine green silks under the other figure's dark cloak, Slade understood why.

The Goldengrass and the Lowlands were more often at odds than not, but Hartwin Saddler and Marten could not be more diametrically opposed if they had tried. Saddler was wont to insult Marten's intelligence, and Marten was usually left red-faced and ready to throw fists. Not exactly lordly behavior.

Hartwin had always been entirely courtly with Slade, though their interactions had been few. Slade comported himself fairly well among people who spoke to him like he was an adult. As near as Slade could tell, the heir to the Goldengrass refused to simplify his speech for anyone, it seemed. When the pair passed through the unlocked gates of honey-brown gold, Slade was reminded of the lump of beeswax stuffed in the bottom of his trunk and he shuddered. Hartwin noticed them and a sly grin slid over his long, equine face.

"Mirebreaker! You brought someone who might actually understand tonight's proceedings!" His smile turned to Slade, "I am genuinely pleased to see you here, tonight, m'lord."

If there was an insult there, Slade could not decode it, so Slade nodded curtly. "Thank you, my lord. Though, if I may be frank–"

Marten stifled him, with a light jostle. "Saddler. You look well."

Saddler extended his right hand to shake Marten's, and then loudly feigned apology when he saw the shattered hand, switching to his left and firmly grasping Marten's uninjured hand. "Apologies! I heard about your incident with Deepreach! Someone had to do it, the man is a brute!" His smirk went predatory as he fixed his gaze on Marten, "And my cousin, Ser Doyle, got him back in kind, shattered the Bronze Kraken's right hand like it was seaglass. Even a plains-shark feasts on octopus apparently."

Hartwin's lilting tone was braggadocious, to be sure, but not unkind.

Marten nodded, "Your man, Osprey, he fought well. Beat me, at least." He gave a solid chuckle, "You're likely safe in Talon Bay."

Saddler gave a gracious toss of the arm, turned toward the interior of the garden. "We three are the first to arrive…" Four brass braziers had been lit, their flames of orange, red and gold dancing in the twilight. They cast long, deep craterous shadows over the faces of the three young men. Behind them, twins in funeral black danced on fruit trees. A dozen fine carved stools, golden wood and purple pads had been circled around the braziers, "But being that it's my grandfather's castle, I have made absolutely sure that we will meet with Prince Talor in the dearest comfort."

Slade watched this practiced politician settle onto a silk padded stool, and had to remind himself not to like him.

Saddler patted the stool next to his own, motioning for Slade to sit, "Lady Joelle Bridge tells me that you're a remarkable young man, Slade. Why don't you show me while we wait?"

He smiled without warmth, but Slade sat anyway.

ILLYSTRE II

"A pair of pretty eyes and womanly hips'll kill you faster than an arrow. Hurts more, too."

Illystre stood over the body that had been Lord Purvon Webb this morning. The tall faceless elves of the continent had left him alone with the boy, respect for The Lord of Espionage. The Priests of Eresh had done what they could for the boy, washing the gouts of blood from his now marble-white flesh. A thin, nearly invisible thread had been used to mend the great valley that had rendered the ribs and flesh and chest asunder. Illystre leaned extra low, his nose inches from the chest. His practiced gaze traced the closing lines of grey so thin it bordered on unseen. Illystre traced the stitched line down the dead boy's chest.

"Spider silk." Illystre was a spymaster, detection and perception were second nature to him, but all the same, he had not heard the tall elven priestess behind him. She strode in robes of starlight, her features behind the blank metal mask that all the devotees of Eresh wore. Though her face was covered, her voice was clear and unobstructed.

Illystre hid his surprise as best he could, standing tall, away from the boy's corpse. "That's kind of you, or is that standard procedure for a death god?"

The woman rankled behind her mask, her tone taking on a tinge of ice, "Eresh watches over souls making their crossing, through the veil of this life to whatever comes next. He is no death god, only a shepard." She lightly touched a thin pendant, pale wood bent into the shape of a crook, and tied around her neck with an undyed hempen cord. "But, the silk was provided by Lord Webb's younger brother, the new Lord Webb."

Illystre nodded, "I see." The new Lord Miles was a younger half-brother and not a season past fourteen years. House Webb had been a high house of great wealth and power in Ozwyk, but since the submission, they had suffered tragedy after tragedy. Lord Miles was the last trickle of an ancient, proud and dying bloodline. Illystre could relate. "Is the boy dealing with the loss well?"

"No, the orphaned child who watched his brother die in front of him is not dealing with the loss well, My lord." The tone was as close to acerbic as the masked priestess could allow herself. "Was there more you required?"

Illystre rose, meeting the place where her gaze should have been, but found the blank metal unsettling. "The other body, where is Lord Tymm?"

"The Royal family has taken custody of what remained." The priestess relayed the queer information without passion.

Illystre Coldhearth clicked his teeth, "I suppose that would be all, then." He opened his purse and pressed two silver coins against her palm. The strange priestess bowed her head, locks of platinum falling. She never noticed the lock of Webb's brown hair that Illystre had pocketed.

Upon leaving the temple of Eresh, Illystre slid into the throngs on Honeyhome's High Holy Lane. The evenings revels were in full swing, bawdy songs rang from the walls of the alley back to the high dome and here again.

"*--blood rained down, it surged o'er his lance. Brave the knight leapt, his maiden crept inside the bandit's manse!*"

The Ryme of the Raider Maiden filled his very pores, along with the haze of the street and smells of sweat, mead and meat. He sunk into his grey cloak, grey eyes flashing under grey shocks of hair. The swell of the commons for the tourney had overflown the taverns and inns and surged into the street, a river of revels. Despite himself, Illystre fought a smile when a pretty maid with red hair and a mostly-open bodice spun through his path. Wine of berry and fuschia splashed from her chalice, sprinkling her bare feet and the cobblestones below. She lazily dragged a finger over his collarbone, smirking, but Illystre slowed for not a moment. He pressed through the throngs of mankind, trained ears of a spy picking through the swirling eddies of sound for pearls of information that he might actually want.

"--price'a barley is makin' it too costly to brew…" came ringing from one of the open tavern doorways. *Shameful, but useless,* Illystre mused.

"--told her that if she didn't send that damn shit-dragon to the road, I'd send her–"

"--still aches when it rains, right where my thigh joins my–"

More complaints and tripe, but no treasons, no thievery. Hnh. Illystre clicked his teeth.

"--she opened up the Webb boy with her witchcraft and her halberd, and she bathed in the boy's blood. It's how them witchwomen stay so young looking. Bathin' in the blood of the young." Illystre paused long enough for the drunken peasant woman to finish launching her opinion all over the sidewalk, along with mead-colored spittle. He ultimately decided against correcting the numerous errors in the alcohol-soaked woman's statement, but did chuckle, recalling that Vellen and Webb were born in the same season, of the same year.

As he turned north toward the dock ward, the street went from ancient, cracked and eroded cobbles (supplied by the old temples, schools and libraries in the district,) to merchant-purchased, freshly hewn and lain greystone. *The spoils of trade versus tradition, I suppose.* The parties only grew louder, the street even tighter, but Coldhearth had a destination within sight, *Rolen's Flushed Filly.* The sturdy little brick alehouse sat just on the edge of the docks, the first building built on land, not stilts, as you approached from the Bay of Bees. The roof was a patchwork of a wrecked dwarven cog from far Tolstagg, and the various chunks of crates, pallets, lumber and carts that went into maintaining and repairing it. The bricks of the alehouse had been mined from the red rock not a daegrid south on the shore. Those sturdy stones were some of the oldest man-made objects on the island. It had once been the corner of a fort, long gone. Then, the remaining bricks had been scooped up and restacked by opportunist and frugal worshippers of Suiden, the sea god. The foundations they had dug remained, though the walls and structures had changed hundreds of times over thousands of years, all built with the same pile of red bricks.

The building had been a courthouse, a jailhouse, a customs office, a shipwright's studio and served half a hundred other purposes, but for the last two hundred years or so, it had been an alehouse of grand renown and ill repute, all in one; exactly Lord Illystre Coldhearth's favorite sort of place. He stepped through the doors, salvaged from the galley of a pirate prince from the icy north. He drew pale fingers over the red-brick of the wall and felt old magic thrum in his bones. *A good place, a safe place.*

He gave a sly nod to the familiar barkeep, and after a silent moment in the corner, the Lord of Spies had been handed a glass of some corn liquor and led to a strangely empty table in this crowded tavern. *Networks are not just for information gathering.* The thought amused him, but the burning clear drink in his hand did not. He placed it before him on the table, but it still stung his eyes like cleaning alcohol. With a sigh, he subtly dumped it to the straw and sawdust at his feet, where it would mingle with various other fluids. Illystre hoped most of them were liquor. When the strange and sad half-elf waitress passed by, Illystre slipped her a silver and sent her for a horn of mead.

She would return, pale like reflected moonlight, hair the black of water mirroring the midnight sky. As she provided the mead, Illystre locked eyes on his quarry. Two Malbes guardsmen pushed through the doorway, the first, leggy, lanky and weedy, the other with a big ugly pustule on the side of his nose. You would need know that these were Malbes men to identify them, granted, Illystre made it his business to know. They wore no uniforms, only wool, leather and simple cloaks. The pair was already swaying as they settled onto stools at the bar.

Illystre's focus on Weed and Pustule left him blind to the approach of a tiny man from below– a tiny man who had been trailing Illystre since the temple. As a small hand touched his knee, Illystre leapt in his chair. He found a man staring up at him, no taller than a barely-weaned child. Paper-white skin with hair darker than coal framed eyes of frozen smoke. Black, white and grey, Totho. Totho was one of the small-folk, a halfling.

Most of the halflings were genial little folk, who lived in the hills farming or in the cities running inns and taverns. Little folks about the size of a six-year old, even when full-grown. This one, however, was odd. He was a pale, plump little man, who powdered his face and kept his black hair oiled and slicked back from his moon-face. Always immaculately dressed and perfumed, the little man was some sort of mage. He served Illystre's sister, the High Lady of the Greatwood. Lady Isolde Ironarm was married to Lord Torvald, who ruled the Metal Mount. The little man had been tasked with gathering some of the more esoteric items that Illystre's late-night activities would require.

"M'lord, might I join you for a drink?" His voice was far deeper and more sonorous than one would assume from such a small framed man. His wide, frog-like mouth parted, "I am utterly parched."

Trying to maintain his focus on the two guards, Illystre simply waved a hand, "Go ahead, but I beg for a moment's silence." The two guardsmen were still chatting openly, and the ale had loosened their tongues to the point that caution was lax and volume was wild. The Lord of Spies was only truly interested in Pustule. The ugly guard had a sick mother, and that likely ugly, but certainly ill woman could benefit from a nice little cottage on the shore with some sea breeze.

For the paltry price of some information about the transportation of a Starheart crown across the yard tomorrow night, Illystre would be willing to give that old woman a mansion on the cliffs. Both men were clearly drunk, but Illystre needed to get Pustule alone. Weed beside him quaffed from a horn of mead, and swung unsteadily.

"Lottie is just unapproachable, I do not understand the workings of the female persuasion." Weed was bemoaning as a thin trickle of yellow mead dribbled from the corner of his mouth.

"Gerron, you lack imagination." Pustule slapped his friend on the back. Pustule's real name was Bertrand. Illystre had taken the time to learn everything he could about his quarry, as was his process. It was also his process to avoid thinking of the person he was hunting as a person. This was not Bertrand, the son of the castle's kennelmaster, a guard of three years, and betrothed to Farrah, who churned butter in the yard. No, Illystre had to make this man Pustule. Pustule had information that Illystre required. Illystre can squeeze a pustule until it pops. It was simply something he could not do to a man.

Beside Illystre, Totho had managed to flag down the pretty half-elf waitress and procure some sort of greyish liquor. It was silvery and cloudy and swirled in the glass, even when Totho set the fine crystal on the pitted table. "M'lord, the changeling ichor was extremel–"

"A moment of silence, Totho." Coldhearth repeated, whispering through gritted teeth.

Pustule took a draw of his own mead before shouting to the barkeep for some bread and cheese. After a moment, the barkeep produced a crusty loaf and hunk of a fragrant yellow cheese with veins of wine running through it. Once the bread and cheese had settled onto the bar, Illystre knew time was on his side. Though he kept a watch on the two off-duty guards, he allowed Totho some of his attention. He loosened, "Sorry, proceed, my friend." He gave an easy smile as he let the hunter off his haunches, just a little.

"As I was saying, m'lord." He croaked, "the changeling ichor was markedly more difficult to acquire than is custom."

Illystre only gave a wide-eyed stare in response, which left Totho flustered.

"And markedly more *expensive.*" He frowned, his thin pale lips pressing together hard, "My lord."

"I was under the impression that Lady Isolde paid you a very generous salary." Illystre generally liked this little man, but he could never allow himself to forget Totho's origins on the streets of Deepsteel, a thief, charlatan, and conman.

"Quite generous, quite fair, but this was extravagance beyond mere generosity. I would end up destitute and starving if I made no effort to reclaim something of my gold." He patted his expansive little stomach. "Truly. Me. Starving. Unfathomable."

Illystre rolled his eyes, more than ready to end this transactional part of the conversation, "Fine." He scribbled some words on a wrinkled piece of brown parchment from one of his many pockets, "Find my squire, Homer, at my pavilion. Show him this paper." He slid the tan hunk toward Totho across the scarred, greying wood, "He'll pay you."

Totho examined the mark warily, unable to determine exactly what the spiky square rune said, "I'm… unable to read this, m'lord."

"You can't. It's not for you." Illystre gave his own grin, a slim grey panther cornering a particularly plump piglet. "Homer can. Homer will pay you." He extended a gloved hand, palm up, "The ingredients?"

Totho sighed, pouting just a little, "Yes, of course, my lord." He began fumbling through his own large brown bag, calfskin, supple and nearly as large as he was, though the weight never seemed to bother the little man. One by one, he produced strange little bundles and vials and tinctures, turning them over to the Lord of Spies. A hunk of crumbling yellow stone in a glass phial, "Brimstone, m'lord." A feather, only an inch long, but black as pitch and scattered with sparkling shards of starlight, Something wrapped in wax paper that clinked like glass. A bundle of dried leaves the color of old blood, wrapped in jute. A small jar of some grease that was nearly transparent, only the slightest pink hue suffused through it. And finally, the strange little man produced a vial of lightning. "Changeling ichor."

The vial was little larger than even Totho's little finger, and inside the substance shone like a flare and sparked against the glass, popping and hissing, but never reducing. Even these few drops would likely cost Illystre enough to fund a small army, but if he put them to work wisely, it would be an investment well-made. Illystre reached for it and Totho withdrew slightly.

"You're quite sure the boy will pay me?" Totho moaned again, no sign of his playful nature from earlier remaining.

"Yes, yes, if not you literally know where the child sleeps. Threats are free, just give me my." Illystre snatched the vial, *"prize!"* The Lord of Spies rolled it between his thumb and forefinger, watching the light inside violently dance and jolt.

Totho's pout grew into a full-on whine, "You are a truly terrible man, bullying an innocent little servant like me." He made his wide, wet grey eyes grow huge and amphibian, an attempt at charm, but Illystre found it more unsettling than anything.

"Your innocence is neighbor to my chastity, old friend." Illystre gave him a wicked smile, and watched as his target, a man with the pustule on his nose, rose from his stool at the bar, "And much like me, they both seem to have long since disappeared." With a quick flourish, the practiced spy dropped a trio of coins for his drink and Totho's.

The grey cloak became his mask, his shield, and his shroud once more, blending into the crowd on the floor. As bodies shuffled across the worn wooden floorboards, Illystre could have reached out and grabbed his quarry by the shoulder if he so desired, but the well-trained, perceptive guardsman had no idea. *Rabble.*

Pustule grunted up to his friend, "Gonna head down to the docks. I need a piss and cool breeze, it's stiflin' in here." Sweat was running in rivulets down the broad guard's forehead. A desired reaction, of course. Illystre had bribed good money to the barkeep to slip the feverwort extract into Pustule's mead. It would have him sweating and running to the chamber pot every half-hour until dawn or so, but leave no lasting harm.

Pustule stumbled through the salvaged doors of the tavern, slow and sweating. He and Illystre were but two of many bodies slipping through the threshold in either direction. He stuck close to an older merchant, fine robes and great mustache distracting from the young man in the shabby grey cloak beside him. After a few short, clunking strides, Pustule leaned hard on a tree. Illystre was afraid that the guard would relieve himself right then and there.

The stout little badger of a man shook himself loose and managed to continue down the path, eventually coming to the cool breezes and blue-black waters of The Bay of Bees. The dock that Pustule had chosen was an older, smaller one. Rickety wood and rope had been bleached bone-white by the sun, before being stained and re-stained cedar red a thousand and one times. Even now, when the marina was stuffed to bursting with boats of every shape, size and quality, this sad little dock only had a sad little fishing boat tied to it. On each side, great ships of great houses turned this shaky little dock into its own isolated alley. *The perfect place to empty your bladder and catch your breath.*

With a deep exhale and a hustling leap, Illystre hopped from shadow to shadow, eventually using gangplank, rope and rail to position himself high above Pustule on the dock below. He squatted high on this starboard rail, as Pustule fiddled drunkenly with the laces on his breeches, a dozen feet under the Lord of Spies' watchful eyes. Illystre waited for the sounds of streaming to cease, supplied a few further seconds, just so the guardsman could shake and stow his cock. Once Pustule turned his back to the sea, Illystre pulled his mask over his face and became The Hunter once more.

Illystre's mask left only his smoke and snow eyes visible. The thing was silvered and gold, fine filigree running through the veins of ancient grey wood. The mask was older than the Lord of Spies, his father, his father's father and all three combined. It had once been something more than wood and gold, made to resemble something or someone, but time had left it eroded and faceless. It had been passed through Clan Coldhearth since before the Old Owl Kings had fallen. Rumors connected it to witchcraft and blood sacrifice. Illystre's sister, Lady Isolde, was an expert in both subjects and could find no correlation, however. Magic or not, Illystre liked the old mask and it gave him a simple divide.

Mask off, he's the debauched and debased Lord Illystre. A useless little playboy propped up by a network of hyper-competent spies and operatives. A politician of high renown to be sure, but no warrior. A spoiled young lord who stood to inherit a powerful ancient keep and respected lordship.

Once the mask of ancient grey ash covered his face, all that faded away. He packed it up and became The Hunter. He was focus and flight and fire, once that mask was on. Nothing could touch him, he was smoke and shadow. He could slay giants and shrug off arrows. The Hunter feared nothing. It was the Hunter who leapt the dozen feet to the dock and seized Pustule in one fluid, rolling tackle. When they clattered to a stop on the old slats, the Hunter was on top.

Before his leap, a silken cord had been wrapped around the Hunter's left fist. A quick practiced snap and its cord was drawn tight in both hands, and pressed tight down on Pustule's throat. Behind the mask, Hunter's voice was a snarl. "You are guarding the crown tomorrow." It was not a question.

Pustule was not as finished pissing as either of them had hoped, but the Hunter ignored it. From under this grey phantom, the terrified guardsman writhed. His mind was too scattered to find words, but he nodded and babbled something close enough for affirmation.

"How many others? Where is it being held?" A slight release of the cord allowed the guard enough breath to speak. Each question was clear, precise and threatening.

Pustule wheezed, "Eight-eight men-at-arms, and two knights. G-grey guard."

Fuck.

The Hunter squeezed with the silks, part frustration at the news, part need for more information, "Where?"

"*'Sinthebaseofthetowervault"* he squat man struggled and rasped, so the Hunter relented lightly once more "Behind the high steel door, the black one." He sputtered, phlegm and sputum rimming his quivering lips. "I'm so sorry, I didn't do nuffin' I just wanted the extr–"

The Hunter choked him again, "Which Grey Guard?"

"*IdontknowIswearIdont.*" Pustule was beginning to unravel, his voice rising to a high squeal.

The Hunter replaced the cord with his left forearm, firm pressure constant on the guardsman's windpipe. With his right hand, he slipped a pouch from his belt, and clinked it onto the roughspun wool of the guard's jerkin. "There's more than enough coin in there to get your ailing mother out of the city, *Bertrand.* I suggest you take her to a safe little shoreside chalet. Join her. Live a quiet, happy, *safe and healthy* life. Make sure you bring your betrothed. *Farrah*, right?"

With a hearty shove, The Hunter flipped backward from the prone and terrified guardsman. Quick as whisper, light as a lie, The Hunter slid back amongst the shadows, and became Illystre again. The fog had begun to pool in the low spots as far in the distance, the assembled lords and ladies were gathering under the great pale dome of the High Hall, their revels rising even over the songs of the gathered commons.

His own slippers of grey slid smoke silent over the cobbles. The night was taking shape into something unpleasant. He ruffled the cloak around himself, sighing. Any member of the Grey Guard would be a serious issue to contend with. *As long as it's not Selach. A sniper could send this entire plan to shattering.*

He knew where to find something resembling answers, but dealing with his sister would mean decoding exactly what her visions meant, and time was far too short for such riddles.

HARTWIN III

"I know you think me a fool, Hart. I'm not blind. Believe you me, son, love is not weakness. Hell, boy, love makes men better."

The problem with secret, clandestine meetings, at least according to Hartwin Saddler, was the fact that you couldn't hire out the work to make you comfortable. Thankfully, Hugo and Doyle had been more than happy to assist Hartwin in preparing the area in Grandfather's garden. Hartwin wasn't especially fond of Lord Dobson Malbes, his maternal grandfather, but Hart wasn't fond of most people. Where Hartwin was often disgusted at his own Lord Father's overly generous nature with the smallfolk and his general soft-hearted nature, Lord Dobson was an entirely different matter. The swollen old lord of Honeyhome was known to never let a coin pass him by, unless it would lead to him farming two more. Malbes was always bedecked in the finest silks and satins, and an amount of gold that even Hartwin found garish. Of course, both of them shared a predisposition for overindulgence and had waistlines that reflected that. They were even opposite in their gluttony. Father would fill his halls with feasts and laughter and drink and song, and Grandfather Malbes was a pallid, bloated old man feasting on the finest and richest delicacies behind closed doors. The measured Hartwin was always mindful, with mother's *focused* aid, that he was a few corn cakes away from such a state, and made sure to carefully curate his diet. Mother was even more *focused* with Lady Harlow. Hugo ate what and when he wanted, he worked it off and then some, in the yard. Swords and shields took fuel to swing, he supposed.

The tall, thin Saddler lordling had been loath to leave Joelle behind, but love and duty frequently set themselves to odds, and

Hartwin most often chose duty. Lady Joelle Bridge usually chose her duty, as well, so the misgivings between the pair were slight, if any. When he slipped from her chambers shortly before Owl's Hour, she had only teased him, "Are you off chasing another maiden, my lord?"

The bed was warm and soft and so was she, but one is only granted certain opportunities to treat with the Crown Prince, so Hartwin dressed himself, and kept his smirk slight in the low light, "If you can find a maiden who does the things you do, she's no maiden."

She feigned offense, but then shot back, "If you can find a maiden that does the things I do, *I'll* marry her." She laughed, her full, sincere laugh, and even though Hartwin couldn't say it, he knew he loved her.

He took a step toward the pink silk door of the pavilion, and she rolled in the furs and blankets, enough of her body visible to stop Hartwin for a moment, curves in the reflected blush light like hills at sunset. She called to him, 'Have fun at your meeting, be nice to the Mirebreaker boy. The little one. He's a good little turtle and I think I… broke him or some such thing last night. Bad joke at the fire last evening, heh."

Hartwin had not told Lady Joelle about the meeting of the young lords, and he had not expected the younger Mirebreaker to be present. He had also learned not to underestimate the resources of the Lord Executor of the Empire's favorite niece. She had known about the fine young colt he had been planning to gift her about three weeks before it was even due to be born. He simply shook his head, chuckling and left the pavilion, his verdant silks wrapped in a plain black traveler's cloak.

His long cantering strides carried him across the yard quickly, as the smell of woodfire and the sounds of drinking songs mingled in the haze around him. The minor lords camped outside the walls were having a much more raucous time than the great lords cramped up in their tower, and from the city below, the sounds of revelry were vibrant and wild. Songs and cheers and commotion still rose from the streets of Honeyhome, even as midnight, the Owl's hour, crept nearer.

When he had requested the keys for the Great Gate Garden's gate, his Lord Grandfather had only given him a wry smile, yellow teeth matching the jaundice in his skin. "Are you bringing some girl? Impressing her with grandfather's wealth?"

"If only." He suppressed a grimace at the lech before him, "Backroom dealings with the young lords, very hush-hush."

Though the old widower was visibly disheartened, it only lasted until the words "backroom dealings" were uttered. His enthusiasm buzzed back, and the elderly lord was more than happy to acquiesce, and even suggested braziers when Hart managed to ask for stools. The old man had offered some servants to the task as well, but that was where Hartwin had to refuse. "Too many mouths share secrets, my lord. Hugo and I can put things in place if they're provided."

There had been some hollow bluster about how it's "Squire's work at best, hardly fit for a Lord and a knight!" But Lord Dobson had eventually agreed.

And now, at midnight, he was here. Hugo had the tourney, but Hartwin had been preparing for a night like tonight for years. Steady hands slid the brown gold key into the brown-gold lock and made a satisfying *thunk* as it twisted them together. He left the gate closed behind him, but unlocked. If one knew, he knew to enter. Getting the first brazier burning became a slight trial unto itself, but once Hart calmed his anxious nerves, it was soon blazing. Wood fire and incense flickered then flared, and soon all four bowls were casting their flames as bright as sunshine.

Hushed voices heralded two figures, paired and barely sneaking. Once Hartwin saw the blue-green of their wools, he smirked. Marten Mirebreaker was a bully and an idiot, but he was easily put in his place. A pointed barb usually left the lordling hot-blooded and mumbling his own attempted insults, but Joelle had asked him to be kind to the younger one. *Fine.* He grumbled to himself, but did recall the younger Mirebreaker's reputation as a budding intellectual. *Also his reputation as a cripple,* he mused to himself, but decided that was best left unsaid.

After a few barbs, and a genuine invitation, he and the two brothers had settled in on three of the stools, poking at the fires, as young men are wont to do when they're outdoors. The discussion had been easy enough, asking the boy about the kings of history he was most fond of, and like a shot, Slade Mirebreaker was elucidating on the failings and virtues of kings long past, dead and buried.

"Duncan the Second was the only Owl King with a lick of sense, as far as I can see. He ended the hostilities with Ozwyk, because the King Katan of Ozwyk loved him so well. He even let him shelter there when the Little Bastard took the throne, and Duncan had his family had to flee his wicked nephew." Slade recited almost by rote.

"Well." Hartwin countered, "King Oswell, his father, is the one who fostered that bond, wasn't he? He took Katan to ward as a boy, and raised him beside his own sons."

"'Took him to *ward?'*" the younger Mirebreaker's face twisted in disbelief, "He had pirates kidnap him and hold him to ransom for a decade!"

Hartwin shrugged, "It worked, though." He unwrapped the bundle of shredded leaf in his pocket and took a pinch, before offering some to Slade.

"Oh! No, thank you. I don't like the way it tastes… or makes me jittery." the boy shook his head.

Hartwin chuckled, "It's mint, not smokeleaf. See?" He raised the parcel, and the boy sniffed it, while his older brother flipped a log in the brazier. "It just settles my stomach and keeps my breath sweet. Ladies like it, I swear!"

Marten snorted, "Well, if that's the case, we'd best all have some." He set his firestoke at the side of the blazing brazier and sidled over, carefully picking a pinch with his left hand. He sniffed it, made a face of pleasant surprise and popped into his mouth, chewing heartily, "Not to kiss and tell, but I recently became, uh, *familiar,* with those Selach twins that the Prince keeps mooning over."

Though amused inside, Hartwin kept his mouth a thin, hard line, "The Selach Twins? I believe they are cousins to my cousin Doyle…"

Marten froze, "*Familiar* in that we–"

Hartwin could contain his mirth no longer, "I cannot stand Ser Doyle, and Prince Vernus is a spoiled little ass, you have done me no offense. As long as you stay away from my sister, feel free to cuckold the boy prince to your heart's desire."

"Some folk might call that treason." There came a new fourth voice. At the entrance to the Great Gate Garden, Prince Talor Artus stood, dressed in his plain wool and leather. The festivities and the tourney had left the heir to the empire drawn and pale, dark rings under his eyes of shining gold, "But since that is likely to be an ongoing theme of our event, I will forgive it for now." He smiled a prince's smile, "And likely because my brother is actually a spoiled little ass."

He was attended by the young Lords that Hartwin only knew by reputation. On his left was the skeletal Lord Torvald Ironarm. Ironarm was thirty-some and a head taller than even lanky, long-legged Hartwin. He seemed too ungainly to move, like a tree stuttering amongst the forest. He moved like a man decades his senior. When one looked at his skin, it was so thin and pale that a watershed of veins in red and blue pulsed to the naked eye. It was said that Lord Torvald was often too ill to leave his castle on the Metal Mount, and gazing upon him, Hartwin believed the tales. Ironarm was Lord of the Greatwood, and though he was married, he had no children to name heir.

If Ironarm was a skeleton, the other Lord beside Prince Talor was a burning phantom. Hartwin had heard the story of Lord Karas Reave, but he had never laid eyes on him. An assassination a handful of years ago had killed the High Lord of Ozwyk, and left both of his sons scarred. Kyne, the younger, the warrior, had lost an eye, but otherwise recovered to become one of the most feared warriors in the Empire– a whirlwind of sword and flaming sorcery. Karas, now Lord Karas, had not been so lucky. Much of the burning elemental magic that had scorched the halls of the Trifort that day had ripped through Karas Reave, scarring over half of his body.

It had been four years, and the scarred Reave still *smouldered.* The High Lord of Ozwyk covered himself in a hood and mask, only his eyes visible. Even so, around his flashing eyes of blue, much of the skin was burnt. The scarred burnt flesh looked more like a log pulled from the coals than soft, human skin. It was ashen black and cracked like a droughted riverbed. A dull red emberglow filled those cracks, and on occasion, a flare of orange or even yellow would flicker bright.

There was no smoke, no stench of burning flesh, but Hartwin could feel heat that was not from the braziers, as these three young lords grew nearer.

Ironarm and Reave gave simple courtesies, nodded, shook hands and made small talk with both Mirebreakers and Hartwin himself. Hart took stock of both, practicing assessments of his discerning eye. Ironarm was polite, and seemed rather well read. His voice was little more than an exhausted whisper, but his mind was sharp and he spoke well. A brilliant mind in a failing frame, it grieved Hart on some level.

Reave was a different sort, though robed and masked, his passion was clear in his tone and posture. He spoke with his hands, as much as his words, an animated orator. "I like your idea of taking the fight to the pirates in their hovels." He excitedly espoused to Mirebreaker when the subject of the eleven raiders to the south came up. "If we could get the king to agree, I could raise the ships."

Marten nodded, "I've got a fair few lords that would agree with you. Axe, Selach and my Uncle, to start." the lordling laughed, though he wisely didn't commit to raising ships outright, Hartwin quietly noted.

Hart found himself speaking, "I don't see why you're not allowed to defend your own borders. We chase bandits and horse-thieves across the Goldengrass, but because the vermin hide across the sea, you need permission? Horseshit."

The gathered lords broke into laughter, save serious little Slade and the Prince himself. Prince Talor had mirth in his eyes, but sparks and flares of thought were tracing themselves across his shapely face. "Bold words, Lord Saddler."

"My father still breathes, I am no lord, merely an honest servant, my Prince." Hartwin knew enough of the political situation on Avalar to know a few light jabs at the king might be endearing, but he would never dare directly insult the prince.

Prince Talor Artus chuckled at that, "I am sure you are at that." The young prince settled to a stool taking inventory of the gathered young men, "We seemed to have gained a Swampman." He gave the younger Mirebreaker a warm, kind smile, "We are better for your presence tonight, my young Lord. Your brother is wise to seek your counsel and even wiser to include you in our proceedings."

Even cold-hearted Hart felt something as he watched the young Slade Mirebreaker go a deep shade of red and mumble and stumble through his thanks. "I- Thank– It is the h-highest honor, Y-your Grace."

"We seem to be missing Hullen Curr." The Prince continued, "And I asked both young men from Fisher to attend. The succession is... undetermined. Strange that neither boy has arrived yet, heheh." The chuckle seemed out of place, but the gathered boys said nothing.

Curr would arrive shortly, short of breath and red-faced. When greeted by Ironarm, gave only a grunt. Hartwin wasn't especially familiar with this Curr, but given the lordling's reputation of gregariousness and charisma, Hartwin found this galling. The heir to Wylde slouched onto his stool, folded his arms and waited for the proceedings to start. Not at all the young man Hartwin had heard of.

After another twenty long, crawling minutes, the Young Lords had begun to grow restless. Ironarm's thin eyelids had begun to hang low, blinks growing long and longer as the time tumbled forward. Slade had leaned back over to Hartwin and whispered "What do you know about the Curr Clan?" His eyes shot to Hullen, then back to Hart.

Hartwin twisted his face in amusement, "Why are you asking *me*?"

Slade sighed, "My brother is a dry well, Curr himself seems unapproachable. You are the only other person here I've said more than a sentence to. The burden is now yours."

Hartwin genuinely laughed, he found himself enjoying this odd little swampboy, "So, it seems! Now, to be more pointed, why do you want to know?"

"Political intrigue?" The young lord's voice immediately betrayed the lie. Hartwin's only response was a knowing stare, until the boy finally spoke again, 'I kissed his sister!" He hissed the whisper between clenched teeth, and Saddler had to stifle another snorting laugh.

"Ahah, I see." Saddler kept his lips pressed tight together, preventing a smirk. "Romance is more dangerous than any battlefield. Isn't she here for Prince Vernus?"

The boy stammered, "Well, yes, I suppose, but you don't think he'll pick *her*, do you?"

Hartwin finally allowed the smile to crack his face, "I would not worry about your Lady Curr." He frowned again, thinking of his sister, "My own sister Harlow, however, may be in danger of that vermin's gripping paws."

Slade nodded, but before they could continue, the gate at the edge of the great garden slammed and shook, rattling loudly. Marten Mirebreaker and Hullen Curr both bounced to their feet, hands going to their blades. Curr went low, lunging forward, a growl in his throat. Mirebreaker pulled his brother behind him, before creeping forward to shield the sickly Ironarm as well. The Ozwyk Prince began to glow under his silks and satins, sparks and embers glowing under his cracked and burning flesh. Hartwin was no warrior, but here, gathered among these other young lords, he found his own strength of steel. He cracked a gloved knuckle, before shakily rattling his short dress sword from the scabbard at his hip. *Gods, don't let me embarrass myself, or... die, I suppose.* Remembering his lessons, he held the blade flat out in front of him as Prince Talor slid into his left line of sight, unlike Hartwin, the point of his blade was steady as the ground they stood on.

Another slam at the gate, followed by more muffled shouting. With the Prince's urging, Hartwin crept forward, his throat suddenly parched. A third slam, even fiercer than the second and finally the voices became clear.

"--can leave or end up facin' my off hand, and I promise you boys, that'll be plenty!" The voice was unrefined, and stopped and started with the harsh consonants of a Fisher accent. Lord Marten visibly stiffened, his blade in his own off hand, as much like the man speaking, his main hand had been broken. *Ser Rolof Deepreach. That's interesting.*

Deepreach himself had no claim to any lordship that mattered. He was heir to Ryleh, a salt-rock-and-seagull-shit clump in the western seas, but Clan Deepreach was a minor political force at best. However, it was told that Lord Fisher's young wife had taken to using Ser Rolof as a blunt object in a multitude of ways. Hartwin had even heard it whispered that Lord Fisher's young son Karl was actually a bastard born of Deepreach. Hartwin tried not to give such court gossip credence, but here, faced with the Bronze Kraken beside the boy himself, the resemblance was uncanny. The boy Karl stood behind his sworn sword, both of them tall, lanky, big-eared and dark-haired.

Opposite the pair were two blonde boys in the livery of Clan Fisher, orange and brown. Autumn tones, western tones. The taller of the two boys, who seemed a handful of years older than the other, shoved a stiff finger into the chest of the Kraken Knight, "I could give a shit, swing on me, yeh bloody coward." The boy stuck his strong chin out and pressed in on the big knight. The boy only came to the center of his chest, but showed no signs of fear or backing down. The younger boy behind him wasn't directly supporting the older, but he seemed to be staring a hole through young Karl Fisher.

Deepreach shoved the boy into the gate again. A fourth slam. The big gate of honeyed gold shuddered, but the boy did not. From his rear, Hart felt Mirebreaker and Curr rushing forward, but the Prince had seen all he intended to allow.

With a word, he became beautiful and terrible, shining and powerful. He unleashed his word and none could disobey

"ENOUGH. THERE WILL BE NO MORE VIOLENCE."

The Kraken Knight went limp, docile as a lamb. He did not stumble, he did not fall, but Hartwin watched all the fury and fight drained from Ser Rolof. He seemed to relax, not drowsy, but contented, settling back against a slender brown elm. Dreamily, he mumbled fractured apologies under his breath.

Whatever the Prince had used on Deepreach, it seemed to ripple outward through the rest of them. The two blonde boys in the Fisher raccoons seemed to settle, and even Hartwin found himself wishing his sword was lighter. Curr's growl faded into a whimper and the sparks from Reave ceased.

And as suddenly as he blazed, the Prince was but a friendly faced young man again. He smiled at Karl Fisher. "You will not need a bodyguard, but I would love to have you and your nephews attend." He motioned to the blonde boys, "Lords Leland and Calun, I presume."

"Aye." The taller boy nodded, "I'm Calun, the oldest of Lord Ludo's grandsons."

The younger boy followed, "And I'm Leland, the son of Lord Ludo's oldest son, the *actual* heir."

From the shadows, eight year old Karl piped up, dark haired in a sea of blonde, "I'm Lord Ludo's only living son, I oughta be heir!"

Hartwin's gut twisted. *This is a western war in the making.* The succession to The Pilfered Throne was divided into three fierce camps, each united behind one of these boys. If Deepreach was any indication, violence was bubbling beneath the surface. Fisher was already a nation of great division, the seas raided the rivers. Hardscrabble raiders from the bare, rocky western islands made the lives of the simple riverfolk hell. The Fisher Kingdoms had some of the most fertile soils in the Empire, but they were controlled by a few Clans. This led to raids from the hungry men from the Scattered Islands.

Some four-hundred years ago, King Arlan III had brought the isles under permanent heel and outlawed the practice of the great Summer Raids. This simply meant that the sails the longships flew stopped carrying family sigils. Octopus and marlin and vulture simply became silks of black. The raiders put on masks and helms and nothing changed. Officially, of course, none of the old Clans conducted Summer Raids, but more than one son of those ancient families had ended up strung up on a shore for piracy, writhing as the gulls and crows took their fill.

Prince Talor brokered no more argument. "If my Royal father and your *sire,* heheh." He stifled a chuckle at his own pun, "cannot sort out this succession, I will have all three of you attend, as simple a solution as there can be." He smiled, and led the three boys, two blonde and one dark, to join the rest of the young lords.

Moments passed quickly as the assembled lordlings regained their places near the brazier. Hart sat, choking through a half remembered dream as he stared upon the deep shadows the dying fires cast in the hollows of his companions' faces and the tall wild shadows that danced against the trees that bordered this manicured yard. Prince Talor took his seat, the darkness shading his face until his father, King Gallus, seemed to sit in his place. The light flickered again, catching the single topaz, a golden eye in the center of his golden crown. The light rose and fell, making the Prince's face dance and laugh wildly, though he was entirely still. After a moment that seemed an age, the Prince broke the gathered shroud of silence. "I... I just demonstrated the power of my line, the gifts of Clan Artus. You all felt a... *touch* of our power, just now, just here. A brushing of a great finger, but not a true strike."

The silence that had shrouded them returned, deeper, colder, older. Among these ancient trees, even the dying embers of the four fires had gone silent, their pops and hisses faded to quiet. Hartwin's eyes followed their circle, finding each face grim.

"And compared to my Royal Father." The Prince continued. His eyes were fixed on some far-away point, golden pricks of starlight dancing in the fire's reflected glare. "Compared to my father, I am an idiot child fumbling in the dark."

He let the implication sit, not a threat but near enough.

"Before I continue, I need to reiterate the need for continued discretion. Our meeting's existence seems to have spread further than I would have liked. There's no accounting for that now, but its contents must remain clandestine." He let his golden eyes flare, "If you will not commit to this, I bid you leave with no ill will, but you need leave."

When none of them rose, the Prince sighed, and continued.

"I will not cloak my meaning longer. I believe my Royal Father is losing his grip on sanity. And given the burdens of rulership and the powers he possesses, sanity is a skill most paramount."

Reave spoke first, sharp and noble, "You have proof of this?" Hartwin nodded slowly in agreement, but said nothing. The mumbled chatter of the young lords seemed to affirm this sentiment.

"Proof you all witnessed this afternoon. Proof was my father using Lord Jack Tymm as a puppet to murder me. My father used his powers to attempt my murder, and Lord Tymm died for it." There was a sullen, resigned obviousness in his tone.

Hart had been there, he had been in the stands when the Prince had killed Lord Tymm in the tourney, but to imply that this was something more sinister left Hartwin feeling hollow. He watched his Prince, looking for any sign of a lie. A twitch, a smirk, a blink, but the prince's face was stone.

Hartwin found his words again, and they surprised even him, "This is treason, your Grace."

"I am well aware, Saddler, but I do not raise this issue lightly. The mere discussion of this matter could mean any of our heads. But the fate of our Empire, our families, our people, demands the risk, gentlemen." The young prince rose, and he turned to each of the young lords in turn. There was no sign of his celestial blood flaring, but his words burned with strength of purpose and the earnest honesty of a good man pleading what he believes, "Our gathering here, in a garden, has a meaning. There is a symbolism to it. We are the stewards of the empire, its custodians. Its *gardeners*. We are the future of the Empire.

In five or ten years, maybe more, perhaps less, we will be the men ruling each nation, and I will preside over all of it."

Hart had similar thoughts himself, on occasion. His own Lord father wasn't evil, he'd never tried to harm any of the triplets. But, the old man was slow to act and indecisive . And when he eventually did act, he was soft. Frustration was not conspiracy, however. Hartwin watched the other faces in the garden, all of them beastly frozen masks, animated by the dancing firelight. Maybe the prince was telling the truth, madness and the strange powers of the Royal clan seemed to go hand in hand. More than a few of the Artus royals had been quite mad, and if Talor were to quietly usurp his maddening father, he would not be the first.

It was Mirebreaker, the older Mirebreaker, Marten, who spoke first, "Supposing you're telling the truth, *supposing,* what do you want from us? I won't lead my men against royal soldiers." He sat, making eye contact with the Prince. He was younger than Artus, but bigger in the chest and shoulders. If his broken hand grieved him, he did not wince when he used it to point or gesture.

Curr nodded in agreement, the sullen, silent Wyldeman, making his case plain, "No need to spill blood for a throne that will come to you with time, unless there's a real danger."

The Prince did not raise his voice, but he added a firmness to his tone that was new to Hartwin's ear. "This meeting has only been called because danger is growing."

Half-remembered lordlings bounded through a dream, before talons and feathers stormed them to shreds, as Hartwin tried to put that nightmare away, shuddering. In the distance an owl shrieked, a knife of ice and iron parting the ribs of the night. Somewhere among the leaves and pines, some little beastling was being devoured.

One of the tow-headed Fisher boys spoke next, the taller one, "Treason is treason, my lord. He is your king, and your father. Loyalty is all we are in the west."

Hartwin brayed a laugh, "Stay loyal to a fool or a monster and you become both."

The boy shot him a glare, "Are you pragmatic or just a grasping schemer, Saddler?"

Never one to stand for insult, Hartwin felt a pang of excitement grow at this cocky little riverlord. He sat, and without fury, devoid of anger, Hartwin spoke. His tone was clinical, dry and careful, but each word was picked to expertly vivisect this *Fisher.* "Since I am unfamiliar with which one of Lord Ludo's lost little lordlings you are, I will grant you are not familiar with me." Hartwin smiled broadly, devoid of mirth, "As such, you will want to find out that I am fiercely pragmatic. Pragmatic to the point that I would never *ever* dare insult a potential ally I've never met, simply because I'm a vainglorious, overconfident, bold, *stupid,* little boy. Especially when I need all the allies I can get to support my *incredibly dubious* claim to my Lord Grandfather's chair. If that offending every person that crosses my path with an unyielding notion of chivalry is your notion of politics, you and I are playing a very different game, *Calvin.*" Hartwin fixed his green eyes on the boy, the smile never moving from his face.

"It-it's Calun, my lord." The boy had gone red from forehead to chin and barely stammered out the reply.

"Given the odds of you holding the Lordship, I can't fathom that I'll need to remember that." Hartwin kept the fixed smile, before turning back to the crown prince, "Apologies, Your grace." Hugo may have his sword arm, and Harlow had her grace and beauty, but not a mind in the Empire would outpace Hartwin. He nodded gently, bidding the Prince to continue.

Artus watched Hartwin closely for a minute, the barest hint of a smile at the corner of his own lips, "Thank you, my lord."

The Prince smirked down at the Fisher lordling, who had cast his eyes to the dust. "I would never ask you to lead your men against my father's. I should hope for his men to be my men in time." He placed a hand on the downtrodden Fisher boy's shoulder. "All of them." The boy smiled weakly up to the Prince.

"Apologies, your grace, I seem to have m-misspoke." He finally raised his gaze to the Prince.

"No need to apologize for debate, my lord." The Prince picked up a chunk of the dry, split firewood, and began feeding the brazier nearest him. The hungry flame took to the dry splintering wood quickly and the dull red glow flared to a blazing orange, "I called this meeting for discussion, not dispensation of my rule, heh." He chuckled again, almost unaware. "I do not seek rebellion; I need competent rule. Through our letters and exchanges, I have come to know each of you. I know your needs and your frustrations, and I see how the crown refuses to meet them." There was a general buzz of accord, and the prince pressed forward, "My Lords Mirebreaker and Reave, just tonight, you spoke together of elven pirates from the continent hassling and harrying your shores and tradeships."

As the Prince swung a perfect tanned hand toward both Reave and Mirebreaker, the Ozwyk lord stood. Lord Karas Reave blustered under his veil, "Yes, your Grace. The crown refuses us ships or even leave to cross the strait and put them to the sword."

"As I am well aware. As part of the crown, I tell you here and now, *take your leave*. Burn them out. The assaults on our people will cease." Artus had moved to the second brazier, and began feeding its flames.

Reave rose, his burnt flesh crackling under his silks. "What of the king?"

A long hard stare came before any words, "Lord Karas, you are blood to my own wife. Your son and mine share that blood."

Reave removed a glove from his left hand. Black leather pulled away from crackling skin. As the night air hit the burning lord's hand, it flared like kindling taking breath. Lord Karas waved his crippled, burnt hand over the brazier, and it flared to orange life. There were no words between them, but the point had been made.

"I will handle the King. I will handle King Gallus in all of this. I do not ask you to rebel. I ask you to judiciously ignore commands you think prevent your competent rule." He didn't laugh, but there was a little playful joy in his tone, a bounce. "If you rule competently, despite the King's protestations, soon the smaller lords and common folk will see my father as we have come to see him, *failing.*" The distaste of failure hung on that word like a shroud of noxious smoke, twisting the Prince's handsome face as he spit it.

Slade Mirebreaker piped up, his voice nasal, "Without intention of insult, Your Grace, permission does not give us ships."

It was the youngest Fisher boy that responded, the dark-haired son of eight, "My mum's got ships. Lots of 'em. Gorge ships. And Reaver's Rock is full o' hungry men to sail 'em."

Slade snapped back, "We can't just set the Scattered Raiders on the continent..." Hartwin watched the dawning realization cross the boy's face, "...Can we?"

The Prince smirked, "Why not?"

Beautiful and terrible. Hartwin saw Prince Talor then, he saw him for the shrewd politician behind the Grinning Prince. Hartwin could see it all slowly reveal itself to him, like fog pulling away from a landscape. *The Shining Island, The Lord Executor's Chair, Joelle. This Prince can give it all to me, but I must give him my best. I must show him that above all, I am indispensable.* To rise like he craved, Hartwin Saddler always needed a mount. And today, he had found him. Hartwin rose, and without a second's hesitation, he spoke, "I pledge what I can from the coffers of the Goldengrass to this purpose. Moreover, Your Grace." Hartwin spoke and took a trio of slow, deliberate steps toward his prince, "Let me be the first of the young lords to pledge my loyalty to your cause." Hartwin fell to one knee, "My prince, I will be your most fervent supporter, because your vision mirrors my own. I see a future where we young stewards lead the Empire into greater prosperity than ever before. I pledge my wits and my wiles to you, my Prince. I offer my sword, too, but I oft find myself struggling there."

From above, Prince Talor gave a gentle toss of his black-as-night tresses, "Your wit and wiles are worth thousands of swords, my Lord." The Prince extended a hand, and Hartwin took it–leather on leather. Hartwin rose to his feet, with the prince's aid, and Talor Artus raised their intertwined hands above their heads and called out, his voice clear, "Kneel, my lords and I shall raise you up. Kneel and we shall ascend together. This world is ours, my lords, we only need to reach out and snatch it. Boldness and youth are our weapons and the elders can fall into our march, or be trampled underfoot!"

With a few exceptions, the other Lordlings knelt. Both Mirebreakers found their knees first, followed by Reave and the Fisher boys. Ironarm shook his head, the oldest of the lords. A decade older, a decade more cautious and exhausted, the tall lord rose, but he did not kneel, "Knees of stone and steel do not bend so well, your grace." His voice whispered, the celebration simmered to a low babble, to allow for Ironarm to be heard, "I understand your desire, and I'll not stand in your way… but you do not understand what you begin here, my Prince." The tall Ironarm lord, bone-thin, skin so pale and thin that Hartwin could watch blue veins throb and pulse from across the fire. "You think youth and boldness are enough to rule." He sighed, "You are children. You are a flicker of candlelight at the edge of a darkness you cannot comprehend. Great and dark and ancient, and it consumes. The smoke and shadow of eternity swirl and storm around us, and you all play… children in a garden. You did not plant it or tend it, you simply think it has always been."

He stepped away from the circle, "I have no intention of revealing your secrets, and I wish you the best, but I'll not participate in such foolish endeavors. The world is too dangerous for division."

Artus watched the Lord limp away, leaning hard on his staff. But the prince made no effort to stop him, merely wistful, perhaps rejected, "As is your right, my lord."

Hartwin watched the sickly, childless Lord of the Greatwood, Mountains of Orre and The Coldwater Lakes limp into the darkness, and was immediately reminded that his heir was a darkly different sort. *A problem for later, perhaps Ser Reuben Stagg will be more tractable.* He tensed his neck, as his Prince released his hand. As he stood there, on Prince Talor's right, the other young lord made his case.

Hullen Curr IV was as wild as the black hound on his sigil. Pointed canines and shags of brown hair gave him a wolfish sort of look, but the way his eyes flashed and his energetic lope did little to make him look more civilized. He snarled, "Cowards and caitiffs, all of you." He said nothing else, but gave Marten Mirebreaker a long, sad stare before swirling his cloak of midnight indigo before making his own way into the distant night.

Once he had fled, the Prince sighed again, "Well, I did not actually hear a *no,* heheh." The laugh was more of a tick than an expression of joy. "He is upset, but Hullen will come around. The Wylde is vast, empty and cold. Grain is hard to grow there. If not him, someone in Rime River must be interested in feeding his people."

From his place on the Prince's right, Hartwin stood above the kneeling lordlings, and he felt the warmest of warm smiles spread over his face like shining silver sun over the great golden plains of his home. Destiny had led him here, above them all.

The gathered nobility would soon regain their feet. Into the night, they would talk. Each of them would raise the issues the crown had failed them on. In turn, the Prince would bring his solution and then the lords would discuss it. Most often, what resulted was nowhere near what Prince Talor had proposed, but as the solutions seemed to please everyone, Hartwin saw the prince's easy smile never wavered.

For his part, Hartwin took some of his Lord Father's advice, a rare occasion to be sure. He listened twice as much as he spoke, he gave deference to lords who had seen things he'd only read. But no matter where the conversation led, Hartwin made sure of one simple thing, he remained at Prince Talor's right hand. He would stand here until he rose above all of them, once more.

Somewhere in the woods, an owl shrieked again. All Hart could think of was storming brown feathers and talons as sharp as onyx, even swaddled in the laughter of impetuous youth.

VANDRE III

"Don't pretend you are some hard thing. You are a scared little boy. You roar and rage because you are hurt, not because you are fierce."

Vandre had an eye for gold, practiced through need and survival, but even he could not tell if the crown in his hands was real or fake. Beside the tired old knight, Clovis leered at the circlet, trying to get a closer look. Vandre wrapped the thing back in rags and called down from the high balcony, "You see where it went?"

The mean little gnome in red grimaced back up, forty feet below, "No." She disappeared under the stands without another word, and Vandre turned to the elf beside him.

"You fucking saw that, right?" Even the seasoned sellsword was shaking, clutching the crown in rags to his chest. Wisps of black smoke still suffused the entire balcony box where they stood, though the night's warm breeze was slowly scattering them.

Clovis shook his head, "I-I am unsure, Ser Jemes." In the midnight moonlight, the elf looked alien. He moved, cautiously, staring over the edge of the royal box, where he and Vandre had found themselves. Their fourth, the wild elf from Ozwyk, was seated behind them. She had settled onto the worn bench with worn purple cushions. Her spindly legs were crossed, her hands were folded in her lap. Under shags of blonde hair, the huge elven eyes were closed, and the slight, girlish features were still.

Vandre impatiently reached a hand to shake her, but the slim Clovis grabbed his wrist. Clovis motioned skyward with his gaze, indicating the circling red hawk owned by the wild elf, "She's doing something. Stop. Use your brain."

Vandre snatched his hand away from Clovis, clearly irritated. He stuffed the rag-wrapped crown into his satchel, before any of his companions would have the chance to object. "She's doing something with the sodding *bird?*" Vandre swirled his cloak around his shoulders, "If I had a lick of sense, I'd throw you off the top of this fucking thing, bash *her* head in and be in the dark before the gnome got back up here."

"You should have started two minutes ago, then." The little red gnome gal hoisted herself through a gap in the bleachers. Hand over hand, she pulled a tight silk cord up behind her, wrapping it tightly as she went. Her deep burgundy eyes never left Vandre. The other two were no threat to him, skinny elves he could skewer on his sword. But this gnome had murder in her tone when she spoke. Vandre had lived long enough to recognize a contract killer when he saw one. Even if he was wrong, there was nothing to be lost by keeping his distance here. Her cord gathered, Scarlet rounded on him, and though she only came to his waist, the threat was very real. "What happened to the crown, old man?"

"It turned to smoke when Webb disappeared." He lied and waited for Clovis to contradict him. When the old sellsword glanced from the corner of his eye, Clovis's face was a mask of stone, keeping Vandre's secrets for now.

Scarlet fingered the long dagger at her waist nervously. It was no Lutinese throwing knife, but a heavy steel thing, blades on both edges. Just the way the edges caught the scant moonlight breaking the clouds showed how sharp it was, "I don't like this." She pointed the blade at Clovis, "I don't like none of this."

Clovis broke the silence first, his high noble voice flush with caution, "None of us like this." He lowered his hood, a light breeze set his long, dark hair to motion, but he was all grace. Vandre watched as the awkward, lanky elfling recast himself into royalty. A hundred hundred generations of old Malvari Kings radiated grace and charm from the boy… And Vandre cursed himself for almost letting the elf boy's magic overwhelm his sense.

The old knight slapped his own cheek with a gloved hand, and saw Scarlet settle onto the bench, nodding cheerily at Clovis. He would have to move now, or be lost. He surged up on Clovis and drove a mailed fist into the elf's face with a sickening crunch. The boy dropped to his knees, sputtering. *I am sorry, boy. You deserved a better friend than me.* The Red Killer was still dumbfounded from Clovis's magic, which only left…

There was a screech, and the talons were on him. The Wild Elf kept some exotic raptor at her side constantly– this hawk of cherry-red, with hooked talons and a hooked beak. Though its master still sat silent, lost in dreams or thought or more, the bird had plummeted down from on high and was raking sharp claws at the old man's scalp and ears. Vandre swung gloved hands wildly, as hot blood began trickling down his cheek, mingling with salt sweat. Furious screams and curses mingled with Clovis's sobs and Scarlet's mutterings. As much as he tried, he could not grab this damn bird.

It slashed and tore. Vandre shrieked as he felt the bird's cruel beak tear a long strip of flesh from the back of his neck. More hot blood soaked his jerkin, running in crimson rivulets down his back.

Eaten by a damn bird. Fitting end for a rat, it seems.

As he lost more blood, he stumbled to a knee. This bird would kill him if he didn't stop it. It was too fast, too vicious. Too strategic… Too human. Blind rage filled him as the simple fact dawned on him.

Grunting, he ignored the bird and kicked the Wild Elf in the chest, where she sat on the bench. She crashed backward, the breath leaving her body in a thumping huff. The bird shrieked and flapped its great red wings, unsteadily finding perch on a banner, safely away from Vandre's reach. Free of its master's magical chains, it saw no reason to continue attacking Vandre, so it retreated.

The old man limped down the stairs, away from the three unconscious bodies in the Royal Box. If he'd had any sense, he'd have killed the three of them, but as he touched the sticky spot where his left ear had been, he decided medical attention was important. Blood was congealing in the small of his back, as he hurried across the tourney grounds.

I should kill them, he thought, *But even so, the dead seem restless here.* He was carrying a Starheart crown that the Late Lord Purvon Webb had stolen, after all.

Moments ago, he and his three companions had crept, silent and breathless, into the tourney grounds. They had been given no information other than the time and the place, simply told to arrive. What each of them had expected, Vandre could not say. He personally had expected some form or other of bullshit, a lordling who thought he was brilliant and mysterious or something that foolish. The whole endeavor had stunk of trap, but his options were limited. He was facing extortion and the headsman. Vandre was used to dancing on the strings provided by nobility, but this was far, far more dangerous a precipice to balance upon.

When the quartet crept into the arena, where the stands had once thrummed with energy, colorful banners, and screaming common folk, only silence sat. The smells of blood and dust hung with old smoke, but the only life was a stately old screech owl, who silently swooped away the second it heard their low voices babbling back and forth.

Each of them had their secrets, each of them had fears and expectations, but not one of them expected to see the dead boy beckoning them forward. Lord Purvon Webb had been impaled on the halberd of Lady Lenore Vellen some ten or so hours ago. A thousand sets of eyes had watched the boy take his last shuddering breath, seen the thick red blood flow in a flood down the shaft of Vellen's weapon and tide over her body.

The whole crowd watched the Priests of Eresh remove his helm. Vandre had seen the boy's face himself, there was no doubt that the boy had perished with a jagged hole in his chest large enough to let light through. But all the same, Lord Purvon Webb stood before the four blackmailed miscreants, with his spider-helm under his left arm and that horrible hole in his sternum letting moonlight pierce his shadow.

As the boy stiffly swung his lanky left arm, he began to speak. Puffs of white smoke hung at the edge of each breath, "Sinners one and sinners four, I offer redemption. I offer life." The face was Webb's, though etched in black and white. No trace of blood or life moved in that boy, no blush in his cheek, no sweat on his brow. His voice was far away, a rattling wheeze as air rushed into the great rend in Poor Lost Webb's opened chest.

Incredibly, Clovis had been the first one to speak. Vandre had understood the elf in that moment, finally. Below his fearful facade was a polished mind, sharp, infinitely curious and dangerously canny. The gore didn't slow the tall elf, as he shouldered past Vandre and spoke, "My lord, my eyes tell me a thing that can simply not be." As the elf unleashed his voice, his left hand shakily clutched a small trinket, bone and stone and brass. White and black and gold. It seemed to produce a light different from the blue moonlight, soft and warm and flickering like a candle flame.

Vandre smirked, *A fuckin' Learner. The kid is a Learner in disguise.*

Clovis lurched forward, his need for answers outweighing both logic and fear. He kept whatever that thing in his left hand flickering, but low to his side. He spoke again, "Are you Purvon Webb?"

The boy spoke again, the puffs of smoke thickening, darkening to a swirling grey, "I have that which you need." Grey tendrils of smoke began to snake from the huge, bloody hole at the center of Webb. Without stepping, Webb crossed the center yard. His long cloak of spider-silk melted into the smoke surrounding him. Silver and grey and swirling, the ghost moved without weight.

Like fog on the breeze, the stick-thin spider-lord floated over the dust and gravel, and passed through the narrow gate where he had taken some of his last living steps. Vandre broke into a run, trying to keep up; Clovis and the rest were on his heels. This grey shade floated, purposeless, but never slowing. As fast as the living chased this dead boy, they grew no closer. Vandre pumped his sore old legs, The Wild Elf beside him moved like a dashing cat, but they closed no distance. Silent and scowling, Webb slowly ascended the great grandstand, finally settling in the Royal Box.

Three stories of stairs set Vandre's heart to slamming and he was sucking warm air between gritted teeth, as he deliberately put one foot in front of the other. The four miscreants clambered into the Royal Box, where Webb waited. The hollow spider reached into the hole in his chest and gripped something sparkling. With a grunt, the grey smoke pouring from Webb turned to black, growing thicker, rolling and spreading across the floorboards. The living began to choke on this black death, as the dead Webb unhinged his jaw with a snapping crack that echoed from timber to canvas. More black smoke began to usher forth from the boy's mouth, now sparking with red embers, stinking of sulfur. Both hands wrapped the metal buried in the meat of his torso, as he wrenched, laughing and mocking, "This is it–" There was a wet crunch and Lord Purvon Webb tore a perfect golden tiara from his broken body, "This is what you've been hired to steal."

The choking air sent Vandre and the rest of his companions to the floor. The old sellsword tried to cover his mouth and nose with his leather-gloved hand, but it did nothing to stall the stinging smoke. They all choked on the floor, writhing on the floorboards. Spots flashed over his eyes– flares of black and ultraviolet shades. Vandre bit down, crooked yellow teeth split his lip, and the taste of blood gave the old man a second wind. He was too woozy to handle his heavy sword, but his dagger came free from its sheath. Vandre stumbled forward, slashing with steel and finding only smoke. Scarlet pressed through the smoke to his right, a cloth of crimson covering her mouth and nose. Her eyes flashed in rage, clutching a crossbow with deadly intent.

Vandre tripped, his worn leather boot catching on something unseen in the smoke. He avoided jamming a wrist, as his sternum whomped into the floor. The old man moaned, sucking black smoke and choking. He reached to his boot, to see what he had tripped on, and his grasping fingers found the fine gold circlet on the rough hewn planks. Greedily, his fingers snatched it, his dagger clattering to the floor. The black smoke skeleton of Webb surged and rushed over the balcony, flying as a phantom upon ribbons and tethers of fog and carrion. It cackled, rushing into the dark of the night along the ground, dripping burning flesh like fat into a cookfire.

Without a second thought, Scarlet had followed, tossing a tether of silken cord behind her so she could slow her descent. On the ground, Vandre had the ticket to freedom that he had come to Honeyhome for. The Starheart Crown.

He limped across the yard, his treasure hidden amongst his cloak and rags. He had to reach the castle. He quickly tossed his hood up, just another pilgrim in brown. He had spent too many of his fifty years as a pilgrim, wrapped in cheap brown and drifting from place to place. Hammerdale had been no home, and he would sleep in a freezing alley before he returned to that stinking city.

One foot in front of the other, though he could feel the sticky blood on his back and neck growing stiff. His small clothes were glued to his back, thick blood going brown. The yard was not empty, but it was far from full. Lordlings and nobles prowled and played, but paid the stranger in brown no mind. He was just another little brown rat scurrying through the granary.

Though the nobility paid him no mind, a brassy voice, girlish but firm called out for his attention, "Ser! Ser! Are you hurt?" Vandre put his head down and hurried away, beginning to sway in his steps. He needed to get to the High Lord. Turn the crown over for a reward. That would get him protection.

Had to get to the… main… bailey.

A young woman in swooping purple and grey silks came up on him. The old sellsword didn't immediately trust his eyes when it seemed like the girl had green skin and curving brass horns, but when he blinked bleary eyes, the strange features still remained. She called again, a kind voice, "Ser, you're bleeding. Let me…"

The pretty green hellheart pressed a soft hand to his face and saw him. She drank the dark deep when she recognized his stern eyes, the nose that had been broken and never quite set, the deep crags of laughlines and scars. She gasped, as the face that she had seen through the eyes of a dead farm boy in a thicket stared back at her, bloody and begging for aid. He smiled weakly, "My lady, I need to– find…" He was unable to find the words, his head was swimming and the world seemed muddy. "Help. I've… I need to get the crown.." He blinked unevenly, swaying. "Please."

He smiled in a silent, kind appeal.

She screamed. "Guards! I found the killer! The farm boys! He's right here! Get Lord Hartwin, now!"

Shit. Saddler. Vandre was struggling, but even his molasses-heavy head saw the danger here. He turned to pull his dagger to slash this green demon girl, his hand grasping in a practiced motion, and found only air. His dagger lay yards away, in the royal box, beside the three companions he'd abandoned. *Shit.*

He reached for his sword but he was too shaky to rattle it from his belt. A tall young man in green silks and a high pointed helm had come running at the Hellheart's call. Vandre swung a fist at him, off balance and sluggish with anemia. The guardsman ducked it lazily and drove the butt of his spear into the old man's gut. Vandre gagged, spit and bile and blood rushed forth from his mouth, as a gurgling groan issued breathlessly.

Another guard rounded behind the old sellsword, and wounded, Vandre lashed out with a mule kick. He swung a heavy foot backward and caught it directly into the second guardsman's codpiece. The guard stumbled backward, as two more managed to seize the woozy old knight by both arms.

Snarling, Vandre bit the fool holding his right arm, full on the cheek, coming back with a mouthful of blood, skin and meat. The boy howled a noise that sent the rest of the yard to running, but the vice-grip of his hands never loosened. The first guard drove the butt of his spear into Vandre' sternum and he fell to the ground, boneless. The guard who he had kicked in the balls returned the favor as Vandre writhed.

Vandre was fading as one of the tall Saddler Guards battered him with a kick to the ribs. *Careful,* he idly mused through the blinding pain, *the elf ain't like to mend those again.* The biggest of the four had pressed his spear into his chest, not knowing that the wounded man was in mail. *Mail is easier than companions.* Dying and bleary-eyed, the old sell-sword tried to focus on the guards in green circled above him, but something about the way the sparse moonlight made their shadows jump made him feel sick so he focused on the spear instead. "...ivegotthecrown." He thickly mumbled, low and rumbling.

The tall guard leaned down, blue moonlight glinting on his great bronze, "What did you say, old man?" Vandre mumbled something unintelligible, his mouth sticky with blood and bile. The guard ignored him, leaning on the longspear harder. "They hang murderers, you scum."

The last sound Vandre heard before was all silent and black was the voice of the green girl who somehow knew he'd killed those boys in the cold night air, "Well, you've earned yourself a terrible little fate, haven't you?"

Then he only heard his own ragged, wheezing rips of breath. Then there was nothing.

END ACT TWO

EARLIER THAT AFTERNOON

A Bridge Between Acts

Three figures sat flickering in the firelight, shadows dancing on the firmament of orange and blue silk above them. The Scarecrow's pavilion seemed larger inside than out, but the shadows needed every inch of square. While the three figures sat silent, their shadows carried on a spirited debate, a projection on canvas. The Bird quorked and fussed at its shadow companions, communicating its intention directly to the Scarecrow and the Bear without words or sound.

Though it made no sound, the Bird's voice rang hollow to the Scarecrow and the Bear, whistling low and sad like the wind in the reeds. The posture was slouched and tired. The bird had been on the losing side of an argument, *"For the safety of my people, I ask you to withdraw behind the veil."*

The shadow of the Scarecrow snapped straight, though its owner never stirred from the place he leaned on his silver scythe. The thin shadow was all angles and limbs, a lanky twisted mire of spikes, *"What of my people, Coronox? After four hundred years, the people of the west are more mine than your elves and changelings skulking through the shadows."*

The mountainous shadow of the Bear rumbled, shifting its huge fanged jaw. Thick hair fell in great shadowed shags down the beast's shoulders and chest. There was more rage and less reason in the great bear's response, *"While you've been hiding in the smoke, the rest of us have been facing the rot head on. It's rich of you to demand anything from us. We have sat on this side, waiting for you. I am a leader here, I have responsibilities. I am depended on. I have a child.*

You will not be taking me into your Unseelie Hell, no matter how noble your reason."

The bird shadow swelled on the wall, becoming great and awful. Great wings of black spread as horns and talons and beak all menaced. *"Your ancestors swore oaths."*

The Scarecrow laughed, *"Dig them up and let him fulfill them, then. I have oaths here, black bird."*

The Bear thundered in agreement, as some scuffle erupted outside the tent's door. *"I swore you no oaths, Coronox, but I've sworn plenty here. If there is aid I can bring you from my seat at Starlight Shore, it is yours. But I will not abandon my people or my family to fulfill a promise made by a grandfather's grandfather who never planned to repay it himself."*

The silks of the pavilion parted, and a tall man, with dark hair and big ears and all three young men spun their heads to face him, shadows settling to normal. The pale boy who had been the bird frowned, "Who the hell is this?"

The tall man tried to speak, "Ser Rolof–"

With a flash of golden eyes, The Coronox silenced Deepreach.

"ENOUGH. BACK TO YOUR MUDDY MIRE, SQUID. FORGET YOUR PURPOSE COMING HERE. FORGET WHAT YOU HAVE SEEN."

The knight went stunned and stiff, burbling like an idiot child under his breath. After a moment, the tall knight excused himself politely. Ser Rolof Deepreach bowed deeply, clicked his heels together, and passed back through the tent's front flap. His memories of his experience were already fading like frost on a spring morning.

As the interloper retreated into the afternoon, The Coronox turned to his companions, and spoke to them, man to man to man.

There was no magic, no force, only a tired man pleading, "I could force you. But I could not hold you. If you two will not see reason, I will be forced to take more drastic measures." Ruffling his huge feathered mantle around his shoulders, the young pale bird-man-thing made his own way for the exit."I will do what I must to protect *my* people. They were once *yours.*" The fury in his words cut at the Bear and the Scarecrow, leaving only fluttering feathers of grey, brown and black in his wake.

ACT THREE:

INNOCENTS

LILAH III

"The Gods told us right and wrong, Lilah. Protect the weak, keep your oaths, tell no lies. These things are hard. They are supposed to be, but that is what makes them worth doing."

After the fracas at the procession, Doreen was severely less interested in Vernus. And she hadn't held much interest in the first place. To hear her tell it, at breakfast the next morning, the entire ballroom had erupted in violence when Lilah departed. Ser Hugo Saddler had almost removed the head from Prince Vernus' bodyguard after the Prince had groped Harlow Saddler. At least, that was the story Doreen relayed excitedly. Lilah was sure there was either more or less to the story. There was simply no way Doreen was telling the events accurately.

Lilah resolved to get the information from a less traumatized source, once the opportunity presented itself. Granted, Prince Vernus was a useless little letch, so the groping part was probably accurate. The odds of Vernus selecting Doreen had plummeted to unlikely, which Lilah was secretly thrilled by though she would never dare show it.

The little red kobold under her bed was bothering her much, much more, however. The hunk of icy-white diamond set into a black dragontooth in her traveling chest even more so. The thing had thrummed in her hand when Verm, that little red kobold, had given it to her, but it was simply too dangerous to keep. Clan Curr would notice this was missing, to be sure. Given the importance and history of *Snowsnarl,* this ancient sword, Clan Curr would most likely want its elemental heart returned. Doing so would be incredibly difficult, as Ellari Curr had become a problem.

It was before dawn and Reuben snored softly beside her. He had made his way to bed only a few short hours ago. Lilah had managed to corral Verm under her bed, and demand his silence. The rusty dragonling only wanted to serve Lilah. Its grasp on Commontongue was tenuous. Through careful, calm cajoling, Lilah managed to comprehend that it swore some debt, as she had saved it. Dedicated service, despite Lilah's objections.

Since she had been wed to Reuben, packed up and shipped off to the cold, rocky Metal Mount, Lilah often felt like a princess in one of the stories stupid little girls love so much. Not one of the princesses who marries a prince and is given every single stupid thing she could fill her stupid empty dreams with. No, Lilah felt like a princess locked high in a tower or deep in a cave dungeon. She was guarded by a vile, beast, weak and stupid and the horrible witch who commanded it. A hateful stag and a hemlock hag. She needed a knight and the Gods had sent her a dragon. *And not even a big one.* If it was a joke, Lilah didn't find it to be a particularly funny jest.

The young mother dressed in silence, choosing a plain dress of an autumn-red, and a soft wool cloak in brown. Lilah needed peace and reflection, and she was not one to flaunt her wealth in the temple. She softly settled herself on the bedsilks beside her husband, fastening soft leather flats to her feet. Sensible shoes for a day walking in the dust, Lilah stretched her long toes apart, sighing lightly. As she rose again, Reuben spoke, groggily, "...Are you going?" His voice was far away, and dreamy, "The bed is warm."

She softly brushed some of his cinnamon brown hair from his forehead, "Yes, my lord. I am in need of some morning devotionals. Prayer for those we lost yesterday, guidance for your sister, as she becomes the Lady of Leaper's Ledge, your continued success in the tourney, all such things." *Two truths and a lie.* Again, Lilah saw the irony, she just didn't especially enjoy it.

From his pile of pillows, Reuben sleepy nodded, "s'goodthing to do. You're good, Lilah." He rolled over, with no intention of joining her or aiding her. Lilah did not mind that, either. She gathered herself and slid into the hall.

The common area of the borrowed apartment was not as empty as she had hoped. Her Lord Husband's father, Ser Mandel Stagg, was standing in the window. The stiff old knight didn't immediately turn to his daughter-by-law, but he often ignored her. He was dressed plainly, a dressing robe of cotton over his small clothes, far from the rehearsed and practiced knight he usually presented. He was silhouetted, all in grey. The light of the silver sunrise over the Bay of Bees had left Ser Mandel a grey phantom. When he heard the door of her chambers click shut, Ser Mandel turned his head and though he did not smile, recognition crossed his face. He nodded in acknowledgment, bowing his head politely.

He held a steaming cup in his hand. The smell of ginger and spice spread through the room, just as warm as the sunbeams the Stagg knight bathed himself in. "Where are you headed this early?" He paused, frowning, taking a moment to correct himself, "My manners. I apologize, Lilah. Good morning."

"Temple, ser. The t-temple, I mean." Her voice was a low, nervous chatter. Her father-by-law always made her feel like a dullard. "With all of the strange, fearful occurrences here, turning to prayer might help me center." She shifted her weight uneasily. Lilah was telling the truth, but something about the way Ser Mandel's huge green eyes washed over her made her feel like she was lying anyway.

The usually immaculate knight crossed from the window to a nearby, low table, where a small porcelain pot steamed from the spout. Ser Mandel warmed his own cup with fresh tea, before looking up to Lilah, "Can I offer you some? It's been shipped in from the Far Fort, very choice." She shook her head in polite refusal, and he settled into an overly plush chair in violet. "You're wiser than we give you credit for, aren't you?" Those big, myrtle green eyes fixed on her and didn't shift. *He misses nothing.*

"You miss nothing." He smiled softly. Lilah wasn't sure she'd seen him smile before, not even with the children. "You may not understand everything happening around you, but you are very, very observant, aren't you, child?"

Lilah wanted to reply, but the only reaction she could manage was a quiet stammer and a nod.

"Do not be frightened, Lilah. I am trying to." He paused, nodding to himself, "*relate* to you." His little white cup steamed, geyser hot, and he dolloped a thick spoonful of chilled cream into it. "My wife is ungentle with you." The cream steamed and dissolved into the amber hot tea. "She is unsubtle and ungentle in many things, but especially about you." That is incredibly unwise of her. I think you could do great things for the Clan and family, if given the chance." He stirred the tea, his broad hands gentle with the delicate cup and spoon. "I think you are foolish and soft-hearted and focus entirely on the wrong things, but I do not believe you are stupid."

Lilah listened, and while she heard the words, she watched her father-by-law. Ser Mandel looked especially drawn and tired in the earliest beams of dawn. She wouldn't thank him for such double-talk, but she still listened.

"I notice things that other folks don't, Lilah. Like you do, I'm more perceptive than most. Stags don't survive in the wood unless they see predators. I guess one might say the same of squirrels."

Lilah chuckled at that, "That's very good."

He smiled again, that same thin, sad smile. "I see most things, Lilah. I... I see how Reuben..." His eyes went far, far away, and even began to mist slightly, "Reuben does not often comport himself as a knight. I may be sterner than I ought to be, I admit this, but I never taught him to lay a hand on a woman."

She couldn't believe her ears. Someone saw. Her voice came rushing back, chattering in breathy, low whispers, "You know he hurts me?"

Reuben's father was stone, but nodded his balding head slowly after a long moment. "I do."

It was then Lilah felt it in her stomach, a sudden sinking shift. Her stomach understood before her brain did. Her mouth had made the words before her brain understood them, "You're... you're not going to help me, are you?"

Mandel looked to his steaming cup, unable to face her. His tone was almost as distant as his gaze. "I am not going to stop Reuben, no. But–"

Lilah did not care to hear the rest, "'Ser, if you choose to stare idly at my suffering, I do not see what help you can offer me." The tired young mother took two hard steps before turning back to her father-by-law, "It sounds to me that you are yet another hand reaching out to put me to your purposes, more work."

Ser Mandel stood, plaintively defensive, "You misunderstand, child, please!" His voice rose and for a moment both feared disturbing the sleepers. "I can still help you. Much like Lady Grete, Reuben requires a more *soft touch.*"

Buck teeth bit a soft lip, as she struggled to contain her fury, "My touches have been nothing but *fucking soft.* It seems that Reuben might need some education on how to touch kindly."

Ser Mandel's face looked like curdling cream, "I know, Lilah. I know. You are absolutely correct." She turned to leave and he stopped her with a touch, "Allow me one question, Lilah. *Please.*"

Annoyed, Lilah looked at her husband's father, and briefly saw the stiff old knight as the small, unimpressive little follower that he truly was. She sighed and consented.

"No matter our feelings, Reuben will very likely be High Lord of the Greatwood. Sooner than later, if we both know my wife." It was no threat, simply reality. Lady Grete would kill for power, Lilah was perfectly aware of this. Mandel continued, "On that day, who would you rather whisper in Reuben's ear? You or Lady Grete? Who would better serve The Greatwood, its people? Your sisters among them."

Lady Grete was not a kind woman, and she did tend to indulge her son's cruel tendencies, it was true. Still, the world was not her responsibility. She resumed her trek toward the door, but the knight had one last snare, "Your son." She stopped in her tracks, heels suddenly stone. Lilah had expected this, but was no more disheartened when Ser Mandel continued, "Your son. Our little Neal. He'll be Lord someday, then. He's a good little boy, Neal, isn't he?" He waited for no affirmation. "What kind of man do you want Neal to be, Lilah? Because I don't want our kind little boy to grow up and be like his father."

There was no lying in Ser Mandel. His plea hit Lilah in the heart, and she paused. "...I will think on what you've said, Goodfather.

In fact, I will pray on it, presently." She smiled at Ser Mandel, "I am in need of friends, Ser, but do not think me desperate." The snap of the door behind her was the sweetest sound she'd ever heard. She strode into the hall, fierce and proud of herself.

Her predawn devotions were about as fulfilling as they tended to be; small recitations and rhymes. She said her words at her altars, but the motion was more practiced than felt today. She lit incense for the Mother, sipped bitter bean brew before the Wandering Silver Father. Even this early, the temple was filled with pilgrims and transients and a few worshippers of noble stock. She gave polite smiles to familiar faces, a wrinkled old Lady from Clan Brazton, the wild Warbear's Lady Wife of Starlight Shore, and others. So many faces, all of them kind, even the strangers. Though the Gods had failed Lilah again and again, she still liked people. She knew better, but she couldn't stop herself.

Honeyhome was a city of wealth and gold and ostentatious decor, and even the temple reflected that here. Though piety, even poverty was a value dear to the Gods, the temples were run by men and men could be purchased. The High Oblate here was a twisted-looking little man in his forties. His dark hair avoided the center of his head, as if his thoughts themselves drove the hairs away with their foulness. Long strands had been combed over his shining pate, above deep-set eyes so brown they were almost black. A scraggly, greasy beard reached the little priest's waist, and you could smell the odor of his body as he crept and sauntered from patron to guest to supplicant.

No matter who the High oblate spoke to, his performance was unaltered: Protestations of poverty as he motioned from marble pillar to gilded post. When he cornered Lilah, his breath reeked of garlic, his eyes slid toward her hips, and his voice was a rough whisper, "Appearances of grandeur are expensive to maintain." Lilah noted the thick chain of gold around his neck. A white-filmed tongue traced dry lips, and he continued, "Even a few silvers can help us serve the needy and maintain the temple, m'Lady." She didn't even have to politely decline, the parasite detached itself when a plumper host stepped into the temple: Queen Natasha and her retainers.

Queen Natasha was a vision. Silk and brocades of her family red and green were swirled with flowers of Artus blue. Sapphires cut to catch every mote of sparkling light lay on her graceful neck, linked by chains of polished yellow gold. Lilah had never seen the Queen in person before. Natasha Harlock was taller and thinner than Lilah, but Lilah thought she was the most glamorous looking woman she'd ever seen. Her face was lean and beautiful, with wide, kind eyes. Though she was almost immediately surrounded, the Queen remained calm, her guardsmen kept the throngs at a distance. The slithering High Oblate of Honeyhome sidled toward the Queen, leaving Lilah behind, but he couldn't get through the gathered commons. The impoverished shoved back and forth for a mere glimpse of the Queen.

This sudden cloudburst of activity was all the opportunity Lilah needed to scatter. She had fulfilled her obligations here. After her uncomfortable morning, she looked forward to some time with Neal and Theasa. The low, sad tones of Ser Mandel's words came rushing back to her, *"What kind of man do you want him to be?"*

She was pressing her way through the gathering masses, when a heavy boot came down on her brown leather shoe. She stumbled, nearly finding herself on the cobblestones, as they suddenly flew toward her face, grey stone, black with grime and grease and grit. A pair of strong hands wrapped themselves around her waist, and like she weighed nothing at all, she was set right once more.

A great pale tower of a boy stood over her, blue eyes fixed on her face. A solemn face was fixed on hers and slowly, he spoke as recognition overtook both of them, "Lady... Stagg. Are you unharmed?"

A flurry of pink palms knocked the young knight away. Lilah's weak slaps did the boy knight no harm, but she would not let Hale Torchbearer lay hands on her. "I am fine, Ser Hale. You were most knightly, thank you." Her disgust was barely hidden as she shoved him away from her.

Offended, the knight downturned his narrow mouth, his grim face looking even grimmer. "Apologies, my intention was not to harm. I did not know that your intent was to be trampled."

Lilah's appetite for weak-willed knights, oath-breakers like these, was at its end. Reuben, Ser Mandel, this Ser Hale; who was taking marital knowledge of his sworn Lord's wife; it seemed to Lilah that knights were nearly as useless as the gods who had anointed them. She simply sighed under her breath, "I am perfectly capable of keeping myself untrampled, Ser. Perhaps it is best you maintain your own oaths, and leave me to my own defense."

She shoved off, through the crowd, fuming. The smallfolk were less densely gathered outside the temple, and by the time she had passed a handful of smaller buildings, she was all but alone once more. In the early dawn hour, silver sunbeams broke the eastern horizon, one by one. These great beacons of silver light filled the east, slowly growing thicker and wider until they simply grew into one another. A silver shield of sunlight dyed the low shadows long and black. Men became fearsome giants, ashwood spearshafts grew into impossibly tall and thin spires, and the black spreading fingers of the wood surrounding the Great Gate Garden clutched the High Dome of

Hivehall like a hand holding a great ivory heart, beating as the breeze rattled ebony fingers. Something about the black of the shadows on the dome made Lilah's own heart beat uneasily.

Across the yard, a few of the young Lords and knights who were scheduled for competition this morning had begun to gather. Bedecked in indigo and silver, the young Lord of Talon Bay, Mortimer Osprey unleashed arrow after arrow into a target. Each shaft struck the target in a practiced spot, splitting the straw and canvas and sinking in the wood backing with a solid thunk. Perched beside him, a big grey sea raptor preened itself fussily. Two young men in green clacked training swords together, deliberately stepping and swinging to warm cold muscles into action. Lord Hinric and Ser Hugo Saddler. Knights and retainers she hardly recognized held shields and pads, scoured mail and sharpened swords. A skinny boy in a blue jerkin nearly ran her down, carrying a huge whetstone in a canvas sling as he stumbled under a weight that nearly equaled his own. A grim knight in a feathery mantle and owl-shaped helm she didn't recognize caught Lilah's gaze. This strange owl watched from the sidelines, but did nothing. Lilah didn't recognize his armor, nor the red and black standard he bore. The great yellow eyes on his helm filled Lilah with a deep discomfort.

Before she could think of this man further, a slightly familiar voice called her name. Lilah saw a Malbes Guardsman, tall and thin, waving his arms to gain her attention. She did not recall his name, though he had reminded her repeatedly. Lilah simply thought of him as "Broomstick" as he was that sort of a painful thin creature. She smiled, though she was truly in no place to deal with such an interruption.

"M'lady, Lady Lilah! Hello! Greetings." Broomstick practically bounced on the balls of his feet, as he jogged up to her, his scaled mail clanking loudly, "Thank the Gods I caught you. Have you seen Bertrand? He went missing last night at the tavern. Didn't show up for duty this mornin'. I told the commander that he was shittin' himself sick" he caught himself, and paused, "Pardon me bluntness, m'lady. But I lied to the commander and got Old Carys to cover for him." He shook a spear toward the staircase that had been his post over the tourney. A frail elder with a drooping grey mustache dozed on a stool, leaning hard on his spearshaft. "I got him covered today, sure, but I cannae keep the commander away forever. You haven't seen him, have you?"

"B-Bertrand?" She stuttered politely, as it slowly clicked together in her mind. "The other guard! The one with the…" Lilah trailed off, unsure of how to politely refer to the enormous boil on the missing guardsman's nose.

"Great big red fuckin' tumor on his nose, yeah." He nodded, "He's mean and ugly, but he's my best mate. Have you seen him?"

She racked her brain, and felt her heart sink. For all of her talk of love and compassion for the smallfolk, the faces of the guards around her all tended to blend together. Even a face as distinctive as Bertrand's was one of many. Lilah was exhausted, too tired to lie, so she answered honestly. "I don't know, I'm sorry. But, if I see him, I'll let him know you are concerned." She gave a tight, dismissive smile and breezed away. He cried once, her name, in an agonized moan. She slipped past dozy Old Carys, and hurried up the spiral stair of the borrowed tower. Hurriedly, she took dancer-light steps upward, always climbing.

Halfway up that spiral stair, the arched wooden door that led to their borrowed chambers swung open about an inch. Lilah had specifically heard it click shut when she left this morning. *A solid little thunk when I left Ser Mandel behind, I heard it plain as day.* After a carefully considered moment, Lilah pushed through the door as her babies were in that apartment, and the black void of death itself would not keep her away.

Lilah shouldered through the door, ready to defend Neal, Theasa and even horrible old Lady Grete with her very life. There was, however, no dragon, devil or fierce beast. On the other side of the door, Lady Grete stood, having a conversation with a handsome young lordling.

He was tall, with a wolfish grin. Brown hair fell in locks to his chin, with a single streak of white. He wore a night blue cloak of soft wool, and black ringmail of the Elder Iron. The shaggy black hound of Clan Curr was stitched, sprinting across the cream of his overcoat. Hullen Curr IV was standing in her foyer.

Lady Grete gave her wide, sharp lie of a smile. She placed a narrow hand on the table beside her, trying to show a casual sense of comfort and failing outright. "Lady Lilah, I don't believe you've met Hullen Curr the Fourth, have you?"

Lilah shook her head, as her heart crept somewhere into her knees, "N-no, My lady, though his own Lady Wife spoke ever so highly of him."

Curr turned toward her, his usually jovial grin gone grey and empty, "Lady Lilah, I don't mean to be rude, or confrontational, but I believe you and I need to have a private conversation." As such, he gave Lady Grete a curt nod, and beckoned Lilah into the hallway. Lady Grete was rarely left speechless, but today, she found no words. Lilah stood silent a moment, looking at her mother-by-law, whose thin face had gone gawking. With the shrug of a woman who has no fight left in her, she followed the Curr boy into the hall.

He may only want to talk to me about the affair his wife is having with his best friend, not the heart of his ancient sword that I somehow seem to have stolen.

As Lilah followed Curr upward further, toward his own chambers, she couldn't help but notice that Snowsnarl still hung from his sword belt, ice blue and threatening.

Even without the magic, that blade is more than sharp enough to carve my heart out before Reuben even noticed I had gone.

She hoped the boy wouldn't do that. He probably wouldn't, not here. She silently followed, and after a moment she stopped on the stone steps and called up to her new companion or captor or whatever Hullen Curr was in the moment. "My Lord, I apologize, but I will not go another step until you explain to me what exactly you require of me."

Curr sighed, looking at his armor and sword and thickly registering the threat he presented to a lone, unarmed, fairly small woman, "Oh Gods! The apologies are mine alone, Lady Lilah!" A charming smile, broad and a wee bit wild, clicked into place on his face, and suddenly Lilah was put to mind of a dog wearing a muzzle. "I just require a private conversation of-of a sensitive manner, and your Lady Grete didn't seem likely to give the space needed."

His motion was gentle, controlled, as he extended his right hand toward Lilah, a chivalric gesture to help Lady Lilah up the stairs. Lilah raised her own little rosy hand, a smile crossing Lilah's face, buck teeth on plump red lips. His right hand viced around hers, iron hard. Harder than she expected, harder than was reasonable. His twin on the left gripped her elbow tightly, and the smile faded from Hullen Curr's face. With the lightest pressure, he dangled her backward, her tiny frame seconds from dashing apart, tumbling down the hundreds of hard stone stairs. His eyes were sad, as he drew her close. His muscles tensed, coiled springs ready to throw her, shove her, hundreds of feet down. "I'm sorry, Lady Lilah."

There was a high keening sound, like the scrape of metal on a whetstone. Lilah saw a rush of rust and claws drop from one of the high timbers above Curr. Hullen's hands released Lilah and she managed to skitter to the safety of a bannister. The little rusty kobold, Verm, was slashing his little red arms and snapping sharp teeth into the head and face of Hullen Curr IV.

The heir to the Wylde tottered. He swayed, and for one breathless moment, he hung weightless above gravity. His wide pale eyes pleaded, his strong hands reached for Lilah, and she barely snatched his trembling wrist.

Years of abuse, pain and anger bubbled up. Another knight had tried to hurt her, and this one would be the last. Finger by finger, Lilah released Hullen's wrist and the weight of his body returned.

There were sixty-eight stone steps between where Hullen Curr the Fourth had held Lilah and the marbled floor at ground level. Crunching, tumbling, breaking and bleeding, the handsome heir to the Wylde had managed to wetly thud to a stop on a landing after fifty-three sharp stone steps. A dark pool of crimson blood spread below Curr's trembling mouth as ragged breaths misted pink.

A thin little voice under Lilah cracked, "Verm… protect Lady Lilah."

Below them, a woman's scream pierced the early morning.

Numb, faraway and utterly at peace, Lilah answered, "We protect each other." Curr shuddered and coughed below them, as a staccato of steps began to flood upward from the ground floor. Guards and men and maids and aid were well on their way. She could hear kind-hearted Broomstick shouting.

"Always." The little squirrel's voice was as hard as her heart.

HARTWIN IV

"You can't be kind just when you're happy."

Hartwin did not want to be in the tower. If all things were equal, he would be more than happy to be dozing in Joelle's pavilion, listening to her snore softly on his chest. Instead, he was lying in a sterile, borrowed bed. In the room beside him, the low sounds of motion through the wall indicated that his brother had risen and was beginning to busy himself for the tourney. Today, Hugo would deal with the strange Bird Woman from the southern country of H'ro Cratis. A pilgrim from a desert land, she had gained a remarkable reputation as a mercenary of great skill and honor. Hugo should dismantle her with little effort, in Hartwin's opinion, but he supposed they held the matches for a reason. The blanket wrapped around Hart's legs took a few twisting kicks to loosen, but he managed to roll out of bed before the silver sun had broken too far above the treeline outside his window.

The tall ginger boy splashed tepid water on his face, hoping the basin could help him wake. It did, but not nearly as much as he'd have liked. He dabbed his face with the linen beside the basin, and took a look in the small mirror on the table. He hadn't shaved since arriving in Honeyhome, and a smattering of orange-brown bristles had begun to spread over his cheeks and chin. He ought to have shorn them right then and there, but he felt wild and decided to wait. Hartwin pulled a thin cotton night shirt over his bare chest, and relaced his breeches. In the warmth like this, Hartwin preferred to sleep without clothes.

Dressed enough for family, the bleary-eyed Hartwin staggered into the shared common area. The Malbes' servants had produced their usual impressive spread, somehow delivering it totally silently in the dark. Bread, fruit, boiled eggs, sausages, dried meats, cheese and other little delicacies from the farms, fields and kitchens of the Honeyhome were spread on the center table, a bounty ready to be devoured. Hartwin pulled an especially plump sausage from the plate and popped it into his mouth. The burst of fat and spice as the skin broke between his teeth satisfied some primal desire deep in the pit of Hart's stomach.

A deep laugh from an unseen corner of the room set Hartwin to jumping, "Don't let yer mother see you eating with yer fingers, we'll both be scolded for your bad manner." His father, High Lord Byrony Saddler, smiled broadly at him. In truth, Lord Byrony did everything broadly, he was a very broad man. A heavy brow, wide shoulders, huge hands with palms like oars, and a thick, brawny torso gave Lord Saddler the impression of a great beastly brute. Even Hartwin was the first to admit that this was an unfair assessment, for all his flaws, his father was no fool and no brute. The old man speared a sausage of his own on the point of his knife, before taking a hearty bite. "They are mighty good, though."

Hartwin bristled at his Lord Father's presence, but swallowed his immediate annoyance. "They're not half bad, Good morning, Father." He gave a lazy half smile, and a lazy half wave, procuring a plate and stacking sausage, bread and a selection of berries on it. Hartwin settled into a chair and resolved to eat in tired, sullen silence. But then his father smashed the quiet.

"Looks to be another warm one, no breeze coming off of the bay this morning." The old man's grey eyes were fixed on the clouds on the window, drifting lazily through the sapphire summer sky.

The weather was not a topic of conversation that Hartwin was overly interested in. He and Prince Talor had some incredibly productive discussions last night, and the Young Colt was more focused on his future than the sky outside. "It does certainly appear that way, yes Father."

His father gave a dissatisfied grunt through his nose, "Awright then, I'll be leaving my pride aside then, Hart, I need your opinion."

Hartwin gave his own little nose-grunt, "Of course, my Lord." He raised his gaze from his plate. "I'm always at your disposal." His father frequently sought Hartwin's counsel, sure, but that was almost always in an official capacity. Hart was one of dozens of advisors to his father in the Lord's Hall, but here, it was only the two of them. His father wanted his opinion and his alone. Pride in that was a foreign, funny sort of sensation, but Hart vowed to make the most of it.

Lord Byrony's face was still as a windless plain, and his voice was low and gentle, "Your Lady Mother arranged this whole damn tourney to get the younger prince to meet your sister, you know?"

Hartwin nodded, "I had an inkling, yes."

They both chuckled, the low rumbling laugh was one of the few things Hart had inherited from his father. Concern was knit over his heavy brow, "The Prince. The boy prince, Vernus. You were there last night, Hartwin. What happened?"

Hartwin pursed his lips and exhaled, tension building through his shoulders and neck. He popped a strawberry in his mouth and found it surprisingly tart. "To be true, Father, I wasn't in the room when it started, I was out on the balcony."

The grin on his father's face was like a wicked child with a wicked secret, "With Lady Bridge." Hartwin's face must have betrayed his surprise, but the old horse lord just kept his smirk, "I'm old, I'm not dead, boy. A Lord has to have his ways." The point of his dagger pierced the center of another spiced sausage, and he continued, "We'll circle back to your pink lady, trust me, but continue."

Hartwin's stomach sunk, but he did as he was bid, "Well, Lady Joelle and I were having a discussion–"

"Necking." His father interrupted.

"*Talking.*" Hartwin spat, "We heard Harlow scream, and ran on back to the ballroom. Hugo was standing on the hellheart, and about ready to skewer the two Grey Guard." Hartwin stood and poured himself a cup of beer, weak stuff, just enough alcohol to kill the worms. He sipped it, "Hugo loves a scrap, I know, but Harlow was *shaken*, My Lord. I believe her. If Harlow says that the boy touched her inappropriately, I don't know why she'd lie."

Lord Byrony nodded, "Have you taken this boy-Prince's measure, Hart? I haven't met him, but your mother claims he hung the sun and raised the mountains."

"I should not speak ill of the royal family." Hart's stomach was in knots.

"You should also do as your liege lord *and* your father commands." Byrony stood, crossing to his eldest son, and laid a heavy, but gentle hand on the boy's back, "I am not asking you to speak ill, I am asking for truth, Hartwin. What kind of man is this Prince Vernus?"

When Hartwin started talking, the flood came and he found that he could not stop. He was no longer the suave, cold Heir to the Goldengrass, he was an upset little boy relaying a story to his dad. "He is goddamn garbage, Father. He is thin and sickly. He dresses like he's blind and no one around him has the nerve to tell him." The words came faster, "He is lecherous and gluttonous and will not be satisfied with whichever girl he chooses. Prince Vernus is a vile. cruel little man who creates chaos and pain and then hides behind the sword of his bodyguard and his crown to avoid consequence." The fire left him as fast as it had filled him, and he defeatedly finished, "In short, I would not like Harlow to marry this boy, no."

Lord Byrony guffawed loudly, "Well, shit. I guess I demanded honesty."

Hartwin felt a sheepish flush rise in his cheeks at this rare slip of control. "Apologies, that was more blunt than was appropriate."

"Maybe, but at least it was straightforward. Too many men try to avoid offendin' you, and refuse to say anything that means anything." Thick cords of muscle tensed in the old man's neck. He shuffled across the room like a depressed landslide, before exhaustedly dropping back into his violet chair. "I don't suppose you have a way of tellin' your Lady Mother not to have Harlow marry this boy, do you?"

"Between Hugo's sword and my words, I don't think that's all that likely, *Dad*." It felt queer referring to the old man so informally, but Hartwin was trying.

"You would be shocked at the things your mother can smooth over." His beady eyes fixed on Hart, heavy with worry. "Hart, is this boy gonna be dangerous for Harley?"

Harlow marrying the Prince would be a tremendous boon to Hart's political ambitions, a direct family link between Clan Artus and Clan Saddler. His need for the High Executor's chair was one of the driving forces of his life, but handing Harlow to Vernus seemed monstrous. His sister was a fragile thing, and that boy would take her apart by measure, just for his own amusement. There was no question, Hartwin nodded.

A cloud of black melancholy settled over father and son. For a few long moments, they soaked in it, snapping sausages in sullen silence. The sausages were somewhat less delicious suddenly. After a long sigh, his father spoke again, the mischievous edge back on his speech. "Joelle Bridge, then?"

Hartwin's face burned red, "I've been seeing her on and off for some time, yes."

Lord Byrony was the cat who had eaten the duckling, grinning wide, "Oh, I know." He folded his hands, "She's a Lady with lands and no brothers or heirs, Hart. She's sworn to the Mirebreakers. They're not just gonna give up that land if you marry her."

Hartwin rankled, "I… It's not about the lands, father."

A familiar warmth spread across his father's face, "Then I'll sit down with Marten Mirebreaker and figure it out. Coin, lands, men, whatever the boy wants, we'll make arrangements."

Hartwin arched an eyebrow, cautious, "...To what end?"

"You love her."

"I do." Hartwin's cheeks were embers of burning red.

"Hart, you aren't a nice person. I love you dearly, but you're not." Byrony chuckled, "Lady Joelle is kind. She's smarter than you, too. Love is transformative, son. Or at least it can be." His eyes were far away again, wistful, "I like the person you are when you're around her, and I think you do too."

For once, the old man had the right of it. Hartwin was self-aware enough to know that he tended to be hard-hearted and hard-headed. Joelle made him feel a touch calmer, gentler. A lord could stand to be gentle, he supposed. Hartwin could struggle with people sometimes. He preferred the command to the request and that often chafed people.

Across the room, the old man continued, "The money doesn't matter. Clan Bridge and Clan Saddler both have more than we could ever need in half a hundred lifetimes." His voice grew a little weaker, the boisterous bass dropping out, "You are more than old enough to know that your Mother and I didn't wed out of love."

Hartwin snorted, "I am acutely aware."

Lord Byrony gave a sad smirk before hanging his big, bald head, "If you are, you know why I'm not going to hand Harley to the prince. You know why I'm gonna move heaven and earth to let my son marry the girl he loves and not some girl that will just expand the herd."

In that moment, in the low silver sunlight, Hartwin saw his father not as the beastly oaf, but as he was, a tired, solid old plough horse. Never stopping, always pushing forward, holding his family and his nation together, even as his yoke rubbed his flesh raw and bloody.

The old man laughed to himself, before Hartwin found himself standing before his father. He took the old man's calloused hands in his own and bid his father rise. It had been almost a decade, but Hartwin embraced his father. The Young Colt managed to keep his tears back, just barely, as he stammered, "T-thank you."

When they'd parted, the chaos took his father again, "I don't mean you shouldn't try to expand the herd, though. I'm not getting any younger, you know, I could use a grandchild. Your Uncle Hinric isn't likely to, and Gods know if I'll ever get Hugo to love any girl as well as he loves his sword."

Hugo's flat voice came from his chamber door, "Find me a girl that's half as sharp as my sword and I'll marry her without complaint." He strode, mail and silks in place, helm under his arm. The broad chested young night stopped at the table, piled with its delicious spread. Like his father and brother, he immediately gravitated toward the sausages and popped one in his mouth, grunting affirmatively, "S'not bad."

Hartwin ignored his brother, "I still have to ask her."

Hugo piped up again, "Joelle? That girl is head over heels for you. She asked me an' Doyle where you were, soon as she got there."

Hartwin's mouth gaped as his father sniggered into his open palm. "How much have you heard?"

"Somethin' about how the boy prince is a pillock, which, yeah, accurate. And then there was bonding and hugging, I decided to intervene before you two decided to start singin'." Hugo sliced a fat, red third off of an apple and ate it directly from his knife. "D'you want me to kill this boy-prince then?"

The broad knight in green was not joking. Hartwin did wish Hugo's direct, simple solution was a viable one, but murder rarely was as simple as it seemed. Before Hartwin could explain the issues with that thought process, Lord Byrony spoke, "Not just yet."

Hartwin wasn't sure if old Lord Byrony was joking. Every lord has dug his share of graves, Hartwin has no illusions about that, but picturing his genial old father ordering a murder was like a horse writing a letter, unlikely and the result was sure to be an especially enormous mess. The tired old lord crushed a crust of bread to crumbs in a thick hand, letting the grains tumble to his plate like sand in an hourglass.

"For the best anyway." Hugo intoned monotonically, "I'd rather like to win this tourney. Seein' as it's for his birthday, they'll probably cancel it if he dies." Hugo poured his own cup of beer, frothing yellow-thin. The boy sniffed it, determined it acceptable and quaffed it in one quick go. "Speaking of, 'm meeting Uncle Hinric and Doyle in the yard, so I best be off." He gave his courtesies, and disappeared out the door.

Hartwin would soon return to his own chambers and dress, not relishing another hot day in the stands staring at lordlings bashing one another with blunted weapons. He dressed himself in the lightest cottons he could find in his trunks, but his mind was wheeling. There was no way life could be so simple. With the support of Father and his coffers, there was no legitimate reason to keep him from marrying Joelle. If she wanted, of course. That was the rub. As confident as Hugo seemed to be, Hartwin doubted himself. Joelle was a beautiful, intelligent, proud woman, with lands and money all her own. She did not need Hartwin, and that worried him.

The thin brown belt had just snaked around Hartwin's waist when a soft knock came at his door. The sound was quiet, tentative, an incredibly unsure little sound. Hartwin cracked the oak door to find his sister's pale face staring back at him. Harlow looked like she'd slept little, her eyes were heavy and framed by black circles. Her gentle little voice warbled, 'Good morning, Hart." Her auburn locks were a cloud of frizzes framing huge mossy eyes. There was a half smile stuck to her face, an attempt at manners.

Hartwin, who had used a few hours to rise and compose himself, greeted his sister warmly, "Harley! Good morning." She stepped through the threshold, grunting softly. The petite Saddler daughter was still all practiced grace as she settled herself in the carved wooden chair beside the carved wooden desk in this chamber. She was dressed in her nightgown and patched old green and purple woolen robe, a garment of extreme age and sentimental value. It was best to let Harlow have her sentiment.

"I was not planning on attending the tourney this morning. I'll make my way out this afternoon, but I'm not feeling well." Her tone was thin, worn.

Hartwin nodded, "Of course. By all means, rest."

"Thank you." She bowed her head politely, folding her hands over one another.

Hart looked over his baby-sister-by-minutes, taking the measure of her and losing enthusiasm about the way she was coming up. "Was there more, Harl?"

She nodded, "I wanted to make sure you thank Lady Bridge for me, as you're like to see her before I am." Even exhausted, her eyes held a knowing mirth, as she had found the energy to tease her brother, "Her aid after the incident last night was most appreciated. Isn't is fortunate that she was right there! She's always around just when you want her, isn't she?"

"Not near as much as I'd like." Hart admitted, somewhat sheepish.

She rose, smirking, "Oh, I know. You want *aaaaaaaaall of heeeeerrr.*" Her voice went sing-song as she stood, "I am going to attempt to sleep a few more short hours before mother-"

Hartwin stopped her, and though he wished to let her leave, to speak of any other matter, he simply had to know. His voice was grim and firm when he spoke, "What happened last night, Harlow?"

"I had one of my incidents, is all, Hart." The words were practiced. Those words belonged to their mother. They were a lie, sweetened to what their Lady Mother wanted the world to know. "I shouldn't have gotten so overexcited. There was music and wine, it was all so very grand."

A slow burning rage was returning to Hart, a volcanic magma in his belly churning as it had when he had first seen Prince Vernus speak to his sister unkindly. It had faded over the middling hours, but it had not subsided, and now it threatened eruption. He swallowed it for the moment, "I don't strictly think that's true, what happened, Harley-girl? Did that prince touch you?"

She nodded, slowly at first, her pretty eyes fixed on some point Hartwin could not see. As she spoke, the tempo of her nodding head sped up, matching her words, "He was very familiar at first, overly so. I was wont to forgive it." She took a sharp inhale, "He is the king's son, after all. And to be true, I didn't find him unhandsome. When he touched my hand, or my knee, I did not scold him. When he unexpectedly kissed me, I did not recoil. I was polite and gracious, even when he may have faltered in returning the favor."

Hartwin gently restored his sister to the chair. She had gone tense, stiff as a fencepost. "That's good, Harlow. You were very polite."

She continued, her cadence and tone unbroken, still miles from this little warm chamber. "Thank you. I did as mother bid, I did as *you* bid. I put on my mask and I smiled. I was the perfect chaste maiden. And that boy tried to make me his *whore.*" Anger smoldered on the edges of that final word as Harlow gripped the hem of her robe between painted nails.

The sausage in Hartwin's stomach had petrified to brick. "I am so sorry, Harlow. I did not know he was so–"

She continued, whether he was listening or not, "He slid his hand under my smallclothes in front of half a hundred lords. He touched me in a place that I have been told is only for my husband. He did it without thinking, and without care for me, because he simply wanted to, Hart." She finally turned to face him, tears were in the corners of her eyes, "I told you that I did not like the look of that boy. I told you, Hartwin. And you made me go."

He could find no words.

She still had plenty, "And then, when I needed you, you weren't there. I had to rely on *Hugo*." She sat forward, suddenly angry. Her posture was nearly as indignant as her tone, "To be true, he did more than you could have. But Hartwin, you threw me to the wolves and then you *left.*"

"I was with Joelle."

"You were already sulking on the balcony when she arrived."

His sister did have the right of it. He had been sullen and selfish.

She sighed, "I love Lady Joelle almost as much as you do, Hartwin. I am glad she was there, and I am truly glad you were with her. I look forward to raven-haired nephews with apple cheeks and freckles." She snorted derisively, "But you dropped me to this boy that you do not know and could not even stay in the room with me."

Tall, lean Hartwin felt two inches tall as his sister elucidated further.

"Like it or not, you are a protector, Hartwin. The women in your life are not granted the agency to do it for ourselves. Give me a sword, and I promise you, that boy will never touch a girl in such a manner again, even if requested." Fire and bile flew from gentle Harlow, "But until that day, I must wait on brothers and fathers and kings. A woman must not defend herself."

There was a hellish crash. Thunder and earthquake and falling roofs and shattering bone shattered their moment of understanding. Something had fallen down the staircase outside their chambers, heavy and hard, violently passing over the small room where the siblings now sat. They sat, idle in shock for a long moment, uncertainty passing between the pair without words. After the final flakes of plaster had drifted from ceiling to floor like so much falling snow, Harlow rose first, taking careful, but rapid steps from Hartwin's bed chamber, through the common area with a bounty of food to break fast. Hartwin followed closely, but when they came to the front door, he placed his shaking hand on the latch before she could.

"At least allow me to defend you here." Hartwin opened the door, and saw butchery.

Identifying the shaking, bloodied mass as Hullen Curr IV had taken Hartwin a moment. The boy's long limbs were twisted into one another, jagged with joints that no man possessed. His scalp of brown hair had gone black with blood, and while Hartwin was no doctor, he could see bits of skull poking through the skin. Hartwin was sure someone had dropped a corpse on his front step, but then Hullen Curr shuddered, coughed, and breathed. Harlow saw and shrieked at the top of her lungs, piercing the early morning silence.

Hartwin knelt beside the young heir to the Wylde and spoke to him gently, laying a hand on his chest. "Curr… Curr, can you hear me? It's, uh, Hartwin Saddler. I think you've had a fall." Curr's eyes did not focus on him, though they were open. If Curr could hear and comprehend him, he could not respond. Blood trickled from the corner of the boy's mouth and stained Hartwin's breeches, red on calfskin.

Thankfully, Learner Powell had been on his way to examine Harlow after last night's incident, so a healer's arrival was prompt. Hellendre, their mother's witch, followed shortly after, veiled as she often went in public. When the boy was carted away, he was still breathing. Hartwin heard Learner Powell tell Hellendre that "was a blessing". *If that was a blessing, let me remain accursed,* Hartwin mused to himself.

News travels fast, and bad news thrice-so, as such, within the hour, the tragic fall of Hullen Curr had become the talk of the gathered nobility. And as gathered is notoriously fickle, it had entirely replaced the talk yesterday's two tourney deaths. Hart managed to take some of the morning with Harlow, who he had hoped to shield from most of the horrible gore. Her stunned silence showed he had failed her there, too. It was later, when a draught had lulled Harlow to sleep that Hartwin and Hellendre dared leave her chambers for the silence of the common area.

It was only then that Hellendre removed her lace veil, burnt orange to match her dress of orange and pale coffee-and-cream. On her skin of verdant green, she was a vision of summer fields. Her jewelry today was coral and aquamarine, a stud in her nose and several in each ear. The cut of her dress was low, exposing her sternum and shapely chest. She was tired, near as exhausted as Harlow had appeared.

"I was unkind to you in a moment of tension last night, Hellendre. That was wrong of me." He let the words hang, and when she did not react, he added that sting, "I am sorry."

Her soft lips remained pursed, and hurt still seemed to seep from her very pores, but she did speak, "You were a real shit-sack last night, Hart." Her big brassy eyes poured at him, wounded. "Your puffy pink princess shows up, and suddenly, I stop bein' your friend and start bein' the help. I'm not blind to it." She shook her head sadly, horns of brass catching the mid-day's light, "I've been through it before, you can't *really* be friends with you highborn folk, but I guess I expected more from you, Hartwin."

Finally, Hartwin shrugged, "I seem to have disappointed many of the women close to me last evening. In my defense, I'm young and in love." He smirked, and Hellendre sighed at him.

"I want to stay mad, but I was already on my way up with a splendid gift for you." She stood, and began rummaging through the satchel she always kept on her hip, "Even before that poor broken pup tumbled into our laps."

As she rearranged the vast contents of her bag, Hartwin asked the question that had been haunting him since he watched the Curr boy draw that ragged pink breath, "Is Hullen Curr going to live, Hellendre? You're a healer. You... tended to him."

Her hands of green paused in their duty for a moment, as the hellheart went somber. "Well, he was breathing when the Learners took him. That means something." Outside, a lone bird's call rose over the sounds of the far off tourney, somewhere, Hugo was likely trading blows in his match. "But, I won't lie to you, that boy was a mess. He might die in bed with the best care in the world looking after him in an hour. He might live. If he does, I don't know how he won't be crippled, if not blind or deaf or a lackwit. He may never walk again. I don't know, Hart. It's as bad as I've ever seen."

They both sat in silence for a moment, before Hartwin spoke, "But, what about your magic?" He paused, and regathered his thoughts, each of them rolling over his face like a breeze through plainsgrass, "Not yours, specifically, well, maybe, I don't know, but magic, some sort of magic could help him, right? Mend his bones, fix his eyes, what-have-you."

A haze of unease settled across the face of Hellendre as she pulled her hands out of her satchel and folded them neatly over one another, "I know a poultice that could knit that boy's broken arm. I know one that could put every one of his shattered ribs to right. Better healers than me could fix his eyes, or let him hear more perfectly than he did the day he drew his first breath. Mages and priests have helped men with broken minds, destroyed by violence or by malady." Her huge brass eyes locked on Hartwin, without pupils, they were just pools of liquid metal, swirling and knowing. "There's even men who can restore life to the flesh that life has left behind. Sometimes it even resembles life. In all these things, there is a price, though. To both healer and patient." Her green fingers slowly brushed one of the curving horns that jutted from her hairline. "Some of us wear the price of power on our bodies, some on our minds or our very souls. Magic is a fickle mistress. To do all the things that boy needs to live, all at once, with magic? The price would be incalculable, there's no telling what might result to both Hullen and whomever tried to help him. It's better to let the Learners do it with their herbs and chants and surgeries. You put too many nails into a piece of wood, and you stop nailin' it together and start hammerin' it apart, you know?"

"Oh." On its own, in the silence, the word hung, this noxious little sadness neither person wanted to acknowledge. Hart asked the next question, difficult as it was, "Better to let the boy die, even then?"

"It's best not to speak on such things." A toss of the hair sent her ginger locks dazzling in the sunlight, "Besides, I said that I brought you a gift, didn't I? Well, actually, I have two gifts, just for you." She gave a wicked grin, "Besides me and a few of your Stallion Guardsmen and yer Lord Grandfather, no one even has the foggiest idea about it."

Hartwin was not a man who enjoyed games with a power imbalance, unless he held the high ground. Here, he was wading through the muck and he did not care for it. Hellendre had piqued his curiosity, but letting her know that would be an admission of loss. Utterly unacceptable. The Young Colt arched an eyebrow and remained silent.

Hellendre pouted, "Fine, be no fun. Well, my first gift is in your grandfather's dungeon, chained to a wall." This shocked Hartwin, and it must have shown in his eyes, because Hellendre's grin only became more wicked, "He's grey and bent and the Stallions may have broken a few of his more fragile pieces, but, he's the one who killed our farm boys back in the thicket. I saw him through the dead boy's eyes."

Hartwin nodded, "A bandit knight for Hugo or father to execute, fine work, but hardly a gift for me."

The pretty green demon-girl snorted a laugh, "That's what I thought, until I found what he was hiding, clinging to like grim, grim death." She reached into her satchel and slowly removed a bundle of brown rags, roughly the size and shape of a dinner plate of pie-pan. Brown, stained rags, smattered with stains of dark red blood, were passed from Hellendre's soft palms to Hartwin's shaking fingers. Bit by bit, he wound back the rags and saw gold. Not just any gold, imperial gold, royal gold, Artus gold. A crown sat in Hartwin's hands. The crown that was to be placed on the head of Prince Vernus's betrothed tomorrow, just before the final match of the tourney.

"This is–" the words tangled and caught in his throat, "This isn't, it can't be"

"It can and it is." Her eyes were fixed on him, "The Grey Guard is keepin' it quiet, but I heard from a scullery who is cousin to the squire that's sleeping with Lady Bara's bedmaid, the low news network, you know, well all the same, I heard that the crown was stolen from the vault sometime in the middle of the night and the King and your Lord Grandfather are furious."

"Holy fuck." Hartwin's airs of nobility had gone. "Y-you should have taken this to the Grey Guard or the king or Father... Why in the hell did you bring it to me, Hellendre?"

"Because the miserable thief asked for you by name, Hart. You wanna go meet Ser Jemes Wyse?"

A memory of perfume tickled the back of Hartwin's nose as his jaw set and he nodded.

DRAKE III

"That's the most sickening thing about you, you don't even seem to like the glory you seem to keep stumbling into."

From the top of the tower, he and Ser Darwyn could see the whole of the city spread below them. Though dawn was rapidly approaching, pockets of activity still burbled. Songs drifted drunkenly over the embers of campfires and the snores of those less hardy. The edges of silver sunlight were breaking over the bay, and the green-grey leaves of the trees danced below the pair, a rolling cascade of waves to match those of the sea, down the cliff. If the circumstances were better, this view would have bordered on the divine. As it stood, Drake was afraid of what would come out of his sword brother's mouth.

Darwyn looked exactly as a man who watched his brother die violently hours ago ought to, broken. The Darwyn Tymm's face usually held a smile so large it approached inappropriate, but here, in the pre-dawn light of Cat's Hour, the Jester Knight was dour. Tymm took a long draw from a bottle of something that smelled like turpentine, swallowed his vomit, and spoke, "Pisswater."

Drake had no time for games, "You're supposed to be in your chambers." He didn't know if he would be able to outmatch Ser Darwyn normally, but felt fairly confident that he could deal with this drunken mess wearing his coat. He had no armor, no visible weapons and was swaying between swigs of some Lowland juniper gin.

"I'm supposed to be one of the six greatest knights in the land." He half-chuckled, half-sobbed, "Was an oaken door and a ploughboy with a spear really going to keep me tied down?" His soft brown eyes almost pleaded at Canar.

"They are trying to protect you." Canar sat heavily. "This night will never end, I swear."

"It's not me they are protecting, Ducky." He offered the bottle to Canar, who shook his head. "You need it, Drake. Night like tonight."

Drake pulled his leather gloves from his hands. Tooled with swirling smoke and dyed a dark mulberry, they had been a parting gift from his mother. While they were very fine, he'd be much happier with his old brown gloves and his worried looking little mother. He clutched the neck of the tall green glass bottle and swigged. Burning pitch and pine flooded his mouth and nostrils, and even the sinuses under his eyes. Drake coughed, sputtering the words, "...Pisswater."

Tymm laughed, taking the bottle back in his shaking hand, dusted with brown freckles. He took his own drink, and swallowed it without issue. "We're ruled by spoiled rich children, Drake."

"I am fairly sure that has been the case as long as there have been rules. Kings talk, men fight and work and die. You and I just so happen to be a pair of men." There was a sadness in his voice, a longing far off.

"Kings used to be men. Proper men." Darwyn gave Drake a look that chilled him and excited him, before clasping Drake's bare hand in his, warm and calloused. "Brothers... shouldn't die for men like these. Born or sworn."

"Then why did *you* swear?" Drake tried his hardest to chill Darwyn in return, but felt foolish.

"I didn't understand the duty when I did, I was just a boy." He took a long, bitter swig, "And great swaths of the less enjoyable obligations were kept in the shadows, weren't they?"

Canar nodded, blushing at their continued closeness, "It certainly seems so..."

"Women? Hah!" He laughed bitterly, "I can give up women, any day! An' I never wanted my father's lands or his castle, those-those were always for Jack..." He trailed off, lost for a long moment at the mention of his brother. "I-I never wanted 'em. I'm glad Josiah is gettin' them."

"Have you spoken to your brother?" Canar had four brothers of his own at home, twice what Tymm had even started with, and now, the two Tymm sons were alone.

"Briefly, he's got so much to deal with. He's the Lord now, he and that Stagg girl will take court at Carnival Hall." His voice was hollow, "...never liked her. Fat little gossip that she is."

"To middle sons..." Drake took the bottle and raised it mockingly before another horrible swig.

Drake had barely finished sputtering when he felt two calloused hands on his cheeks, and Ser Darwyn was kissing him. Drake had, admittedly, considered the prospect. And now that it was occurring, it wasn't unpleasant. Darwyn's hands were strong, his body was warm and he smelled like sweat, but in a good way. Almost like a horse after a long day's ride, an acrid sour sort of smell, but not a bad one. The kiss was all passion and fire, two fumbling boys, unsure of what they were doing.

Drake's finger traced up Darwyn's chin, and he tasted the foul Lowland gin. The sad little grey duck broke the kiss, "Stop."

Darwyn looked at him, pleading, "What, hey, Ducky..." He trailed off, before gathering himself, "Drake. ...It's you and me, man. You get it. Through the smiles and the smoke, you see me." His hands had fallen to Drake's cloak, gripping the grey wool. "Smiles and smoke, it's all bullshit, but there's no bullshit here... Please."

The Jester Knight was trying not to sob as he tried to kiss Drake again, and Drake had almost let him. He wanted to kiss Ser Darwyn, not this drunken mess wearing his coat. "No, Dar, not like this, okay?"

Rejection and grief crackled across Darwyn's freckled face, followed by a mournful pang of realization, "We have to kill 'em, Ducky. It's the only way. Vernus is a bad nut, and I don't think the Crown Prince is better. Neither one of 'em should be king."

Drake pulled away, removing the hands from his collar. The drunken Ser Darwyn stumbled after him, still sobbing. "You're drunk."

"The tourney tomorrow, Drake. You could do it. The prince can die in the smoke." Tymm pleaded, but he didn't understand what he was asking for.

The Smoke was sacred. The Smoke was an ancient magic, a ritual of his father
s and their fathers, passed to Drake. He was not its master. He could not control The Smoke, no more than he could control the land he lived on or the seas he swum. The Smoke was the balance of fire, air, water, earth, and effort. Drake looked at his sword brother and spat what came next, "I have given up my lands, my brothers, my sons-to-be. I will not give up my god. I will not profane The Smoke for revenge."

He would leave Darwyn there, letting him sob against the dawn as it devoured the stars. A predatory shriek echoed somewhere in the tree below, as an owl set to its morning meal. Exhaustion clawed at him from all sides and another trying day loomed ahead. The scant few hours of sleep the young knight would manage would need to be enough. He stripped down to his smallclothes and collapsed into the bed he'd been allowed to use. He would sleep only briefly, and he was haunted while he did.

Smiling skulls gave way to smoke that choked. Talons rended, stories ended, a broken sword mended. A pretty boy king, a tentacled thing, mirrored maidens with a broken ring. Smoke of white. Smoke of grey. Smoke of black. The visions painted themselves in smoke of thousand shades, all smoke. A burst bladder of wine, flaming pitch and woodbine, fruit rotted on the vine. spider 'round the moon, spire tumbles to lagoon, always waking just too soon–

It was Shoreshrike who woke him. His lamplight kept low and his touch soft, the big Northman was surprisingly gentle and unsurprisingly terse with details, "The King wants all hands on immediately, no one has said why. You got five minutes, then we're meeting in the hall to draw Day's Command." He stopped, halfway to the bedroom door. Ser Jurgen Shoreshrike swung his big snowy head to Drake, "Uh… Sorry for waking you."

Drake felt sick as he tried to clear his head, shaking his pale blonde shag. He dressed quickly, rough wool breeches, a smoky lavender tunic and his grey cloak. Spinning to the rack near the door was his belt, with sword, dagger and Smoke. Gloves of mulberry leather covered his hands as he went to work. Like an unwanted dawn, the sleepless knight pressed ever on.

Drake hurried his way to the veranda below. It was the same place he had sat with Sozen some hours ago, transformed by daylight. The silver sun set all the dew on the glassy yellow-stone to shining, gilding the entire terrace in daylight and dewdrops. Sozen had beaten him there, the placid, slow blinks of his eyes made Drake wonder if he'd ever left at all. Gnash Selach arrived next, carrying the huge Commander's Tome under his left arm. Even burly Ser Gnash shrugged at its weight. The lineage of the book went back centuries. This was the seven-hundred and sixty-fourth volume. The previous fifty or so were housed in the basement of the Ashen Bastion back in Avalar. Any older than that, and they were shipped off to the care of the Learners in Still Waters. Every day, the Grey Guard drew lots to elect a Commander from their six, and every day, that commander would make an entry in the Commander's Tome. It was an uninterrupted record of all that the men of their fraternity did, stretching back to the very origins of the order.

Drake was no reader, as a practice. He found books to be a chore, most often. However, the summer of his twelfth year, Drake had taken a tumble at a pool of water and broken his left ankle. Boys heal better than almost anything, old Learner Gedon had laughed, and he was right, even now, his ankle didn't bother him. Back then, however, he'd been forced to stay off his feet for a month. It was initially a misery, until his father brought him a gift. Lord Malcom had done much the same sort of injury in his youth, and had been similarly miserable. The curly headed Lord smiled at his son and presented him with a set of old leather books. These were no religious tomes or dry histories. These were songs, and stories and bawdy tales of knights and warriors and adventure. The stories of "Ser Kjellan Ice-Eyes, The Bard-Knight of Barrow-Hall" had been written centuries past, but those were the sort of adventures that Drake imagined the Grey Guard lived every day.

The reality was not quite as grand, but Drake had found the old tome fascinating on the occasions he'd carried it. Whenever he'd drawn command, his time with the book had been a highlight. He had drawn command nine times in the three months he'd been on the Guard, and while that seemed infrequent, statistically speaking at least, Drake didn't mind. He was but a Grey Duckling, content to follow, observe and learn. He appreciated the opportunities to lead, as well, but another part of him was thankful that the most dangerous occurrence on one of his command days was a drunken mummer making japes at Queen Natasha during dinner.

When Selach brought forth the lots from the inside cover, Drake secretly prayed that he would not draw the short. Selach drummed his sturdy fingers on the book impatiently, "Where is everyone? I am dying to get rid of this heavy thing."

"Maybe that's why they feel so late." Sozen intoned, as mild as a warm breeze, "Because you are in such a hurry." His eyes were closed, his legs were crossed, and he clutched a bundle of purple and white nightshade flowers in his hands, "If you stop hurrying, they will be here."

Selach thought on that, screwed up his big face, sending the dark tattoos under his eyes twisting, "Fuck you, if they hurried themselves, they'd be here and I'd be done with this goddamn book."

Drake fidgeted, sworling two small smoke beads over his gloved knuckles. *Did everyone mean Darwyn, as well? Is he still sequestered or is 'all hands on' truly 'all hands?'* He said nothing to his brothers, simply sat on his tongue and waited for the other half of the Guard.

Ser Cole Canden was a big man, and Shoreshrike was even bigger. Though neither of them had taken the time to doff their plate armor, there was no hiding the cacophony of the two massive warriors approaching, barking conversation back and forth. When they had greeted their brothers and settled, Selach spoke again, "Are we doing this without Tymm? Is he still out?"

The stern Old Goat, Canden grunted, "Six is six unless one is dead. Tymm isn't dead. He'll be here." Canden was the oldest of the six, bald as an egg.

Selach groaned querulously, "Your soft heart is noted, Ser Cole."

Sozen opened his midnight sky eyes, "The work might be good for him. Let him focus on The Line, not his loss."

Shoreshrike, eyes like chips of blue diamond, bowed his head, "There's peace in duty."

If Drake were an impartial sort, now might be the time to bring up the fact that Ser Darwyn had openly advocated regicide a mere four hours ago. Drake said nothing. Thankfully, Ser Darwyn slunk onto the veranda like a sly beggar at stewhouse, catching every eye. His arrival removed the temptation from Drake's tongue at least. He mumbled, "Apologies, you would not believe the day I have dealt with."

Drake couldn't tell if he was still drunk or just so drink-sick that it made no difference, but Ser Darwyn Tymm swayed with every step. He had barely dressed himself, his tunic was the same as yesterday's: wine stained and wrinkled with sleep. His eyes were bloodshot, his ginger locks uncombed, and the stink of wine clouded around him. He gave an unsteady smile and quipped, "Were you expecting someone else? I've arrived. Work to be done."

Selach and Canden exchanged a look, but no words. Ser Auberon rose, his eyes of night opening. The Monk Knight circled Tymm, tapping the iron ends of his stave on the smooth yellow cobbles. Sozen breathed so deep that Drake worried that the old monk would end up drunk as well, but after a circle, Ser Auberon was staring at Drake, not Ser Darwyn Tymm. "You are one of us, Ser Drake. Notably silent, however." Those damn eyes like a night sky bored into him, wind through smoke.

His words left his mouth before his mind had sculpted them. "If he says he is ready for duty, he is ready." The young knight spit the next words, "We've got enough children to nursemaid without him acting like one."

Selach laughed, "The Duck gets it." He set the six lots in the little wooden cylinder and spun it, "Lots to be drawn, boys. Work to be done."

Six was the magic number, though for centuries, it had been but five. Ozwyk had submitted itself to the Empire some eighty years back, after its own near fall. With that, the kingdom had gone from independent rule to one of six angry siblings, squabbling for attention from the Crown. As such, the ranks of the Grey Guard had risen from five as well. The six painted wooden pegs spun in place, and slowly clicked to a stop. One of the six had a hidden tip, down in the ceramic, painted Grey. Selach snatched his lot, and sighed with relief when it was unpainted. "Thank God. Yesterday was quite enough."

He passed the little cylinder to Ser Cole, who gave an unamused little utterance when he also pulled a plain peg. Shoreshrike and Sozen each pulled a plain peg on their attempts. The four plain pegs left a hard lump in Drake's chest. Any one of the older knights would have served as a fine commander today. Any one, just not Drake, not today, not facing the King's fury for whatever misgiving had occurred over the course of the evening, not a day where he would need to try and keep Ser Darwyn on a short leash.

The Jester Knight reached to take a peg, still swaying, but Drake beat him to it. He deftly snatched a peg of his own, and felt a mix of relief and terror when the tip was painted slate grey. Darwyn jeered, "I was gonna pick the other one anyway, are ya happy, Ducky?"

"Thrilled." He lied.

As previous day's command, Selach was to open the proceedings, and he did with a report of yesterday's occurrences. The broad chested knight had tattoos in indigo on the tops of his round cheeks. Once, in the field, he had been caught without eyeblack, and "The Great Grey Shark" had been unable to find much purchase with an arrow in the sun's blazing glare. He resolved to never face such an issue again. He had tattooed eyeblack in Selach indigo on his face permanently. This was the way with Ser Gnash, decisive, permanent action. No fear, no looking back. One shot, get it right. Always the archer.

As Selach began relaying his report, Drake wished he possessed some of that decisiveness. "Well, there's no easy way to say it boys." Ser Gnash began, "We are in the shit–"

Ser Cole bleated an angry interjection, "Language! Can we at least keep the curses out of the first sentence of our meeting? Some illusion of knightly order!" The shining dome of his skull had gone red and a few sparse beads of sweat had begun pooling the folds and ridges of his forehead.

Gnash sighed, "It's my report, I should bloody-well give it how I see bloody-well fit, but fine; There's no easy way to say it, brothers." He paused dramatically, staring at The Old Goat, "King Gallus is livid. Last night, the Starheart crown on reserve for the Princess-to-be-Chosen disappeared from the Brazen Vaults under Hivehall last night."

It was the usually calm Ser Jurgen who rose first, rage tinging his voice, "How in the world did that happen?! I had personally picked the six Artus guards taking shifts. Two men on a shift, three shifts a day. Lord Malbes added two of his own best men to each shift." He sputtered, mind whirling as his thick hands went to his snow-white hair, "Those vaults are forty feet underground! How?!"

"Queen Natasha tended to the crown yesterday evening, before the Cattle Ca–" Ser Cole gave Selach a withering look, and the archer corrected, "Debutante's Procession. That was the last time anyone was in the vault with the crown." The other five knights whispered murmurs, but Selach continued, "Learner Franz entered this morning, shortly after dawn. And the room was empty. The crown had been the only thing held in that particular chamber. All four men working seemed sober, sane and awake, they swore no one came and no one went."

The ever-steady Ser Auberon spoke, measured and calm, "We can not possibly search the High Learner."

"Nor the Queen." Selach added unhelpfully.

"Nor the Queen," repeated Drake, misery overtaking sense, "So, we cannot possibly imply that the two most likely suspects are even suspects, before we even start the investigation. That is damning at best."

Selach continued, "The King and Council have managed to keep the theft secret, as of now, but we are working on a timeline. Information will get out. Servants will gossip. Even here, I imagine the trees have ears." He gestured at the tall greenery around their little veranda. Last night it had been black and menacing, but once daylight returned, the comforting verdant shades followed. "The King wants the crown found with the greatest urgency, suffice to say." The broad archer in indigo continued, his voice still tense, "There's also the matter of the two dead Ozwyk Lords inflaming tensions in the city. Three men from Clan Wyre strung up a boy from Clan Dolan when he said to expect more fairy-boys to die in the next round. And that's just the worst one. The spearmen are reporting a couple dozen brawls in the pavilion rows and city streets. Lord Webb, the new Lord Webb, wants Lady Vellen arrested, and the Reaves have done nothing to calm the commons or the lords."

Drake immediately saw an opportunity, "Ser Darwyn, this is your duty today. I want you to spend the day treating with the nobles from your fair island. Start with Lord Karas and work your way down. Your brother Josiah and Lord Miles are also paramount. Find out what they want, what we can do to put them and their people back to peace." His voice held none of the tremor that often afflicted him when he commanded the more experienced knights. He was sure of this course. It would keep Ser Darwyn far from Prince Talor, Prince Vernus or any of the other royals. It was a stop-gap, to be true, but it would get The Grey Guard through the next day. "Find Lord Arkady Wyre, as well."

Tymm nodded, brown eyes sparkled with a knowing look, "Sure thing, Ducky. Sorry, *Commander* Ducky. Lord Arkady gave me my first hunting hound, we're old pals."

Drake ignored the less-than-respectful jape, and bid Selach continue, which the Shark quickly did, if simply to fill the awkward silence left by the exchange. "Beyond that, there's still a tourney today and a dance tonight, that we are expected to secure." He stopped and chortled through his nose, "Oh, also, the heir to the Wylde went boots over butthole, down about seventy-five stone steps in the tower the high families are in. He's not expected to live."

This was news to everyone. The heart went out of him, "Hullen Curr IV?" Selach gave him a grim little bob of a nod, and Drake felt ready to vomit. "When was this?"

"About an hour ago. Lilah and Lady Grete Stagg both attest that the boy came past their door, stinking drunk and singing loudly. Seems pretty open and shut, but the Clan Curr is demanding satisfaction. So, in short, good luck Ser Drake."

Drake sighed, he would need all of it.

Somehow, he and his brothers had managed to divide the duties that needed to be done, and that was enough. Drake would spend the morning with the King himself, which was normally an enviable duty. Today, however, the normally grim king was downright sour and snappish. Drake would be allowed to choose his own companion for the day, and he decided on Ser Jurgen. The big northern knight was the most taciturn of his brothers, which was the sort of brotherhood required today; steadfast and silent.

They would head from the morning brief to the King himself. The narrow faced king pounced into Drake's immediate line of vision. "Ser Drake, welcome." He placed his bony hand in Drake's, "My family has been most insistent about the location of the crown, and I am inclined to agree." He gave a tight smile, strained behind exhausted eyes. Prince Talor coolly retained his distance from the two Grey Guard and the King. Drake had initially assumed it was due to the contest between himself and the Crown Prince this afternoon, but the Prince maintained a silent divide from his father once he and Jurgen peeled off to speak to Prince Vernus and Queen Natasha.

"Where is my crown?" Vernus's voice was a cicada buzz of a whine, "I cannot be expected to name my betrothed if I cannot crown her."

His sister, Princess Bara, circled him, needling him as only a sister can. "Vernus will die a maiden!" She skipped, as the slim-armed princeling swatted at her, lazily. "Maiden!" She chanted, drawing out the vowels, 'Lady Vernie the Spinster!" Her nursemaid, an irritated looking spur of a woman, knelt low, trying to catch the Princess's attention. She would initially try sweet words, then seizing the girl, then finally produced a sugared candy, and bribed her into leaving her harried older brother be.

"I can't have her tongue out, woman." Vernus hissed at the woman's back, "But she is your responsibility, and should she speak so uncouth to me again, I will have yours out with hot pincers."

Fiery Queen Natasha, herself harried under her glamorous airs, grabbed her sixteen year old son by his right ear. She pinched the pink skin and cartilage between her thumb and forefinger, twisting just enough to cause the Prince to wince and moan. "My Prince." She twisted just enough to make Vernus go to his tiptoes, "Grelli, there, fed *you* from her own breast not that long ago." She locked her blue eyes on her son's not-quite-golden ones, "That woman is more than a milk-cow and herd-hound. She tended to your ills and needs and loves as well as I did, and she is due respect." She released the boy's ear and he crumpled to his knees.

Both hands shot to his ear, which he cupped, "Ow. Owowowowowowow." He watched his mother, and he hated. He was an angry little man with an angry little heart. In that moment, Drake was very, very, glad Vernus was not the regent.

The Queen gave Drake her winning smile, teeth perfect snow-white. "Apologies for the Prince, we have all become very tense with the theft of the crown, but his behavior is absolutely unconscionable." Graceful, always graceful, she placed a lily-white hand on Ser Jurgen's stark white plate. "Ser Jurgen, what have you and your brothers discovered?"

The big man went rigid, shoulders as steady as the crenellated stone wall behind them, "Beg pardons, your Grace, but Ser Drake is command today."

Drake nodded, "That's true your Grace, but I can brief you, of course."

Queen Natasha took Drake in, and gave an unsure smile, "Of course, I seem to have forgotten the *unique* command structure of the Grey Guard. Please, Ser Drake, by all means."

Here of course, came the impossible bit. The Guard had learned nothing in the preceding six hours. Whomever had gotten that crown out of that vault must have been a phantom, but he could never *just say* that. His mind churned like seawater on the rocks, desperate for some sort of way of phrasing that to the Queen.

The Dashing Duck saw no way around this issue, so he would simply bull through it. "Your Grace, I could lie to you. I could give you flowery words, and try to sell you a story that is simply not true." The sigh that escaped his chest was downright funerary, "There's no merit to that, no honor to it. We know nothing more than we did when you last spoke to Ser Gnash this morning." He wrung his gloved hands into one another, "The vault is a solid stone structure with one point of egress. That point was guarded the entire evening with no interruption from your exit to the High Learner's entry this morning, but the crown is gone. The walls are undamaged. Um." His words suddenly caught in his throat, nerves tense, "The Learners and, uh, the Saddlers sent their sorceress, but none have been able to find any arcane evidence, let alone determine its source or nature."

The queen knit her eyebrows together, mind whirling. From a distance, her older son, the Crown Prince strode to the gathered trio. He smirked at Drake, "I know it's bad luck to see a maid before the 'wedding' this afternoon, but I suppose we'll need to ignore tradition." His strong hand gave Canar a hardy slap on the back.

Unsettled, Drake gave a weak smile, "I suppose we will."

Three hours later, Artus was driving his two balled fists and a double axe-handled pair of forearms into the boiled leather and ringmail on Drake's back, sending him to his knocked knees. Drake spun, hand to ass to hand to knee to toe back to his base. Both boys had been disarmed, and lost their weapons in the mud pit that had once been a dusty arena. Shortly after noon, the solemn iron gray clouds that had spent the morning haunting the western horizon had finally rumbled their slow progress above them, and with them a driving rain that would soak the afternoon's proceedings. By the match between the Crown Prince and the Dashing Duck two hours later, the dusty arena had turned to a slop of mud and grit and blood.

Talor croaked a low burble as Drake drove his knee into his sworn Prince's stomach. Artus stumbled backward, and the young knight spun his head under his helm, searching the mud for a glint of metal. His dagger, his sword, even Artus' big broadsword– just something, anything to put an end to this damnable contest. The Prince's big tower shield lay a half dozen feet away, spattered in yellow-brown mud. Drake dismissed the slight temptation instantly, he was not accustomed to that heavy hunk of oak and iron. He would likely end up off balance, Artus was much stronger than he was. Drake swung a purple leather mace of a fist at the Prince, who half shifted, causing Drake to miss his intended target of Artus's stomach. Instead, Drake smashed his hand into Talor's armored hip. A flare of pain shocked through his entire arm, but he shook it loose and felt nothing broken as he stumbled away groaning.

As Drake turned, still shaking nails of pain from his hand, he saw the golden pommel of Prince Talor's broadsword, half buried in the mud, not four feet from both combatants. Drake instinctively reached for his belt, looking for Smoke. When his fingers found nothing, he stuttered. It was that momentary mistake, that slight second, that would cost him everything here. He had intentionally decided to not pack his capsules. Despite the temptations, despite the possible need, using the Smoke here seemed *profane*. To use his most sacred weapon against his charge would be a distortion of its purpose, even in a tourney. Tymm's mocking voice rang in his mind. *Honor is a convenient excuse for a man too cowardly to make difficult choices, Ducky.*

Had he been able to make a smokescreen, Drake would have quickly taken the sword from the muck with speed and stealth enough to end the battle in a stroke. Without it, he dove, slipping through the slime and mud, and Artus dove with him. The Prince was taller and stronger, to be true, but Drake was the middle of five-fucking-sons, brawling in the mud was the cradle he had been raised in. He shoved, he shook, he bit, despite mouthfuls of mud. The struggle for dominance depended on who ended up on top, both boys knew. Drake had grapevined his skinny legs around Talor's muscular left one, desperate to not end up on his belly in the mud. Artus had gripped Drake's left wrist in his overpowering right hand. Drake started tossing wild haymakers into the prince's ribs, but chain and padded jacket left those strikes impotent.

Horror entered Drake's heart as he watched the Prince's gold eyes flare, but he never felt the fingers of royalty stroke his psyche. Instead, the Prince reached out with his left hand, and tendrils of golden light followed his arc. Swimming slowly like sunlight made molasses, the trio of long golden fingers reached and swirled. Gently and deftly, they wrapped themselves around the hilt of the prince's sword, like vines made of the celestial prince's will. With a lazy toss of his hand, the hilt flew to him. Drake reached, batting, swinging, trying in any way to intercept the blade. More yellow brown mud flew, trailing behind the shimmering sword. A bit slopped onto Drake's lips as Talor caught the sword.

Blade in hand, practiced grace returned to the handsome Prince. The way he swung the point to Drake's throat was almost artistic, objectively beautiful. The point barely scraped the dyed leather of Canar's gorget, barely leaving the trace of a scratch. Drake spit more mud, and writhed vainly. The Prince smiled down from his helm, eyes still sparkling with pops of golden light, "Do you yield?"

Drake stopped his struggling, he laid flat with a massive exhale. In the face of such overwhelming power, what choice did one little grey duck have?

ELLARI III

"We rarely get a chance to face our sins head on. More often than not, your demons will dance in your dreams, making you gorge yourself on guilt."

His eyes were closed. More than anything, she was thankful that Hullen's eyes were closed. Ellari stood above her husband, watching Hullen more still than she'd ever seen him. Her hand found his, swollen, twisted, broken, but *warm*. As shattered and terrible as he looked, Hullen was still alive. They were alone now, finally, and he was still asleep. Asleep or dead, his breath came so shallow that it was sometimes hard to tell.

Hullen had been stretched out on a long, narrow bed in the breezy solar owned by Clan Malbes. The Learners had all attended to him. All of them. There had been so many that Lord Hullen, her Hullen's father, had to send them away, leaving only the quartet of Learner Maesh, the Curr's own healer; as well as Learners Franz, Vaughn and Halidon. Franz was the High Learner of the entire Empire. Vaughn was well renowned for his breadth of knowledge having traveled far and wide, across three of the four continents. He had written several books, most notably The World of Gyent which Ellari had devoured as a young girl, reading it cover to cover in days. It was still among her most treasured possessions. She had dreamt of meeting him as the respected spitfire Lady Executor, not half a grieving widow. He had been very kind and very gentle, but she had wanted discussion, not soothing platitudes. Learner Halidon was the Learner of the castle here, these were his facilities.

The four old men had gathered around the broken young one and done everything in their considerable skill to set him right once more. His twisted limbs had been splinted, the gashes stitched, and the great soft spot on his skull had been covered in a plaster. Hullen had not since returned to wakefulness. She had asked all four men when her husband might wake again, and was given four different answers.

Tired, grey Halidon was little help at all, "Oh, to be sure, too much is uncertain, my Lady." He wound thin fingers into themselves, "He is receiving the finest care."

Learner Franz was plainly honest, "Your husband is deeply, gravely wounded, Lady Ellari. The fact that he still draws breath is as much a blessing as there is likely to be."

Maesh had brought both Ellari and Hullen into this world, as well as Hullen's siblings. He was a sweet old bull of a man, whose stern face was a lie, there was not another stern thing about Maesh. Big hearted, clever and kind to the children, Hullen's fall had left him a husk. There was no joy, no laughter, only a single minded focus: he would save Hullen, no matter what. Of all four men, he was the one who labored the hardest, and when Ellari tried to question him, his only response was a brief pained look.

Finally, Ellari had approached strange Learner Vaughn, the traveling Learner who had come as a special guest of the royal family. The short, round little man did not exude the presence of an educated man. With his black-and-iron-gray shaggy hair bound into a loose knot on the back of his head, and his big bushed beard reaching the middle of his dust stained robes, The Learned Sojourner looked more vagrant than genius. He had spent the least time of the four examining Hullen. He gave the broken Curr a cursory once over, and then set his considerable talents to assisting Maesh silently, offering no suggestion, nor critique.

This set Ellari to her fury. When she finally got Learner Vaughn alone, she struggled to contain herself, though she managed to question him with no twinge of her annoyance coloring her tone. "Learner, when will my husband wake?'

Vaughn gave a still little rasp, and Ellari realized he was chuckling, "Oh, no fuckin' way that one wakes." He shrugged, almost dismissively.

Ellari felt her jaw fall. With no thought or effort on her part, her hands had gone to iron vices on Vaughn's lapel. She jerked him close, her face mere inches from his. Her hot breath sent the whiskers in his beard trembling. "What purpose does helping Maesh serve, if Hullen is going to die?"

Vaughn shook his head, wriggling loose of Ellari's grip, "I am helping a good man struggle against impossible odds. Apologies to your husband, but his battle is over. Barring a miracle, that is. And I don't see the Golden Boy here." He turned, giving a slight nod to Maesh. Working in just brown roughspun, the Wylde's learner had discarded his black and white robes, leaving them in a heap at the feet of the chair he had collapsed into. He was not more than three feet from his patient, but the agony on his face said more than any word could. "That man is going to put every drop of himself into saving that boy. When nothing works, I need him to know he did everything he could do, and that he did it right." Vaughn sighed deeply, "I'm sorry, Lady Curr. There's nothing I can do for your husband, but I can help a good man not lose himself here." He gave her a sad smile, and returned to Learner Maesh's side, comforting the tired healer with a hand on his shoulder.

Ellari, Lord Hullen and Lady Gail had been the first allowed to see Hullen, his wife and his parents. The ruined noise that escaped

Lady Gail's mouth had settled into Ellari's heart and would likely live there for the rest of her life. Lord Hullen was not a man prone to displays of emotion, but even he fell to his knees, and hot, angry, devastated tears flowed from his pale eyes.

But Ellari didn't. She saw the man she had wed, and shared a bed with lying shattered. Hullen was bloodied and shuddering. He was a mass of broken bones and bruises. The boy's breath came in wheezes or sobs. He looked like a toy soldier that had been crushed under the heel of a boot. She didn't cry out, she didn't weep. The most she could manage was a strained, "Gods" under her breath, no more than a whisper. She tried to cross to Hullen, it would only be about five quick steps. Onetwothreefourfive.

Her mind screamed, her feet refused to hear.

Walk, she cursed herself internally. She ground her heels against the rough stone floor. *Just lift one damn foot, you fool.* Finally, her body did respond, though not how she wanted. With no will she could explain, Ellari spun from the scene and hurried into the hall.

She had to get away. There was too much here, she had to get to–.

Hale.

Ellari unleashed a squeal of shock when she found herself face to chest with her Tower. He caught her, strong hands on her narrow waist. They locked eyes, and hesitated for a moment just lost in the touch, in one another. Her bottom lip trembled and the only thing Ellari wanted in that moment was to kiss him, but that would have been monstrous. He released her waist after the barest ghost of a squeeze. His tone was all business, as the sobs behind him indicated they were not alone. "How is he, Ellari?"

Ellari's eyes followed the four gathered before her, as she stumbled a trio of steps back. Hale was pale, his narrow mouth set. Beside him, Hullen's other two sworn swords, Esben and Chaddar were just as grim. Lady Masha leaned in Esben's huge arm, red-eyed and weeping loudly. She had wrapped a silk around her tiny tight fists, and would occasionally wrench it tighter before an explosively loud sob.

Words failed her. As intelligent as she was, these gathered few staring at her left her dry-mouthed and stuttering. "H-he's…" All she could picture was Hullen's twisted limbs under the rapidly working hands of the Learners. "Hullen needs all of our prayers." She stared up to Hale, the pools of black-blue that were his eyes refused to meet hers. "All of us."

Masha nodded between the sobs, great tears rushing down her cheeks. She threw herself at her cousin and Ellari wrapped her in her arms, desperate to bring her solace, peace, or comfort, but failing to find all three. The scared girl shook in her arms, searching for a sense that left the world this morning, "What happened?"

"We know very, very little. He fell, it seems. The blood on the stairs indicates that he tumbled a long distance before he stopped." She swallowed her emotions once more, "We were very fortunate that the Saddlers and their witch found him almost immediately. We owe Hartwin Saddler his life."

Esben spit on the ground bitterly, his voice a gentle rumble of distant thunder, "The aid is welcome, but I fear any debt to that horse trader. That boy is fulla himself."

It was the ice cold gaze of Lord Hullen Curr III that turned the hissing whispers of the five youths to silence. The Lord of the Wylde was not a huge man, but he exuded authority without needing size. Pale hair, pale eyes and a soft voice gave the presence of a man who was already half a ghost, and the ancient black warhound that padded behind him was his reaper, Mistral. The pair entered, a fraction of second after the old lord's words, "I don't care if that boy is full of himself, his entire family and this one. We will be thankful for his aid."

Esben's podgy cheeks went purple with embarrassment, and he sputtered a frightful apology as the Lord coldly addressed the five of them, "Masha, your Lady Mother requires you to attend her." Masha dabbed the tears from her eyes and nodded at her lord father affirmatively. The sad, skinny girl would gather her skirts and rush away, totally focused on her duties as a sister and daughter. Her sobs matched the rhythm of her trotting feet, which Ellari would have deemed amusing, if it wasn't so sad.

The old lord put his hands in Hale's, smiling sadly up to the tower-tall boy, "I do not wish for this to weigh too heavily upon you today. You have earned a great victory, a great honor for this Clan, and for yourself. I know you love my son more than a brother." Hale's big black-blue eyes were fixed on the floor, but for the slightest hint of a second, Ellari knew they were on her. She could *feel* his eyes on her. "You *must* put Hullen aside and fight with a clear heart and head, Hale." Hullen III continued, "Or better still, hold him tighter in your heart and let him be the wild wolf heart that beats for your own. Honor your sworn lord with a victory."

Hale could not lift his gaze from the floor, he only mumbled his best assurances.

Beside him, Esben and Chaddar gave him what encouragement they could. Though their spirits were certainly dampened, Hullen's two loyal friends ignorantly vowed to help his disloyal one prepare for further glories while their sworn lord lay infirm, possibly dying. With Lord Hullen's encouragement, the three boys would retreat to the yard. Hitting things made more sense than feelings to soldiers, Ellari supposed.

Then she was alone with her uncle. She was alone with her father-by-law. The moment the boys stepped out of sight, three long cloaks swishing down a long hall, the tension went out of Lord Hullen's shoulders so quickly, he nearly collapsed. The big hound nosed his palm gently, and the faded looking lord choked back a sob. Tenderly, Ellari put a hand on her Lord's bobbing shoulders, and she felt his agony.

Lord Hullen had never once done wrong by Ellari, save marrying her to his son. He had been a kind and gracious provider, to be sure, but his merits went far past such basic matters. When Lord Hullen grasped the depths of Ellari's cleverness, her canny political manner, he took her under his wing without a second thought. Though some of his older lords griped at the skinny teenage girl sitting at his right hand, the High Lord took no argument. The girl was given a mind for ruling, and he would use it, and someday, if Hullen the Fourth was wise, he'd use it as well. The memory still filled Ellari's chest with a warm pride.

"Why was he out so early, Ellari? Why didn't he bring Dirge?" His voice, so strong moments ago, was the quavering of a reed in the wind, thin and hollow.

Ellari had her suspicions to be true, but she couldn't possibly share them with Lord Hullen. *He spent the night with Reuben Stagg and did not wake me. I would imagine he learned about my ongoing affair with Hale, oh, I'm fucking Hale, by the way, but I imagine he learned about that and was off to do something drunkenly rash and he fell down the stairs.*

"I could not say, My Lord" came out of her mouth instead and she wished she could drop dead.

"This was clutched in his fingers." He lifted a small, fluffy scrap, brown-red, no bigger than a playing card. Ellari took it carefully, stroking it, her shaking fingers finding it sinfully soft. A piece of fur prepared for some gentle, noble purpose. Lord Hullen looked to her, some strength returning to his voice, "He managed to keep this in his shattered fingers. Whatever it means, he knew he needed it."

Ellari turned it over and gasped. She knew exactly where this squirrel skin had come from and she knew the woman who wore it. Before the day was through, Ellari Curr would need to find Lilah Stagg and ask her some pointed questions.

Before that spar, there were other contests to deal with. The sky had turned iron gray and angry and a slow, steady, driving rain had taken all of yesterday's heat from the air. Ellari, and most of the rest of northern stock were especially thankful, but even the southern lords seemed more comfortable, as long as they were dry at least. The commons looked miserable, a wooly flock sodden. There was some lack of propriety in Ellari being in public so soon after her husband's fall, so Ellari made no grand entrance with the boys. She slipped in the contestant's door, and in her cloak of moss-green, she sidled up among the squires and knights, hoping to remain unseen.

A slim, serious boy with a shaggy head of brown hair scooted from the spectator's fence to allow her to draw closer. Here, a great awning of yellow canvas kept the gathered squires and nobles more dry than not. The boy, who could have been no more than twelve, was dressed in the trappings of a squire, navy and a violent mint, with the eerie, awful lanternfish of Clan Marianos silver in a badge on his jerkin. Ellari reached into her satchel, and secreted a tiny parchment parcel, about the size of a gold coin. She tapped the boy's shoulder, and when he looked up, she dropped a small wrapped caramel directly onto his forehead from a hand that appeared empty. It bounced into the boy's cupped hands, and he squealed with delight, before stuffing the whole thing in his mouth, waxed paper and all, bits of drool flying.

She had been so engrossed in her small act of prestidigitation, she had not noticed the Lord in all grey beside him. Without looking, he dryly intoned to the boy, "Taking treats from a mysterious source usually leads to all sorts of trouble, Homer." He patted the boy on the head, as Homer, presumably, stopped chewing. "And you generally ought to remove the paper before consumption." He had something of a lazy, bored tone, practiced in its lack of regard. "You're embarrassing us both in front of the Lady Executor."

"D– Oh, I am sorry my lord, my lady." He wiped a muzzle of caramel from the corner of his mouth, sheepishly.

The Lord in Grey turned to Ellari, and gave a relaxed smirk, "Don't worry, m'lady. Your discretion has been noticed." When she immediately tensed, spinning her head in search, he corrected, "Oh, no, just by me and I suppose Homer, now." He tiredly placed a hand on the fence before them, idly cracking a sharp little splinter of wood loose. There were bloodstains beside it. He rolled this pencil thin wooden pick between his fingers, before dropping it to the dust, "I don't care, of course. Illystre Coldhearth, Lord of Spies." He winked after introducing himself, "It's my job to know everyone's secrets, but the secret about secrets is the worst secret of all, Lady Curr. Most every single secret people keep is dreadfully boring, personal and entirely un-unique." A sweep of the hand pushed locks prematurely silver from his forehead. "Matters of coin and land, loyalties" he trailed off, grey eyes boring into Ellari, "But matters of the heart are the nastiest little secrets of all."

Ellari pulled a second caramel, shakily pulling the paper from its sticky surface. It tore between her fingers, and she dropped the candy into the dust at their feet, "Sh-shit."

"How rude of me." Coldhearth gave her a wide smile, so wide the red of his gums stood against the white of his teeth. "You've been through so much today, of course you need an escape." Coldheart uncorked his wineskin and pressed it to his lips, but Ellari could tell he drank only a third of what he mimed. "We were so very sorry to hear of your lord husband's accident, Lady Ellari. Hullen is such a dedicated man. Wasn't it terrible, Homer?"

The boy nodded, chewing still, "Tragic, ser."

A roar went up from the arena, as Lord Hinric Saddler cut the longbow his opponent was carrying in two. Lord Mortimer Osprey cursed under his helm, charging. He wielded the uneven halves of his longbow like batons, and swung wildly at the Lord of Finance, resplendent in his shining armor and oiled mustache. The Little Horse Lord sidestepped the Lord of Talon Bay, and raked his cavalry sabre across the younger man's back. From under a glorious mustache of his own, Lord Osprey groaned in agony. Uncharacteristically, Coldhearth himself cursed, "Apologies, I just cannot *stand* Saddler." He turned back to Ellari as Osprey shouted his submission, "Well, that's that, then." He lifted a parchment with the lists scrawled on it, in a looping scribe's hand. A perfectly trimmed nail traced the names and stopped about halfway down, "Well, the next match scheduled is your husband's man, isn't it? That Torchbearer boy."

Ellari screamed inside, but swallowed her terror and fury. "S-Ser Hale Torchbearer, yes. We're all so proud of him, having bested Ser Kyne Reave."

"As well you ought to be, you and all of you Wyldefolk. It's not every day that some nephew to a minor lord defeats a warlock prince, you know." There was a grey fox leering at her, mocking the Curr girl. The bored lord gathered himself, stashing his wineskin and patting Homer on the back, "Come along, Homer. The next match holds nothing for us. There's been enough northern boys battered for my taste."

And they were gone.

Ellari would stand there for a moment, shifting anxiously, before she felt the caramel in the dust squish under the toe of her shoe. She could have wept, but that was for little girls. It would be a few minutes until Hale's contest, and Ellari would busy herself being as uninteresting as possible. Perhaps her efforts were worthwhile, as no one else took notice of her and the horns would soon blare the arrival of the combatants. High in the royal box, Prince Vernus rested, his feet up. The look of boredom on his face was indescribable. Two men had died for his tourney, Webb and Tymm and now Hullen had suffered here in Honeyhome too. Bloodshed like this, all for this little worm, Ellari found it sickening.

Sober, brave cheers greeted Hale, who to Ellari's shock had traded his trappings of Torchbearer red and yellow for Curr indigo and cream. Chaddar and Esben had as well, though they were no longer in the tourney, having both lost. Any glory today was for Clan Curr, for the Wylde.

"For Hullen!" came the cheer from Ser Chaddar Goldenlocke, who swaggered even in his grief. A fairly large contingent of the crowd echoed him in rhythm, chanting for a fallen boy they'd never known. Hale raised his shining black greatsword, *Wayfinder*, and the chants swelled into cacophony.

Her shining tower, her Hale dressed in the trappings of a Curr lord gave Ellari's heart a wicked thrill that she hated as much as she loved. *If you were the Lady of the Wylde and he your consort...* Her thoughts went back to the broken boy laying in the solar and she wanted to weep again. She gripped the fence ahead of her tightly as a young blonde woman in pink and teal sidled next to her. She paid Ellari no mind as the horns and herald roared the arrival of Hale's opponent, the Lord of Brimstone, Lukas Axe.

Axe was north of forty. A big man, near as tall as Hale and wider by half. Axe was as thick necked and sturdy as the burly burgundy bull on his standard. He was adorned in boiled brown leather and black chain. A pair of short red horns spiked upward from his helm, not longer than a thumb. *Hardly horns of a bull, those are the horns of a devil.* Most notably, Axe did not carry a weapon. He could not. Instead a short maul was strapped to the stump where his right hand had once been. Tales said that Axe had lost it in the mouth of a crocodile in the lowlands, on a hunt. Ellari found that notion preposterous. Alligators lived in the lowland swamps, not crocodiles.

Once the courtesies had been observed, the two combatants began a slow circling dance. Hale gripped his long sword in both hands, the blade parallel to the dirt. Slow rivulets of rain streamed down both men's helms, and their wools and leathers were quickly growing in weight, as they swelled sodden. Hale struck out first, stabbing forward at Axe, the ebon point of *Wayfinder* carved a ragged pale gouge into the black paint of the bull's shield. The big man snarled, and slammed his maul directly at Hale's left knee. Ellari's heart left her throat as her Tower spun to the right and the head of the hammer found only squelching mud.

The older knight was more canny than he appeared, flicking the mud upward with a stunted jab. The yellow blob arced skyward and found its home directly in the eyeslit of Hale's visor. The entire left half of his helmet was spattered with mud, and he bellowed in blind torment. Sightless, he slashed forward, the great black blade swinging at waist level, desperately hoping to connect with anything. From the side, Chaddar screamed, "There's no honor in that! Mud in the sodding eye!"

Hale pivoted, his left hand releasing the pommel of *Wayfinder* and fruitlessly pawed at the eyeslit, clogged with its clump of yellow mud. Tall, narrow and dark, with a flash of yellow atop, Hale had become the lighthouse on shield. Axe smashed his weighty wooden shield into Hale's hip and the big tower crumbled to the muck. Driven to one knee, the blinded Torchbearer tossed his sword aside and simply grappled the brawny Axe. Ellari knew from personal experience that Hale was surprisingly strong and *vigorous* for a man so lean, but against such a burly foe this may be folly. Hale wrapped his long arms around Axe's waist and drove them both forward, in a desperate attempt to get Axe on his back.

Axe brought the maul down across Hale's back, one, two, three times. Each shot a ringing drumbeat that sent a cringe through every member of the crowd, no matter which combatant they supported. Hale shifted, jerking his head in a suffering howl. The rim of his helm caught on Axe's sword belt, and the two were stuck together. Torchbearer could only struggle, his ear glued to Lord Lukas's hip. For his part, Axe refused to waste a single second, unleashing another barrage of maul strikes across Hale's battered back.

Something primal surged in Ser Hale Torchbearer, screaming a blooded howl, Hale tore his head backward. Every bit of muscle in the tower-tall boy strained and stretched, and finally, the leather thong binding the helm to Hale's head snapped as his chin pulled it tighter and tighter. Hale looked fierce and feral as he flipped his head free. Ebony strands of thick hair had loosed themselves from the tight knot at the back of his head, and Ser Hale reared to his full height, his left eye closed with grit, his right blazing a spectral blue-black.

He had traded his helm for his eyes, Ellari immediately knew, but would that be enough to turn the contest to his favor, or was he asking to die? Hale launched forward, fury and fire and passion and hate. Like rolling thunder, tall grim Torchbearer somersaulted forward, his left hand settling on *Wayfinder.* He hacked at Axe's shield, great splintering hunks flying like sawdust at a mill. It was all the big bull could do to stagger backward and keep his shield up. Ellari hooted, something like joy entered her for a split second. Axe raised his maul, and Hale clipped the head from it with a hooked little strike. The heavy hunk of iron fell to the mud and fetid water at their feet, slipped into a wet footprint and would likely never be seen again, as brown water sloshed over it. *How many of these fights just become boys wrestling in their fanciest clothes?* She snorted at how strange and stupid men are, because in that moment, the whole thing felt absolutely asinine.

Axe had lost the head of his maul, true, but two feet of hardwood handle still jutted from the stump at his wrist. And when he cracked it into the exposed temple of Ser Hale, Ellari realized the contest was far from won. Hale's hand went to his ringing ear, so Lord Axe tried to swat the other. Hale managed to parry the blow at the last second, using *Wayfinder* to send the stiff blow stinging into his shoulder, rather than his head. Hale stutter-stepped away from the blow, set his base, and spun a great whirling overhead chop at Axe.

The determined Lord of Brimstone raised his shield. There was a sickening crunch and a groan. Both Axe and Torchbearer strained, pulling apart to no avail. Hale had buried his sword deep in the shield's metal core. There would be no parting them without a smithy. Axe realized this first and tossed the shield aside. The rapidly shifting added weight to his weapon sent Ser Hale stumbling forward. It was the brawny bull's turn to sidestep, spinning with an unexpected grace. As Hale stumbled past him, Axe spanked him, right on the rear, with the broken maul handle. Torchbearer spun, fury twisting his face at the offense. "What in the hell is wrong—"

Hale would never finish his rebuke. Lord Lukas ducked himself low. Even from her far place in the stands, Ellari saw the thick muscles in Axe's thighs go taut. He surged upward, sharing a vicious headbutt with the unhelmed Torchbearer right in his strong chin. Ellari watched as his beautiful blue black eyes lost focus and he tumbled to the mud. The Gamesmaster would sound the horn . Seconds later, Hale was miles away, unable to continue. He lay in the mud, moaning, as the rain washed the filth from his pale face, black strands stuck to his forehead. The slightest trickle of red blood from the corner of his perfect lips. The only thing she wanted was to press her thin lips to his.

For Hullen. Ellari thought, ready to be sick.

VANDRE IV

"Sooner or later, you're gonna fuck up. Sooner or later, you're gonna end up at the mercy of the Gods. You best hope they are kinder than they are just."

At this point, Vandre was willing to see if he could live without ribs. Tear them out and let him be done with it. He'd buy a breastplate, if he somehow lived through this. The tired old sellsword wasn't confident of that outcome. He'd been in prison before, but, as he touched the thick steel collar at his neck, he realized; he was in much deeper peril than he had thought initially. He leaned against the wall, tired. His back and ribs screamed, shifting like a sack of glass and gravel, gifts from the guards, grimly groaning from his grumbling guts. He raised his manacled wrists to find that his left ear was still mostly in place, though a sizable chunk was missing. The rest of his head and face was little better, right eye swollen shut and raging purple, a fat lip, several huge gouges from the claws of a raptor, and his nose might have been broken.

He hadn't even bothered looking for the crown. He knew it was gone. As was his sword and ringmail. At least they were kind enough to let him keep his boots, though the shiv he kept tucked in the left one was gone. As he lay in this pitch black cell, Vandre folded one hand into the other, and he did something he'd not done since he'd left Hammerdale behind, he prayed.

He didn't pray for escape, he and the gods were all well aware of his guilt. He didn't even know what he'd been arrested for, really. It happened so rapidly, and he'd been weak from blood loss. No matter, whatever it was, he'd likely done it, if not here, someplace else, then. Sure of his guilt, Vandre didn't pray for deliverance, he prayed someone would remember to feed Beauty. She had never asked for any part in this, and had been as loyal an animal as he had ever owned.

Trying to reconstruct the night only led him to further questions. He had robbed the others shortly after midnight, stumbling across the yard couldn't have taken him a half hour, not even as busted up as he was. How did the green girl know the crown had been stolen, let alone that he'd had it? Even the presence of the green girl was troubling, Vandre didn't even trust his memories of the incident, trying to determine what happened was like grabbing handfuls of smoke.

From the far end of the dungeon, the low flicker of orange torchlight began to blush on the wall. In total black, your eyes become hungry for any light they can find and search greedily. Vandre sat himself as straight as he could against the wall, as tall as he could manage. The chain around his neck was too short to allow the old knight to stand, and his hands were manacled, a couple of feet of short chain binding them as well. The floor under him was dirt, but something was piled on it, something soft and a little moist. Vandre hoped it was chopped straw, but he had little way of being sure.

He was injured, dazed and chained to a wall. When he heard boots clacking on the stone growing nearer, the old man clenched his fist in want of a weapon. He might die here, but he resolved to make his killer *hurt*.

The tired old fighter could tell that three figures had entered, but in the dark, the blaze of the torchlight reduced them to striding shadows. The one in the center was the tallest, and carried both the torch and a long spear. The injured Vandre tried to place his face, his standard, his armor, but nothing seemed to hook in Vandre's memory.

He parted his swollen and bloody lips, dragging a parched and cracked tongue over them, "Water."

A husky voice behind the spearman grumbled an affirmation, and the tall man dropped a waterskin in Vandre' lap. It was then that the clink of gold horseshoes from the spearman's scale gave Vandre the answers he was searching for. This was a man of Clan Saddler, not Malbes. He removed the cork from the skin and drank the tepid water down greedily, until his belly ached and for some time past that. He coughed, gagging up the last few swallows, but settled shortly afterward. The spearman hung his torch in a sconce on the rack, and knelt low. The spearman was an affable looking man in his early thirties. Like most of the Young Stallions, the finest horse soldiers in Daneau, his mane of long chestnut hair streamed to his shoulders, washed, perfumed and shining. Vandre reckoned he might be able to grab a handful of hair and– *Die stupidly in the dark. You grab him, you die in the dark.* He sighed and settled back into the wall, suddenly limp. "Okay. What did I do?" Between bloodied lips and a sticky tongue, the old man sounded like he had not stopped drinking in months.

From the shadows, the third figure spoke, a woman's voice, but brassy and clear, "You killed four farm boys outside of Stonestall."

Vandre looked to the torchlight in its sconce. For a moment, it was an orange cookfire, grown too big, casting shadows on a thicket of trees. The torchlight left the two rear figures shadowed, but one was definitely a woman. "Before I confess to anything, yer gonna need to tell me who I'm speaking to." The old man knew he was being difficult, but as he had already been beaten bloody, he felt like he had little to lose, especially with the headsman looming large in his mind.

The response was a low rumble from the first voice, a great shuffling mountain in black, "Strike him."   And the spearman did. A mailed fist broke through the fog of injury, as the spearman smashed his bruised abdomen, right under his sternum.

The wind rushed from Vandre' lungs with a groan and he hacked blood and mucus. Long moments passed and the only sounds were Vandre sputtering and the torch doing the same. Salt tears trickled from the corner of his eyes, as he struggled for breath, "...I-I did." He grunted up at his captors, "...It were them or me, and I chose them." He spat bitterly, "I'd do it again."

The spearman turned back to his shadowed companions, and the woman voiced one passed a bundle of shadows between them. The Spearman passed back into the light, holding a glimmering circle of gold. It rattled to the cobbles and straw. Glinting light on its point was the only thing that stopped the claustrophobic cell's spinning. He focused on the light and tried not to gag.

"How did you get this?" The spearman nudged him with the toe of his boot. "Now, old man."

Vandre's head was spinning, he could only focus on the horseshoes on the spearman's armor. "S-saddler." He mumbled, "I wanna talk t-to Hartwin Saddler." He had met the young lord once, in passing, but a dying man is a desperate fool. Blackness at the edges of his vision pulsed as he struggled to stay awake, "Purvon Webb... Saddler." The dead danced in his mind as he heard the woman's voice burble something and promptly lost consciousness.

He was somewhere in an old memory with a young love when he woke, still groggily unaware of his place. The warmth of the air around him was an immediate indicator that he was no longer in the dark cell, as was the silver sunlight. He tried to move, but found himself still shackled. His wounds had been bandaged with pristine white linens. The room had a... window. Vandre slowly rose, exploring the space. A small room, to be sure, but a room. He had been laid in a plain-looking bed, but it was stuffed with goose down, not straw. The room had a small clay chamber pot, with a cover and a wash basin, full of clean water. A pitcher of wine sat beside a cup and a small bowl of fruit, centered on a little round table.

Vandre put an unsteady foot on the wooden floor, followed by the second one. With a groan, the old knight willed himself up to his feet. He took a shaky step toward the tall window, sliding his feet across the floor rather than daring to pick them up and shift his weight. He came to the panes of glass, set into honey brown gold. Shaking fingers touched the door handle, and it swung open. Vandre, eyes still readjusting to light, swung his head out the window and into the light.

He found nothing. As the blazing white daylight faded with a squint, the old man could see the vast black blue Shining Sea on the horizon. Directly below him, he could see the ground, a fresh green lawn, manicured perfectly. He was in a tower, too high up to jump, even if he was twenty years younger and healthy.

Behind him, something smug said, "If you want to die, I poisoned the peach as a prank."

The young lordling was called the Young Colt, but when Vandre spun his tired head, Hartwin Saddler looked more like a snake. The Heir to the Goldengrass had crossed to the bowl of fruit, tall and thin, and bedecked in green. Sharp green eyes were fixed on Vandre. "Maybe it was the apple, I forget." He reached into the bowl of fruit and plucked the red, ripe apple and held it out to Vandre, "I think we can make a deal."

Vandre shook his head, and mumbled words of refusal that were almost a sentence.

"No?" Saddler shined the apple to a gleam on a green silk sleeve and then took a huge, horsey bite of it, a spray of juice flying into the air. "I didn't poison any of it. If I wanted you dead, you'd be buried in a pauper's grave." He offered the bowl to Vandre again.

The old man took fig, and cautiously bit it in half. It was sugary and heavy and earthy. It was good. He chewed the dried fruit, parched. He eyed the pitcher of wine, and then looked to Saddler. "After you." His voice felt as dry and cracked as his lips. But caution outweighed need, for the moment at least.

Saddler gave a derisive little snort and poured himself a cup. He sworled it, showing the thin red fluid to Vandre, "A piss-poor vintage, but entirely safe." He quaffed his little half cup in one go, before passing the clay cup to his prisoner. Vandre took it, pouring himself a cup of the wine. He sipped it, if it was piss-poor, Vandre must have had terrible taste.

"Do you know what you had?" Saddler wasted no time.

Vandre didn't like to waste time either, "I reckon it's the crown that Prince Vernus is gonna crown his little lady with."

Saddler neither confirmed nor denied, "Where did you get it?"

Vandre ate the rest of his fig, and reached for his wine, chains rattling, "Sure is hard to eat with these big ugly iron bangles." He shook his wrists to create cacophony. "I've never cared much for fruit, either."

Saddler's face lost all sense of feigned kindness, "I'm willing to chat because I think you might be useful. This room, the bed, the food, the *light*... They are entirely contingent on your continued cooperation." He paused, pulling a thin knife from his belt. Silver and hooked and wicked, it was about six inches long and gleamed in the sun. "Your cooperation is not required. I can take this, and I can start cutting you, Ser. I'm not great at torture, the knife will slip, especially if the handle gets *soaked."*

Vandre plucked a grape from the bowl thoughtfully, before deciding that he might as well push back, "I've been cut before."

"I'm sure you have, and by worse men than me." Saddler smiled, very, very broadly, like some ape threatening violence. "I happen to know several. If I can't get the information I need, I can send for my brother, Hugo. He tends to be more hands on with his interrogations than I am, but he's much more effective. Failing that, I know the Lord Inquisitor is here, that spymaster, Coldhearth. I'm sure he'd love to try his hand at such a tough nut to crack." Saddler took a grape of his own, and crushed it on the table beneath his palm. Red juice oozed between long, pale fingers.

Vandre simply nodded along, trying not to let his terror show.

"Perhaps I can have my mother's witch come in, you met her. The green *ifre-croi* that caught you in the yard. She can see into your thoughts. That's how she knew you killed the farmboys."

The old man stopped chewing.

"That's how she knew that you're not Ser Jemes Wyse. That Ser Jemes Wyse is dead, and you're a bandit with delusions of chivalry." Saddler's tone had gone sharp. "I can have her come in here, and reach into that pathetic cesspool you call a mind." Saddler wiped a smear of thick red grape, juice and pulp, on Vandre's forehead, "And Hellendre can rip out the information I need, and hopefully not mess the place up too much."

Terror had gripped the old man's heart. Were he not injured, he might have risked attacking the boy. Saddler was younger and taller, sure. But he was lanky and no warrior, Vandre could have dealt with him easy enough. A castle full of guards, those would kill him, but his point would have been made, at least. Instead, he sulked into his chair, a broken old wretch.

"Or." Saddler continued, plucking another grape, "You can be a nice puppy and I'll keep giving you treats." Saddler pressed the grape to Vandre's lips, and pushed it into his mouth with a thumb.

Every single instinct made Vandre want to kill this boy, but he chewed his grape and he answered, "The ghost of Purvon Webb gave me the crown in the Royal Box at midnight. On the tourney grounds" The thought made Vandre feel crazy when he kept it inside, saying it out loud was even more maddening. "I haven't killed anyone since the farmboys." He added, awkwardly.

Saddler didn't laugh. He didn't even smirk.

"I had been south, working a job in The Witchwood, guarding a caravan against bandits. Then one day, Belbert, the head merchant's head steward came to me, with a little bundled roll of parchment, edged in red." He frowned, "Now Belbert was smart and Belbert had worked these kinda jobs long enough to know what kinda men he was hiring, so when I got the letter, the seal was broken." Vandre shifted uncomfortably in his chair, "Now that letter said the same thing about Ser Jemes Wyse as you just did. Kinda thing that would get me executed in half-heartbeat. But Belbert said… It said something about my dyin' father in Honeyhome. No matter who I showed it to, it was about my dyin' da' in Honeyhome, even though I read someone threatening to expose my dearest, darkest secret."

Saddler watched him closely, Vandre could feel the Lordling searching for an inconsistency, a lie.

"The best part is… My old man has been dead forty years. And he never spent a day north of the Lowlands."

Saddler narrowed his eyes, a curl of auburn hung over his forehead, "Strange story. Sounds unbelievable. Probably true." He looked over at the bandaged old man, "Well, go on."

Vandre nodded, "Somewheres around your fine city of Stonestall, I realized that I would be needing a horse to make it to Honeyhome by the time this letter told me to be there, so I stole one. Fine gelding. Right out of one of your Daddy's yards."

Hartwin gave an amused little snort.

"'Coupla the local farm boys must have taken exception to such a fine animal going missing, so they found me and tried to take him back. Scrap happened. The horse ran off into the night and the boys died." Vandre kept details honest, but sparse. He was past exhausted and this may yet go on for some time. A rattling cough set the old man to groaning at his busted body.

"The boys *died?*" Saddler was incredulous.

"...I killed them." He shook his head, "To be true, the horse killed one. That wasn't me. Kicked him right in the head."

Saddler rose, and his great green eyes roamed over Vandre's broken body, "Still, how old are you, forty-and-five?"

"Two-past-fifty."

"Still." Saddler had allowed just the barest hint of a compliment ride out of his lips, "few men can fight three-on-one and walk away. Especially against men half his age."

"They were unarmed." Vandre downplayed.

"They should have armed themselves." Saddler gave his little snorting laugh again, "Hunting for horse thieves is deadly business, it would seem." He drummed an impatient finger, "Your story is still several days from Honeyhome."

"Right, sorry. I managed my way to Hope's Hill and met up with another man with a letter from the same source, that elven alchemist I was traveling with when…"

Saddler grinned, as Vandre refused to meet his gaze, "We *met*. I instructed you on a better way of bathing and… …I loaned you horses?" He was confused. "That doesn't seem right." The point of the knife in Saddler's hand found his thumb.

"The… elf. He charmed… you." Vandre sipped the wine again, it was loosening his tongue, but he was so thirsty. "I think, I don't know. I reckon he's a Learner."

"Motherfucker."

"He and I made it here, and set up my pav– my tent. Tied my donkey off, and we got set on by two more miscreants. We fucked around with the matches a tad, used the elf's drugs, made a little money, humbled some miserable bastards. We had a good time."

"Albin?"

"We thought it would be funny." Vandre admitted, referring to the drugging of a sober, pious lord. "But good times end, and we were summoned to the tourney grounds at midnight. We arrived and…"

He stopped. There was no way the cocky young lordling before him would believe the rest. It was too fantastic, too wild. To be true, the old man didn't totally believe the events himself. He downed more wine and continued, "We arrived and the dead boy was waiting for us. Webb, that little Ozywk that died in the first round. He had a hole… big, bloody hole… could see the moon right through his… his… chest. He floated on smoke– He tore the bloody crown, right outta his ribs."

Saddler looked at him for a long, long time. The Lordling held his tongue, merely twisted the point of the knife against his thumb. A strong jaw covered in wiry ginger brush ground back and forth. For a moment, Vandre realized he could hear the tourney outside. The commons had gathered in force, sword sang on sword, and the world moved on without him. It would be much the same after this noble boy had him on the gallows.

Saddler produced the crown from a hidden pocket in his clothes. He set the fine gold on the table with nary a tap. Finally, the lanky, stern boy spoke, his voice rough and whisper quiet, "I do not think you are mad... ...I do not know if it occurred in that exact manner, but I don't think you're crazy."

Vandre exhaled for what must have been the first time in a month.

Saddler continued, his volume rising with his confidence. "There is a level of strangeness here that I cannot comprehend, despite my learning and wit. Unlikely, even impossible things keep occurring, as you well have seen...– I suppose I should not call you Wyse." Saddler turned the knife point on the old man, shining wicked. "Your name. Your real name. Now."

"Vandre." The old man said it pained him, but he said it.

"As you have clearly noticed here, *Vandre,* there is something most strange occurring in Hivehall." Saddler put some verbal odor on the common-born sort of name, "That simple fact gives me pause when it comes to dealing with you."

The old man lifted his lined face, windburnt and sun-worn. He exhaled, "I'm old, kid. I'm tired." He finished the last cup of wine, and his head had begun to swim, "...And I'm out of drink. You got what you want, so I figure, if you want something else, you'll blackmail me. If you don't, I'm already dead."

"Astute."

"I didn't live this life this long bein' stupid."

Saddler took another of his long, hard looks. Vandre could see wheels rolling, calculations whorling and debates occurring in a few short seconds. Finally, his tight little slash of a mouth opened, "You did not." Saddler passed a small green square of fabric, a handkerchief, to him. "Your forehead." Vandre wiped the sticky juice and pulp away and Hartwin Saddler continued, "You are clearly an adaptable sort, and if you killed those four boys alone, you are clearly not lacking with a blade."

Saddler chewed his bottom lip, screwing up his face in an annoying sort of way, "I have men that are good with a blade. I have men that are adaptable. But I don't have men that have those skills and no other value to me whatsoever."

"Disposable and useful, I'll have them carve it above my tomb." Gallows humor fit this situation, Vandre supposed.

"No need to be so maudlin, I think I've found a use for you, and that means I don't intend to have you hanged for murder and theft." Saddler smirked, offering an escape.

Vandre knew that he was trading a noose for a bridle, but service was preferable to Hell. The old man nodded. "I might be receptive to that, sure."

"I am a well protected man, Vandre. You know of my brother, I'm sure. But both my uncle and cousin are extremely skilled knights as well–"

"Your brother and your cousin might be, but I seen that dandy Uncle of yours rattle that pretty saber poorly. He's not nothin'." Vandre interrupted, hastily. The wine's warmth was in his cheeks now.

Saddler smirked, "Like I said, astute." He continued, "Which is nothing to say of my two-hundred Young Stallions, the finest mounted soldiers in the Empire. I have a small army and capable men to command it. I will inherit the coffers of not one, but likely three of the richest Clans in the Empire when my father and grandfather die. I am not a man who wants much. But, still, there is more to be done, more that I need. And for that, I need men whose honor I can stain."

Vandre laughed, sending blazing red spiderwebs of agony through his chest. He coughed and sputtered, "Of course, you mustn't have knights and soldiers kill people! It would not be proper to have a killer commit murder."

"You are jesting, but you are right." His long face held not a scrap of mirth, "There are things that a lord must do that are ugly, unsightly, maybe even evil. For the greater good."

"The greater good?" Vandre questioned.

"The greater good." Saddler repeated, "Sometimes hard choices need to be made and harder actions taken. Sometimes, one innocent needs to die in order to save ten."

"Must be nice to be the one decidin'."

"It's Hell." Saddler nodded, slowly, sadly. "And you're going to join me."

Later, the green girl would return, and tended to his wounds with magic that rivaled even Clovis, if that was even his name. They called her Hellendre, and she would take some getting used to, Vandre decided. The girl was bubbly and pretty and more kind than she ought to have been, but there was something about her big brassy eyes, great shining beads of metal, that put him to shivering. But her touch was gentle and by the time she had taken to his bruised and battered chest, he was feeling bold so he spoke up.

"Are my ribs broken?" She had servants bring a big brass tub into the room, and he was currently soaking in a stew of steaming hot water, oils and herbs. Vandre breathed raggedly, nude, bruised and pink from the hot water.

Her voice was musical, brassy, everything her gentle hands were not, "Aye. Probably, and judging by the way you breathe, it's not the first time."

"It's not the first time this week."

Bells of laughter tinkled, "I'd believe it. Not to be judgemental, Ser–"

"Stop with that, I ain't pretending to be a knight."

"Not to be judgemental." She corrected, "But, I've never seen a man so scarred. Do you lose fights on purpose? Do you like getting stabbed?"

He glowered, "Nah, I just seem to be good at it."

"Getting stabbed and living is a skill of itself." She grinned, and her canines were pointed.

"I'd rather have been good at sums and been a merchant." He groaned as she pressed her palms on a dark angry bruise, hard, but when she lifted them, the pain was gone and so was the purple. "Or that, that is a skill I could stand to learn."

She smirked, "I'd love to teach you, but I come by it natural" She blinked her big brassy eyes, heavy-lidded, "Same as my good looks."

"So, the Learners, they're all born with it, too?" His tone was curious, but careful.

A little toss of the head sent her auburn ringlets dancing. "Some of 'em, sure. But most of them *learn* it."

Vandre held onto that, still wondering what became of Clovis and the rest. She would leave shortly thereafter, and he would be allowed to dress himself in peace. His dusty brown cloak had been replaced with one of fine laurel and fern greens. His ancient bronze ringmail had been traded for black scale. New smallclothes, breeches and boots. A chain to snap around his neck, with the sigil of Clan Saddler. A medallion of his new position. A leash.

He dressed in silence, a new man in new clothes. Ser Jemes Wyse would be given his name back; it seemed, Vandre no longer needed it. The girl had done good work, he moved almost painlessly. Once dressed, he stepped to the window and tried to catch his own reflection in the glass, the small cell did not hold a mirror. It was difficult, but the tired old man could see he was mostly whole. His left ear was missing a sizable chunk. There were a few new scars on his face, his hairline had been left a ruin by the bird's talons. The long gash on his neck was now a great purple scar, near eight inches and ragged. He had not started with a handsome face, and life had not improved it.

The old man would soon be gathered and sent to the armory, where he was given a new long-sword. It was castle made steel, and wicked sharp, the hilt wrapped in honey-smooth calfskin. When Vandre held it, he liked its balance, though it was both longer and lighter than he was used to. He would want to swing it in practice a few times before he needed to swing it in earnest. Next, the weathered old blacksmith peered at him with crooked eyes and a notched smile, "Yeh carry a shield?"

Vandre nodded, "Round, if you got it. Three hand, maybe three and a half."

The sooty old smithy cackled, "Just the thing, just the thing!" His great gnarled hands slammed a round oak and iron shield on the rough table in front of him.

Unscarred, undented, devoid of device. A clean start.

He smirked and decided he'd keep the donkey

SLADE III

"They say war makes strange allies, but that ain't it. Fear, love, greed. Those make strange allies, war is just the symptom."

While he sat waiting for Marten and Ser Tullus, Lord Byrony Saddler smiled broadly at Slade. This big man sipped a clay cup of warm honeyed milk, a favorite of Slade's on a rainy day, and when offered, the High Lord accepted vigorously. Slade clutched his own cup in his left hand, keeping his crippled right hand in his lap. "It's been ages since I've had this stuff, thank you, son."

Slade nodded politely, though he generally hated being called 'son', he let it pass. "My pleasure, my Lord." The big man folded his hands over themselves, and the quiet awkwardness hung between the pair.

Saddler took a longer, deeper draw and cleared his throat. "How have you been finding the tourney?" Slade watched this red-faced old man gurn at him, and went for honesty. He was too tired for much else.

"I am not much of one for tourneys, but I have found the library to be incredible. We don't have much in the way of books at the Moss Mont."

"You sailed up, didn't you?"

"We did." The answer seemed silly. *Why would anyone ride through the swamps?* He swallowed his irritation, "Every Mirebreaker is a sailor, they say. I know we tend to rivers and swamps, but the ocean is water all the same."

"Well, if you're not opposed to ridin'- maybe bring a knight or something, someone you like and trust." He seemed to trail off, finding his point again, "But you and a few retainers could ride south with us, take a look at our stacks. My father was a great reader himself. Our collection ain't what they got here, but it's sizable enough. You can ask my Hart if you don't believe me. He's read damn near every one of them." The big lord chortled, "But if you're interested, I'd love to have you at Stonestall for a few weeks. I know Hart would as well."

Slade's stomach did an excited little twist. He did not especially relish the prospect of that much riding, but the bookvaults at Stonestall did have a reputation he wanted to investigate. "I would have to discuss matters with my brother and uncle, but I would certainly enjoy that, my Lord."

"Good, good! It's been too long since I've had fresh ideas in the court, your visit could be just the thing!" The big man grinned again, and Slade found himself thinking of his Uncle Tullus, and realized that these two were men of the same stripe, coarse, but ultimately kind, sensitive and good.

The doors swung open, and both Uncle Tullus and Marten made their way to the table. Uncle Tullus had a contest this afternoon and had disregarded the normal airs that a meeting like this would request. He wore a tunic of Mirebreaker myrtle, plain leathers and a bronze chain. Lord Byrony seemed entirely unbothered.

In contrast, Marten was dressed in his finery, befitting a young lord. He was wearing a tunic of autumn ochre, nearly bronze, under a velvety calfskin vest dyed in soft greens. Matching boots and gloves in their own jades. He had clasped his finest cloak, a swirling brocade of swamp flowers in brazen thread on black. He clasped the whole thing with a dragon turtle pin, yellow gold and green emerald eyes. He was every bit a Lord, all smiles and congeniality as he extended his hand to the Lord of the Goldengrass.

They exchanged polite courtesies, and settled into their seats, Uncle Tullus on Marten's left and Slade on his right. *As he always promised.* Joy swelled in his chest and he exhaled, satisfied; it was time to be a Lord.

Marten opened the proceedings, "What do I owe the pleasure, Lord Saddler? My stables are plenty full."

Saddler's tone was warmth itself, his sonorous voice flowing over the whole room, "No such horsetrading, M'lord. But trading all the same, and in matters such as these I find it better to stay real direct." He paused, a great ponderous mind searching for words too small for his ideas, "My son, Hartwin, he's in love."

Marten squinted, nodding along, slowly, "Well, that is… very good?"

"It is, to tell it true, she's a damn fine young lady." There was a bit of mirth in his tone, "You all know her plenty well, she's your wealthiest bannerwoman."

Slade frowned, "Lady Bridge?" *Oh, I know her indeed.*

There was a slow nod of confirmation from the Horselord, and Marten immediately shifted, tension building in his shoulders, "I don't know what your game is, but we can not part with the incomes her land provides, my Lord. And she's the only heir of that ancient line, there's no way she'd possibly abdicate."

"I wouldn't ask you, m'lord. Clan Bridge has incomes you need, the Goldengrass doesn't. But we do need Lady Joelle, well at least my Hart does."

Slade had liked Hartwin, despite himself, his older brother would likely be less charitable. Hartwin and Marten had never gotten on, and even last night there had been jabs between the pair. Marten pressed his lips together, eyes narrowing to predatory slits, "What are you proposing, Lord Byrony?"

"Well, it is certainly a unique situation, and I have a number of unique solutions." Saddler unrolled a large map, sheepskin and the whole of Daneau was laid out before them. Huge hands, covered in coarse black hair gently smoothed the vellum, rivers, roads, forests and cities dancing under his digits, "Well, I could offer a historical recompense, Codd Stone was taken from the Lowlands and given to my grandfather's grandfather or some such thing, during that little southern rebellion you all had down here–"

Slade peevishly interrupted, "Clan Mirebreaker stayed loyal!" Marten placed a hand on his forearm to calm him, and Uncle Tullus gave him a withering look.

The mirth on Lord Byrony's face only grew, "And that's precisely why there is still a Clan Mirebreaker to negotiate with. But that said, Codd Stone and Clan Dolan could be granted back to the Lowlands, in exchange for Cobalt Bridge and her incomes.

Before his brother could say a word, Slade burst outward again, "Absolutely not. A non-starter, my lord. Cobalt Bridge makes thrice what Codd Stone does, even with the ports. And Cobalt Bridge isn't raided every summer. No way."

Marten raised an eyebrow, "What he said."

Saddler and Uncle Tullus exchanged a look, and the old knight gave a dismissive toss of the head, "They're the lordlings, I'm just here to make sure they eat a vegetable once in a moon."

Both older men chuckled, and Byrony continued, "I'd be lyin' to say if I expected that to work, but I had held out hope." He pointed directly at Cobalt Bridge, a river port, a sea port, surrounded by fertile fields and fine marble and cobalt mines. Even the keep of Rain Tower

Hall was known as one of the most picturesque castles in the Empire, a sturdy spire of grey marble overlooking the fjord where the city sprawled. "Always lead with the low offer."

Tullus laughed, "Fuckin' horse traders."

"Some men are good with swords." He smirked at Marten, "Some of us have other skillsets." His glance shifted to Slade, "In that case, I have a much more tempting proposition for you. Keep it, keep the whole damn thing. Hart and Joelle and whatever staff they need can serve as lords until they need to serve in Stonestall. By the time I'm dead, which should hopefully be a few more years." His eyes sparkled with a youthful exuberance, "They should have at least an heir to sit the chair."

Marten stifled a laugh."Your son would never submit to serving as my bannerman, even for a few years."

"You ain't seen how much he loves that girl."

Slade was more interested in the practicalities of such an arrangement, "So this hypothetical Clan Saddler of Cobalt Bridge still pays all of its incomes to us. That's fair enough, I suppose. He's just asking to change the banner on the castle really."

Byrony shook his head, "Keep the crawdad for all I care. Hell, you might even convince Hartwin to get a second son to take Lady Joelle's name and it can stay 'Clan Bridge' if it bothers you."

Marten stared at the map for a long time, "It's not that I don't trust you, my Lord. I do, Lord Byrony. I even like you, my late Father spoke very well of you." Lord Tullus chuffed in agreement, and Marten smirked, "It's not that I don't even believe that your son might *actually* love Lady Joelle. I just don't see what benefit this brings The Lowlands at tremendous risk to my own family. No intention of offense, but a mind like your son's… that's a real threat. He's a fox in the henhouse, so to say. Because sooner or later, maybe long after you're gone, I reckon your son takes a run at me."

Byrony chuckled, "I figured you might say something like that. And I think I have a real elegant solution for that, something that helps us both out."

Slade burrowed his tongue against his bottom teeth. Marten placed his hands on the table. He had father's wedding ring on his left pointer finger. Father had huge bear paws like Ser Tullus, like Lord Byrony. "I'm listening, my lord." Marten's hands may not have been as massive, but he was only eighteen. He was yet to stop growing.

"Harlow."

The name hung like the ringing of a bell. Harlow Saddler was the flower of the Goldengrass. Slade had only seen her at a distance these last few days, but she was beautiful, graceful and regarded as the most desired maiden in all of the Empire. She was being courted by Prince Vernus himself.

"You're not the only one your father spoke well of, Marten." Saddler looked over the young Lord. Tall, strong, handsome, Marten was a prize, to be sure. But the old man focused on Marten's right hand, in the cast. "I heard how you broke that hand, son. Maybe not a wise act, but an honorable one."

Slade felt embarrassment hot on his blushing cheeks, and couldn't lift his eyes from the floor. He simply focused on his thumbs tworling over one another and listened.

"We protect ours in the Lowlands. The swamp's too dangerous to survive without family." Uncle Tullus made a defense. *Funny, you were furious when it happened.*

"So it is in the tall grass, too." Byrony smirked, "I'm sure you heard what happened with Harlow and that Prince last night, as well?"

Slade had not, Slade intentionally avoided as much court gossip as possible. Marten nodded, "If whispers I've heard are true, my little cousin acted improperly. Prince or not."

"There's no lying in my Harlow, m'Lord." Saddler espoused.

"Just your heir." Marten replied. His face was still, a wooden mask of an ancient prince.

Slade had had enough of his brother's attitude. "Marten!" he barked, "The Lord is offering you the most beautiful young noble in the country, he's offering a permanent tie to the richest lords in Daneau." Exasperation took his voice, "Hartwin Saddler is only an ass to you because you get so angry! He's been nothing but nice to me!"

Marten stared, the expression on his face hardening, but not as much as it ought to.

Slade tensed, he knew he was in the murkiest quagmire now. Nothing to do but hold your nose and press on, "Sometimes, you just need to swallow your pride, because the worst person you know is still a person, Marten. If you're gonna let money stand in the way of two people who love one another, you're not the man my Dad raised you to be." In the resulting quiet, the only sound was wooden chair legs scraping as Slade slowly rose.

Marten grabbed his wrist with his plastered hand. He looked up to his younger brother, his words tracing the word 'okay', as his eyes pleaded apology. He turned back toward Lord Saddler, "I suppose meeting the girl couldn't possibly hurt."

"Perfect! It's settled!" Slade rose again, "I am sorry to be rude, but I have a previous engagement in the library who is very likely growing impatient."

As he hurried to the door, Uncle Tullus called at his back, "Impatience will be the least of your worries if you are not at the tourney this afternoon, Slade."

Slade hollered back, "Send Gar to get me!"

It was Marten who answered, "Garland has his own things to do! It's not his job to fetch you!"

Slade stopped, before crossing back to Lord Saddler, who was grinning through all of this, "Apologies, how rude of me, I don't mean to run off like that, but there is a pressing matter." Marten made a barking noise behind him, until Uncle Tullus shook his shoulder. Slade knew the barking was meant to deride the young lady waiting for him, but nevertheless, he continued, "...that I must attend to. But, were I to accept your earlier proposition, you'd allow me my choice of companions along?"

The old lord grinned, nodding. "Sure, son, whomever you'd think would enjoy the reading."

He had just the girl in mind.

Once he had returned to his chambers, he was a whirlwind of activity. He not only needed his notes and charcoals, but he would also need his book of maps and dates to plan this trip south. Gar would certainly be happy to ride as his protection. The big smithee was no warrior, but he would be more than enough to keep Slade safe on the road, at least among the procession and in the great doors of the Stonestall. Lady Masha would certainly agree to tagging along, Rime River seemed almost as dull–

"Slade?"

Aunt Carmine had quietly inserted her head through the partially ajar doorframe. Her face seemed drawn, there was tension in her posture. Slade lifted his head, "Oh, yes?"

She carefully opened the door, slowly. Fog silent, she padded through the threshold. "Slade, honey. I just spoke with Lady Jasmine." A slow, sad smile spread over her cheeks, "She told me that you spent the afternoon with Lady Masha Curr yesterday…" She trailed off, and Slade could not place her meaning.

"I did, yes." He frowned a little at her uncharacteristic gentility. Lady Carmine was a woman who was capable of tenderness, true, but she generally leaned toward the uncouth.

She sat on the bed, and patted the place beside her. Slade settled in, his thin body towering over her. It had only been in the last year that the second son of the swamps had outgrown his aunt. While he enjoyed feeling like a man grown, some part of him longed for the comfort of time past. "Have you been getting close, Slade?"

He nodded, "Yes, I think so."

"That's what I thought." She placed a soft hand on his knee, "Sometimes, Slade, things happen; out of our control."

Slade blinked in confusion, "Did something happen to Lady Masha?" He could feel his body tensing, heart pounding.

"She is unharmed, Slade. But her brother, the heir to the Wylde–"

Slade interjected, "Hullen."

"Yes, Hullen." She bit her bottom lip, pink as a peony. "Some time this morning, Hullen had a fall down the stone spiral stairs in this very tower, hun. He–" her voice, usually all guts and gravel, cracked under the weight of tragedy. "The Learners don't know if he's going to live. Lady Masha is very needed by her family."

Slade often had a hard time with his feelings. He was often almost numbed to things, unsure how to react. But then, sometimes, especially when disappointed, an awful fury would brew in his belly.

This horrid, awful anger would feed itself, thick and hot and acidic, just under his ribs. It would squeeze his heart, stomp his lungs and he would spiral into despondency or resentful rage. The boy was a strong willed, logical sort, and he hated feeling so out of control. This news, this horrible theft of a future that he hadn't even gotten to ask for, sent him to that overwhelmed, tempestuous place.

He did his best not to rage, though hot tears had begun streaking down his cheeks, "Is she well?"

"She is not, Slade."

His throat constricted itself, like he was trying to strangle himself from the inside, "I see." He stayed as silent as he could, because if he spoke, the whirling emotion inside him would spring forth, swarming like angry bees.

"I am unsure of what you need, Slade." Carmine's tenderness remained, but trepidation had begun to stain her speech.

"There is nothing to be done, Aunt Carmine."

He would not go to the library that morning. Instead, he would attend the tournament with his brothers. He didn't care for the light or the noise, but Jamen and Marten were the best comfort he knew. He cheered as sad Lady Lenore used her witchcraft to stagger the beastly Ser Sancho Madapple. He watched Ser Hugo Saddler slash and jab his way to a victory over the bird-woman from H'ro Cratis. He wondered to himself what sort of family this man would be if Marten took Lord Byrony's offer. Harlow seemed like a good, kind girl. Slade liked Hartwin, despite knowing better. But there was something about this third triplet, this Hugo, that set his flesh to goosebumps. Pitiless eyes of green, always hunting. He wore a horse on his helm, but all Slade saw was a tiger.

Other matches began to drag one into another. A Saddler Uncle disarmed a bowman. The Crown Prince wrestled one of his Grey Guards, that smoky raider Duck, to the mud. But when the horns announced the mystery knight, this Big Turtle, Slade looked up from his book. This man strode through the rain, clad in a gorgeous green and orange plate. It was near as fine as the shining bronze Uncle Tullus wore, even rivaling Marten's striking helm and ringmail. The mystery knight parted the raindrops, when he swung his immense two-handed sword to the clouds matching the shade of his steel. Something about a chivalrous knight like that, a bastion of all a knight should be, gave Slade's heart the slightest balm. He was brave and strong but sought combat for its own sake. Mystery knights won no honor, no riches.

Horns blew again, and some shaggy Wyldeman appeared on the march. He was not one of Lady Masha's Curr men, they had all come to watch Ser Hale Torchbearer lose a few matches past. This man was as big as any man Slade had ever seen, clad in a tunic of clanking bronze disks, each the size of a coin. His shield was a rough hewn, well beaten thing, gouged so deep that Slade could not recognize his standard. He was dressed less like a knight and more like a bandit. A great orange and brown cloak that looked like autumn foliage covered his shoulders and a beard to match poked out from under his leather and iron helm. His long sword was a wicked piece of steel, beaten and notched with use, and poorly repaired and maintained. Slade tapped his older brother in the ribs with an elbow, "What in the name of the celestials is *that?*"

Marten gave a braying laugh, "That is *Lord* 'Red' Ronnie."

Slade mentally parsed through the list of lords he knew and came up short, at least until he got another look at the standard: a hairy forest giant on a burning field. "Tallman? Isn't that." He lowered his voice to a whisper, leaning in extra close, "Gar's *other* family? You know, where his mom was from?"

Marten nodded, "Yeah. When his ma… y'know, passed, they sent him off to Uncle Tullus." Garland's mother had died giving birth to him, in no small part to his great size, Slade would have to imagine. Slade could not possibly imagine feeling so… *unwanted.* Marten snorted, "Shame he ain't here to watch this guy get his shit kicked in." The regal lordling who had met with Lord Byrony a few hours ago had slowly slipped back inward to his brother.

The Turtle clanged his sword on his shield, once, twice, thrice. Tallman did the same, sending flakes of orange paint and slivers of wood tumbling to the mud below. The peevish little games master made his announcements, trying to shield his bald pate from the rain with a large silver serving dish. When he was done, he sloshed through the mud toward the gallery. The horns tootled one final time and Tallman was immediately knocked to the mud.

Slade wasn't even sure he'd seen the Big Turtle move initially. Marten was just as dumbfounded. A seasoned warrior himself, he muttered, "No right to be that big and move that quick. None." under his breath.

The big man had not used his big two handed sword, no, he'd lifted a huge boot and kicked Tallman full on in the sternum. It was not a move any knight would have expected, and one could hear the surprise in the rush of wind torrenting from "Red" Ronnie's lungs. For his part, Tallman refused to be helpless. Even from his back, he was dangerous, kicking up toward the Turtle's knees and instep, anything to take away his base.

Tallman eventually would connect with a wild thrust to The Turtle's knee, staggering him. 'Red' Ronnie scuttled to his feet, pouncing on this opportunity without a second thought. The Turtle dropped to one knee as Tallman resumed his vertical base. Tallman swung that big ugly notched steel downward at his opponent, but the Turtle swung his big sword up so quickly the air snapped behind it. The crash of steel on steel rang into the crowd, who swelled its echo like thunder, screaming raucous cheers. Slade cheered the loudest as the Turtle set his own base and through raindrops and sword slashes that fell nearly so rapidly, the mystery knight pushed his way to his feet.

The powerful anonymous swordsman had become a favorite of the crowd and it was easy to see why. This Big Turtle was Glinda the Greenskin come again, a generational talent, and not one soul in the crowd would speak to his true name.

Tallman was no longer able to rain down his overhead blows. The orange bearded Wyldeman was taller than the Turtle, but only by a meager handful of inches. They had switched to a more elegant form of swordplay, the Turtle would try for a cut with his great, heavy claymore and Tallman would parry with his barely-lighter longsword. As quick as the Turtle was, the sheer size of his weapon was the disadvantage. Even Slade was fairly sure he would be able to parry it.

Tallman was clearly ready to continue this game forever, but the Turtle did something unexpected, rather than try for Tallman, he started chopping wood. The Turtle hammered away at Tallman's less-than-sturdy shield. Paint and wood flew in concert, and on the fourth strike, the shield shattered, sending a weighty hunk of oak flying into the front of Tallman's helm.

Tallman stumbled backward, and again, rather than his sword, The Turtle chose his fists, once more. With a grunt that may have been a "Fuck you." The Turtle planted a plated gauntlet between Tallman's eyes, and the legs went out from the Wyldeman. The commons and lords alike burst into delirium at this unknown paragon besting a terrible barbarian from the icy north. As the horns made another clarion call announcing his victory, the Big Turtle raised his claymore, and Marten sighed, "Poor bastard has Prince Talor in the next match, tonight…"

That hurt Slade's heart. The Prince had been kind, intelligent and genial in their meetings, but something about his power and the blaise way he used it left Slade very, very concerned for this new mystery knight. The Prince had already killed one combatant accidentally, to be true.

By the time Aunt Carmine had made her way to the arena, the rain above had slowed from a drizzle to a gentle sprinkle and the silver sun was even trying to shoulder its way through the clouds. She had dressed in her finest contest armor, swirling silks of Lily greens, yellows and pinks over enameled plate and gilded chain. She was a frog princess, she was The Bloody Lily. For this contest, she carried her long curved scythe sword and nothing else. It was her favorite weapon, Slade knew.

The horns sounded once more and the crowd erupted into furious cheers, as Uncle Tullus made his appearance. In his youth, Ser Tullus Mirebreaker had been the most renowned tourney knight of his age. He had won more than enough gold to secure a comfortable lifetime, and that was discounting what was due to him as his inheritance as a second son of a Great Lord, and nephew of a queen. He hadn't taken to the arena in nearly a decade, but both he and Lady Carmine had stepped into the tourney after Marten had assaulted Prince Vernus, but this match was a welcome reward.

Uncle Tullus carried a pair of short, thick short swords, almost more spades than daggers, and had worn even thicker gauntlets than

Slade usually saw him using for sparring. Again, he leaned to his brother, "What's he up to?"

Marten's face was stern, "I have not the foggiest."

In the slick muddy slop, the spouses would slam swords. Aunt Carmine was quicker, as Uncle Tullus swung his heavy gauntlets, his wife could have dodged twice. Her sickle sword flashed and rang on Ser Tullus' armor, but could find little purchase. If Aunt Carmine got too close to a joint in his armor, the Snapping Turtle would simply swat it away with one of his great armored gauntlets.

And seemed to be the match, Uncle Tullus on his back feet, drinking in blows on his thick metal shell. If his intention was to wear down the Lily, she did not seem to be slowing, Slade mused.

She cried out, "Twenty damn years I've been waiting, and this is the best you got? Yer a damn turtle hiding in his shell!" In fact, Slade saw the pace of his aunt's whorling slashes increase in speed and viciousness.

Uncle Tullus's mouth moved under his big blonde horseshoe of a mustache, but his words were too low to be heard by anyone but Aunt Carmine. The Bloody Lily gasped indignantly and sped her strikes further, wilder, harder.

And then one of them made her stumble off balance, ever so slightly. In her fury, her chase, her *need* to best her husband, she had gotten angry and Lady Carmine got sloppy. Ser Tullus Mirebreaker was not called the Snapping Turtle just because he was short and squat. Ser Tullus had become one of the most feared warriors in the realm, despite being short and squat, and that was because he had an uncanny ability to pick his moment. He would draw his opponent exactly where he wanted them, and then...

SNAP.

Ser Tullus spun his whole body, and both heavy iron gauntlets, in a quick low arc, just enough to send a slightly off balance Lady Carmine sprawling to the muck with an echoing squelch.

He towered over his wife, "I'd prefer not to stab you, love." He winced at a rapidly stiffening shoulder, "But we both know I will."

And then there was a sound, at first low and rolling, but it floated upward, echoing through The Bloody Lily's helm, finally settling into a noise Slade loved well. Aunt Carmine was laughing. Loud and clear, in her voice that was not unlike a flute that someone had stepped on. The laughing woman sat up, and tossed her sickle-sword aside. "Fuck you." She barely got the words out between her guffaws, "Fine, fine, knock the little frog in the mud, yeh big bully!"

The way the stands cheered filled Slade's heart for the rest of the day. He looked to his brothers, his aunt, his uncle; even Gar, wherever he had gotten off to. Knowing what Lady Masha was going through, only yards away, Slade was incredibly thankful for the people and things he had, and right then and there he realized he was bright enough to obtain the rest. He just had to find his "hows".

ROLOF III

"You have more strength in your body than some whole clans, boy. But even you can't struggle against some things. Some things are too much to be battered or wrestled. Sometimes, you just aren't big and bad enough."

Magic was a coward's toy, Rolof had decided. He wasn't an especially cerebral sort, but after Prince Talor had put him to a dreamless sleep in the Great Gate Garden, even he had begun to notice the unaccounted hours of this awful trip. Rolof had woken up in his chamber– no memory of how he'd arrived there. The thin blanket had wrapped him so tightly, for a moment, he had thought he was back in Ser Doyle Selach's net, taking a beating once more. His body was still stiff and sore from the tourney, and he felt his right knee groan as he stretched his limbs from cold stone. The sun was higher in the sky than he would have liked. He probably had missed the opportunity to break his fast, which irked him further. He grunted, finally finding his feet, and when rough calloused heels found the bare chilly stone, he remembered that he'd left his son.

The bulky bronze Kraken bulled into the shared common space, bare-chested. He was covered in coarse black hair and a lattice-work of well earned scars. Rolof was certainly not a sentimental old soldier, but he had a torrid, violent tale to go along with each one. The ragged line that curved from his shoulder blade to ass-crack? A gift from a Clan Crowe scythe-man when he was seventeen. The puckered circle just above his hip? One of the forest folks from Clan Ludna had shot him with a little dart, nothing more than a needle with a yellow dandelion puff of feather fletching. He had yanked it out with no second thought, but some foul magical ichor on it had caused his whole hip to swell up over the next three days, fiery crimson, melon-round and oozing a black puss. He had needed a healer then, but he would let no land-loving Learner near him. It would be a priest of Gargol from Clan Gorge that saw to his ills.

As this man with wire-grey hair peeking under his black feathered headdress and a huge hooked nose saved Rolof's life, he spoke. He spoke strange words in a black tongue and drained the throbbing, swollen mass with a knife of black iron. The old man held it in a sputtering brazier until it glowed the same cherry-red and fire-hot as the malignancy on his hip. When the old priest brought them together, Rolof's screams had sent the rigging of the ship above him to shaking. Through his travels, Orin Gorge would become one of his constant companions. It was Gorge who had introduced him to Lady Larissa, his niece. In a way, this was all the old priest's fault, but Rolof would not speak ill of an old ally who died well.

Old memories scattered faster than the serving girls who had nearly been bowled over by Rolof as he burst into the common room. Save the terrified maids cleaning up the remaining foodstuffs, only Lord Ludo remained. The old lord had just begun his tenth decade, but remained nearly as sharp as he was in the prime of his life, even if his stamina couldn't maintain such standards. The old man was pawing at a yellowing tome, seeing glasses perched precariously on the end of his round little snub of a nose. Lord Ludo raised his head at the commotion, and when Rolof skidded to a stop, bareheeled and naked from the waist up, the little old raccoon gave Rolof a long stare, "I am reasonably sure I purchased enough clothes for you to wear this whole trip, Ser."

Dumbfounded, Rolof opened his mouth, a dull groan escaping as he tried to think, "Oh, holy shit— I mean, I'm sorry– APOLOGIES, My lord." He finally settled in. "I woke a bit… out of sorts."

Ludo returned to his book, "I can see that, Ser Rolof." He smiled under his glasses, as a cup of something steamed beside him, a medicinal stink flooding the room. Despite the decade of cuckoldry, Rolof didn't bear his high lord any bad blood. Lord Ludo was more often too fatigued to give Rolof any attention beyond the occasional simple order. He was generous and kind and far too distracted to notice a decade of infidelity and a "son" that looked nothing like him. "They've all had to head to the tourney grounds. Ser Sancho is in the earliest match once again." He paused, thoughtful, almost more to himself, "Suppose that's fortunate. Keeps him from drinking all night." He turned back to Rolof, smirking at his thought, "Anyhow, how's the hand, lad?"

Rolof raised his hand, the two smallest fingers having been wrapped together in silk by the Learner. "Two broken. Little ones, barely need 'em to hold my sword."

A slow, wide grin crossed the old man's face, if Lord Ludo wasn't so pleasantly oblivious, Rolof may have thought he seemed amused at Rolof's injury. "Good, good. We can't have my wife's bodyguard far from her body, can we?" He gave a lecherous laugh, "And what a sweet little body it is, I think I made myself another son last night! The gods may have taken my leg." The ancient lord shook the peg at his right leg, looking cherubic and childlike in his old age. "But at least they left me *that*! Matter of fact, I feel more virile than ever; maybe I'll make me some *twins* tonight!" The old man cackled with glee, even rising to nudge Rolof's shoulder like they were old friends.

If I dashed his head against the hard stone floor, not one soul would question him falling at his age. Rolof tensed and squeezed his left hand. He could palm the little Lord's head like a playball if he had a mind to. *It would be so easy, like cracking an egg.*

His thoughts of violence faded when a puff-cheeked old woman in a heavy black velvet dress, ancient and ill-fitting, entered. The short, round old matron guarded by two swords in a matching black mail. Lord Ludo hobbled to her, leaning hard on his cane. "Lady Adelpha, such a pleasure to see you!" He took both her spotted hands in his wrinkled ones, "It has been far too long, coz."

She squinted rheumy eyes, sniffled a watery nose and spoke in an austere wheeze, "Ludo, my Lord, you look nearly as bad as I do." They both guffawed and Rolof moved to excuse himself.

"If you do not mind, I'll be off to the tourney." He took a long step back to the door, the old woman's eyes roaming over Rolof's broad bare chest in a hungry sort of way.

"Pray, hold just a moment, Ser Rolof." Lord Ludo was not asking. He pressed a hoary-haired old hand to the old woman's ear, and they both giggled like schoolchildren and wore grins that gave the Bronze Kraken a watery feeling in his belly. The old woman gave Ludo a short nod, and his face glowed, "Wonderful. That should do it for now, Ser Rolof. Make your way to the tourney grounds. My wife's body is unguarded. Who knows what sort of churlish ragabrash may try to dishonor her?"

"What sort of–" Rolof just nodded, and went to dress himself. *Better I had just killed him, I think.* There was little time for more thinking as Rolof hastily assembled some clothing and his sword. The two broken fingers slowed his dressing, but he would shortly be racing across the castle yard, dressed in his leathers and wool, his great falchion at his hip.

Finding the Fisher Clan contingent was as easy as following the banners in flapping orange and brown. When the boy saw him, the tension in his chest eased. *Even without my name, he is mine. Let that old man flap his gums, I'll make Karl a Kraken yet.* He was glad to see the boy safe, and even gladder to see Lady Larissa grin and blush at his approach. He shouldered politely through Fisher cousins and aunts and sisters. *A bellowing bunch of widows and their brood.* It was true. Lady Larissa was the only woman in the family that had wed that was not widowed. He only had to wait for the old man to die. He wasn't too proud to wed the widow of the high lord. Then he and Larissa and the boy could sail back to Ryleh and live a good, quiet life away from the lords and their dealings and foul mainland magic. Let the mainland be his place to raid and reave; the rocks of Ryleh and their deep green waters were a place of rest.

He pressed in beside his charge, and she quickly brushed her little hand in the small of his back, wary of his injuries, not ungently. "Ser, I see you slept in." her voice was as gentle as her touch, a whisper, "Well earned, my love, Karl has only raved about your performance last night and the grand discussions."

The last thing Rolof recalled, the Artus boy, Prince-of-the-Black-Salt-Sea, had spoken to him, and he had needed a rest. Fog covered memories; gold and green and swirling. He tried to recall more, but deep in his mind something bid him to think not on it, so he didn't. Something on his face must have spoken to his confusion. He looked to Karl for answers and the boy only gave him a mischievous grin. *Filthy mainland magic.* Rolof did what he always did when he didn't understand or recall, he agreed and said thank you and scowled. "Thank you, m'lady." Rolof scowled.

As she settled to her bench, turning to gossip with Lady Cecily Madapple, one of Lord Ludo's many grand-daughters and wife to Ser Sancho. Rolof gave Karl a nudge with his boot and the boy made some room for him, "We will have words later, boy." He grunted into Karl's ear as he sat. The boy only sniggered at him. "How are the preparations for the witchling? Is Sancho ready?"

Karl spoke excitedly, "I think so, Ser. He spent all mornin' gettin' his axes shining sharp. He had an extra horn of ale, and only blood pudding to break his fast."

"Blood-drunk, lovely." Rolof was oddly fond of Ser Sancho, though he reckoned one day he may need to kill him.

Horns announced the arrival of Ser Sancho Madapple. Though he was no hero to the commons on most days, great cheers met his grim march through the rain to the center of the arena, ready to open the festivities. The slightest green miasma permeated the ringmail veil that hung from his crested helm, hiding his scarred features. The scars and miasma were a remnant of a fever in his youth and its subsequent arcane remedy. Rolof had heard scant few details, but a witch was said to be involved. The whole thing made Rolof uncomfortable.

After the witch had left a corpse of Lord Purvon Webb, both the commons and the lords alike had turned on Lady Lenore Vellen. Once the horns heralded her arrival, the stands erupted in enraged jeering. Vellen was pretty enough, pale, too skinny for Rolof's tastes, admittedly. Vellen was a shy slip moving down the pathway, every screech and boo a stone slung at her. She carried her halberd limply, and each droplet of the light rain seemed to weigh on her. As this girl, maybe a third Ser Sancho's size, stood across this damp arena from a great monster, a hunk of something foul flew through the air.

A lump of human excrement hit the witch-girl square on, in the face. Thrown from somewhere amongst the groundlings, Rolof watched the crowd burst into even wilder cheers than even when Ser Sancho had arrived and he laughed inside. *No one loves a sorceress.*

Hot, angry tears practically steamed in the rain, as they trickled down her filthy cheeks. She raised her long cloak of midnight indigo, and gently dabbed her face, and when it dropped, her left eye was glowing a ghostly green, literally steaming some smoky miasma of her own. The pair stood ready and the horn blew, signalling the end of Vellen.

Or so Ser Rolof Deepreach had assumed.

The entire arena went silent as Ser Sancho unleashed a hellacious howl, lowered his head, and charged forward, rain thickening as he bulled through it. Vellen stood, waiting. At first, Rolof had assumed she was simply ready to die, but there was too much fury in her ghost-eye. The closer Madapple roared, the brighter she shone. There was a horrible lump in Rolof's stomach.

The earth herself filled Vellen with light, a hundred hundred filaments of that same ghostly green sprouted and curled like delicate vines of ivy. An enormous thrum seemed to emanate all around them, a huge pounding *buzz*. They swirled around her, and she left the ground briefly, her silhouette blazing through her clothing. Ser Sancho slashed, and Vellen dodged it without moving, without effort. A pale hand touched the mail over Madapple's steaming cheek, and the green miasma of Madapple swirled into Vellen's ghostly hand. The great giant dropped the axe in his left hand, the one in his right flew a good ten feet and tumbled across wet dirt, leaving great gouges. He fell, leaving gouges of his own as Madapple tumbled across wet dirt, in concert. The big man snored lightly as Vellen lowered herself to the dirt. The witch knew she had won, and left him lying without another motion. The stunned silence of the arena turned to screams of hatred at her back, but the Witchling wasn't listening.

The boy broke the silence, "Whu-what was that, Ser Rolof?"

"Magic, boy." Rolof ground his teeth together, "A shortcut and a trap." But still, something deep within him thrilled beholding Ser Sancho downed at a touch. *The things I could accomplish with a fraction of that influence.* He squeezed his unbroken fingers. *Magic.*

"Is that it, then? Is Ser Sancho out?" Karl rose from his bench to better see the happenings in the arena, but there was little to see. Madapple was groggily finding his limbs again, but it was too late. He had been defeated.

"Seems so." He placed a hand on the boy's shoulder, ready for a long, wet afternoon.

That evening, Rolof could not have said what drew him toward the library in the far northern ward of the castle. In truth, he could barely discern books. Words had a way of dancing on the page that dizzied him, but he knew his letters and could sign his name. Rolof had sent updates to his father every half-year, ever since he'd left Ryleh behind. He was near as shy as a maid as he quietly slipped into the vast stacks.

An age-spotted Learner, in his bisected robes dozed, flecks of spittle bubbling from his bottom lip. Deepreach was unsure if he would be able to wake him if he tried, so he wandered on. He expected silence, but somewhere deep ahead, there was the slightest rustling and ruffling of motion. He pressed on, following the sound of pages and murmurs as they snaked between the shelves of these thousand

thousand tomes. No flame was allowed in the library, but the slow orange and pink of sunset cast its own fires across the shelves and floors. Great spanning crystal windows kept the room filled with adequate light during the day, even well into sunset.

As he drew closer to this mysterious reader, the heavy thud of his boots on the tile must have betrayed him, as the rustling stopped and this reader called out in a high, slightly monotone voice, a boy's voice, "Lady Masha? I knew you'd–"

Rolof rounded the corner to find that bony little Mirebreaker boy. The looks of mirrored revulsion between them passing any sense of decorum. This Slade was surrounded by great stacks of books, three or four, each of them containing at least a dozen hefty volumes. Parchment and charcoal and notes were scattered haphazardly across the table before him. The boy looked disheveled, to say the least. His hair stuck up in several different directions, charcoal and ink stained his eight fingers, and his vest and breeches. To set the final vision of weariness, the boy's eyes were red with the strain of hours of reading. The boy had initially held a look of happy anticipation, but it instantly fell to a scowl when his blue marble eyes found Ser Rolof, "Oh. It's you. Hello."

Deepreach grunted, "Boy." His eyes roamed over the table, lingering on the titles of the books; Fae Beasts and the Unseelie Hells: An Learner's Telling, Discerning the Eldritch, Dark Words on Dark Wings, and piles more of strange volumes. In the center of the table, the parchment was scrawled with drawings, a high writhing dome, a female figure that echoed Vellen's light this afternoon and...

A flash of pain seared between Ser Rolof's ears, deep flares of burning yellow light, a screech of a raptor and talons swirling in his mind. He stumbled, catching himself on the table with his smashed hand. He winced a curse under his breath. Mirebreaker leapt to his feet, taking a long step back, "Ser?"

The Bronze Kraken stabbed at a drawing with a thick finger. A huge twisted… man-bird-thing had been scrawled in charcoal. Feathers and talons and huge angry eyes. Though the boy only worked in charcoal, the knight knew the creature had eyes of yellow. "What is this… *thing?"*

Mirebreaker watched him, wary, "It's a drawing. …Are you unwell?"

"I'm fine." Rolof grumbled, "What is it a drawing of? I've seen that thing."

The skinny boy's hollow cheeked little face drained of color, "Where..?"

"I don't know…" The big man was suddenly very helpless, a great lost child, "I know I've seen him. I was sent by my lady… there was a bear."

Slade's eyes went wide, nodding. The boy lowered Deepreach to a chair gently. Inside his mind, Rolof pried and reached, his own tentacles of will struggling against screeching black talons. "I need you to tell me everything you know, Ser." The boy was entirely serious, all the venom from him.

Rolof's big barrel chest pounded, barely holding his heart in. His mouth had become cotton, "I think it's Gargol, God of Reavers. The Carrion Crow." Rolof had made offerings to the black bird before stringing black sails and bringing flame and death to the mainland, true, but he had never expected to see the Death-Devourer himself.

Mirebreaker twisted his face before tossing his head dismissively, "No, that doesn't fit. This thing speaks."

Deepreach grabbed the boy by his ink-stained lapel, "You've seen it too, haven't you?" Desperation was rising in his voice, but he didn't care. "They keep going into my memories, boy. The magic users. Great big swatches carved out like wheat in the field." The boy pulled away, frightened by his intensity. "If they know you've seen them, they'll carve up your brain too."

The boy was not comfortable.

ILLYSTRE III

"Everyone has a plan until they get stabbed."

The old man turning on the team and stealing the crown was not ideal. In truth, the old man had only really been a useful idiot at best. He was the career criminal that Illystre had needed in case the plan had managed to hitch itself on a challenge. The sort who knew how to adapt, the sort who could die and not be missed. Those sorts of men, men on the fringes, came with inherent risk, but Illystre could not have imagined Vandre would have made off with the Starheart Crown.

The old man getting arrested for a totally unrelated crime in the yard? Illystre was starting to believe in the gods, but he clearly must have offended them.

His position on the Lords Ascendant had gotten him into the twisting dungeon tower. Below him, honeycombs of cells were stacked onto one another, descending to depths even the Lord Inquisitor himself feared to question. Ten stories of barracks and "cells" spiraled above him. The cells were, in truth, just locked rooms with narrow windows. They were generally reserved for high birth prisoners. *So why in the world is my painted wooden knight up amongst the noble-born prisoners?*

He was on the ground floor of the Hangman's Tower, a cheerfully named octagonal tower near the rear of the castle. It was situated on a high rocky cliff, and the way the wind buzzed its little narrow arrow slit windows was said to drive men mad during storms. Less well appointed than the more public facing buildings, this tower was all rough worked white stone, mortared in strange yellow clay. Yellow torchlight cast a glow that made everything inside jaundiced. Illystre grimly recalled an old tale of a bard fed to the dogs in this very tower, he thought. He had tried to steal hounds from an old Owl King or some such trifle. Now that he came to think of it, it may have been the tower that the Curr boy fell in. *A dead pup in the Dog's Tower, ominous.*

He had every intention of using his privilege to make his way up the stony stairs, but he was blocked by the mountainous sweet-stinking Lord of Honeyhome. Lord Dobson Malbes was still in his dressing gown, still. A swirling thing of purple and gold samite, it was as garish as the rest of Honeyhome. The old man had not bothered to tie shut his robe, and his white haired chest and belly were exposed. His decision to forgo pants was also… *noted.* He was backed by three of his own Malbes spearmen.

Illystre swaggered, charm would need to be his weapon here, "Good morning, My Lord." He nodded toward the Lord's exposed manhood. "Seems we both rushed to get here." He flashed a wide, white smile, as the old Lord harrumphed.

He straightened his robe, tying it messily, "Lord Coldhearth, unless you've committed a crime, I see no reason for you to be in my dungeons."

Illystre took a quick sniff, under the heavy perfumes, the trained spymaster caught whiffs of wine, herbal ointment and mint. Malbes gripped the handle of his cane so tightly that his white knuckles blazed against the puffy swollen red of his hands. He was huffing after descending the stairs and the spearman behind him carefully watched the old Lord's shuffling slippers, and the path ahead of them. Illystre remembered the Lord Malbes of his childhood: a powerfully built old warrior, slightly out to pasture as he reached the middle of his sixth decade. This pale, flabby codger was hardly the same man, though in the moment, his beady eyes still blazed in fury.

"Information is my business, Lord Malbes." He never let the lazy smile slip, "And the pitter patter of servants' feet tells me that you have a most interesting prisoner upstairs."

Malbes frowned, "Bullshit, none of my servants know anything about my granddaughter's prisoner."

Harlow? That's not right– Isolde saw the witch take the old man... Her visions are never-

Unsure what game Malbes was up to, Illystre conceded, "I'd rather not reveal my sources, My lord, but suffice to say, knowledge of your prisoner and his… prize has made its way to my ears, as is my duty." The silver-haired spy buried his face into his hood and tried to make this declaration an intimidating growl.

Malbes snorted, bitter as stale coffee, "Your duty ends at my walls, boy. 'In his castle, every man a king.' If you want to find yourself in my dungeons, keep at it. Otherwise, you'll let me and my family do our business."

With his three big, brazen bee bodyguards, Malbes moved to shuffle away, but Illystre called after him, "He's lying about his name. He's no knight."

Malbes stopped, his tracks freezing under his feet, "We know that because of what my granddaught– How do you know that, Coldhearth?"

Illystre grimaced, trying to be fiercer than he felt, "It is my duty to know. Despite appearances to the contrary, my duty is *paramount.*" Before the old man could answer, Illystre heard the snap of a door and muffled conversation. Rage bubbling beneath the surface, Illystre rounded on the old man, his grey cloak swirling. "Who was questioning the prisoner, *the man who stole a crown from The Crown?* What treasons are you plotting, Lord Malbes?!" He hissed between his teeth. This was all a false fury of course. He knew Malbes was planning nothing. Illystre had hired Vandre and the rest. Well, he'd blackmailed them. It had been a mix of research, threats, bribery and a sprinkling of his sister's divination, but a ragtag assembly of thieves had been gathered to serve as scapegoats, and this Vandre had to go and *completely fuck it to tatters.*

In short, Illystre was man enough to admit he was projecting his frustrations onto the old lord.

The spearman stumbled forward as the old man sputtered, "My grandson!" He leaned on his cane, "Kalistah's oldest boy, Hart, he's up there questioning him."

Illystre paused in his fury, a sudden stillness as he thought. He had only encountered Hartwin Saddler once or twice. His recollection was a skinny, sullen teen. A ginger stalk of grass with pimples, but that was nearly a decade past. His reputation had grown into a callous, shrewd young lord. *Young, smart and too stupid to understand that being smart is only half the battle. Fabulous.*

The Grey Spy did not need to wait long for the Young Colt. It was Hartwin Saddler's muffled conversation at the top of the stair, and it would soon be his boot heels descending it in a clicking staccato. Upon seeing Illystre, hooded and dour, Saddler shuffled a parcel in his hands, before meeting Illystre's gaze with a cold smile. "My Lord." He intoned through gritting teeth, "you seem to be lost."

Illystre eyed the parcel, "I am not what's lost, m'lord. But perhaps you and I should have a discussion."

Saddler sighed, before nodding. "I was about to deliver it, my Lord." He held his hand out, a bundle the size and shape of a dinner bowl, wrapped in bloody rags, "For the record."

370

Illystre reached out for it, fingers so close, but the Lord called out, "Hartwin, do *not* turn that over."

Both young men stalled for a brief moment, before the slim horse-lord pulled back, taking himself and the crown out of reach. Saddler smirked, "Of course, Grandfather. I suppose we ought to negotiate."

Malbes set a fine table, no one could argue that. Rather than sit in the dungeon, Lord Malbes had *insisted* that Illystre and Hartwin "discuss matters over meat and mead, like men", despite both younger men's protestations that it was midmorning. So it was that they were led to a grander space, a cozy nook nestled near the kitchen. The room was warm and inviting, smelling of fresh bread and caramelized sugar, as natural light poured in through ivy and nightshade covered windows. The softness, the warmth, the sugary invitations, it all felt false enough that Illystre was on the lookout for the hook.

Saddler sat at the far end of a six foot table made from garish, expensive striped wood from the far forests of Ajua. In the boy-lord's defense, he looked to be enjoying his surroundings no more than Illystre did. He held the crown in both hands, though a violet velvet cushion had been provided to rest it upon. The stiff little lordling gave a shake of the head as Illystre took his own seat opposite Saddler.

In the center of the table both meat and mead had been spread. Two great pitchers of Malbes mead sweated in the humidity, fine cool dew beading along their stonework. Dried and cured slices of salted meat and hard cheese were stacked in swirls on a platter. *Commoner's food. Subtle as everything else the old man does.*

With a sigh, Saddler started, "There is no reason this needs to be difficult." He shook the crown, "I was genuinely headed toward the barracks of the Grey Guard."

There is nothing so dangerous as a smart man with half the available information. He's like to jump to the entirely wrong conclusion and be confident until the ground goes out from under him. Illystre grinned, lying, "Wonderful that I stopped you, Saddler." Coldhearth extended a grey-gloved hand to one of the pitchers, and poured himself a frothing golden glass. A small taste found it surprisingly sour, Illystre enjoyed that. "I believe the Shining Command may be involved." *More sour lies in sweet words.*

Saddler stiffened in his chair, before leaning forward, "Do you mean that, truly, my lord?" Illystre gave the barest nod, watching Saddler's great green eyes go wide enough to see little brassy flecks in the iris. The heir spoke, "I thought as much, my Lord. It's that Tymm knight, isn't it? Rumor is that he has turned mad after our Prince had that… *unpleasantness* in the tourney with his brother."

Unpleasantness. These Lordlings will use any turn of phrasing to keep from feeling for another man, won't they? He chuckled inside, noting that he was exactly no better. "That may well be, the rot could go deep." Illystre carefully removed a glove, then the other, before motioning for Saddler to hand him the crown. When the boy shook his head, Coldhearth sighed, "There's two guards at the door and thirty-foot drop out the window, I am not going to flee with your prize."

The Young Colt was as skittish as his namesake as he slid the crown across the striped wood, pushing with long, strong fingers. "I suppose you won't. Why on earth would the Lord Inquisitor need to steal from the Royal Family?"

If Illystre had not been so entirely sure of his deception, such a line may have unnerved him, but he had left no trace. Isolde and Totho's sorcery had allowed him to summon a phantom last night. Illystre understood the magic less than those two, but the lock of

Webb's hair, the changeling ichor and the other strange ingredients made something that looked like the boy. Isolde assured him that it was not Webb, but the sadness in his eyes haunted Illystre. It would have taken a ghost to get into the vaults, so Illystre made one. Send the ghost into the vault, and drop the crown to his marks. Ever so simple.

And then the goddamn old man had ruined everything. They should have been arrested with the crown, yes. But not so soon, and *not* by these Saddler men. He did not own any man among them, and that made this much more difficult.

His intent had been simple. Give the crown to the group of ne'er-do-wells and force them to sit with it. Once the theft of the Starheart crown had been discovered, Illystre could arrest his marks, becoming a hero in the process. Of course, while the crown was in his possession, he could also switch it for a duplicate.

The same duplicate he currently held looped in his sword belt, hidden in his cloak. The taste of victory was near sweet on his tongue, cutting the sour mead. He only needed a moment to swap the two crowns, and then Saddler could do whatever stupid damn thing he wanted.

Stealing the thing would have been easy enough, but Coldhearth needed the royals to not miss it. He had to steal it, replace it, and give the Lords and Ladies the blaggards responsible for the theft. The fact that their albi, the ghost of a dead boy giving them the crown, was ridiculous was a fortuitous accident to be sure. Illystre would have much preferred a smash and grab, but politics require a deft touch.

He sat here, so close, with no way to distract this boy, so he did what came naturally, he bullshitted, "And why would the Grey Guard? That's what I intend to find out." He watched Saddler. The young man was overpuffed with ambition, plain as the freckles on his face. He wore the brash intelligence of youth like a helm, visor down, blinding him to all around him. If there was an opposite to a useful idiot, Saddler was it. *An ineffectual intellectual?* This boy was likely very good with the other Lordlings, but here, he was a foal before a grey panther, and he didn't realize how deep he was in it. What came next was rote, "You are an observant young man, Hartwin…" He let the familiar term hang for a moment, "I *may* call you Hartwin, yes?"

The boy who would be lord nodded, "Yes, My Lord."

"Your Uncle Hinric sits on the council with me, a peevish little man." He sipped the mead again, "And your sister is like to marry the Prince, I hear." Saddler visibly bristled, and Illystre liked that, "Hugo is likely to win the whole tourney, as I can *personally* attest. Where does that leave you?"

"I am the heir–"

"Glory born into, not glory earned. I see you, Hartwin. Ambition is your burden. You see your purpose clear as day, don't you?" Illystre thumbed one of the points of the crown. It would be sharp enough to break skin with less pressure than seemed safe.

The slow smile that crossed Saddler's gaunt little face was wide enough to snap his skull in half, but the young lord simply chuckled, "Oh, oh I do, Lord Illystre. Clear and bright. Shining, even."

Illystre liked this, even moreso. "Good. I think you and I see many situations facing our Empire in a similar light, Hartwin." The boy eyed him cautiously, "Friends on the Council are hard to come by and I think you could have two by the end of this conversation." He poured a cup of mead and slid it to the young lordling, sloshing not a drop as it stopped inches from the edge of the table in front of him, "Drink. Your Lord Grandfather commanded us." A disarming flash of a smile and the boy gripped the cup, downing it quickly.

"Oh, thank god, it's sour. If I had one more honeyed cloying drop, I would like to retch." Saddler shook his head. "Fine, fine. Let's get to horse-trading . Then, what do you propose, Coldhearth? What's your game?"

Illusions of sweetness were gone, so were formalities. "I would like to examine the crown… more thoroughly." Illystre saw no point in lying to the boy about that.

"Hellendre, my Mother's witch–"

Illystre interrupted, smiling at the thought of heavy lidded brass eyes and plump lips. "I've met her."

"Hellendre has cast half a hundred spells over that thing, and there seems to be nothing wrong with it. If it's been corrupted or cursed, she cannot tell."

"My intentions are nothing so simple, capable as your witch is, she is not searching for what malfeasance I am searching for." His eyes traced the lines on the little crown, each an exact twin to his forgery. A hundred tinkerers would never see the differences, even searching for a hundred years. "But to do what I need to do, I need time, *My Lord.*" Saddler smirked despite himself, "All you need to do is give the Royals *this crown.*" he slowly pulled his forgery, holding it in his left hand. "Instead of the one our wanderer had. That's it." He handed Saddler the forgery, before setting the original on the fine violet velvet cushion in the center of the table. "Examine it. It's identical. Have your witch look it over. It's completely safe."

Saddler turned the forgery in his hand for long minutes, occasionally checking the real crown for confirmation or denial. After he had examined the forgery thoroughly, more than once, he set it on the striped wood beside him, "Perhaps I do this thing for you. Perhaps I do this thing and I don't ask questions. Perhaps, I even keep silent about it. You say this brings me your friendship. What kind of friend is a man like Illystre Coldhearth?"

"A loyal and generous one, Hartwin."

Saddler nodded, "Good, then I have need of a boon, friend." His tone was motivated, tense, bordering on desperate, "If I do this thing, this crown gets nowhere near my sister. Harlow will not wed Vernus Artus."

Illystre nodded, "Honestly, were it my sister Isolde in the same position, I would be asking the same. This is a thing I can do for a friend, I believe. The boy prince is tractable and distractable, as it were. I'll dangle him something sweet and shiny, and he should forget about your Harlow." Something wriggled uncomfortably in the back of his mind, "Didn't your Lady Mother go to considerable cost to arrange this event, in the hopes of pushing your sister as a bride for the prince? Won't she be furious?"

"I should hope she is." Saddler's mouth went tight again, "She meant to hand my little sister to an abominable little wretch."

Without betraying his own thoughts, in a tone as grey as his cloak, Illystre whispered, "That sort of talk may be called treason."

"It is simply the truth. I have not defamed the boy, nor do I wish ill on him, I just will not have him wed my sister." He picked up the forgery as he rose, leaving Illystre alone in the room with the crown. "It's a matter of friendship, my Lord."

The door clicked behind the Young Colt. Getting in bed with a budding schemer like Saddler was, admittedly, a risky proposition, but it would simply need another high tithe to be laid to gain his prize. A trembling hand snatched the golden ring from the velvet and the Lord of Spies felt the world suddenly grow smaller around him, his circle of awareness a dim campfire casting light against the shadows around him. It was his.

His prize was quickly stowed on his sword belt, just as his forgery had been. Even the weight was the same, familiar as he bounded his way out the now unguarded door. His joy nearly overwhelmed his reason as he found himself outside his chambers, where his sullen squire Homer waited for him.

The boy tossed his head of shaggy brown hair, and spoke as only a bored teenager could, "Two of your men came by, brought a serving girl from the castle, my Lord."

Illystre narrowed his brows, "Which two?"

"The big one, and the mean lookin' one with the eyepatch." Homer was chewing on the corner of some pastry. The boy had an awful sweet-tooth. Thankfully, youthful appetites seemed to keep him trim.

"Which big one?" Illystre rolled his eyes, specificity was not among Homer's strong suits.

"The southern one, Leo."

"Ah, and Carlyle." Leo was a bit of a blunt instrument, but the one-eyed Carlyle had a way with the serving staff wherever Illystre seemed to send him, so this had the stink of promise to it. This was good news, why was the boy still so tense, "What else?"

"Your Learner is back, m'lord." The boy watched Illystre's face, which stiffened.

"Set my Learner up in the back solar. Inform him that he may sit on his hands until I arrive." His tone stone on stone. "I'll see the girl first."

Homer took him into the small common room, where a serving matron sat in a wooden chair, eyes white and wide. When he entered, swirling in his greys and silks, the little woman gasped. She was a squat, toady woman, hair a dirty blonde that was more unruly than a castle servant ought to have displayed. After her loud gasp, she crowed, "You're the spymaster, ain'tcha?"

Illystre only gave a silent nod. *This one is happy to spill her secrets.* He tossed a silver coin to her.

"I knew, I knew, me'lord!" She fixed her bulging eyes on Illystre, which did no favors in the manner of her amphibian appearance. "I seen't somethin' that would turn yer hair white, me'lord."

He dropped his hood, shaking his mane of premature silver, "Doubtful, but continue."

"Funny, funny. Funny little lord." She babbled, "I were makin' my way upstairs, from the laundry way in the basement of the tower, all the way up to the high chamber where them Ozwyk are stayin'. I were carryin' my baskets, so I used the back stair, the servants' stair. And I seen't what happened to that Curr boy. It weren't no accident, m'lord. Nobody seen me, but I seen them."

Hullen Curr IV's fall had been a tragedy, to be sure, but foul play? That seemed less than likely. Still, Illystre flicked her a second silver, "There was a girl, real, real pretty, she was. Hair like beaten copper, soft skin, big lips, but she had fangs, like some kinda monster. She had a demon, some kinda hateful imp, slashed the boy up, and then the girl threw him down the stairs. That poor noble boy."

"Did you hear any names, see where this succubus may have gone?" If Curr had not been alone, anyone else with him had to have disappeared without a trace. *Unless...*

"The little imp led 'em both right into the servants hallway, m'lord. Like it knew it was there. I hid. I climbed high and I hid in the shadows and the gods were graceful. They went down the stairs, because I was hidin' up."

Illystre rounded on her, sliding her a stack of five heavy silvers. "What was she wearing? Colors. Fabrics. Badges. Sigils. A name. Anything."

"It was real dark, my lord. I-I couldn't see much." She frowned, "She had a big furry thing on her shoulders." Illystre took his hand from the stack, and she snatched it.

"What is your name?" Illystre watched her bite a coin between browning teeth. Satisfied, she pocketed her bounty.

"'m called Yellow Ally, on account of my hair." She gave another wide froggy frown, "It were prettier when I was young."

"Well, Ally." Illystre gave his cold grin again, "You have provided me and the kingdom with a great service today. …Should these things turn out to be true, of course."

"Oh, my lord, I swear, on my–"

"I'm sure." He let the barest threat hang in his tone, "But should anything we've discussed here turn out to be inaccurate, you'd best correct it. Or I'll need to send some of my men to discuss the discrepancies with you? Are we understood?"

She nodded as the color drained from her face.

"Excellent. Be on your way." He dismissed her with a wave. Once Homer had shuffled her off, Illystre gathered himself and made his way to the solar. Cogs spun and ground as Illystre grappled with this new information. Curr was now the second young Lord to have an attempt on his life, as Smilin' Jack Tymm nearly murdered the Crown Prince. Though both boys still lived, Illystre had begun to see a worrying pattern.

The Lordlings would need to wait, as he needed to speak with his Learner. He felt his fury rising as he entered the solar. He fingered the light Lutinese throwing knife on his hip, as he stepped into the silver sunlight. His Learner waited, seated in the sunlight, long fingers spread, drinking in the warmth.

Illystre growled at the elf, "Learner Clovis. I would *absolutely love* to hear what you have to say about our overnight."

Clovis grimaced, his pale eyes blazing.

DRAKE IV

"Compromise has a bitter taste. So does medicine. We do neither for amusement, only survival."

Drake had been standing behind the King when a serving man, a Malbes man, whispered in his ear that Hartwin Saddler was requesting to speak with the Day's Commander, about a pressing, urgent matter. Had King Gallus Artus III not been sitting directly within earshot, Ser Drake Canar would likely have told this messenger that Hartwin Saddler could directly fuck himself, and speak to tomorrow's commander.

Had the King not been there, of course.

But he was, so Drake bowed in deference. He left Ser Jurgen with the King and his gathered councilors and High Lords, and he followed this little man in purple down a winding corridor of glass and bronze.

Saddler waited, not in some opulent lounge, but down a dank back hallway, several floors down, between a neglected gallery and the chef's rarely used dining room, the sort of rooms that existed just to be rooms. When Saddler's gaze met his, and he saw which Shining Command Grey Guard he would be speaking to, he rolled his eyes like an annoyed brat. "Precisely the ugly duckling I had hoped for, Ser Drake."

Drake gave him no such satisfaction, "Lord Saddler, how may I assist you?" He strained a smile, but a "If we could make this brief, it would be tantamount, as Day's Command–"

He felt his tongue turn rubber when Hartwin Saddler shoved something cold and metal into his gloved hands; the missing Starheart

Crown, "You're the only one of those Grey-Shields I know to be too honorable to be involved in this."

"In what? What the hell is this, Saddler?" Canar jostled the crown inches from Saddler's face.

"Well, I should hope you know what it is. Little chance of finding it if you don't." Saddler's dry attempt at wit twisted his long face into a smirk.

Drake fumed, "Where did you get it?!"

Saddler sighed, "A sellsword." He took a step back, reaching into a pocket and producing a small waxed parchment bundle. The cool smell of dried mint leaves filled the tight little hallway. Saddler placed a pinch in his mouth. He looked to Canar, before extending the little pouch. Drake took a small pinch of the mint leaves and quaffed them. The cooling oils spread over his tongue and down his throat. Saddler spoke again, "He had killed some of my father's peasants on the Goldenroad. Some paltry matter about a horse."

"Fine, bring him to me." Drake made no attempt at sounding like this matter was a request.

"Alas, I cannot, Ser." Saddler's tone was not as apologetic as his words were, "We did to him what we do to all horse thieves. We hung him. My grandfather's gallows are full of men like him, we only found the crown once we had searched his meager possessions. He had secreted it in a false bottom of his trunk."

Drake's stomach felt tight as he palmed the crown, "D-Did this sellsword have a name, Saddler?"

"Near as we can tell, he claimed to be a 'Ser Jemes Wyse' from the Brinegate Panhandle, but that seems to be a fabrication." Saddler hummed to himself satisfied as a new thought seemed to bloom, "Or a stolen identity. Suffice to say, an old man in orange and green with a treecat on his jerkin swings for the crows to feast upon as we speak."

Drake had no doubt of this, unfortunately. He slowly spun the crown in his fingers, searching for mar, damage or theft and finding nothing. "How did he get in the vault, Saddler? My brothers have had it locked down for days. How did a common sellsword dance into a sealed vault?"

Saddler shrugged, "I don't imagine he did it alone. One of your brothers may have helped him, I do not know." He backed away, leaving the crown in Canar's hands, "I found it in a dead man's trunk, but I do not want this glory. It's yours. Or give my grandfather's headsman a sack of silver, I do not care. But Clan Saddler had no part in this victory." Saddler was hiding something, but Drake could not tell what.

"What's your game?"

Saddler frowned, "If I return that crown publicly, it ends up on my sister's head, Ser Drake."

Canar felt his jaw tense, "Isn't that the sort of power you keep chasing?" Drake liked nothing about this.

Saddler shook his head, "Call it brotherly love, call it ego, but I will not wed my sister to a monster for personal gain." He smirked, "You might understand the need to win your own glory."

"If you think the Grey Guard is involved, why give the crown to me?"

Saddler shrugged, "Some of your brothers might be involved, but you're not, Canar." Slim and tall, Saddler was a lean shadow as he faded back down the hall, "You're like me. Predictable. I will always do the best thing for me."

Drake waited for the insult, "And me?"

From the dark, the Young Colt made his reply, "You're honorable. Boring, but honorable. Realm needs men like you. Be seein' you, Ser Drake."

There was no more from Saddler, Drake was left alone with the Startheart crown. He briefly considered finding a window to chuck it out of, which seemed simpler. It felt heavier than it ought to have for something so delicate. He would eventually decide that a sack of silver to the Malbes' headsman felt like the least odious lie of omission, and thus he made sure the kindly faced old executioner was well paid for his part.

When Drake set the crown before the king and queen, he told no lies. "The crown was discovered in the trunk of a Ser Jemes Wyse. Under a false bottom, it was concealed."

The small sitting room where the King and Queen had taken Drake was overfull with hunting trophies. Dead things hung on the walls, sat the shelves and even the chandelier were made of bone and antler. The king and queen sat a lounge together, on which was tossed the skin of a great golden-white bear, ancient and extinct. The last of the gold-bears of Borrowhill had been hunted out some two-hundred years ago, so this fur was a seat for royalty indeed. Elk, deer, wolves, a griffin, a drake, a tusked bear, glass eyes stared from dry sockets, without blinking.

After a long, tense quiet, King Gallus spoke, "I see. And where is this man?"

"...He was apprehended by some local law for horse thievery and hanged, your grace." Drake's eyes never left the floor, "The crown was found amongst his things, once he was dead."

Queen Natasha rose, taking the crown in her hands. The Queen was known to be an educated occultist in her own right. She examined it, she seemed almost careless, but her eyes were focused and when she put the crown back on the small table, she nodded with a strong certainty, "Where is his corpse?"

"We are trying to recover that specific carcass, Your Grace. With the tournament, there's had to be a glut of hangings, to the point of mass graves. And the record keeping of the local guard is not exactly pristine." And again, Drake sighed, it was true. He would not lie to his charge. He reported the facts as he understood them, the simple, brutish reality. There was no need to invent phantoms or delve into maddening dreams. The truth, as presented by Hartwin Saddler, was grim enough.

King Gallus spoke, stern again, but not devoid of warmth for the young knight, "There are ways to extract the truth, even from parts of a body, Ser. *We need that corpse, Ser Drake.*"

Drake nodded so readily he worried he had injured his shoulder, already stiff from his loss in the tourney today, "I could not agree more, your grace. Arcane means are likely to be the only way we will ever find out what happened to that crown. We ought to be content in its return for a moment, while I have some men search the corpse pits."

The King and his Queen shared a silent look between them and then she spoke, "We are content in the return, to be fair, the gods are good. However, too many questions remain, Ser Drake. We need this corpse, desperately. Someone tried to kill the Crown Prince and steal a crown. The body is too important to be left to mere soldiers."

While the implication was clear, Drake wanted no part of it. Still he would not lie and he would not deny a command.

Instead of dinner with his sworn brothers, Drake had wrapped the bottom half of his face in a red woolen scarf his mother had knit for him, lining its layers with sweet smelling flowers and herbs, and made his way to the great stinking corpse pits. The day's rain had left much of the city a sloppy mess, and as Drake rode through the afternoon sun, the air was growing warm and humid. Drake was no great rider, and he struggled on this borrowed horse when it caught the scent of corruption. As he rode this moody gelding, the stink of death rode a low breeze upward from the hollow ahead. It was a grassy little half-sphere carved out of the earth, low enough and far enough from anything important that it served as a convenient place to dispose of refuse from the city.

There were two great, open pits over this wide low field, one filled with trash: rusted and rotted and things past repair piled in an open stinking hole. And beside that pit was a second, smaller one, filled with a different sort of refuse. Black clouds of flies crowded both, though the crows, gulls, vultures and dogs favored the smaller pit.

As he came to the squat spiked fence of sharpened pine boughs, the salty blonde gelding would not take another step, so Drake dismounted, tying the thin leather lead around the black tar and wood palisade. He squished over soaked sod sinking slightly into soft and sodden soil. A practiced reaction to tension, a muscle memory coaxed his left hand into placing three glass beads filled with The Smoke between his fingers. He rolled them over fingers, over each other, and he breathed through his scarf. Scavengers bustled and chattered at the charnel pit. A trio of figures in black moved around the great crater, unloading a cart of corpses like farmboys tossing heavy bundles of hay. He called out loudly, all three black-hooded gravediggers stared up to him, but none of the white, gaunt faces made response.

There was a shuffling behind the cart, and a fourth black hooded figure unfolded itself from the ground. He shuffled around the front of the wagon, wobbling and bobbling. A short, wide little ball of a man in all black waved back to Drake. The Dashing Duck approached, hand extended. "Hail, goodman! I am Ser Drake Canar of the Shining Command."

The stumpy little man in his black hood practically bounced over, babbling excitedly as he tossed his hood back, revealing a big bald pate, and a mustache that hung near to his collar in grey-brown braids. "My lord, my lord! How may I be of service? I am Lead Fossor Delber, and I am at your service entirely, My Lord. Do not mind my collaborators, they lack the anatomy or ability to answer you. Strong backs for digging, though." The three shuffling hoods never slowed in their labors.

Drake gave his head a toss, "I'm no Lord, friend. Just a knight in over his head." He tried to let his tone give reassurances his covered face could not. "I'm looking for a corpse, Fossor Delber."

"Well, this is certainly the place for that. Executions aplenty with stabbings and rapes and treasons at the tourney. And you get all sorts of folk from all sorts of places together, with all sorts of airs, folks start gettin' sick, so…" He gestured toward the wagon of nude corpses, "We have bodies by the actual wagonload, my lord– Ser."

Drake toed toward the edge of the charnel pit, but decided not cast his gaze downward. *I'm not that curious.* He looked down at his little man, who came to his chin. Drake was not especially large for a knight, but this man was tiny, but nearly as wide as he was tall. If not for his fine, delicate features, Drake would have guessed he was a *Jortmunn.* "I am looking for a specific body, Lead Fossor. A horse thief who was hanged this morning, he wore a jerkin with a tree cat on it."

The little man nodded so hard Drake was reasonably sure he heard something rattle, "Oh yes, t'aint every day we get a knight. But,

I'm afraid…" The Lead Fossor shifted his weight from heel to heel, "Well, he's down in the stew."

"I am assuming the stew is…"

The Lead Fossor hopped toward the edge of the pit, so close a dirt clod tumbled down, out of sight, Drake heard a sticking plop and shuddered, "Down there, yes. Space in the pit was becoming limited with so many… guests needing a final rest, so we came up with a new sort of solution after seeing that Tymm boy die in the tourney."

Drake thought back to the green acid dissolving the flesh and skin from the face of Smilin' Jack Tymm as the glass vase shattered over his grin.

"If he has been *stewing* since this morning, what is left?" He swallowed hot bile, still resisting any temptation to inch closer.

"The hardest bits of bone, I suppose." Delber lifted a long pole and began poking at the contents of the pit, squelches, hisses and clacking like wood on wood echoed up with each jab. Feathers scattered as crows and vultures took to wing, harrying and fussing all the while, "Teeth, knuckles, kneecaps, skull, like as anything."

Darwyn isn't even here and his damn family is still giving me headaches. "You're using the Tymm compound, yes?" Delber nodded, and Drake wanted to retch.

There was nothing else to be done. Drake thanked Lead Fossor Delber. As he pressed a corroded silver into the clammy little palm, the Dashing Duck wondered if the next sixty years would be this difficult, or if they would get easier when his mind went after about fifty. He tried to give silvers to the three gravediggers who never paused in their toils, but Delber stopped him. "They have no use for their silver, but it can go toward their debts accrued."

I have had enough horror.

He would return to the irritable little horse, finally pocketing The Smoke glasses as he crossed back through the palisade. The ride up the hill in the late afternoon sun, spikes of silver still struggling to push through the cloak of irongrey clouds. In his own cloak of Grey, the commons parted for him, calling kindly. He was a hero of the raids, a beloved bodyguard of the Royal family, and his shield and cloak made him obtrusive to the point of fame. A woman raced from her market stall, jostling a fine hunting knife in a horn sheath. She chased him for too many long strides, before Drake waved her away. "I have picked my blade, madame. I am sure yours is fine, but I am a man wedded."

She looked confused as he patted his short sword and rode away, finally pulling the herb-laden scarf from his face, as the courser trotted across slick tan cobbles. The tourney had turned the main street into an extended market square, and crowded as it had become in the dinner hour, Drake feared his mount might take a bite of some peasant boy's ear or boot an old woman into her stall, so he disembarked, electing to lead the miserable animal. He weaved through the swelling masses, drinking in the chatter, the smell of smoke and ale.

Jostling through the crowd, a less observant man would not have noticed the slight change in weight at his belt. To be fair, a less observant man would not have been worthy of The Smoke. The skinny boy likely thought he was snatching a purple plum prince's pretty purse, but the Dashing Grey Duck was a different story. Drake whorled his reins tight around his fist and jerked the insubordination from the horse, urging them forward on purple leather soles.

The boy was quick and small, and he was not dragging a less-than-cooperative gelding behind him, so as long as they remained in these tight quarters, this deluge of man, there would be no closing the distance. Drake would not lose sight of the boy, this thief would not take the smoke. The little cutpurse was a thin little whip, lashing around ankles and feet, snapping and leaping across the cobbles.

Either youthful inexperience or a jolt of fear led the boy to abandon the actual safety of the crowd for the perceived safety of a mostly empty alley. The teen stuck his chest out and broke into a sprint, "Outta me way, folks!"

Drake finally let chivalry go in pursuit of right, he threw his dagger. "Halt!" Drake called, a little desperate. End over end, the steel and gold tumbled, finally striking the thief. The blunt little end, shaped like a scallop shell, struck the skull of the running lad, right where his neck met the stubble of his dark brown scalp. The kid stumbled, went limp and tumbled to the stones.

The thief whimpered a bit as Drake finally towered over him. He rolled over, clutching the bag of glass capsules to his chest. He was a scrawny thing, with sparkling eyes of hazel. He groaned, rolling to his back, a wide, pained smile crossing his sun-bronzed cheeks. "...I halted, Ser."

Drake snatched his satchel of Smoke back, scowling down at the lad, "Stealing from a knight is a rapid way to lose a hand, lad." He could practically feel his sword hand buzzing at his belt, but he tensed his fingers on themselves, rather than hilt. "What do you think you were doing?"

"Well, m'lord, I saw you, lookin' rich and noble and fine. And I figured as you were wearing more silver than I'm ever likely to see in me life..." His hand went to the back of his head, likely finding a nasty knob, "Well, a snatch and grab might feed me fer a week."

Drake looked down at this underfed boy, and sighed, "How old are you?"

"More than ten, less than twelve." The boy sat up, still wary of the sword, "The priest, uh, the *High Oblate." H*e stumbled on the noble term, "ain't exactly sure."

"You live at the temple?" Drake fixed grey eyes on the boy, who despite the question, had only eyes for the gems in the hilt of Drake's sword.

The boy nodded, sharp chin and round cheeks, still bare as the day he was born, "When there's room, yeah. Packed full of pilgrims this week. I found a spot under an old stable. It keeps it dry enough." He coughed conveniently, "Nothin' to eat down there though."

Drake sighed, "Get up."

"Ser?"

Drake offered the thief a hand, and the boy took it, scrambling to his feet. Drake grabbed the boy's shoulder and spun him, shoving the boy's chin to his chest. Drake brushed the rapidly rising goose egg under the boy's scalp, bristled black and brown. Drake frowned, "Sorry about the lump, but you're like to live." He stepped around the boy, meeting his gaze again, "Are you alone?"

"...Why, ser?" the urchin slid his ragged feet backward, "Boys don't live long on the streets followin' strange men home…"

Drake swirled his cloak of grey around him, "Do you know the Grey Guard, son? I am Ser Drake Canar, The Dashing Duck." Drake smirked, savoring the taste of theatricality in the moment.

The boy blinked dully.

"A knight sworn to help the innocent and downtrodden." Drake tried to elaborate.

"Yer going to feed me?"

It was Drake's turn to blink dully, "Y-yes." The boy would quickly become much more friendsome, all smiles, though his hungry eyes continuously danced over jewels and precious metal that Drake wore. Drake smirked to himself, "Have you ever been on a horse..? –I don't know your name."

The boy paused, clearly thinking of a lie, "Cyp. My name is Cyp." Drake let it stand, for now. "No, Ser, I don't believe I have."

Drake would help the boy into the saddle, though the knight kept the reins. Drake, walking in his purple finery, and this Cyp, riding in his rags, would weave through the commons, up the center road. As they moved, Drake managed to learn the boy's story, at least as the boy had been told it; he had been born to a tavern worker down near the docks. She was young and pretty and decided a baby was more of an anchor than she could endure. The boy was left in the care of the tavern keeper, when his mother hopped a galley to the continent. The old tavern keeper would raise him through five, but eventually the grey old tavern woman would die, and Cyp would be on the street at the age of six. Theft, begging, charity and luck had kept him alive so far.

Cyp's happy little squeal when he saw the high walls of the Castle made Drake grin to himself. "You ain't takin' me inside the walls, Ser?"

Drake laughed, nodding, "I am."

They would take the mean little horse back to Lord Dobson's stable, and Ser Drake Canar led this ragged child into the borrowed barracks kept by the Greys. He would sit the boy at the shared table in the living space, where the remains of a picked over dinner sat cold.

Surrounded by cold bleak stone and a half eaten soldier's meal, the boy struggled to breathe for wonder. From the stack of logs on the hearth to the row of beds with fresh linens, Cyp had never seen such luxury. He could barely murmur a question of permission before

392

hungrily attacking the food Drake's Sworn Brothers had deemed unfit for a knight,

Within the hour, the boy would be asleep in a padded chair, snoring lightly. Cyp was tired enough not to stir when two of the brothers returned from their duties, bantering broadly about the tourney results. "Stagg underestimated the Selach boy, the reach of a pole arm can prove disastrous if you don't know how to counter." Ser Auberon Sozen dryly droned.

"Of course you'd claim it's the equipment." Ser Gnash Selach retorted, "Can't just admit the Selach men might be built better."

Sozen snorted, his eyes on Ser Gnash's thick waist, "Built heavier, perhaps."

Rather than rage, Ser Gnash Selach fixed his sharp gaze on the snoring boy wrapped in Drake's blanket. "Ducky, have you picked up a stray?"

Sozen approached catspaw-soft, he circled the plush brown chair and its sleeping contents. Ser Auberon took one look at this half-starved stray, and shook his head, "No, no, Gnash, our Ducky has picked himself a *squire.* "

Drake could only give a sheepish grin.

END ACT THREE

INSIDE A DYING BOY

A Bridge Between Acts

The woods were a deep and dark place, ancient. Trees with bark like ink twisted together above so tightly that it was impossible to tell where branch began and night sky ended. A bitter wind whipped and tore, a cold breath whispering death.

The broken hound limped through the undergrowth, blood matted its fur in clots going black. This shaggy cur loped, panting agony, blood and slather running from its open maw. Heavy lids kept pale eyes half open. Thorns and stiff, sharp dry branches raked the body of this poor blooded beast.

The Hemlock and the Stag.

The young cur had known better than to trust them, *Hemlock bore poison.*

The dry dead undergrowth tore at a dozen wounds on this creature's flesh, and ripped new ones where none had been before. Each step was agony, and truly, this cur was looking for a soft spot to lie down and die, but the thicket around him was dense with dead wood and twisting weeds. *No respite.*

As shattered as the body of this young pup was, the spirit behind the eyes gave no indication that thought had slowed. Though its eyes were half open and clouded with injury, purpose still shone in his black pupils.

My mate... My pack-brother...

He fell.

Amongst the twisting black trunks, the barbed vines and the rot, this dying boy fell.

He still breathed, though he could not stand to walk. The night was coming, and safety was far away. *No respite.*

The blood of the beast would not let him die, it would not let him rest. Facing the end, this cur thrashed and raged, still more barbs and thorns and spears and stones rending his skin. More blood poured, more than Hullen could have ever had, great steaming rivers flowed over stone and loam, soaking the brown earth black.

It would be easy, all he had to do was die. Close his eyes, and stop breathing.

Ellari.

There was a thrum. It filled him, lifted him, buzzed through his broken bones, painlessly. Dimly aware, the dog sensed light at the edges of his eye lids, and his left eye slowly fluttered half-open. Motes of light danced above him, below the ceiling of twisting branches. *The stars are so close...*

The thrum began to pulse in time with the tiny swirling stars, and with his own slowing heartbeat. These will-o-wisps danced and warmed him, their light swelling and falling in a gentle rhythm. They slowly settled like a spring snow, uneasy, into the dog's shags of brown and black fur, and more light dawned.

There was an angel. She was made of these motes of light, these stars, these *fireflies.* As this nude woman made of light approached and laid a thrumming hand on the dying beast's brown, a sad little gasp escaped her thousands of tiny mouths in chorus, as one voice, "..zzzthiszz... you are a cur. A beassszzsst -tt-. Butttzzsttilll, you have done no wrong. You are born of the hunting hounds and the warbears. There is a beast inside you." The longer she touched him, the clearer her words became, until the dog realized he was no longer hearing her with his ears.

Her hand was warmth and light itself as it stroked between his ears. The long gash on his skull slowly knit. "I can heal the beasts. The bear, the dog... but the boy must find his own way." She gripped the scruff of fur at the back of his neck, "Or I can bring you an end worthy of a hunter. The choice is yours." From behind a mask, this head made of a thousand shining bees, this swarm that crowned itself a queen, offered the only choice that ever mattered, "I can offer you life, at a price. My Prince, the real King, The Coronox needs soldiers. The war is coming. *Do you wish to live, Hullen Curr?"*

ACT FOUR:

SAVIORS

LILAH IV

"There is blood to bind and blood to separate. Family veins are full of both."

Flickering torchlight glinted orange and sputtering on the big liquid metal silver eyes of the rust scaled little drake as he dragged Lilah by the hand, down the dark stone stair as a rush of humanity shuffled up to the broken body of Hullen Curr. Four inches of wood, mortar and stone kept the girl and her little dragon hidden, secreted on the servants stair. Her heart was pounding in her chest, she was clammy and slick with nervous sweat. Verm's little clawed hand clutched her fingers, there was blood and meat under his sharp black nails.

He hissed in his clicking and snapping draconic tongue, too flustered to remember that Lilah didn't speak it. *"Drekki guldo. Gon Han!"* Verm muttered fiercely against the black dark and great stony maw that threatened to swallow them both as they scuttled half blind down it.

When Hullen fell, Verm had urgently taken Lilah's hand in his and yanked her to a small alcove where a door was not so much hidden, more made to be completely ignored. The wood was painted to match the wall, even the moulding and wallpaper. Verm slid a claw up the seam, found whatever latch he was looking for, and pulled Lilah through the door and into the dark servant's stair.

Girl and dragon rushed over stone stairs, heels and talons clacking. The staircase leveled to a narrow landing, Lilah planted her heels and felt her lungs burning and a hot knife of pain in her side. She snatched Verm's attention, her voice not as quiet as it should have been, "Where are we? What is this?"

"*Tarruk tall*– Er- Back stairs. Secret." He kept his little horned head down, creeping forward, "Verm… always finds places like this."

Lilah followed, "This is how you sneak around, isn't it?"

Verm shrugged as if it were not incredibly impressive, "*Mioldrekki* need do things like this. Big folk not like us, we are vermin." His little clawed hand traced the stair's inner wall, searching for a lost… something. "Any kinds of little holes or tunnel, we find. We use." He found what he was looking for, making a cheerful little chirp as a portal of light opened. Verm swung a secret door open, and Lilah stepped into the light.

Lilah barely had time to blink the brighter light from her eyes. She was in a high ceilinged chamber, with tall windows wrought in honeyed-gold, as her eyes scanned the room in the dim morning light, she saw a sampling of familiar items. Reuben's boots poked out from under a bed in the center of the room. Little Neal's pile of toy soldiers warred with a gigantic furry beast played by his sister's stuffed bear on the center of a fine woven rug. When Lilah saw her own dressing robe slung over the back of a stuffed chair, she realized Verm had returned them to their borrowed chambers.

The door clicked shut behind Lilah, but there was no sign of Verm. He had taken to the inner warrens of the castle to whatever little devotion he deemed important next. Lilah took tentative steps around the chambers, moving toward the bed first. When she saw that it was empty, no Staggs to be seen, she fell into the bed with a sigh and a sob. Reuben and the rest must have made their way into the castle proper.

The linens and feathers of the vast, cushy, yielding nest gave her welcome respite. Burying her pretty face in the pillows left her blind and mute to the world around her, which was as preferable as anything, she supposed. Reuben was not scheduled until the final match of the second round, so Lilah had no special hurry. Lady Grete and the nursemaids would hardly let her near the children anyway. She would think of anything but Hullen Curr, with the sad resignation in his eyes.

She shrugged her torn squirrel-fur mantle to the floor and pulled the heavy quilt over her body. Sleep would not immediately find her, but she was verging on a doze when she heard the hidden door swing, she tensed in the bed, pretending not to hear. The sound of her ragged breath drowned away everything else; as did the great, fluffy, comforting pillow. She chose bravery and decided to call out, "W-who goes there?"

There was no immediate answer, just the quiet clack of steps on the floor. Something clicked and clacked around the bed, before there was a light shuffling, and whomever had snuck through that secret passage was in bed with her, under the quilt.

It squirmed from her ankles, up her leg, over her belly, and it settled between her breasts. Rust colored scales and big silver eyes emerged from the soft folds of the blanket as Verm's little head appeared on Lilah's sternum. They blinked at one another, belly to belly and chin to chin. "Verm made sure. We are safe. We take care."

Lilah nodded, placing a heavy hand on the little drake's brow, "We take care, Verm. Thank you." He was no heavier than an especially fat house cat, and just as warm and cuddlesome, so it was little time before they both had fallen asleep from sheer exhaustion.

Sleep was not restful. Was it guilt? Was it the kobold sleeping on her chest? There would never be a way to be too entirely sure, but the tired young mother slept. And worse for her, she dreamt.

She and the children were walking through a wood... THE wood. The Greatwood. Ancient spires of pine, and oak and hemlock rose into a great green-black firmament of leaf and bough. Scents of fresh growth and the earthy aroma of old rot mingled here, where green leaves fell to brown loam. Silver sunlight dappled through the canopy, sparkling over the Lilah, children and the soft silks and velvets the three wore. Far in the distance, parting the trees, a tall tower penetrated the canopy of leaves, stacked layers of dark red brick on one another, causing this erect tower to almost undulate in the sunlight.

The beasts and birds of the wood chirped and chattered in the trees and dense brush. Happy little songbirds and busy chipmunks hopped amongst her and the children, but something kept pulling her forward. Like red strands of light, something warm filled her chest and bound her to that far tower. It reeled her tugged at her, dragging her deeper into the wood. It pulled faster, hurrying her and harrying her. On their short child legs, the boy and the girl could not keep up, and though she clutched their hands close, branches of hemlock wound themselves around her babies and pulled them into the forest, deep into the brush and away from their mother.

Still she was inexorably pulled forward, the strands growing less ghostly, more ghastly slowly swelling into tangible, throbbing strings of the same dark red as the far tower that they presumably connected to. Warm wet gore dripped from these strings as Lilah saw them join her own spiderweb of veins, in her arms, her chest, even her cheeks. They wrenched her through the wood and the beasts and birds fled from her. Stags bucked and leapt in flight, a broken bat flapped on tattered wings. A turtle struggled in the muck and mire as it fled, snapping at anything that came too near. The only animal that stayed, the only thing that watched, was the owl. The owl with his pitiless yellow eyes.

She was pulled toward the tower, still. And then she realized she was. She was still and the world was moving around her. She pushed, she pushed with her heart and her blood. And her love kept the tower at bay. The grim trees pulled back, and the grasping hemlock arms of iron led her babes back to her. She pushed and the threads of gore faded once more.

The silver sun dappled her and her babes, and even the rusty little guardian skipped with them. But still the eyes of yellow watched. The owl screeched and it was too late.

The trees opened with thousands more pairs of yellow eyes and Lilah saw what she had missed. The beasts had not been fleeing from her. The trees had been protecting the babes.

Beaks and talons and beating wings were upon them. Then nothing.

Blood. It is in your blood, beast of the trees.

Breathless and sweating, she woke with Verm still dozing on her chest. The dream was already slipping away like fog in the morning sun. She tried to grasp whatever sent her to such panic, but it was like trying to grab smoke. Verm made a sleepy churting sort of noise and Lilah smirked despite herself. He was much less ugly up close, she decided after a few long moments pondering his little mutt face. She liked him, he was little and weak, like her. Her breath was slowing as she puzzled exactly how she intended to take her little protector back to the Metal Mount. As Reuben was heir to the great ancient castle, and as that was unlikely to change, Reuben had lived there most of his life and Lilah for their entire marriage. It was likely to be another long sail back to Black Pearl Bay, and then several day's ride north along the old Steelsong Road, through the Greatwood and even a bit into the Mountains of Orre.

The tourney would end tomorrow, and there would be no concealing her new... *friend* on the weeklong journey home. She would also not leave Verm behind. The little kobold had given much to her and she would repay his love with love.

"Wake up, Verm." She whispered, and the big silver coin eyes fluttered open.

"Verm not sleeping, guarding." His tone was serious in the way a toddler is stern.

"Do you like it here, Verm?" Verm looked at Lilah's chest, and she shoved him off of her playfully. "I meant in Honeyhome, why are you here?"

The struggle to unbind himself from the bedding kept Verm from answering for a moment, but when he did, his eyes were far away. "Verm came with van, some sellers. Others singers. Verm was supposed to pick pockets while the singers sang, but Verm got caught."

Lilah nodded, stroking his little horn with a finger.

He purred, "They sent Verm away, said 'You are bad, Verm! We not want you!' So Verm went, and was hungry for a long time."

"And then you saw all the tents and smelled the food, you tried to get something to eat."

"And now Verm killed guy. Verm just wanted cheese."

Lilah sighed, "That is the human experience. I just wanted cheese and now we killed a man." She laughed until she sobbed and then laughed some more.

Almost numbly, Lilah would rise, carrying her tiny defender. She would take him to the basin, washing away Hullen Curr's blood from his little talons and teeth. There was a sharp pebble caught in the hard scaly skin of one of his toes, and Lilah managed to dislodge it, despite his whining protestations. She would wash his scarred and skinny body, washing road dust and old blood from him. The water was cold and he would squirm, but Lilah would deliberately get this little creature freshened. She peeled his filthy rags from him, and replaced them with some of the plainer items she had packed for her son, as Verm and Neal were of a size, though Neal was bigger around the chest and shoulders. The little drake looked ridiculous in fluffed ruffles, but Lilah would need him presentable. *But first...*

"Verm, can you get into all of the apartments from that back stair? All of the chambers in this great guest tower?" She flipped the sharp thing in her palm over and over, "The one the Curr family is using?"

Verm nodded warily.

The clack of dragontooth on wood hung in the silence. "Then this needs to get back in that room, Verm." She slid dragontooth heart of *Snowsnarl* from her palm to the little kobold. "Can you do that?"

He picked it up, big eyes even bigger, somehow.

"Or..." *Or throw it in the fucking ocean and forget about the whole damn Clan Curr. Their affairs and their swords and their dead heirs.* She frowned, "Just... get it in their chambers." A little clawed hand stuffed the tooth among the folds of his borrowed clothing. He moved to the secret door once more, little shoulders slumped. Lilah called to him one last time before he disappeared, "You have to be unseen, Verm. Even if it takes hours, no one can see you. Just do it and come back to me, and we will never see those dogs again."

He gave a little chirp of agreement and scurried through the door. Lilah took the time to make herself presentable, now. She had not been dressed especially well for her temple visit, and the near assault and subsequent trauma nap had left her looking ragged. She changed into a lace and brocade affair, sweeping Stagg bronze and leaf. Her belt and boots were a calfskin so yellow it was almost lemon, and so soft that Lilah thought them velvet when Reuben gave them to her. She straightened her locks and repainted her lips, a striking Rask red. By the time she tied the silk and emerald over her throat, she felt like a Lady.

Now, if only I can act the part.

Though her heart was with the little kobold hiding in the walls, looking to un-steal a precious heirloom, she had preparations to make, protections to make. She passed into the shared space and found only Lady Isolde Ironarm. The Lady of the Greatwood. As far as High Ladies of the Empire went, Lady Isolde was not the practiced picture of grace that a Gail Curr or Kalistah Malbes was. No, Lady Isolde was squat, churlish and held little interest in either governance or high society. She was only a handful of years older than Lilah, but had a habit of treating the Rask girl like a child, but not unkindly.

Lady Isolde was, as always, wrist deep in some arcane practice. She and her husband, Lord Torvald, were always busying themselves with some sort of book or spell or alchemy, all in the name of 'research'. What they were researching was never clear, at least to Lilah. They were, however, frequently visited by Isolde's brother, the shadowy Lord of Spies, Illystre Coldhearth. The trio had been nigh-inseparable since arriving in Honeyhome, so Lilah was somewhat surprised to find Lady Isolde here, but not disheartened. She might be exactly the person Lilah would pry the most honest counsel from.

"The Curr boy is still alive." Lady Isolde droned without looking up from whatever steaming clay bowl she was poking at.

"What?" Lilah was caught off guard.

"I figured you'd want to know. That's all everyone is talking about." She lifted her eyes, "...Oh. He fell, I thought you knew." She looked over at Lilah, "I thought you were at the temple."

Lilah straightened, "I was. I got back. And I was tired." She tried to sound self-possessed, "So, I took a nap. Because *I* wanted to."

Lady Isolde raised an eyebrow, "Good for you." She turned her attention beside her and muttered, "Give me a pinch of the red salt."

Shielded by both the table and Lady Isolde herself, something with a deep rumbling voice resonated at the Lady, "Of course." and a pale hand produced a lump of something the shade of blood. *Totho.*

Lilah spoke, letting her distaste for the strange little man burble clear, "Oh, I did not realize it was not just us ladies." She gave a smile so false she could taste it, but she smiled, "Totho, a pleasure to see you."

The pale little man popped his head around Lady Isode, a yellow grin parting his ivory skin, "M'lady, the pleasure is completely mine." He wobbled to her, taking her hand in an oleaginous kiss, "I am far often too bereft of your *significant charms"* His eyes rested in the same place Verm had slept a few short minutes previously.

Intentionally. Lilah thought to herself, *I avoid this little perverse little rake as much as possible.* Thankfully, Lady Isolde was rarely involved in matters of court, and thus neither was her attendant. But, here they were, right as Lilah needed advice. "Lady Isolde, might I trouble you for a conversation?"

She sighed, "I do seem to be the matriarch of this Clan, apparently." She chucked, "Sure, Lilah." She folded her hands, "how can I help you, dear?" She smirked, eyes glinting grey and green, dancing like she knew some secret and would never share it with the rest of the world.

"There are no other ladies quite like you. Especially the high ladies." Lilah began.

"That's hardly true, Lilith Sage at Mistwatch, hell, even Lady Greenfingers in the Witchwood." Isolde adjusted her wide brimmed hat, felted fur in slate grey. "Plenty of witch-women about."

Lilah shook her head, "I don't mean your magic. I mean…" She stuttered, trying to phrase what came next softly. "Your manner is so singular. There is nothing you do that you do not wish to do. You do not seem to care about courtly etiquette… At all."

Isolde gave her throaty laugh, followed by Totho's rumbling chortle. "There is plenty I do that I do not wish to, cousin-by-law." She poked her steaming clay cup with a thin wooden dowel. The dowel came back shorter. "Hmph. But, no, I do not care about courtly etiquette. It is a slow, silly thing. I have much to do and little time for the rules of pigheaded old men who died before my grandfather was born."

Lilah's tummy tensed, if those words were not treason, they were baked in the same oven. Her tone went soft and high, questioning, "That does not bother you? …You and Lord Torvald." She whispered, "*do not have any heirs!*"

Isolde laughed again, "We do not. I do not imagine my Lord Husband is even capable, and I am not especially interested."

Lilah still could not comprehend what she was hearing, "But, what of the *line?*"

Isolde snorted, "I am descended from stewards who inherited the seat of kings, Clan Artus themselves only came into the empire through marriage and inheritance, no conquest required. The line means nothing to me, Lilah. Besides, you and Reuben seem to have that well in hand."

Lilah rankled, unsure of the implication. *If her husband plans to die childless, someone needs to reign over The Greatwood. Better*

Neal than Lady Grete or Reuben, my son has a heart in his chest, not a black pit. She did not say this, of course, instead she offered humility, "We have been blessed."

Isolde and Totho both gave her long looks, but neither said anything, so Lilah continued, "My point is, my Lady, you seem so unconcerned with how the rest of the gentry perceive you." Lady Isolde gave half a shrug, and Lilah proceeded further, "Even the crown–"

Isolde cut her off, "I have never once gone against the crown, child. Those words are dangerous at home, here, they are deadly. I will ask that you mind yourself." Her cherubic face had gone cold, totally devoid of mirth and joy, the effect sent chills through Lilah's shoulders and spine.

"Apologies, I did not mean to imply–"

"I am certain you didn't." Lady Isolde suddenly held as much power and mystery as the wood itself, something primal and dark pacing through her compact frame. "Please, Lilah, your point."

It all tumbled forth from Lilah like she was emptying her sick stomach, "How do you do it? Again, apologies to you for my boldness, but I do not comprehend how you can simply." She chuckled, "Do whatever you want and parade around with your strange little pet oddity!" She gave a dismissive wave of the hand to Totho.

"Oddity?" Totho twisted his face into a sneer, "You're like to get no more kisses with such an attitude."

Lilah rolled her eyes, "Good. I am running sparse on perfumes to cover the reek of your breath when it lingers on my hand, anyway."

Lady Isolde brayed with laughter as Totho's alabaster cheeks picked up the barest hint of blush. Isolde nodded, "That's the right of it, right there."

"What is?"

"Gettin' angry enough that you don't care." Isolde smirked up at Lilah. "I'm the High Lady. You're next, not Lady Grete. Are you really going to let your husband be a *mama's boy?*"

Lilah could not quite reconcile Lady Isolde's words with reality. Realistically, she *knew* that her awful mother-by-law would never actually be Lady of the Greatwood. Hell, She and Ser Mandel would never sit the Seat at Bronze Bough. For all the terror Lady Grete could put in her, what was the real threat? It was Lord Torvald who held any real power, and he was kind. When he died, Reuben would take the Regency, again, not Lady Grete. She gave a breathless exhale of disbelief, "I-I guess not."

Lady Isolde shrugged, "Stop asking permission to be happy from a Lady that doesn't care if you live or die, Lilah. There's a hole in my sister-by-law's heart, and you're surely not going to fill it, so stop driving yourself mad trying."

Lilah nodded, "I think– I think that is precisely what I needed to hear." She wrapped her arms around the strange little High Lady, and embraced her. "I do not know if you comprehend everything you have given me today, but it is huge, cousin-by-law."

Isolde smirked, "I do not, but perhaps that is for the best."

Lilah would thank her, and even apologize lightly to Totho before spending the rain soaked day at the tourney. From her place under the dry canopy, she thrilled as Ser Hugo Saddler defeated the veiled Al Eh'Syar of Hro'Cratis. Lilah had seen the exotic bird-woman at the Debutante's Procession last evening, and under the veil she was a stunning creature. She was perhaps a year or three younger than Lilah, and had beautiful copper skin and shining black hair that fell about her chin in tight ringlets. Her body slunk and curved like a predatory cat, and her accent dripped warmth and mystery. Her gorgeous face was hidden under layers of silk and mail, as were those slinking curves, as Syar dressed herself in the style of a freerider of the Scorching Sands.

As Lilah watched this far-wandering traveler twirl the heavy axe she carried, counter balancing the huge thing with her own weight, she prayed that Prince Vernus may select this bird-woman instead of Doreen. As Ser Hugo Saddler caught her big axe on his shield, and knocked it flying, Lilah realized that was a flight of fancy. The tournament held few more joys for her, but there was a single moment when she had not dared to expect.

Hullen Curr's three sworn swords made their way to the arena circle dressed in jerkin, cloak and leathers in the colors of their fallen high lord. Excepting the adulterous Ser Hale Torchbearer, Lilah liked the gesture, though Torchbearer's participation left a bilious sensation at the back of Lilah's mouth. Hale Torchbearer stole a glance at a skinny bo– no, girl. The girl was wrapped in a substantial green cloak, hiding her fairly effectively. A split second glance in her direction let huge pale eyes shine, and she could feel Ellari Curr staring at her.

The impropriety of it all left her just shy of shaking. Curr's husband was half dead, in a borrowed bed, and she was here watching her lover. Sure, Lilah may have been the one who *put* Hullen in that bed, but no one knew that. *This woman has no sense of decency.*

After the silent encounter with the Curr girl, Lilah's demeanor had turned as grey and sullen as the soaking sky above. Though the clouds would lift during the back half of the second round, Lilah's mood would not. By the time Reuben had lost to some household knight, she was fuming.

The match had been lost by no fault of Ser Reuben Stagg, even Lilah could see that. The Shark of the Goldengrass, this Doyle Selach, was as canny a fighter as Reuben had ever seen, and his combination of net and trident was like nothing he'd ever encountered, in twelve years of tourneys. Even through all that, though, Reuben may have had a chance, *if* one of the leather straps that held his shield to his left arm had not snapped. Later inspection would find that it seemed to have been mouse-eaten, though Lilah specifically recalled it seeming fine when he'd left it beside the bed on the previous evening.

It was no matter, with his shield flapping freely, Reuben had been knocked to the muck and the commons cheered, as this previously unknown hedge knight marched on to victory, becoming one of the final eight warriors in the tourney: Lady Vellen, Ser Hugo Saddler and his Uncle Lord Hinric, Lord Lukas Axe, the crown Prince, the mysterious Big Turtle, old Ser Tullus Mirebreaker and now this Selach boy, who rode for the Goldengrass. With this Selach, three of the eight remaining belonged to Clan Saddler. *Perhaps the little tumor in a crown will choose Harlow Saddler and spare Doreen.*

There would be four more matches after dinner, and a grand ball after that. She would return to her chambers, to prepare for feast, fighting and festival. The warm, practical dress she had wrapped herself in all day would not be acceptable for such ventures. This day had started with prayer, a simple devotion at temple. After everything that had occurred today, Lilah Stagg was starting to believe her trust in the gods may have been misplaced. It was when Verm slipped back through the hidden door that Lilah could finally breathe again.

The little drake whispered, "Verm got it put back. Wrapped it in big green cloth in trunk, super safe."

Reuben was out of the tourney. The stolen dragon's tooth had been returned. And finally, she had a person, a dragon, in whom she could place her trust. *If I am to be a High Lady, it is time to be one. Let us broker no argument. Verm is my sworn sword as much as any knight.*

Lilah took his little clawed talon in her soft, pink hand, and led Verm into the common area, to meet the rest of his new family.

VANDRE V

"Layin' in a bed of vipers don't make you no snake. You ain't safe just because you think you're friendly."

The old man had managed to avoid being put to work until after dinner, when the distasteful duty of serving as Saddler's bodyguard for the ball and tourney was given to him by a smirking little footman with wandering eyes. He strode through the hallway, his new cape streaming behind him, as his new boots thudded satisfyingly with every step he took across the tile. As he passed by the lesser men, he let the medallion on his chest glint in the Silver Sun. For the first time in his life, men stepped aside when Vandre approached.

The chain around his neck still chafed.

Vandre made his way to the Lord's Tower, where another pair of Malbes guards moved to stop this scarred old sellsword. But he cleared his throat and nodded toward the winged horses on his medallion. "Nah, boys. I got an invitation, I'll bring back a treat for you, I promise."

He would eventually find himself at the Saddler's door, where two of the Young Stallions stood sentinel. Each of them gave him a sidelong stare as he smiled, stepping over a large red-brown stain in the tile. One of The Stallions opened the door, announcing him, "Arriving is Vandre of Hammerdale, Sworn Sword to Hartwin Saddler."

A derisive snort followed, "We know, Elbert. We've been *waiting.*"

The Stallion murmured an apology to an austere woman seated next to Hellendre. The Hellheart smirked, dressed far finer than the simple shift she had worn to heal Vandre this morning. Some gorgeous brassy damask and celadon silks clung to every curve of her plush frame. Vandre felt every one of his years, but something about that dress made him feel much, much younger. She spoke, her usual bold tone somewhat muted, "Vandre, goodman, allow me to introduce Lady Kalistah Saddler."

Lady Kalistah was a woman about Vandre's own age, and she was the spitting image of her eldest son. Ginger hair, freckles, and sharp green eyes were twin to Hartwin Saddler. She wore her own green, a plainer gin viridian, but in fine silk and lace. Her greying red locks were tightened into a dense bun, pierced by a fine golden comb, studded in peridot. She took a long look at this new sellsword and pressed her fat pink lips together. This stern High Lady took a long inhale and spoke, "They often do say to respect a man who lives to old age in a young man's profession, however, it seems our Hartwin may have taken the adage too far with this one."

Vandre frowned, but he let this roll off his back, "I am younger than I look, My Lady. Many hard years behind me. If I were a horse, they'd call me 'rode hard and put away wet,' heh." He nervously approached, a hand extending in greeting until Hellendre cleared her throat at him.

A dyspeptic look crossed Lady Kalistah's face, "I have no time for horses."

Hellendre rose, affixing the lid to a jar of a sweet smelling poultice, before cleaning her hands with a small tea towel. Once cleaned, she rose and called out "Harlow!" before turning back to Vandre. "Hart had a little prior engagement, as did Lord Bryony." Her gaze slid to Lady Kalistah, "And as Hugo is preparing for his match with Lady Lenore, Hart figured that this would be a fantastic opportunity for you to meet Lady Kalistah and Harlow, get a little work in, too."

"You are to escort us to the tournament ground where we are to meet with my Lord Husband and Hartwin." Lady Kalistah expounded. "Three unaccompanied women is salacious. Someone may think us streetwalkers." There was no joke or joy in her quivering voice.

"Mother, you are outrageous." Harlow Saddler entered the common room from an arched doorway in the back corner of the space. Her voice was breathy, and she was hardly more substantial. She was a wisp clad in wisps of her own green silk, a long cut up the side of her flowing skirt went near to her hip, exposing a perfectly shaped leg, with a petite foot clad in a brazen sandal. Her neckline was near as dramatic, diving from her shoulders to her navel. The girl was thin and petite, but had enough of a woman's figure to increase Vandre's heartrate. Jewels that cost more gold than Vandre had even seen in his half-century sparkled on her ears, throat, fingers and toes, "Though I feel like a sheet-selling wench in this gown. You can see my... well... my everything."

Lady Kalistah took no complaint, "You look perfect. You won't have that body forever. Enjoy it."

Hellendre swung her own thick hip, "I don't even have it now, if I put that thing on, you would see green skin bouncing out every which way." with a chuckle. "Yer perfect, Harley. The prince ain't gonna be able to look at another young maid, I promise."

Harlow's face shadowed slightly. *She ain't dressing for the prince, is she? There's something else happenin' here and I don't like being in the middle without knowing what.* Vandre watched this younger Saddler with eyes that had practiced. She didn't move like a noble, she carried herself like a cutpurse. She was always tense, ready to move, but hid it. To the untrained eye, they saw a lax, even skittish little fawn.

She reminded Vandre of a tavern girl he'd met some years back during a job near Codd Stone. She had been a pretty little wisp too, older than the Saddler girl, but not much. She kept her dark hair down in her face, though. She dressed nice, let the patrons look at her all they wanted. She wore a lot of low cut things too.

One night, some local ploughboy grabbed her ass. When she spun, the hair flew from her face, and her eyes had something hateful in them, and her hand had a knife in it. A jagged scar ran down the tavern girl's cheek, from the corner of her mouth to near her left eye. Vandre remembered the tears flowing down the line of the scar as he and a few other patrons pulled her off of that stupid kid. That Saddler girl's scars may not have been plain on her face, but the next boy that touched her was in for just as nasty a surprise.

Chella.

He hadn't thought of her in years. She was married with a litter of her own young ploughboys and tavern girls, now. *Or dead. Not everybody keeps pushing, old man. Not everyone is too stubborn to be killed and too damn mean to die.*

Harlow glided to her mother, taking the older woman by arm. Her mother fussed performatively, not needing the help, but the pair crossed to the main door. Hellendre slid her own arm into link with Vandre's "I suppose that leaves you with me. Don't be getting any ideas, now." She smirked, leaning forward with a whisper, "I don't mind if you look down my dress though, *everyone does.*" She pressed her significant charms together, great green hillsides, and winked.

"I couldn't begin to keep up with you." He shook his head as they followed mother and daughter.

"Maybe not, but the fun is in the tryin'." Hellendre laughed a little, as they passed past the stain on the stoop.

The remaining trek to the tourney grounds was more quiet than not, only the occasional pair of leering eyes at Harlow's dress or Hellendre's horns. As they approached the arena, Hartwin Saddler waited, with a heavyset girl in pink hanging from his arm. He raised the other, getting the attention of Harlow with a wave.

Saddler approached, with this pretty, thick-bodied girl. She had dark hair and apple cheeks and was positively *mooning* up at the tall young noble. Saddler himself was dressed immaculately, wools creased and pressed and leathers shining. The girl in pink wore some satin that accentuated her chest and hips in a flattering enough fashion. Saddler greeted his mother, then sister, then Hellendre. Finally, he turned to Vandre, "There's mud on your boots, Tend to it."

Vandre looked to his feet and saw a single smear of yellow-brown across the toe of his left boot, "So there is, my lord." The old sellsword searched the immediate area; *a trough, a blanket, an especially big leaf, anything.*

The panic must have been dawning too clearly on his face, because the fat girl finally spoke, "You are being cruel, Hartwin." She turned to Vandre, eyes of seawater above pink apple cheeks. "He thinks he's funny when he's just peevish." She gave a pearly white smile, "Lady Joelle Bridge of Rain Tower Hall."

"Vandre of Hammerdale." He nodded politely, hoping for no follow-up questions, as Hammerdale is far nearer than Cobalt Bridge than was entirely comfortable. Thankfully, there were no more.

"Vandre has recently come into my service, Joelle. Highly recommended by the Lord of Spies himself." Hartwin smirked knowingly at Vandre, "Don't let the grey hair fool you, this one is as fierce as they come."

He could feel those big seafoam eyes on his scarred face, so he tried to look extra grim.

Soon, the four younger nobles would pair off and hurry inside, leaving only Vandre and Lady Kalistah. She watched the receding backs of the next generation and there was something very still about her. It seemed the only movement was a wet sheen of moisture on her eyes. Vandre offered the High Lady his arm. After a small sad sound, she took it, pursing her lips, but taking it all the same.

As they slowly made their way into the arena, through the low grandstand tunnel, Lady Kalistah leaned to Vandre, and whispered to him in the dark, "My son wants to marry that walrus."

Vandre tensed up, "Lady Bridge?"

She turned to him with a knowing glance, before recoiling slightly, "Is part of your ear gone– Yes. Lady Bridge, the pink marshmallow."

Vandre tenderly touched the missing hunk of ear, "Gifts from the trade."

Lady Kalistah would fume in silence for the remainder of the walk, and noticeably stiffen at her Lord Husband's husky voice calling out in greeting. Vandre had seen the High Lord of the Goldengrass from a distance several times over the years, but this was the closest he'd ever been to the man he'd stolen no less than three horses from over that same time period. Lord Byrony was a barrel chested man, balding and powerful. He was a heaping handful of years older than Vandre, maybe ten. A broad smile crossed his face as he greeted the gathered youths and then his Lady wife with a warm kiss on the cheek. Lady

Kalistah gave a tight smile that did not reach her eyes as she detached from the sellsword and took her husband's arm.

Vandre extended a hand to Byrony, who took it in his great meaty paw and shook it heartily. His big, warm grin never faded, and though he likely still could have crushed Vandre's hand to powder in his huge hand, he was firm, but not ungentle, "You, my friend, must be Vandre, then. Hart has sung your praises! Glad to see another old boy getting a payday." He laughed freely, elbowing Vandre in the ribs.

Vandre felt the corner of his mouth creep into a smile, "Glad to see some mirth in this family."

Lord Byrony froze. His great wide mouth tightened, his eyes hardened, but only for an eternity of about three seconds, before breaking like a landslide into an avalanche of laughter that Vandre found himself echoing. The big lord slapped his tall, stern heir on the back, "Where did you find this one, Hart? He's alright."

"If he's not less insolent, he is liable to find himself right back in that same hole." Hartwin gave his own smirk, that was not devoid of insolence. "Or someplace even less habitable."

Vandre nodded deferentially to his new patron, "Apologies m'lord. Old men swappin' jests is a mite more comfortable for me than court and courtesy." He cast his eyes to the smear of mud drying on his boot, "But I am a quick study, I promise this."

Lady Bridge was the first to speak, "You've done no harm, Hart knows he's got a stick up his rear, but we're workin' on it." Lady Kalistah noticeably darkened, but said nothing as her son went a shade of crimson that near enough hid his freckles.

The older pair, the High Lord and Lady would be invited to sit in the royal box with Clan Artus and some associated High Lords. Clan Saddler was represented in three of the four remaining contests. The

High Lord and Lady were all smiles, as they led Harlow up to the high box, past two Greyguard, the Big Orca in plate and the Little Grey Duck.

This put Hellendre back on Vandre's side, and Hartwin and Joelle in front of them. The hellheart leaned close and spoke low, "You did real well with the High Lord." Vandre gave her a curt thank you, and she smiled, her pointed canines apparent, "He likes men who get things done and dislikes bullshit. If you hadn't stolen a horse from him and murdered four of his peasants, he'd probably even like you."

"It was only three." Vandre corrected, "The horse got one, that don't count."

"I am sure the High Lord would see the difference." She chuckled, like brass bells and silver sunlight sparkled on her horns.

The quartet would take reserved seats in a box in green and brazen hues, among Young Stallions and Saddler cousins and knights and serving girls. Of all the boxes of nobles wreathing this arena, the Saddler stand was nearest to bursting. Garish oil lamps and mirrors surrounded the whole structure, bathing the whole stadium in dancing orange and gold light. The jewels and satins and fine metals glittered in lamplight, an inferno of wealth and opulence. Vandre was clad in finery he'd never even imagined owning a day past, and still he felt like a vagrant compared to this shining nobility.

He was allowed a seat between Hellendre and Lady Joelle, but before he settled, Saddler took him by the arm and hissed, "Your best behavior, friend. These women are both dear to me. There will be *no* impropriety, is that understood?"

Vandre shrugged, "I'll be so goddamn chivalrous you'll have your brother knight me."

"I'll hold you to that." Saddler gave his equine grin, "I desperately want us to all get along, I do mean that."

The horns would blare, and Lady Lenore Vellen would step into the torchlight. The stands would erupt into boos once more. No one dared hurl refuse this evening, not after her display earlier in the day. Vandre was shocked to see that this little witch had toppled Ser Sancho Madapple, but he knew better than to question. Beside him, the green-skinned Hellheart was uncharacteristically still, save some ebony and onyx beads wrapped around her shaking fist and the slow tremble of her lips in muttered prayer.

The horns blasted once more and Ser Hugo Saddler stepped forth to raucous cheers. He carried a gilded sword and gilded shield, and in his green tunic and crested helm, with its high horsehair plume, the young knight looked like a hero from the old tales. *He'll need to fight like old Durant the Demon to best the girl who beat Madapple, I have no doubt.* Ser Hugo pounded his sword on his shield thrice, setting it to ringing like a bell, as the commons erupted.

Hartwin Saddler leaned sharp elbows on sharp knees and fixed his chip of emerald eyes on the witch in the arena. His tongue probed his bottom lip as thoughts swirled over his stiff countenance.

Ser Hugo stepped forth and whaled on his shield several more times, hard. Reverberations shook through the sword, and Saddler's veiny arm. *What's this boy doing? He's going to be out of breath before the match starts, and that's if he doesn't take the edge right offa his sword.* Vandre thought to himself, but before he could think further, he could feel the hot breath of Lady Joelle bridge on his stump of an ear.

"Hartwin and I are going to be married, you know." Her voice was soft, calm and sweet, her hand never left the crook of her lover's arm.

Vandre nodded, "It'll be my pleasure to serve you as well, then."

In the arena, horns blared. Ser Hugo kept pounding away on his shield, a steady rhythm of hard thwacks keeping the low ringing rumble echoing from every stone in the arena. Vellen swung her halberd in a long looping figure eight, relying on the length of the polearm to keep the more seasoned knight at bay.

To his right, the murmured prayers of Hellendre were increasing in speed and intensity, but Vandre's focus was to his left, as the friendly Lady Joelle continued, "Hart and I share everything, Vandre. We tell each other everything. It's the only way a... *relationship* between two folks like us can function." Her words left Vandre's gut feeling watery.

Hellendre still prayed, her words growing faster. Saddler was still pummeling his shield in the arena, sweat on his brow, sword shaking. Both the beads in Hellendre's clenched hand and the golden shield had begun to glow faintly, pulsing in rhythm. Vellen swung her halberd a half step slower than she should have. Saddler stepped aside lazily, still smacking away at his shield.

"He tells me *everything.*" Bridge chuckled, "Things no other livin' soul knows."

Hellendre had begun trembling slightly beside him, the black and grey beads taking on a dull orange glow in her green hand. Hugo kept pounding, Hart kept watching and Joelle kept whispering, "I know that they're tradin' Harlow to the Mirebreakers, because Vernus is a little shit."

Vellen swung again, her ghostly left eye had begun to shine with its own magic.

Bridge continued, "I know about your horse thievin'."

Hugo caught this strike with his sword, and with an easy flourish, cut the head of the halberd from the shaft, sending the black metal to the ground with a hard, ringing clang. He celebrated with a few more hard shots to his own shield, which had begun to blaze with its own shining light. The beads in Hellendre's hand shone just as bright.

"I know about Ser Jemes Wyse, and I know that Illystre Coldhearth wants your hide." The kindness in her voice never wavered, which was even more chilling. "I know about the crown, old man."

Back in the arena, Vellen tossed the shaft of her halberd aside and raised her palms. Her motion was slow, deliberate, and calculated. Tendrils of light began to sprout like seedlings from the ground around her. Beside Vandre, Hellendre's whispers returned to the common tongue, *"DoitdoitdoitdoitfuckinnowHugonownownowNOW."*

Saddler surged forward and slammed his glowing shield into the unprotected midsection of Lady Lenore and every mote of blazing white from the shield flashed like a potassium flare. Thunder echoed from every stone, timber and body in the arena. Vandre felt it in his chest. Lady Bridge seemed to not feel it whatsoever. "I know exactly *who* and *what* you are, nothin' more than a bandit."

Vellen lay in the dirt, writhing. Smoke curled from some of the silks on her armor as they still smoldered. Hellendre slumped in her seat, breathing heavily. The beads were black again, though fresh burns coated the witch's left hand, a line of circles where the heat of the beads had sizzled. Ser Hugo flipped his helm off of his head, hooting in victorious joy, as the commons screamed salutes toward his singular skill.

"If you think you can use my Hart, or god forbid, hurt my Hartwin." Bridge continued, still the picture of genial grace, "You'd best make sure you kill me first. Because I will spend the rest of my life making the rest of yours as miserable as possible."

Vandre simply nodded.

"I'm but one-and-twenty, I have a long time to be your friend." She squeezed her lover's arm lightly, "but it's an even longer time to have me set to your suffering."

A huge, oblivious smile on his face, Hartwin turned to Joelle, "Jo, did you fucking– sorry- did you see that?"

Her huge teal eyes settled on his long face, "It was a spectacular display, to be true." She smiled still, never showing a tinge of the violence she had just promised. "Just getting to know the new help, love. I'm sure he'll behave perfectly."

There was a certain hardness in the girl's soft face that Vandre could only bow to, "Chivalrous enough, m'lord. I promised." He gave a crooked smile he did not feel.

SLADE IV

"You never know what a man is hiding, be it behind a helm or a smile."

Sabre clattered on claymore. The Big Turtle groaned as he shoved the Crown Prince backward, arms and knees locked as the pair crossed swords. Dirt ground under tooled leather as the Prince roared back, laughing wildly, "Brave lad. Big, big brave lad!" They both heaved and split each taking a step backward, flickering in the lamplight.

Slade cheered as loudly as the rest, maybe even louder, as he decided that he loved his Big Turtle so well. With Marten beside him, and a horn of ale in his hand, the tourney was downright amusing, hell, he would even call it *fun*. Jamen had been kept in the tower after dinner, so Aunt Carmine and Marten had allowed Slade a horn of ale. He had taken a light dinner in the library, so the ale had sent his head swimming and his thoughts drifted back to his evening, mere hours past.

He was happy to leave the memory of his dinner in the library behind. The research itself had not been encouraging, and the lack of Lady Masha Curr had disheartened him even further. The fact that he had not seen her wasn't surprising, but when the footsteps rang out behind him, he had still dared to hope. The hulking Ser Rolof Deepreach had been the latest in that series of disappointments, but Slade was content to let the big knight feel the scorn in his greeting.

At first, he'd thought Deepreach drunk, possibly wandering lost in search of something to drown his sorrows in, or a place to empty his bladder. Though the big man did seem confused, there was no stink of wine or rum on him. His attempt to identify the man-bird-thing as the Raider Devil-God Gargol was a possibility that Slade had researched and dismissed. Gargol was a feral thing and this thing-man–bird showed intelligence.

It was when the Big Kraken started babbling about his brain being carved up, that Slade had grown uncomfortable. But Ser Rolof seemed genuinely distressed, and Slade could not look at this man, who was shaking and sweating and frightened, and not aid him. Despite the hurled insults, despite Marten's broken hand, Slade took pity. He helped the big knight lower himself into a seat near the table. The antique wood groaned under Ser Rolof's considerable weight, and Slade hurried around the small table. He poured water into his small copper cup, from his own skin and handed it to Ser Rolof, who quaffed it, before spitting it across carpets imported from beyond the sunrise.

"What the hell is that? Water?" Deepreach croaked, "I need wine, boy. I have the *horrors,* boy."

Slade squeezed more of the water from the skin to the cup. "I do not have wine, and water will keep you from retching. *Drink.*" He slid the cup back to Deepreach who indeed did drink it warily.

"That does help, I suppose." He said after about five minutes, and as many little copper cups of water. The Bronze Kraken had noticeably calmed, his breath evening out and color returning to his face. "Thank you, boy." There was something sheepish about him, a shyness after his show of weakness, "I ought not to have said that thing at the party. I were drunk and I thought it was funny. Now, I know that ain't a defense, but it's a reason."

Slade had nodded, not accepting the nonapology. "What brings you to the library, Ser Rolof?"

Rolof's thick finger prodded the charcoal drawing of the Bird-thing-man again, "That filthy fucking thing, I think. And the Prince maybe, I'm not rightly sure any longer." He seemed to tense again, but Slade reassured him and he continued, "I keep findin' myself dealing with witchcraft and demons and all sorts of things I got no notion of."

Slade gave him a reassuring look, "Ser, that's what brought me here. The night of the party, I saw that same thing." Slade brushed the charcoal sketch with his crippled hand. "I cannot explain it, I cannot define or understand it." Something thrilled in his little chest at the unknown, "And I have gone through every text allowed to me in this library, and found nothing."

A look of curiosity crossed the big knight's face, "What do you mean 'allowed to you?'"

His hand gestured toward the scroll of black vellum from Almythira. It sat high on a shelf, far out of reach in a locked glass case, likely magically warded as well, "There's that up there, I believe it is some sort of ritual from the far off Beastlands, but there is little way to be sure." He shrugged, "I do not believe it contains anything valuable to my research, but if it's locked away, I would imagine it's extremely powerful."

Rolof simply nodded, before running powerful hands through thinning hair. "So, there's no way to protect myself?"

Slade would have to leave the distraught Ser Rolof there. He had no further aid for this man, no answers for his questions. Noting the time and the tourney, Slade would need to make his way to the arena. Deepreach would give him a hazy farewell and even a notion of gratitude for the water, but would make no move to rise. Slade gathered his things quickly and left Ser Rolof there amongst the stacks.

Back in the arena, the Turtle swung his claymore in a high arc, clattering down on the Prince's heavy shield. This had been the longest bout of the entire tourney thus far. The Turtle and the Crown Prince had been slugging it out for nearly ten minutes, and though each clearly felt the weight of their weapons and armor, neither showed any sign of yielding.

Again, Slade's thoughts drifted back to when Slade had finally made his way from the castle's library to the nearby arena, Uncle Tullus and Aunt Carmine were waiting for him. Uncle Tullus impatiently waited, not for Slade, but the missing Marten. The stout knight was scheduled to take the arena against Ser Doyle Selach shortly, and was summarily anxious. Slade could see blushed fury rising in his cheek, as he muttered curses beneath his blonde mustache.

When Marten did arrive, he could not hold his grin back, he leaned close to his Uncle, "She's very pretty."

The stern old knight smirked, "Aye, I've heard that."

"Kind, too." Marten's sparkling smile turned to Slade, "She reads, too! And she sings like a dove!"

"Doves coo." Slade corrected, "And murmur, they don't sing."

Marten sighed, "Fine, what bird sings, Slade?"

"Nightingales, thrushes." Slade began to list the birds he had committed to memory some years back, "Finches, blackbirds–"

Though he could continue, Marten hushed him, "Thank you. She sings like a finch, then, Slade." Slade gave a satisfied little 'heh', and Marten continued, "She's a catch to be sure, Uncle Tullus."

"And she's richer than the Golden Boy himself, Marten." The Snapping Turtle grunted. He was nothing if not pragmatic, "Are you gonna marry the girl or what?"

Marten bounced his head of black curls, "I reckon I ought to. We're gonna need the coin anyway." The blush on his face betrayed his desire for her beyond his duty.

"Coin? What do you need coin for?" The Snapping Turtle immediately grabbed this nugget.

Marten smirked, "The Prince and I have some ideas, Uncle. We'll discuss them later. First you have a tourney to win for us, and I need to find a ring. Where is Garland? He could make something, couldn't he?"

A ring brought Slade's awareness back to the present arena once more: The ring of the heavy steel sword of the Turtle smashing off of the Crown Prince's shield. The Turtle roared again, a deep baritone echoing and rumbling into incoherence in his beaked helm. Prince Talor was drenched with sweat, his dark hair matted to his forehead, under his helm. He panted, chuckling to himself under his breath. He gave the shortsword in his right hand a lazy spin, loosening his wrist, "Who are you, lad?" He slashed, but the Turtle parried. "Heh, yeh fight like your shell is on fire, Turtle." The Prince jested, golden eyes sparking faint flecks of green.

Still silent, The Turtle bounded forward, trying for a thrusting boot, like the one he had leveled Lord Tallman with. But Prince Talor was much swifter than the big Northman. He spun out of the way, taking the brunt of the Turtle's heel on his heavy tower shield. The boy Prince spun, and the heavy oak and steel rectangle fell to the wet chalk, gravel and sand below. Seizing his opportunity, the Turtle stiff-armed the prince, and managed to snatch the Prince's tower shield from the sodden ground.

Slade screamed in excitement, ale and cheers and song and smoke bringing this evening to some dizzying crescendo. "Get it, Ser! It's right there! Throw it!"

And he did.

With a twirling heave, like a man at a festival anvil toss, the Turtle tossed the near twenty pound slab of oak and steel, sending it sailing like a kite. It took to the air and sailed gracefully, crashing back to the firmament, sending clods of dirt flying with a loud clangor. It was a good fifteen yards up the ramp that led to the pit, and The Turtle was between it and Prince Talor. The Prince smirked, still swinging his short sword, "Well, that's just not fair. You're much larger than I am."

Marten leaned to Slade, his voice a whisper, "The Prince can't sit now. One smash from the Turtle and he's done." And Slade instantly saw it was true, the Prince's entire manner had changed. He bounced from toe to toe, practically crackling with vigor. The tip of his gilded sword never sat still, a buzzing fly that the Turtle must constantly watch.

For his part, The Turtle did not look nearly as in control as he ought to have. Under his armor, Slade could see his wide shoulders sagging the weight of plate and heavy steel claymore. He had slowed a quarter-step, especially after the sheer exertion of hurling the heavy shield.

The Turtle moved first, perhaps foolishly. He threw his entire body into a great overhead chop, which the Crown Prince easily pirouetted away from. The Prince swung his lighter hand-and-a-half sword in a raking spin, catching the Turtle in the shoulder. Flakes of enamel powdered out with a grinding thud as the Turtle stumbled, his pauldron dented.

The Big Turtle tried again, another huge overhead slash. "He looks like a farmboy pounding a fencepost." Slade muttered to his brother as the Prince dodged again, this time sending a precision cut to the side of the Turtle's beaked helm. Off balance and likely knocked senseless, the Turtle tried that overhand slash a final, exhausted time.

"Or like a smi–" He didn't finish the phrase, he and his brother gasped in duet. They knew who this mystery knight was.

The Turtle swung his sword like a smithee at an anvil. For a third time, the nimbler fighter dodged. This time, he rolled right, catching the heel of the big man with his sword point, which sent the big man clattering to the ground like a kitchen cabinet in a cyclone.

The Prince held his swordpoint to the heaving chest of the Turtle, "Do you yield, Ser?"

The Turtle nodded, raising his hands. The Prince stepped away, sliding his shining sword slowly into its scabbard. The Big Turtle slowly rose, removing his helm. Under sweat soaked blonde curls, the great blue Mirebreaker eyes of Gar the Smithee showed proud. From the deck, the staging area, Ser Tullus Mirebreaker shouted himself hoarse with pure pride. Red faced, huffing and sweating, Gar bowed his head in deference to the Crown Prince, "I yield, Your Grace, but I am no knight."

A look of genuine confusion crept across the Prince's face, "Surely, you're jesting. What is your name, my good man?"

"Gar." The big smith stuttered, "Garland, I mean."

"Who do you ride for, Garland?" The Prince's confusion had blossomed into a bemused little grin.

"Well, we sailed, I, uh, don't have a horse." a rosy flush deepened in the cheeks of the towering smith.

The smiling prince stifled a laugh, as a pair of attendants approached, offering both men some linens with which to wipe the sweat and dust from their faces, "No, Garland. Where are you from? Who do you fight for?"

"I am a-a smith at the Mossmont, your Grace. I do not fight, I am no knight, Prince."

"That is patently untrue." There was no jest in the crown Prince, no laugh, no smile. "Kneel, Garland."

The silence in the arena was pregnant with purpose and possibility as the colossal knight dropped to his exhausted knees, his heaving breath finally slowing to a calmer rhythm. As the plate armored knight clattered to a genuflection, more flakes of green enamel fell to the ochre grit at his knees. The prince's gilded sword screeched free from its scabbard, and the Prince raised it high in the silver sunlight.

The Prince's voice was a clarion call, burdened with purpose, brimming in glory, "Garland, I charge you with the duty of a guardian. I charge you with the duty of a shield. Women, children, the infirm, the elderly. They will gather behind you and you will defend."

The flat of his golden blade tapped the right pauldron, the one that same sword had dented deeply moments ago. "I-I will."

The prince continued, ritual and pomp in the dancing orange and gold lamplight, "I charge you with the duty of a warrior. I charge you with the duty of a sword. Dark forces, hateful beasts and evil men will gather, and do their malfeasance. You are to bring them justice in the law of the Empire. You are not to seek conflict, but to enforce peace." A second tap on the other pauldron.

His throat tight with emotion, Garland choked, "I will, your grace."

"I charge you with the duty of a martyr. I charge you to die at these duties if need be. You become the next link in the great chain of chivalry, Garland. I charge you to be a knight." A final tap of the sword flat, to the crown of Gar's gold curled head, gentle as a mother's kiss.

"Yes, my prince, I will."

Gar the Smithee knelt, and Ser Garland the Gallant stood. Tears rolled down Slade's cheeks as his big cousin bathed in the love he'd given the world, paid back in full. Slade and Marten gripped each other by the hand, and even his Lord Brother was blinking back tears.

"Well, Slade, looks like he's moving out of the forge." Marten laughed, and Slade laid his heavy head on his brother's shoulder.

"He did it. He made his own armor and he fought the Prince to a standstill." Slade smiled.

From beside them, Aunt Carmine shook her head, chuckling, "He sure did. He's a good boy. I hope his father is as proud as I am, *whoever* his da' may be." Her raucous, knowing grin said more than her words ever could.

ROLOF IV

"Bravery in the face of the unknown is noble. It's stupid, but it's noble."

Ser Rolof hurried out of the library, taking extreme care not to wake the snoring little Learner at the desk. Though the world still shifted under his feet, the cobbles felt like soft sand, he made his way into the torchlight on the streets of Honeyhome. The big man parted the stream of peasants headed toward the arena. The third round of the tourney, the quarter-finals, would be starting shortly, though Rolof held no more interest. Too many Saddlers still running their way through the lists.

He pushed his way against the stream, heading back to the castle. He was at least a head taller than nearly every one of the commons, so the rabble stayed out of his way. Given his stormy mood, this was for the best. The Mirebreaker boy had seen the damn bird, but the little Lordling lacked answers, as well. Perhaps Rolof's efforts would show results.

The further he got from the arena, the fewer people there were, which, again, suited the big knight just fine. By the time Rolof arrived back within the walls, the only figure he saw was a small man in all grey rushing into the far trees hurriedly. He left the grey phantom to his business and kept his path to the Fisher Clan apartments. Once up the stony stairs, Rolof slid inside the door, hoping to take his prize to his quiet chambers alone, but instead, he was met with Lady Larissa. She was completely shame-faced, and wrung her hands, "Ser. I thought you were going to the Tourney…"

"I had some readin' I wanted to do before we left." Rolof craned his neck, searching for the source of his lady's distress.

The noise Larissa made was incredulous to say the least, "Reading?"

"Yes, *reading.*" He put extra emphasis on the 'g', trying to sound like a proper lord. He strode into the space, and there, he still sat Lord Ludo and ancient Lady Adelpha. The big man knelt for his lord, "My apologies, my lord. I did not realize I was interruptin'."

Ludo gave his little squawking laugh, as Larissa settled into her lord husband's side. Rolof's skin crawled as he watched his woman slide her hand into the small of *her* husband's back. The little Lord wobbled over to Rolof, Lady Larissa on his arm. He spoke, "Oh, no, no! How fortunate, you are not interrupting anything!" Ludo slapped Rolof on the back heartily, "Sit, sit! We actually needed to speak with you, so this is a blessing indeed!"

Rolof settled into the chair and beside him, Lady Adelpha blinked at him through her watery eyes. She seemed so small that she could barely see over the table, like a child seated amongst the adults. Her great puffed cheeks had been slapdashed with rouge, and her coral lipstick was little better. The table before him had been lain with a few pastries and a light dessert wine, not a variety that enticed Rolof's appetites, so he politely declined when offered. This strange old woman had clearly had most of a bottle of the wine herself, and was swaying lightly as she continued to stare at Rolof. "M'lady." He greeted her politely.

Ludo took his own seat, where Lady Larissa hovered behind her husband, her hands on the old man's shoulders, her eyes pleading apologies. The old man gave Rolof a sharp smile, "Well, how have you been finding the tourney, Ser?"

"Well, I broke my hand, but the liquor is cheap, so we'll call it a wash, I s'pose." Rolof gave his own grin back, "How about you, My Lord? You've barely left the castle."

"Well, at my age, all that sunlight and loud noise tires me too rapidly, and I can accomplish my purposes in the castle just fine." The old man looked to his equally ancient cousin, "The swords and dances are for the younger sort, but I have plenty to get done, I do, I do." He gave his high tinkling cackle, "But, so do you, Ser."

"I do, m'Lord?" Rolof's voice was tentative, crawling slowly from his throat.

Larissa cut in, leaning over Lord Ludo's shoulder, "Have you met Lady Adelpha, Ser? She's Ludo's cousin, and she's the sister to Lord Grimgrin of Goldleaf Manor."

Even Rolof knew how rich Clan Grimgrin was. While they didn't possess the vast tracts of land of Clans like Saddler or Curr, Clan Grimgrin sat on a particularly fertile set of mines and supplied the Empire with the gold, silver and copper that was used to make every coin from the Lowlands to The Wylde. They had amassed a great deal of wealth and power over the centuries, though, in recent years, their bloodline had thinned to a trickle. Lord Erasmus was an ancient man, and had never sired a child, though he had outlived nearly as many wives as Lord Ludo himself. *Meaning, that old bag is his heir…*

"I have heard, Ser Rolof, that many a marriage pact has been made and sealed at this tourney." Ludo smirked, "And it's high past time you wed, my friend, you're nearly thirty."

You motherfucker. Rolof saw the trap being laid and tried to desperately keep his writhing tentacles out of it.

"And you have given me so much." That sharp grin never wavered, "Larissa and I both. And for that, Lady Adelpha is to be your reward."

The old woman gave him a gummy grin, "You're much bigger than my last husband, Ser. I-I like that." She leaned against him, "When my brother passes, I'll inherit the whole castle, the lands, and the mines– all of it. And we'll be ever so rich."

Rolof squeezed his broken hand, relishing the feeling of the hot knives in his fingers. He took a sharp inhale through his broad nose, "I can't… I cannot thank you enough, my lord." He considered killing the two wizened elders then and there, but there was no way to dispose of their corpses. He looked to Larissa, but there was no aid from her. There were more arrangements to be made, but Rolof was given less agency than a child. They would take residence at Stolenstone Keep, so Rolof could continue his service to Lord Ludo. He would continue to keep Larissa safe, he would keep her close. That was some small relief, he supposed.

He would sulk back to his small stone chamber. All these lords and ladies with their politics and magic and pages of written words, he groaned. There was no fighting all this damn sorcery, and it was sorcery. Darkness greeted him, in this cell with its little moldering straw mattress. He heaved his bulk onto the bed, and relaxed his body, reaching into his pocket, pulling out his prize.

Rolled black vellum.

The Mirebreaker boy had said it contained power. Alone in the library, the temptation had clawed at him. He had crept, snuck and made sure the old Learner had well and truly been asleep, and he was. Breaking the lock on the little glass case was an easy task for Rolof's huge hands. It would be days, if not weeks until the missing scroll would be noted. This scroll of black vellum from the Beast Lands of Almythria. This power. This was his way of making things fair. Power like this and Rolof would never need to listen to stupid little old man again.

He realized he needed light and rose, smacking his head into the stone ceiling in the low cell. He cursed, stumbling forward. He would fumble in the dank, finally lighting his brazier. A dim red light filled the room, and Rolof returned to his mattress and his reading. He unrolled the scroll beside him on the mattress. Scrawls and spirals of some sort of red-brown ink seemed to be some sort of writing that Rolof had no concept of. Hunched figures writhed in strange, exotic positions, some beasts, some men, most both.

Something rattled free, clattering to the cold stone floor below his feet. Something had been rolled inside the scroll. The big man searched with his broken right hand, probing the floor blindly. Near the floor, little light from the brazier could reach, so Rolof was working almost entirely by touch. As he reached under the bed, something sharp prodded the heel of his hand. With a grunt of pain, he drew his hand back and found it bleeding.

The big knight sucked at the wound, the iron and salt taste of blood coursing over his tongue, clinging. When he pulled his hand away from his mouth, he found a clean gouge, deeper than he'd expected. He was readying himself to reach under the bed again, when the knock at his door shocked him to his feet.

As he quickly wound the scroll back up with his left hand, he shouted to the door, "Jus' a minute!" He stuffed the scroll among his bedding and sucked more blood from his wounded hand, before quickly binding it in a hunk of one of the plain muslin curtains that hung near the window. He tore a strip, about a foot and a half, cursing all the while. He quickly wrapped the little cut that seemed happy to spill so much blood, hurrying to his chamber door.

Lady Larissa was waiting, her huge blue eyes apologetic above her cruel hooked beak of a nose. Her little hard lips squeaked a "Hello, love."

"In." He grunted, swinging the door open and beckoning her inside. She did as bid, for once, and once inside, the big man snapped the door shut firmly. "Just when in the hell were you going to tell me about *my new fuckin' wife,* Larissa?"

"It was the old man's idea!" she pleaded.

"Of course it was!" Rolof balked. "He *knows.* He's figured it out, and he's punishin' me!"

Larissa laughed, "No, love, he has no idea." Rolof watched her move, a lean scavenger, hungry eyes always hunting. "He thinks he's doing you some great honor."

Furious and incredulous, the Bronze Kraken leaned inches from Larissa's face and hissed, "I should like to see what his idea of punishment is, if this is how he wishes to honor me." He kissed her then, rough and hard. She struggled against his grasp for an instant, surprised, but melted into his embrace soon enough. His passions inflamed, Ser Rolof raged onward, "The old man is angry that you are *my woman.* He is angry that I have fathered such a fine boy on you, when all of his boys rot in the ground. All of these damnable schemers and lords, I should kill every damn one of them."

Larissa's teeth grazed his neck as she sighed into him, "Exactly. That's exactly what we will do, my love."

He broke the embrace slightly, staring down at the Lady, "Do not tease me, woman."

"I am not, good Ser. You will kill every one of them. At a specific time in a specific order, very discreetly." He could feel her draw in closer, nuzzling into his chest, breathing his musk in deep. "And I even have a way to keep you away from the ancient old cow, for a few months, at least. You will follow my instructions to the letter, Rolof, and I promise, you and I will rule the Fisher Kingdoms with our Karl and we will be richer than Old Lord Malbes himself."

I have no wish to be richer than Lord Malbes. I am not made to rule. I am made to reave and raid. My home is salt and smoke and death, not these high chairs and secret meetings, thought Rolof. He said, "I will deny you nothing, my lady." instead.

She traced a finger down his thrice broken nose, before finally breaking the embrace with a spinning step, "Good boy." She took a look about his cell for the first time, as their liaisons in Honeyhome had all been on her terms. As her eyes looked upon the musty straw bed, Rolof watched her decide to keep her charms to herself in this space. It was plain in her posture and her face when she turned to face him again. "I ask you to make a difficult choice, my love, you can face the marriage bed with Lady Adelpha or you can risk your life on a fiery battlefield."

He laughed as if she did not know his answer.

"As I suspected." She said, "Karl tells me that there is a clandestine initiative with the younger Lords. A fair few of the southern lords are greatly dissatisfied with the Royal response to some paltry attacks by elven pirates or some such misery."

Rolof had heard the big Lord Axe expressing something to that effect in the mead tent. He and his wanted to go burn the pirates out, but were being forbidden by the Crown. "Seems all a king is good for is gettin' in a man's way."

"That's precisely what the Prince told Karl." Larissa beamed, "As such a little coalition of ships is being assembled to sail south and send these knife-eared pirates straight to hell. *You*, my sweet, will be leading a fleet of Fisher Ships, and as it happens, I've made sure your new bride's lord brother will captain his own vessel into such a dangerous situation. He's a proud man, and is ready to win honor in battle one final time."

"Treacherous idea for a man his age." Rolof felt his mouth curl into a sneer.

"Extremely. After the wedding, you'll sail south and meet some Lowlands ships, and Ozwyks, too. Then, across the strait to glory… and inheritance." She would kiss him this time, her tongue probing his mouth hungrily as he gripped her bony little hips in his hands. She would break the kiss with a wicked laugh, "My sweet beast, what are we going to do with months apart?"

"Enjoy every moment until we are separated." Rolof tried to kiss her again but she pulled away.

"My absence has likely already been noted by one of those awful old widows." She flattened her smock over her stomach. "I must be off."

"It is just like you to raise my passions and leave me wanting, woman." Rolof settled onto the bed with a huff.

She smirked at that and disappeared out his door.

Once he was sure she had gone, he slid to his knees, and resumed his search for whatever little sharp thing had clattered forth from the scroll when he'd opened it. On his hands and knees, it was a much simpler matter to find the mystery item. At first, he thought it scrimshaw, the intricately carved bone and ivory of the Scattered Isles. Carving the stuff was a popular hobby on board galleys, where time could be plentiful. Once he pulled it closer, rolling it from under the bed with a fumbling grip, he found it was an intricately carved stone, not bone. Cold to the touch and harder than steel, it was a little round stick. It was rounded at the bottom, and beaten with use, and more of the strange runes dotted every inch of it. Somewhere near eight inches long, it tapered from the rounded end, where a carved stone blade had been hewn. It looked like someone had combined pestle and knife, and Rolof had seen nothing like it.

It was such an odd little thing, that Ser Rolof Deepreach took a few minutes to realize that not only had the nasty little gouge the thing left in his hand stopped bleeding, but when he pulled back the torn linen, there was no mark, no mark, no hint of a scar.

Ser Rolof was even more taken aback, when he bent his hand, and all five fingers had been healed.

Magic. He smirked.

DRAKE V

"Sometimes bravery, kindness, justice... Sometimes, they are discretionary. Sometimes, the bravest thing you can do is mind your own business. Stick your nose where you shouldn't and you may just lose it."

Drake Canar had only spoken to the Lord of Finance a handful of times, and even those were little more than pleasantries and chivalry. In truth, Drake didn't care much for any of the Saddler Clan, and the smug Lord Hinric was no exception. Even still, the beating being laid on him by Lord Lukas Axe seemed a little extreme. His maul repaired, the Lord of Brimstone, in his devil-horned helm, was beating back the Saddler in green. Every strike of the hammer-hand drove Lord Hinric and his cavalry sabre further onto his heels.

Seated a few feet ahead of Drake, Lord Byrony Saddler laughed to King Gallus in a hearty rumble, "Serves 'im right, I suppose. Sword against hammer is hardly a contest; the man with the maul is in plate!"

King Gallus agreed, chuckling, "Your brother is a stubborn little peacock, is he not?"

"Tell me about it. I've been trying to get that "confirmed bachelor" to settle down and wed, but I think he's too content with his big strong orc houseboy and his little pretty elf houseboy. Looks like it's up to Hart and Hugo to further the line." The old Lord of the Goldengrass carefully watched the King's reaction. His eyes were so green they were almost grey, like distant grass in a summer's haze.

The Queen, Lady Kiara and Lady Kalistah Malbes had left the box, uninterested or likely, unwilling to watch the Prince take on the monstrous mystery knight The Big Turtle in the next match. Drake had watched this huge knight bulldoze through two of the biggest, strongest men in the lists, and had honestly hoped for a chance to beat the monster himself.

The King, Lord Byrony, Prince Vernus and Lady Harlow were the nobles left in this royal box, high above the stands. "Your brother's household is his business, Lord Saddler, not mine."

"Nor mine." The old Lord laughed, "still, I'd like to see him settle down."

Drake didn't mean to speak, but he did, "Perhaps this is his 'settled down,' my Lord, Your Grace."

King Gallus smirked and Drake panicked. *Has he looked into my mind? Has he seen my thoughts?* In that moment, where his most sacrosanct secret may have been stolen, Drake tasted a morsel of the fear that this Clan Artus could inspire. *They are not of this world, I swear it.*

"Precisely." The king's tone was mild. "As long as your brother continues his sterling work as Lord of Finance, I see no reason to question his home life whatsoever."

Byrony snorted, "I should hope he continues his *gold works,* but I digress, your grace."

"Clever." Nothing in the King's tone implied mirth, but he was polite at least, Drake mused.

Horns heralded the defeat of Lord Hinric back in the arena, as the commons cheered. In the box, Lord Byrony chuffed, "Shame, I was really hopin' to watch Hugo batter him."

"Your nephew, that Selach boy…" The king's focus was on his son, seated beside Lady Harlow in front of him.

"Doyle! Yeah, he's a damn fine young man, Your Grace." Byrony excitedly spoke, nodding.

"He need only to defeat the most celebrated tourney knight of the last century and my own heir to give you the Goldengrass final you want so well." The King laughed, "But a damn fine young man should have no issue with that."

Lord Byrony laughed freely at the King's jest, but Drake could see Prince Vernus fuming at the mention of his older brother. *It would only be too delicious for his brother to outshine him on his own birthday,* Drake mused to himself.

Beside the Prince, Lady Harlow was stiff as a board. Drake had not allowed Vernus to move without his notice, not an arm, not a hand, not even a finger. The girl did not recoil from the Princeling, true, but she maintained a considerable distance from him. *Plenty of room for her father and her priest,* Drake smirked internally, *Good.* She was dressed in little more than a few wisps of silk, which seemed strange for a meeting with a boy she seemed to disdain.

An intermission took to the flickering lamplight of the arena, and a trio of jesters in motley of green, blue and red took to chasing one another and tumbling across the mud and dirt. Lord Byrony rose, gesturing for the king to follow, "My liege, perhaps I could interest you in a bit of gentlemanly mockery?" Under his bristly black beard, square white teeth glistened, "I hate to be less than lordly, but my baby brother just was embarrassed in front of a crowd, and I can imagine Your Royal Highness may enjoy helping me rub it in."

It was then that Drake saw these two men not as they were in front of him, but as they had been decades past. Even in middle age, these two old nobles could once again become jackass boys, pulling immature pranks and sniggering as they scurried away.

For the first time in his months of service, Drake heard The Emperor of Three Islands curse, "Fuck yes, I do." King Gallus Artus hopped to his feet like a man ten years younger.

Lord Byrony snatched one of the two wine bottles from the little round table next to Harlow, and scanned the two Grey Guard with them, "Which one of these men has a better humor, Your Grace?"

King Gallus rounded on Drake and his companion, Ser Jurgen Shoreshrike. When it came to mischief, there would be no question, the King knocked his knuckles on the breastplate of the knight that had served him for years and left the Duck that had only served him for months standing alone. Over his receding back, the King bid Drake to 'tend to the Prince and the lovely young Harlow.'

Once alone, both of these noble youths set to a course of action they would never have dared in the presence of their regal sires. Harlow took her left hand, pink and dainty, and tipped in perfect rose-painted nails, outstretched it, and gripped the little brass and wood corkscrew sitting beside the wine bottle.

Vernus placed his hand on the petite little lady's thigh.

She did not scream. She did not rage. Her gaze never even left the tumbling fools in the arena. She passed the corkscrew from her left hand to her right, palmed it, and pressed the sharp twisted tip into the stitched seam at the fly of the Prince's breeches. "My Prince, I believe you need some instruction in the treatment of maidens."

Drake's glove went to his shortsword, but he waited. His trembling hand refused to unsheathe his blade. *Protect the line.* His vows screamed at him.

The beautiful little heiress pressed the coil of brass into the white cotton of his breeches, as he squirmed and squealed, "What are you doing, Lady Harlow?"

"I am returning your touch, as wanted as it was on me, Your Grace."

A wet spot flooded the front of Vernus's breeches as tears began streaming from his copper-patina eyes. Drake watched as his Prince's fear dribbled to the floorboards. *Defend innocent maidens.* Another vow, dueling the first.

"Unfortunately, my Prince, I have recently accepted a different marriage proposal." She pressed with her palm, twisting, "Lord Marten Mirebreaker and I are to be wed. He is a *handsome....*"

She jabbed, "...Kind..."

Another jab, "...Chivalrous, capable Lord. With a good heart and loving family. We will be very, very happy in Okoboji. It's a beautiful city, have you been?"

Sobbing and sniffling, the Prince shook his head.

Harlow snarled through gritted teeth, "We will be sure to invite you to the wedding, Prince Vernus."

Vernus is not the line. Ser Auberon's words echoed through his head, as he watched the reproductive future of the Empire balance on the needle sharp point of a corkscrew.

"If you ever lay a hand on me again, Prince Vernus, I will take a keepsake of this manhood whose ascension you seem to be so proud of. I will dip it in my grandfather's gold and wear it on a chain about my neck." Harlow pulled the corkscrew back, "Perhaps a bath is in order, your Grace, something reeks like piss."

The boy prince tipped his chair, scrambling and sobbing out of the Royal Box, taking the stairs two at a time. A stream of wet little drops trailed behind him, and though he tried to cover himself Drake was sure his golden shame would be clear for the world to see as he fled to his father or bodyguard, or more likely, his palanquin and eventually his chambers. His shrill screams of "Biiiiiirse!" echoed through the grounds, even over the song that the three jesters were howling in the arena.

As he fled, Harlow set the corkscrew on the table, wood on wood, a satisfied little click. She sighed to herself, settling into her chair, "Ser Drake?" she turned to Drake, a wide pretty smile on her face, "Would you mind pouring me a glass of wine? I've developed a thirst, but I don't seem to be able to stop my hands from shaking."

Drake could not remember the last simple task he had taken so much pure satisfaction in.

There would be a ball, and little sleep for the Day's Commander, but he would, in the early hours, alongside his five grim grey brothers, return to their borrowed barracks, where the boy Cyp still slept. Selach and Shoreshrike had no interest in the sleeping child, but both Sozen and Canden pulled him aside, while Ser Darywn paced the shadowy corners of the room, just on the edge of the light of the brazier.

Canden poured himself a horn of ale from a small cask on offer, and Ser Auberon Sozen took one as well, which was uncommon, but the day had been eventful and all of them were sapped to their very cores. Canden's gruff gravel voice began, "You did good today, Duck." He poured a third horn of ale and stood, carrying it to Drake, who took it in his gloved hands.

"Thank you, Ser Cole." Drake sipped the ale, it was bitter, nut brown, heavy with hops. "I did nothing more than my duty." *Nothing more,* he reminded himself.

"Don't be modest, Drake." Ser Auberon complimented, "Days like the one you just watched over do not come every day, they are the crucible that forges great knights."

From the shadows, Ser Darywn laughed, "Yeah, nothin' inspires greatness like trauma."

Sozen sighed and Ser Cole Canden grunted, "Enough, Ser Darwyn, unless you have something beyond childish japes–"

"If I ain't around for my japes, what are you keeping me around for?" Tymm spit from the shadows, "Why is there a common born urchin in our barracks, Ducky? There are easier ways to get lice."

Maybe it was the exhaustion, maybe it was inspiration born on the back of Harlow Saddler, but Drake finally fired back at Ser Darwyn, though it was with a lax sense of calm, "Because I need a squire, Darwyn. A knight of the grey is expected to take one, as you all have."

Darwyn's squire was a useless round little boy of Clan Goldenlocke called Roquefort. He had been all but foisted onto Darwyn by his now late brother, for political reasons, and for once, Darwyn had lacked the wherewithal to object. Darwyn despised the spoiled little brat, and in the interest of fairness, Drake held little love for the boy either. Suffice to say, the subject of squires was a prickly one for The Grey Jester. "That's not a squire, that's a street rat you washed."

"Any boy may serve as a squire." Ser Auberon gave a withering look into the shadows where Darwyn seethed, "As long as he serves nobly. The service is noble, not the birth. Any boy that can earn it can be a squire, any man can be a knight."

"That's no boy! It's a scabies ridde–"

"Enough." Drake's voice found its bass, "If there is a problem with the boy I have put to squire, I will tend to it myself." The Dashing Duck took to his feet, "And I have only fed an urchin. I have yet to interview the boy. If you take issue with feeding and clothing a poor orphan, perhaps you need to reexamine your goddamn vows."

Darwyn raged out of the shadows, his brown eyes blazing like burning copper, orange hair streaming behind him like a flame, "Tell me that when you have tested your vows. You are a squire, you do not need one."

It was restraint that kept Drake from pulling his short sword, but it was pride that led him to cracking a glove wrapped in purple leather into the Grey Jester's jaw, sending him to the floor with a tumbling thud, "I said enough."

Ser Cole and Ser Auberon interjected themselves between the pair of younger knights, "Hold, hold, no more." Ser Auberon's voice was as placid as always, though both palms on Drake's chest were stone.

"Ser Cole." Drake huffed, "Tymm seems unwilling to listen to his Commander, please see him to his chambers." He rolled his wrist, turning away.

Canden lifted a smirking Tymm to his feet, though the younger man would quickly break away from his grip. All Tymm did was smirk and then blow a quick little kiss to Drake. Part of Drake wished he were a worse man, less shackled by honor, so that he could hit him again, or carve the smirk from his lips, but no matter what, he would be a good man.

Cole Canden and Darwyn Tymm would disappear through the oaken door, taking the small cask and their horns of ale along. Ser Auberon shook his smooth bald head, "You know, when he draws Day's Command, he can send you to dig latrines or slay a dragon or some other suicide mission, don't you?"

"Then I will just need to kill a dragon, that day."

Auberon's laugh was a warm one, "You may indeed do that, Duck." He turned toward the door, finishing his horn of ale with a long quaff, "I have endured quite enough excitement for the day, so, if you're done with me, Drake, I'd like to–"

Drake sighed, interrupting, "I'm not entirely done, no." Again, he felt like half a boy when dealing with the other Grey Guard. Sozen was his brother, true, but he was an older, much wiser, brother. He continued, tentative, "If you would not mind assisting me with the boy. Despite what I have boasted to Darwyn, I have not offered the boy anything beyond food and a warm bed for the night." Drake fussed with his horn of ale, nerves keeping him from desiring drink. "I… have never interviewed a squire before. My last squire was my little brother, Donal." He laughed, "I would appreciate your assistance in this, Ser Auberon."

The older knight turned to him and fixed those eyes like the night sky on Drake. So dark they were black, studded with pinpricks of shine. After a short moment, he spoke, "Why?"

"What? What do you mean?"

Sozen laid his hands on the table in front of them, "Why do you want me to help you interview your squire?"

"Well, I have never interviewed a squire–"

"You said that." There was another chaotic twinkle in Sozen's black eyes, "I have never interviewed a squire for you either, Drake. I have no idea what you could possibly want."

Drake couldn't respond with anything more than a few awkward stuttered consonants.

"The boy was sleeping in an alley this morning, so you don't expect him to take your letters and scour your mail immediately, are you?" Sozen smirked at his brother.

"Well, no."

"Yet, you still brought him back here." Sozen shrugged, "You want a project, Duck. And that's fine, you're a young man. A squire like that is real good for you, but you gotta pick him. I'm getting lazy in my old age. My last two squires were incredibly well trained, good little soldiers, no work required." He gave Drake one last placid grin, "I wouldn't even remember where to begin, but I'll send the little fella in for you."

Auberon will disappear and a moment later, a sleepy teen would stumble through the same door, a scrawny stick of a boy. The gregarious old washerwoman had procured some clean clothes that more or less fit Cyp, though they seemed tight about the waist and hip, which was odd for such a starved thing.

"The other knight, the bald one-the kind bald-one. He said you wanted to talk with me, Ser?" He rubbed the sleep from his eyes, but carried none in his voice.

"I do, son." He smiled, trying to keep this strange, half criminal child at ease, "Can you take a seat? Are you hungry, Cyp. Is that your real name, really?" Drake fixed his eyes on the boy and watched him slowly settle into the chair across from Drake.

"It's short for Cyprian. The tavern woman gave me that name, her name were Loubelle, but she's been dead so long, it don't likely matter." His tone was shockingly bitter for a child, "I'm still stuffed from that feast earlier, Ser."

"I'm glad to hear that, we can't have a growing boy like you going hungry." Drake had brothers, but he had no idea how to handle a child that was not his own family, a fact reflected by Cyp's visibly growing discomfort. "How do you normally get food? The temple? Begging? *Stealing?"*

Cyp nodded, "A bit of all three, to be honest. I am not proud of the beggin' or the theft, but there's precious little work for a boy my age in times like these. Everyone is so fat and happy, 'cept the poorest that have nothin'. Good times like this, everybody has twice as much, 'cept twice as much nothin' is still nothin'. So, it's just twice as hard to buy bread."

Drake nodded, showing no judgment on his face.

"And I didn't ever steal from an honest man, I didn't. Ivar, that baker, he puts saw-dust in the-the bread when flour gets too expensive. Alak, that fisherman, he'll steal from other men's traps and smash 'em, so it looks like the currents got 'em. I can help you get lots of these dishonest men, Ser! I promise, you don't have to take my hand!" The boy had burst into tears, and terror had crept over his face.

"Your hand?" Drake laughed, "Gods around us, no!"

The boy's tears paused, his face grew confused, "I don't understand."

"You are brave and quick." Canar gave a small smirk, "Braver than smart, but that might be more common than you think." He felt his knuckles throb, "But we're all learning."

The boy smirked back, "I still don't follow, Ser."

"Are you afraid of hard work, Cyprian?"

The boy shook his bristled head, "No, Ser."

"Do you like a warm bed? A full belly? Clothes?"

Of course the boy did, "Yes, Ser, it's all been real, real fine."

Drake settled in his chair, folding his hands over his flat stomach, as he slouched back, "You said you never stole from an honest man, right?" The boy nodded, so Drake continued, "Then you know what honesty is, what it means to keep an oath?"

Solemnly, Cyp spoke, "T'ain't nothing more important than a person's word, Ser. When you're sleepin' in an alley, all you have is your honesty."

"Cyp, do you know what a squire is..?"

The next morning Ser Drake Canar's entry into the Commader's Tome would read as follows:

Twenty-second Day of Long Light: Ser Drake Canar drew Day's Command. The proceeding is his report of the days' events:

In the early hours of the day, through means yet to be determined, the now Attainted Knight Ser Jemes Wyse stole the Starheart crown to be given to Prince Vernus's betrothed. He was captured by agents of House Malbes and executed for an unrelated crime before he could be questioned. The crown was found among his possessions.

Ser Drake Canar faced Crown Prince Talor Artus in the second round of the tournament of Honeyhome and was summarily defeated, when he yielded to the Crown Prince.

Cyprian of Honeyhome was granted the position of squire to Ser Drake Canar.

The final rounds of the tournament come at dawn.

HARTWIN V

"Bendin' the knee is real simple when you believe in the reason you're kneelin'. The pride ain't always worth it. Lose yourself."

His palms were sweaty.

He was here to seize everything he had ever wanted. She was in front of him, pink and perfect. The low torchlight turned the tooled jewels across her prodigious bust into a glittering cascade that hugged her soft curves exactly the way Hart wished he was in this instant. The pink silks clung to her hips and stomach and Hartwin felt himself grow a little flush just looking at her. Then she smiled at him, perfect white, and his knees went weak as he said it. "I love you, you know?"

She laughed, that musical titter, "I know, Hart. I love you."

The little chamber had long been one of Hartwin's favorites. Unlike many of the old dining rooms and meeting halls in his grandfather's castle, Llyewn's Refectory was not a garish or gaudy place. Ancient maps and charts hung on the walls, treasures of a simpler age. *Here be monsters,* the edges of the maps read. Hartwin smiled, *I am the only monster they need to fear.* The cozy little stone room was nestled deep in the castle and sat above one of the ice-houses in the cellar, so it was generally a more palatable space on hot summer days. It was called Llyewn's Refectory, because a King had died in this room. Nearly eight centuries ago, the Bloodsinger sweltered with fever, as Learners prayed the cool room would bring him aid. It did not, and King Llyewn Mertens died from a mace wound to the thigh. *The Bloodsinger had been a fool*, Hart mused. *Too headstrong by half.*

"Hart?" Joelle's voice was a snap back to reality. "You're staring."

The tall boy shook himself, "Sorry, thinking about the sheer history of this castle." Despite the calm expression, he was nervous inside, ready to bolt like a rabbit. "

"You've mentioned, a king passed on the floor, in here, or some such."

"He died trying to get cool, pressing himself to the cold stone on the floor." Hartwin intoned, half smirking, "A wise man would have just gone downstairs."

Joelle guffawed, prodding at the dish in front of her with her fork. It was a pasta from the continent, a recipe Hartwin's mother favored. Flavored with lemon and basil-leaf, as well as some sort of hard, crumbling cheese, it was the finest dish Hartwin knew, and he was out to impress. Gently, he rose, moving with a careful purpose. He lifted the wine bottle from the table and felt it heavy in his arms. He practically floated to Joelle, before refilling her glass with a fine white wine, made from Coralspear Grapes, plump little gold things, sweet and tart. The night's conversation had been intense. He shared it all with her, the old horse thief, the crown, all of it. As always, she'd taken it all in stride. She had long since passed being shocked by Hart's political machinations, she just wore a dry little smirk through it all.

"This is all very fine, Hartwin." Joelle winked at him. "But I planned on sleeping with you anyway."

"In that case." He snatched her glass playfully, before returning it to her side. "No, no, I had an ulterior motive for inviting you to such a private room." Her aquamarine gaze glittered near as bright as the jewels she wore. "I–" The words would not come out, he choked on them. *This is your one shot, your one opportunity.* He scolded himself. *Do not let it slip, Hartwin. Capture it. Seize your destiny and your dreams.*

He breathed cool, crisp air, and he began, "I am not an easy man to love. Drive for something great clutches at my heart so tight that I think sometimes it does not beat like other men. I am cold and I can be cruel, Joelle." He bowed his long, lean face, suddenly solemn, "I preen and strut, and declare myself king, moving us to a new future. I am too fantastic for an average life, The Young Colt..." He caught himself, "And I'm self-centered, heh." He refocused his efforts. Long freckled fingers from the Lordling gripped the soft rosy hands of Lady Bridge, "Father likes you, Jo. I don't know why that's important, but it is. My father is not the kind of Lord I wish to be, but I think, if he were not a high lord. If he were just a horse farmer, and I his son, I think I would like him a bit better. He is a man with good sense, and he likes you."

She shook her head, "I don't care how your Lord Father feels about me, nor your mother, nor your siblings. Just you."

He pressed his stubbled face to her forehead, lips just brushing her hairline, gentler than the breaking of dawn, "When I see the future, I see you, Jo. No matter what castle I dream of ruling or what chair I see myself in, you are the woman beside me." He felt the blush creeping over his freckled cheeks, "Only you." It was true, in his heart he knew it was true. "I want to spend the rest of my life as your defender, your humble servant and your dearest ally." He kissed her lips, then. He felt his own tears mingling with hers as their cheeks touched. She knew what was coming, she was too wise not to.

As he knelt, he kept her hands in his, "I am not much of a man, Joelle. I will likely never be able to defend your honor with sword or axe. But I will be such a force that no one would ever consider besmirching your honor in the first. I am clever and cunning and I am yours. I love you, entirely, and here and now, I ask you to wed me." Her fingers closed around the gold ring he pressed into them. She gripped it, hard, and wept.

"Red…" she was sobbing, blubbering almost unintelligibly, "I–I will." She slid the ring onto her finger, and wrapped herself in him, kissing him tenderly.

It was moments like these where Hartwin knew that he was right in his trust of her, his love of her. She was wise and good, and she saw the world in the same shades he did, even if she seemed to think the hues were a bit brighter. She would ask questions, once settled, and even manage to feign the proper amount of offense at the arrangements being made behind her back, but it was the last question that she asked the most tentatively, "You're getting me. What did you give Marten Mirebreaker?"

Hartwin looked up to her, still on his knees, "I knelt. Well, that and Harlow."

It was harder to tell which thing shocked her more, both sent her eyes wide. "You knelt to Mirebreaker? *Harlow is going to wed Marten Mirebreaker?"*

Hartwin nodded, "Like I said, father likes you."

The tournament would follow, three Saddler matches, two complete, one remaining. Hugo would crush the Vellen witch, and Uncle Hinric would fall. Seated in the high stands, with Hellendre, Joelle and his bodyguard, Vandre, Hartwin thrilled at his brother Hugo's victory and grimaced at Hinric taking a savage beating from Lord Lukas Axe, but now, all eyes were on Ser Doyle.

The Shark of the Goldengrass and the Snapping Turtle danced in the dirt. Doyle would prod with his golden trident, and Mirebreaker would catch it on his shield. Ser Tullus carried a small kite shield on his left arm, and carried a short, heavy hammer in his right. Mirebreaker had not used the same weapon twice in any round, and this fighting style was not something Hartwin had expected. As Hugo was not there to offer his wisdom, Hartwin quizzed his new sellsword, "Vandre, what is the Snapping Turtle playing at, here? He has no reach."

The scarred old sword squinted, "I'm not rightly sure, m'lord. He might be playing defense, but he ain't got no way of handlin' the net when it comes out."

Doyle would stab more viciously, trying to goad the old man into action, but the old man would only catch it on his shield. When he could, Ser Tullus would crack his little butcher's hammer into the haft of Doyle's weapon, but only the enamel on the hardened wood seemed to be damaged at this point.

Joelle would pipe up next, "He's fighting a net with a blunt weapon, it makes no sense." Hartwin felt the corners of his mouth creep into a grin. *Clever, clever girl,* Hartwin thought to himself.

The net would come out after another frustrated trident stab failed. Doyle unhooked it from his belt and tossed it with a practiced spin. It unfurled, and the old man spun his little kite shield up, the point first. Hellendre saw the plot first, those big brassy eyes missed nothing, "His shield is jagged, look!"

She was right, the bottom edge of his shield had been nailed with a line of metal teeth, the sort of thing that was used to scythe wheat: simple farmer's iron. But these two dozen sharp little combs caught the fine wire of the net and shredded it to tatters with a single hard slash.

And then came the hammer.

Tullus kept his shield raised, and kept himself low. Doyle raised his trident with both hands and attempted to stab down on the old man. Doyle stretched himself tall, angry and proud. *Unprotected.*

Hartwin saw it. Vandre saw it. Joelle and Hellendre both saw it. Every eye in the arena saw it, save The Shark of the Goldengrass.

The little hammer hit Doyle in the hip hard enough to change his direction in mid-air. His diving stab turned into a painful ass-over-tea-kettle tumble into the wet sand. The older knight straddled him and smacked the Shark with the shield and Hartwin felt himself begin to chuckle. A second smack from the shield turned Hart's laughter into a full on guffaw, and Doyle's submission left Hartwin laughing loudly, despite Hellendre's attempts to shame him.

"Doyle is your blood." She nagged.

"He is!" Hartwin sniggered into his hands, "I still think he is a prat, though!"

Once the horns blew and the hands were raised, the lists would end for the evening. The common folk would flood to their tents and taverns and mead halls, a flood of the filthy rabble enjoying their beer, grime and debauchery that came with such a tourney. The Lords would attend one more dance, one more show to mock and humiliate one another. As the quartet descended from the stands, they found themselves reuniting with Lady Harlow.

His sister descended from the Royal box, on the arm of the Dashing Duck of the Grey Guard. Saddler watched the blush rise in his sister's cheeks, and the sway in her steps told the story of her sipping a bit of wine while she watched the knights. Canar smiled to Hartwin, passing the giggly gal to Lady Joelle. Ser Drake whispered to Hartwin, extending a finger, "A moment, m'lord?"

Hartwin painted disinterest clean on his face, "I can't imagine what you'd need with me, Duck."

"I need nothing." Canar's grey eyes sparkled under his blonde fringe, "I just would like you to know that I think your sister is much less fragile than you think. That young lady can tend her own affairs just fine."

Hartwin listened and he watched this Canar, "Thank you for watching her, Ser Drake. I shan't forget this." He extended a hand, which the young knight shook firmly. "Be seein' you, Canar, I will make sure of that."

He and the Grey Duck shared a knowing look, but parted all the same. Hartwin almost regretted the lies he'd fed the boy about "Ser Jemes Wyse" and the crown. Almost.

Upon arriving, they had been greeted by the scowling visage of Lady Kalistah, her arms crossed as she watched her witch, her children and her daughter-by-law-to-be swagger in, followed by the tired old sword in green. Hartwin could feel the disgust in his mother's gaze skitter across his skin, and onto the flesh of his beloved beside him, she simply shook her head, "You and your father have ruined everything, Hartwin."

He grinned at his mother, "I haven't the foggiest what you're talking about."

Lady Kalistah shoved Joelle away, taking her place on Hartwin's side, hissing in his ear, all snapping anger, "Your Lord Grandfather and I went to significant effort and expense to bring this grand event together. Coin and favor both, beyond your miserable knowing, were spent putting this tournament together–"

"Well, thankfully, Hugo is like to win most of that coin back for you." Hartwin bit back bitterly.

Lady Kalistah gave venom of her own, "Will he win back Harlow? Trading her off to some dusky swampboy, for what? That cow–"

Hartwin had heard enough, "Mother, if you happen to be fortunate enough to outlive father, Lady Joelle will be your High Lady. You will not defame her. Not, 'You will not defame her in my presence.' You will treat her with the same respect you would treat the Queen herself, because as far as you are concerned, Mother, she is the Queen of the Goldengrass."

The low grind of Lady Kalistah's teeth against each other was audible to Hartwin, even over the sounds of the bards. She said nothing, only pulling away from her son with a huff. Furious, she would take the old sellsword, Vandre by the arm and drag him toward the barkeep. The old man's eyes pleaded to Hart, but he was too overjoyed to care.

He would blink, and be spinning with Joelle on the painted tile of Coomb's Gallery, her boots clicking in perfect time with his. The singers were old favorites of Clan Saddler, hired specifically by Mother for their skill and breadth of songs and tales they knew. They were currently singing *"Horses and Hayflowers"* , a ribald, but well loved song about a Saddler lord who had an equine reputation as a lover, from decades past.

Hartwin was especially fond of *"Horses and Hayflowers."*

He pulled her close, smelling lilac in her hair. Across the floor, Harlow had linked hands with the older Mirebreaker boy, and spun. Her auburn ringlets flared like copper flame and her smile nearly split her face as both she and her new betrothed laughed, overcome in youthful joy and sweetwine.

The younger Mirebreaker boy was dancing with some daughter of Clan Curr with a hard little face. Lord Father was bringing the boy, this Slade, south to visit the library at Stonestall. The chance to bond with this boy wouldn't be the worst thing, Hartwin thought. *He has a good head on his little shoulders, maybe a worthwhile little scholar to have in the family.*

A hand on his shoulder brought him back to the gallery. Joelle lifted her head from his chest, and her eyes went wide, "Hartwin. It's the Prince."

Ready to spar, at least verbally, Hartwin wheeled, "Your Grace!" He was shocked to find the older of the two Princes, Talor, instead of the younger.

"Oh, Lord Hartwin, is my brother upset with you all." The smile on the Crown Prince's face indicated that he did not share such an opinion, "He's not used to being denied. I think it'll be good for him."

"Your grace." Hartwin repeated, his face changing to a smirk as the bards ended the old Saddler song.

"You did say that." The Prince chuckled, "Lady Joelle." He turned to Jo. "If I might be so rude as to borrow your partner, I've got a small discussion for our Hartwin."

Other ladies may have bowed, practiced and demure, but Lady Joelle Bridge gave the heir to the empire a playful scowl, "Fine, I'll give you a few minutes, I suppose." She let go, but gave his bony rump a smack, "Your access is limited, Your Grace, but he is *always mine.*" She and the prince shared a hearty laugh as Hartwin felt himself grow crimson. "Be quick, Red."

As the Prince and the Colt left Lady Joelle with a gaggle of joyously drinking southron ladies, the men on the stage started the low and sad strumming of *"The Day The Shadows Stole Lyra"*, and the dancers slowed, pulling closer. "I'm missing a slow song, Your Grace, my lady will be furious.

A squawk went up from behind them, as one of the gathered southron ladies saw Joelle's ring and screeched. The prince gave a little snort through his nose, "She's like to be fine, I think." They crossed the floor, where a menacing old Grey Guard joined them, tailing at a distance, once they'd left the ceramic of the dance floor.

"I hear congratulations are in order, then." Talor was earnest. "For you, Harlow and my very lucky cousin."

On the dance floor, Harlow's head had come to rest on the Mirebreaker boy's shoulder. His hands were linked behind her, in the small of her back. They were close, yes, and there was a tenderness, too, but the Lord of the Lowlands treated Harlow Saddler as a precious gift, a blessing, a lady.

"My sister seems to be smitten with your cousin." Hartwin dryly intoned.

"You did this, then." It was no question, so Hartwin didn't deny it.

"I didn't care for the way your brother treated Harlow." Hart shrugged, "I bear the boy no ill will, but I won't have Harlow wed to someone who made her feel as such. Prince, pauper or priest, no man hurts my family." He heard the chill in his own voice, before warmly tacking on, "Your Grace."

"Good." Artus's voice was nearly as cool as his own, "I like that about you, Saddler. You are ruthless in pursuit of what you want. Ruthless, but never stupid. You flaunt tradition, but you never mock it."

"There is success to be learned in tradition, if nothing else." Hartwin said.

"Too true that, but often we wrap ourselves in tradition and ceremony, and forget how damn much it weighs." Hartwin expected the prince to chide him, but instead, there was mirth in Talor's voice, "I like what you've done. It was brave. It was the sort of thing we'd discussed at the meeting."

"I was always a devoted student." Hartwin japed.

The pair came to a small bar, one of many spaced about the hall. The Prince set himself on a stool, and bid Hartwin join. Before they could speak, a serving man was on them, offering wine, ale, mead and stout of every shade and temperature, until the Prince interrupted him, "Red. Something dry. Gods help you if it's honeyed."

Hartwin snorted, "Whiskey."

They would nurse their drinks, talking of the upcoming plans to raid the elven pirates that had been harrying The Lowlands. Clan Saddler had ships enough to keep their shores and ports safe, true, but they were no great sea power. However, they had men, and they had coin, and Talor's many, many plots required both. He needed Clan Saddler, yes, but more than that, he needed *Hartwin.*

"You see it like I do, Saddler. I find some of your methods a bit harsh, I will merit this, but I need a mind like yours at my side when I take the crown." Artus sipped his wine.

"Your Grace, I will offer what Stallions and Coin of my own to the cause as I can." Hartwin let his whiskey sit on the table, "But I want no cloying words than I do anymore of this sweet mead, if you want my aid, you want my aid, not my coin."

Artus smiled, putting aside any ceremony, "Well, shit, Hart, I'll drink to that." The smiling prince raised his glass, and when Hartwin clinked his against it, he was reminded of a dream. *Beautiful and terrible.*

"To our next King." Hartwin bowed his head.

Artus smiled with half his mouth, "And our next Lord Executor."

A coach waited for the Saddler contingent, something Hartwin had arranged to keep him and the ladies away from the rabble. When there was no seat for the bodyguard, Vandre shrugged and heaved himself onto the high bench beside the coachman, greeting him with a sly, "Hello there."

Inside the coach, Hartwin sat with his sister, his betrothed and his witch. They prattled on about something or another, a dog, maybe? He found himself unable to listen, content with Joelle's head resting on his shoulder and the slow satisfying clop of hooves on cobbles, as the wagon lurched along. His thoughts drifted to what lay ahead. He had agreed to ride south to Rain Tower Hall, upon the completion of the tournament. It was not a proposition he truly looked forward to, but Joelle had agreed to ride, rather than sail, and that was a blessing.

Winning the loyalty of Joelle's swampmen would be a trial with no doubt. The Goldengrass and The Lowlands had never been friendly, and the changing allegiances of wealthy Clans and important ports was always a concern. Cobalt Bridge was both. A reputation as an *ambitious* lordling would also serve as another hindrance, Saddler knew. Men would look at Joelle, look at her coffers, and then look at Hartwin. Telling them that he truly loved her would mean nothing, no matter how much he did. *I will just show them my worth and loyalty.* He determined it simply. *The swampmen are men, my brilliance cannot be denied.*

"Hart." Joelle sleepily murmured up at him, "You have that smile you get on your face when you spin your plots."

"Me?" he felt downright joyous, "I don't plot. I *dream, Jo.*"

Harlow quipped, "He dreams more than he *does.*"

Hellendre then poked in, "He dreams big, Harley-Girl. It takes time to put your ass in that many thrones."

The three women cackled, and Hartwin pouted, "If you three do not start being kinder to me, I'll go ride outside with the coachman and send the sellsword back in here."

"Oh, don't do that." Joelle continued, only slightly less sleepy. "He is scared of me."

The Young Colt scrunched his face, as the wagon jolted over a bump and the sellsword audibly cursed outside, "And why is he scared of you?"

She giggled, "Because I *scared* the fuck out of him."

All three women cackled again, and Hartwin kept pouting. Bored of needling him, the women turned their conversation to the events of the day, Joelle continued to fight sleep on his shoulder, one hand wrapped around his upper left arm, the other lying on his chest. Glasses, and a bottle of some brown liquor clinked in a chest in the center of the well-appointed little carriage, but none of them had much thirst. And aside from that, they had all imbibed plenty.

The carriage jolted again, and above the heads of the Saddlers, the weight of something significant thudded onto the roof. The canvas sagged under the weight of something scrabbling and beating, as shouts of panic erupted from Hart and the girls.

Vandre's gruff cadence came from the bench seat outside, a little rectangular window behind Hartwin's head. Hart slid it open, with a clack, "What the hell is that?"

"There's an owl on the cabin, m'lord." Vandre's eyes were wide and wild, brown fire flickering through the little slatted window.

"Well, get rid of it."

The sellsword paused, fear plain on his scarred, old face, "We are near enough the tower, m'lord. I'd rather not upset the thing, it looks a trifle fierce."

Hartwin clacked the little slats shut petulantly, "It's a bird. Just a large bird."

Hellendre was calm, her big brass eyes staring at the sagging center of the ceiling. Focus poured off of her, nearly palpable in the little space. Harlow's voice was a whimper, "I don't like it, Hart."

He didn't either, but saying as much served no purpose but to worry her further, instead, he just gave her a gentle shhhhh, as Joelle clung to his arm tight. Hartwin was no use in a fight, but if it was to come to danger, protecting his sister and Joelle was his duty. *Hellendre, you're on your own,* he joked to himself.

They had been near enough to the tower where the highest nobles rested, it seemed, as the carriage would stop shortly, and the huff of the horses could be heard as they rested in the cool night air. The whole cabin squeaked and shifted, following Vandre's climb down from his bench. That same cool air would flood the little cabin as the bodyguard swung the scrolled wooden door open. Though he dutifully aided all three ladies down the step to the fine gravel of the walkway, his eyes never left the roof of the carriage.

Hartwin was the last to climb down, noticing the shaking hand of the old man on the hilt of his new sword. The sheer terror on his granite mask of a face set Hartwin's chest to pounding. The bird perched on the roof's wooden crossbeams, two eight or ten foot poles of hardwood. In reality, it was probably not much larger than a particularly vigorous rooster, but clad in feathers so black they seemed to drink the moonlight, it looked much larger. As Hart settled to the gravel the silent bird stared into him. Yellow eyes, huge and hateful locked with his and Hartwin shivered as this silent black predator alighted to wing, and rose into the sky, lazy black spirals against a blue cold moon.

ELLARI IV

"You can't bullshit gravity. Everyone falls. Action, consequence."

Masha sat sobbing over a piece of parchment as she scribbled with her little cut quill. Tears trickled down the crease of her wide nose as she sniffled. She looked up to Ellari, wide eyed and pleading, "How do you tell a boy that you really like him but you'll probably never see him again?"

Ellari just stared at her cousin.

"...Right. This is silly. It feels silly in the face of what happened to..." Masha had to swallow more sobs. "It is silly. I'm so sorry."

Ellari bit down, straightened her pale mask and blinked. She was a blank canvas, a dry pitcher, a husk. "Your needs and feelings are not silly Masha. What have you written down?" Ellari's voice was whisper quiet. She had gone numb watching Hale in the mud and she still felt nothing.

She cleared her sniffling nose and read outloud, "My Dear Lord Slade..." She trailed off, then broke down into tears, great heaving sobs, "Gods, I'm so *selfish*."

The word cut through the clammy skin on Ellari's chest, parted her ribs and stuck her dead in the heart. *Selfish.* A dagger of pain and guilt. *Selfish.* She felt something, at least. *Perhaps it's the only thing I feel because it's honest. Perhaps I am selfish and I deserve this.* She thought. *I shall be free of Hullen, a good man will die and I will never be High Lady of the Wylde.* Her stomach lurched, greasy and warm. The dinner course served had been mild, a stew of chicken, leek, garlic and potato, but even so, it sat angrily in her tummy.

Half-answering, Ellari droned, "You wrote that you're selfish..?"

Great tears burst forth and the teenager buried her face in her arms, sobbing into desk and parchment "No, I was twyin' to -hrrrrk-" she stopped, taking a panicked, wheezing sob of a breath, "wite somefing deepeh, but I can't get passssst the openiiiiiing." The muffle of her arms around her face and the rumbling of the wooden table under her made her just barely intelligible, but Ellari had grown accustomed to translating teenager tantrums into something more useful.

"Just..." She pictured Hullen's face, and tears welled, "tell him that your time was all too brief."

Masha nodded, scribbling, though tears dribbled and upset the ink. When the younger girl moved to dab at the parchment, Lady Ellari stopped her. "No, leave the tear stains. Men love when we weep and wail for them. It makes them feel gallant." Her own voice felt unfamiliar, she sounded like some bitter old widow. *A glimpse of what's to come.*

If Hullen were to die, she would likely be shoved aside in favor of Hullen's younger brother, Devlin. Devlin was fifteen and currently serving as a squire and page for their aunt Velda's husband, Lord Calder Greeneye at their castle, Korpiklaani. Arrangements were being made for him to return to Rime River, the ancestral seat of Clan Curr. *Either they will hand him the Regency, or perhaps they'll marry me to him instead.* That was unlikely, of course. After two years of 'wedded bliss' she had not given Hullen a son, Ellari knew what was being whispered when she left the room.

It is as likely to be Hullen's fault as mine, but why take the risk? Have Devlin marry some pretty little Greeneye girl to have a whole gaggle of heirs, it's the sensible thing to do. The whole situation made her stomach set to fluttering under the greasy sick warmth. And… Poor Masha and Slade. Ellari was canny enough to see why they would never actually be allowed to pursue a relationship, the two Clans already shared plenty of blood: Little Daryon, son of Lord Hullen III's nephew, was grandson to the Snapping Turtle, Ser Tullus Mirebreaker. The Mirebreaker daughter, Jasmine even lived at Rime River Keep with her son, as she was the widow of Lord Hullen's youngest brother. Even if the pair were a sweet match, there was no political incentive for Masha and Slade. Curr and Mirebreaker were already family.

She could never tell her little Masha this. *Perhaps, in a way, it's fortunate that they will be separated before she could feel deeper for him.* Ellari knew the pain of loving a man forbidden. *I will not allow myself to hope Hullen dies. Not even for my Tower.*

It seems the only thing I can allow myself to feel is guilt. Interesting.

As Masha scribbled away once more, Ellari set about puzzling the event. The squirrel skin had begun to wriggle in her mind. Squirrel meant Rask, and Rask likely meant Lilah Stagg, born of that stock. Lilah Stagg had been wearing a mantle of squirrelskin, like some barbarian. *How many of those poor little things had to die for that awful little shrug? What a madwoman.*

There was to be a ball tonight, of course. Something would need to be done. Ellari could not find much of a center through all of this, merely a path. Her future had already been mortgaged. This girl knew something, even if she wasn't involved. *Hate, I still have hate.*

And there was Illystre Coldhearth. The Lord of Spies set Ellari's stomach to quivering and she found herself dampening with nervous perspiration. *Fear. I still feel fear.*

There was no way to be free of all these tangling cords without action. She was a hound bound and this Curr would be free, even if she needed to rend her way to escape. *Coldhearth cannot kill a dead woman, and I have no future if he speaks. A dead woman feels no fear.* Ellari folded her fear up and set it aside. She would feast on it later. She held her hatred in her heart. She would need that for Lilah Stagg.

"We need to go to the ball, we have to get ready." She rapidly stood, for the first time in five or six hours.

"What?" Masha raised her face from her tear-stained missive, "No, no one expects us, in light of Hullen–"

Ellari cut her off, a snap in her tone that she had not truly intended, "We have to!" She softened, "For Hullen…"

There would be no further argument. Though time was brief, both young women managed to armor themselves in the dresses and finery that had been packed all the way from frigid Rime River for the occasion. Ellari wore a slim, modest thing, a smoky grey-blue satin, studded with a hundred and a half beaded glass stars. She wore a woven shrug of the finest wool, woven from shaggy camels bred by the mountain tribesmen. It was sinfully soft and woven to show leaping Curr hounds under Ironarm Hemlocks. It had been her mother's and Ellari loved it very, very much.

Masha had been given something much finer, as she was the maiden on display, as it were. Lady Gail and Masha had personally slaved over the dress. When the bolt of silk arrived from Addagio, a city far on the warm Merchant's Sea, Lord Hullen III had scoffed at the expense. When he saw his wife and daughter weep at the pure snow white as they gazed on it, he took his protests back. The mother and daughter had settled on a cut that was modest and ladylike, but free of frump. Lace of tundra cotton dyed indigo edged the hems, and a spray of midnight blue pearls imported from some coldwater continental city swirled from her neckline to her belt. Ellari wrapped Masha in her mantle, a soft furry thing of white fox fur. Ellari gently kissed her cousin on the forehead, "You look like a princess made of cake. You're gorgeous."

Masha blushed, stuttering her thank yous, but a knock at the door of the chamber announced the arrival of their escorts. Ser Esben Hornblower was through the door first. He was a big man, but Ellari still only saw a big boy. He had always been all chest and shoulders and belly, bulling about on legs that seemed a little too thin and a little too short. Ellari had once found a drawing of a great shaggy ape from Assorra in an old book. When she compared this ape to Esben, Hale had given her a stern look, but he smirked a little wickedly all the same.

Today, he was dressed in sea green and cobalt, the colors of his Clan, wools, and a fine cape outlined in silver thread. He was not unhandsome, Ellari mused. Esben was too outspoken by half and not much of a thinker, but he would tunnel through a mountain for his lord, and Ellari loved him for that. He was the older brother that she had never had. When he saw the young ladies, his big red tomato of a face split into a grin, "Ladies, you both look rather comely, don't you!"

Hale was through the door next, a pale phantom, silent. Simply seeing him seemed to slow her pounding heartbeat. Wools in ruddy crimson and autumn ochre served as his sullen reminder of his ancient Clan. He bowed politely, and his huge sword *Wayfinder* was strapped across his back, as if he were playing bodyguard, not escort. "We should not be going with you, it should be Hullen." His tone was funerary.

"It should be." Masha groused, "You are no substitute for my brother." Her eyes lingered, before taking Esben by the arm, and turning her attention to Ellari, "If we must go, let us go, then."

Esben made his one concern clear as they rounded the corner out of sight, "This event has wine, correct..?"

Once alone, Ellari fell into him. Her skin had not warmed his since Hullen's fall, and his touch was the solace she had so desperately craved. In his grasp, she was secure for just the moment. They were stealing seconds, and though she only wanted to tarry here, she could not. "I believe Lilah Stagg was present when Hullen fell." There was nothing more to say, though she wanted to spare him, he had to be told.

Ellari had spent four years with Hale, and she had never felt his body tense quite like he did when those words met his ears, "W-what did you say?" His hands had found her waist, though really she had little shape to speak of.

She felt his hands tighten on her waist when she spoke again, "Lilah Stagg, Rask, what-have-you, I believe she was there when Hullen fell."

"I saw her... moments before." His usually soft voice was barely perceptible, "I accidentally knocked into her, as she was leaving temple." His hands squeezed Ellari gently, "I caught her, just like *this*."

Ellari wriggled loose, "It would have been better to let her crack her jaw on the cobbles. It would have purchased us a few months of silence." She uttered coldly. Shame immediately shrouded her as she pulled Hale into the hall, following Esben and her cousin, "I am sorry. I truly do not mean that, Hale. This is all so... *much.*" The warm greasy feeling in her gut had worsened, and the back of her mouth had gone watery.

Taciturn in his humor as always, Torchbearer merely agreed, "It is indeed."

Honeyhome was a city of opulence, grown far beyond wealthy on trade with the Dwarves on the continent. Hivehall was a monument to grandiosity, almost profane in its displays of wealth. Coomb's Gallery, named for the ancient Malbes lord who raised the first keep of Honeyhome, was an affront to god, man and good taste, with its sheer splendor. Every surface shone with some sort of reflected light, be it metal, satin or jewel. Vines of silken ribbon, strung in Artus blue and gold hung in gentle swooping firmament, allowing the moonlight to filter through the glass above and shine on the ballroom floor below.

The center of the floor was cleared, a great tiled dance space. A septet of musicians played *"The Timbers Witch and her Owlet"*, a lively old song from the Greatwood, though only a few nobles had taken to the floor. She smiled a greeting to Lord Ivan Helm, a northern Lord who was making small circles with what Ellari presumed to be his four or five-year-old daughter, as she jumped and jigged wildly.

Ellari's pale hand brushed the front of her dress. A twist of the neck, and she could be kissing her Hale, but that meant destroying them both. The quartet settled at a small round table near the back of the hall, as far from the bards as could be managed. Hale refused a seat, standing at a column nearby, "I am not attending for mirth. I am attending my sworn lord's sister." He would take a long drink from a horn that Esben had pressed into his hand, "And his wife."

Masha would hide her face when the royal contingent strode in, led by all seven Grey Guard. Between parted fingers, Masha peered at the knights. Even Ellari noted her gaze lingering on handsome young Drake Canar, looking like a fairytale knight in his purple and grey. Behind the guard came the royal family, first the Crown Prince and his

476

wife, Lady Kiara. The future king and queen were clad in matching samite of blue and gold. As the royals began their Grand Procession, the bards began to play *Under His Eyes*, celebrating the Emperor and his get. Talor and Kiara were the picture of absolute grace, followed by the King and Queen themselves, and the page called out, "All rise, for Emperor of Daneau, Avalar and Ozwyk and her nations, The Last of the Stars, King Gallus Artus, the third. He is attended by his Lady Wife, Queen Natasha, born to the Court of Harlock, the Lady Kiara, his daughter-by-law, his heir; the Crown Prince, Talor of Clan Artus." a raucous cheer went up from some of the younger and wilder lords, but the Prince stifled them kindly, with a smile and a wave of the hand, "And our honored guest, on the sixteenth anniversary of his birth: Prince Vernus Artus." His cheers were more polite than raucous. Ellari softly clapped, Masha put her head down.

The King himself would step to the dais, raising his arm to cease the chittering of his lords. "Thank you, my true thanks to each of you gathered here on this day." He crossed to Prince Vernus, warmly draping an arm around the boy. This prince was not clad as perfectly as his father or elder brother. Though the items he wore were tailored, the yellow silk of his shirt seemed to bunch under his chest, and his breeches rode too high when he sat. The crown on his head wobbled perilously, as he bowed his head in deference to his sire, "Today, Prince Vernus turns sixteen and thus is named a man. I pray today that he becomes the man I know he is capable of. That he relies on the wisdom of trusted counselors and learns to listen."

Vernus nodded, either deeply considering what his father had just told him or too dense to understand it, but it mattered little, because it was his turn to speak, "Thank you, truly! You all do me the truest and greatest honor by watching me ascend to manhood!" The King gave him a little shake of affirmation, and the boy continued, "Now, enjoy the wine and the dance. Lord Malbes spared no expense, after all."

The broad smile on his face lasted long enough to cross the stage to his enormous bodyguard, who tossed the younger prince a wineskin. Vernus suckled at it greedily, as lordlings returned to their revels. Masha gently poked her head up, "I-Is he looking for me?"

The music, the warmth, this… *thing* in her gut, it had all set Ellari to sickly sweating, "The prince seems quite distracted." She gestured toward the stage, where the identical Selach twins, Elise and Ameile, had cornered the prince and were mooning over him. It wasn't until she saw the smirking lord behind them that Ellari found another emotion she had lost somehow. *Fury. Rage. Hellfire.*

Ellari had found her feet and was ready to rush toward the Lord of Spies on the dais, when she noticed Masha had also risen and was making a very slow, winding, mindful path toward the corner table where Slade Mirebreaker was laughing with his brother and their new knight. Sighing, Ellari scanned the room for Esben, but he had apparently wandered off already. With her head pounding and belly rolling, Ellari called to Hale, "Ser Hale! Tend to Lady Masha, she is going to talk to a boy. No funny business."

A flash of concern crossed Hale's dour face, but he nodded, leaving her command unquestioned, "As you wish." With a sly little grin, he spun on his heel and followed Masha into the herd of nobility.

Ellari picked up her glass of sparkling pink wine, and tasted it. It was, like everything else in this castle, damnably sweet, "To hell with this." She dumped the glass in the little bowl of flowers on the table and rose again. *I have had enough shit drizzled in saccharine.*

Despite the hammering at her temples, despite the hot, sour fluttering in her guts. Ellari crossed the ballroom. As she grew closer,

478

Coldhearth's voice became clear, still lazy and far-away, "I think that whole ordeal with Lord Morsk was overblown anyway. It's only embezzlement if you get caught, if you ask me." Vernus laughed uproariously. One of the sisters, *Elise*, she thought, *it is hard to be sure*, laughed, and then her sister followed a quarter second later. *If you were uncareful, you may think it was totally in time, but there's the slightest delay, isn't there? Interesting.*

"Well, I would not go so far as that, My Lord." Vernus declared, his voice a persistent whinge, "The Lord Executor is a man to be trusted and feared and Lord Morsk Selach defamed that." He smiled at the twins, "Through no fault of his exquisite nieces, mind you, but still. The Highest lords must fall the furthest, and there is no higher lord than the Lord Executor. Granted, I tire of the bloated bladder that currently serves." He sniggered through his nose, a high, unrhythmic noise.

Coldhearth politely chuckled, pressing a square of stormcloud colored silk to his lips as he did, "Oh, be nice, Lord Bridge has his uses…" He trailed off, noticing Ellari, "But it seems that the ball is not the only thing being attended to, Lady Curr, have you had the pleasure of meeting our *honored* prince, Vernus?"

The Prince may not have noticed the jape, but Ellari did. She did what she always did around petty little men, she smiled wide, kept herself polite and outsmarted them. *Coldhearth wants you to play, you know. You're giving him what he wants.* She warned herself but knew she was too angry to obey. "I have not. The pleasure is mine, Your Grace." Her smile never wavered, which made what came next all the more devastating, "If you're struggling with *Lord* Executors, might I suggest you try a *Lady* Executor for the crown instead. It has worked wonders in the Wylde." She ran her tongue under her bottom lip.

"According to my Lord Uncle at least, being a woman, I am incapable of understanding such overwhelming business."

There was a pause, and then Ellari, Coldhearth, Elise and Prince Vernus all exploded in a shared burst of laughter. Amelie followed an instant after. The Prince laughed the hardest, and as he dabbed tears from the corners of his eyes, he spoke, "Very good, Lady Curr, very witty." His manner softened, "I was truly sorry to hear of your Lord Husband's accident, my Lady. Hullen Curr held a sterling reputation."

"Thank you, Your Grace, we all pray for a recovery borne on swift wings." She dropped the crown of her head, "If I may steal The Lord of Spies from you, for a conversation, at least, I would very much like to. I have reason to believe my husband's fall was *not* an accident, and his considerable network would be very beneficial to my peace of mind." Ellari kept her tone warm, but firm. *This one responds best to being mothered.* "In fact, seeking Lord Coldhearth is the only reason I have left my husband's side."

The Prince gave an impressed little gurn, and gave his leave to Coldhearth. The Lord of Spies dryly quipped, "Well, at least I have left you with a pair of reasons to stay entertained, Your Grace."

Prince Vernus cast his eyes downward at the twins' twin dress lines, "Two pairs, I should think." He smiled as Ellari's skin crawled under her silks.

Coldhearth would lead her to a suspiciously quiet table, half tucked between the servants' doors and the high wooden bandshell erected behind the bards. They were mostly unseen, and the sound from the music would make any sort of eavesdropping next to impossible. *He's the Lord of Spies, finding places like this is his duty, of course.*

480

"If this is about that tosh at the tourney this afternoon." Coldhearth began, "I could apologize, if you'd like, but I'd be lying." He settled into his seat, all of his practiced chivalry back to dust in the wind.

"I do not want your apologies, I want your knowledge." Ellari bristled, knowing this one would not be as easy to curtail as a lascivious princeling. "Whether I was *in* love with Hullen or not, I love my cousin. I could not have imagined this tragedy. I have never wanted harm to come to Hullen."

She felt his eyes on her, those practiced eyes of cold smoke. And though not a word she spoke was a lie, she still felt stinging guilt coursing up her tensing spine. His quiet contemplation complete, Illystre spoke in a gentle tone, barely above the noise of the singers, "I believe you."

"Why?" The incredulity in her voice was heavy, and she leaned forward, taking hold of the gilded candlestick between them, just for something to grasp. Her head was pummelling itself, and bile had begun to creep up the back of her throat as her stomach raged onward.

He sighed, "I am torn, Lady Curr. Very torn."

Fearing vomit, she blurted, "I don't have time for games, m'lord."

"I detest sharing information I do not have to." He cocked an eyebrow, "And what I have is part of a larger puzzle. 'Nothing is more dangerous than a smart man who only has half the information, and does not know it,' Lady Ellari."

"Let me remind you of something that is constantly thrown in my face." Every word felt wobbly, her mouth watery, "I am not a man."

He smirked, waiting.

"And thus, I know what patience is." She could feel her head bobbing low, the thrum of her headache was boiling between her ears, "I will look before I leap, I am nothing if not *cautious.*" She raised her gaze, searching the room for Hale. Something was more than wrong with her, she needed her Tower. A bead of sweat ran from her head and dribbled onto the table. *Coldhearth had to have seen that.* She burped, and vomit flooded her mouth. She swallowed hard, and followed that with a long sip of water from the pitcher on the table.

His gaze, those hard grey eyes, cataloged each of these physical failings. He lay his hands in his silk gloves on the table, "Are you unwell?" There was no smirk. He was tense, ready to stand.

"I am fine." She snarled through gritted teeth. "What do you know?"

He stood, rounding the table to her, "You are ill, m'lady."

"If I am ill, then fucking hurry." She was sweating again, trying desperately not to spill her guts or alternatively foul her skirts. "But I am not ill."

"So, you're not." He settled, "Fine. But you need to share first" This sly grey fox had her cornered. "How do you know that your Hullen didn't simply stumble?"

Past the point of ceremony, Ellari pulled the hunk of squirrelskin from the place at her belt she had tucked it. She slid it across the table, trying to keep her hands from trembling. "Lilah Stagg wears a mantle made of such vermin." She groaned, "Hullen had it clutched in his hand when the Saddler found him."

Whatever Coldhearth had expected, this little fur wasn't it. He raised it, examining it carefully, stroking the dead little thing, "Hmph. You're sure of this?"

"Entirely."

When he said what came next, all the fire in her gut froze for a split second. "A washerwoman saw Hullen attacked by a woman and some sort of... *imp.*" He shook his head, "I know Lilah Rask. She's no murderer, and certainly no sorceress. My sister knows her better, I could–"

"Thank you, Lord Inquistor." Ellari was numb again. Her head pounded, her stomach burned, but she would not allow herself to feel it as she rose. She began to slink away, swaying.

He called after her, this cunning spy, but she was no longer listening. She trudged forward, one heavy step, then another. Her eyes found Hale, finally across the ballroom. He immediately saw her distress. He gave little Masha a look on the dancefloor, as she spun with the Mirebreaker boy, but he broke away from duty to tend to his love. She would catch her as she fell, his great, strong hands wrapped around her slim little waist.

Consciousness would return to Ellari soon after, Hale and a pretty green-skinned *ifre'croi* loomed large over her. Worry lined Hale's long face, his blue-black eyes never left her. The hell-heart spun her head, and called to an unseen figure, "Learner, she's awake!"

She could hear the music and the murmur of gathered lords rumble through the walls. Though she had been laid out in a quiet, dimly lit little den, she was not far from the ball. The burly voice of Learner Vaughn huffed from just out of sight, "Good, good." Ellari let her head laze to the right, and found him busying over some sort of steaming mug of potion. Strong smells cooled her sinuses, pouring from the small table where he prodded his concoction.

"Don't be frightened, love." The green woman smiled, "You had a bit of a tumble, and the Learner and I are tendin' to you. You've had a day, to be true." She pressed a soft hand to Ellari's head. This gorgeous devil smelled of spice and incense and sweet fruit, hot in the summer sun.

The Learner appeared, this gruff little man. Hellendre pulled back, and Vaughn leaned low, watching her eyes watch him, "Do you know where you are, Lady Curr?"

"I believe I'm still near the ball, I hear music."

He nodded, "Very good." He straightened, shoving the warm clay cup into her hand. With a wave of the hand, thick fingers pushed the steam into Ellari's face, "Drink that, and inhale as much of the steam as you reasonably can. You should be fine."

"Is that some sort of healing drought?" Hale's eyes stared at the steam curling around Ellar's round pale moon of face.

"It's spearmint tea." The little man in the bisected robes corrected.

Hale glowered from his corner, "What happened to her?"

Ellari knew before the Learner and the green girl exchanged a knowing look. She had known two weeks ago, but had hoped against hope that it had been the travel or the ship or any other strangeness in her environment. It was the hellheart, the gentle seeming one, who pressed that soft hand to her head and asked, "When was your last... *lunation,* love? Your monthly flower."

It *could not* have been Hullen's, but an heir *would* keep her in Rime River Keep. An heir *would* put her in the Blizzard Chair. Her voice was a mouse creeping from her mouth. A tiny, quiet thing, seeming so harmless, but truly carrying a foul pestilence. "It seems our lord Hullen blessed us before his fall after all..." Ellari gave one more lie, ice creeping over her numb heart.

ILLYSTRE IV

"All magic has a cost, prophecy worst of all. You see, you only find out the price of a prophecy once you've already bound yourself to pay it. That's the nastiest bit, innit?"

It was somewhere beyond midnight, and the Hunter was somewhere even deeper than the deepest gold-vault in Honeyhome. He and the others gathered sweltered in black robes and carved wooden masks. All but Isolde, only the speaker's face was allowed to be bare. Peat smoked in braziers, casting red light and deep shadows in every jut and crevice of the hewn stone walls. Illystre's throat burned with peat smoke and acrid herbal incense Lady Isolde had set to smoldering. Swirling smoke and scarlet light had united with the bitter potion he had been forced to imbibe, and his head was swimming.

He resented using the mask for this. The Hunter was his most prized weapon and this old mask was central to it. Tradition is tradition, and tradition breeds power. Besides, everyone was in these black robes and masks of various beasts and heraldic symbols. He stroked the ancient grey wood. *Better blank than strapping a tower to my face.*

A dragonfly's bulbous glittering eyes. Stitched sackcloth and buttons. A shrieking wooden bat. A great fierce bear. Masks danced on figures made of shadowed robes. A gurning fox. A viper in crimson and blue. A cat with dancing eyes.

Beside him, Lord Torvald sat, a mask of hemlock, carved with spreading branches. The grain of the wood hid the pale, translucent skin of his brother-by-law, with its snaking blue and purple veins. The sickly Lord of the Greatwood raised his voice as much as he could, calling across the round table they all surrounded, "If our speaker is ready to view, we may begin."

Dull red light filling her eyes, her voice and her very manner, Isolde spoke, "I am ready, my lord."

The cavern was so deep, Illystre was unsure if the swelter came from the bodies gathered in the little space, the brazier or the burning fires of hell herself. Ten souls had gathered here, in this cavern rooted deep below the high dome of Hivehall, this long forgotten sepulcher: Nine believers in the Prince and Isolde to speak to the Gods. Each of the nine believers had a solemn part to play here, and it balanced on the blade of the knives placed at each of their seats.

Magic took power and there was no more potent source of power than sacrifice. *And what sacrifice is greater than the blood of my veins?* Illystre jested to himself as he drug the old bronze knife across his palm and watched a crimson dribble coat the channels and runes of the carved stone table before him. All nine of the masks gave their blood, even Lord Torvald who needed his more than most.

The blood flowed, no longer from their hands, but the blood on the table flowed and coursed. From each donor, it followed the maze of channels, as it moved its way to the center. In the center of the table, a woven braid of black thread hung barely brushing the center of the table. As the blood puddled in the little dish-like depression therein, it brushed the low fibres of the braid, and the blood began to climb, Illystre's bile rose as he watched long strings of red gore congeal upward. It climbed and coated until the blood of these nine lords and ladies had made a tall, narrow candle of crimson on a wick of black. Like a living beast given purpose, the blood of their bodies had taken a life of its own and done its own will.

Isolde rose, and cut the wick, about an inch above the tip of the candle. She thrust the tip in the brazier just long enough to light it. She would clap a lid on the brazier. Without warning, Illystre was blind, as the dank stone cell was plunged into darkness. One of the women behind the beast masks gasped and whispered, but he could not determine what was being said.

Isolde's hard little voice cut the whispers, heavy with ambition, wrapped in ritual, "The candle burns shedding its life-light, the light of the future. Those who gave their blood can see it no more than they can see their own faces, so I must speak what these shadows show us."

The Lord of Spies shifted in his seat. He misliked losing his eyes. A flock of fluttering breath, shuffling feet, scooting chairs, his ears only told him a jumble. His nose was little better, the heavy incense covered almost everything but its own herbaceous smoke, though Illystre did get the slightest whiff of burning iron, like a forge too hot or an empty kettle left to smoke.

His sister croaked through the hot, choking room, "Nine masks. Nine shadows…"

"Speak, my love, we listen." Torvald's voice was dead branches in the wind.

"An– An octopus, tentacles consume a… face, a- a man's face." She stuttered and slurred, something pushing against the very tremor of her throat. "A great shagged beast in the ice, A falling tower, no, a burning tower, a falling burning tower…" Her tone was growing lower, and in the dark, Illystre could feel the whole great stone table tremble. "I see a humble creature, a woodland beast astride a dragon… A strike of lightning, storms above fetid water…." She had begun to slur more, and Illystre felt the entire slab of granite shift, and heard Isolde's body slam into it, the breath leaving her in a rushing groan. "A horse stumbles on its plow." She wheezed. "A gold eye is snapped shut with a smile, something in the world is missing... Wings and feathers and talons. Night isn't safe, but day can't stay..."

The whole table was jolting and jumping, Isolde was slamming something heavy into it, and she gave a roaring slur in a voice that was not her own, "The Prince waits for the crown in the shadow of the tower lent, brother of witches, Grey phantom, lord of spies, he waits for you alone."

Then silence and stillness and nothing but dark and Isolde's struggling, pained wheezes.

It was the Scarecrow who broke the silence, "We need light, *now.*"

Torvald's barely-there voice answered, authority in the pitch, "There is a torch near the door. We just need to open in, Lady Vadala, if I'm not mistaken, you are the nearest. Might you try to find it?"

A brash young voice, a woman's voice answered, "Yes, my lord." Her fumbling in the dark led to success with a narrow line of orange light falling across the table, before spreading into a rectangle of torchlight, just enough to see. The girl in the grinning cat mask stood beside the open door.

The only blood on the table was Lady Isolde's. Every drop of the donor's blood had crawled into the candle and the candle seemed to have burned to ash. Still, there was blood spattering the table, great splashes of it. The heavy thing that Isolde had been slamming into the hard stone was her own face. A puddle of blood pooled under a gash above one eye, and the other was rapidly swelling shut. Both nostrils dribbled blood from a nose likely broken, and her bottom lip was split, adding to the painting in red on the table. She murmured, incoherent on the table.

Both the Dragonfly and the Fox hurried to Isolde's side, the stern voice of a lady from under the glittering eyes spoke, "It should have been me, I am far more experienced looking to the future."

"Sounds more like hindsight to me." came a placid girl's voice from the Fox.

Lord Torvald turned to Illystre, "There was precisely one thing in her words that I understood, brother. You have a delivery to make."

The Hunter rose from Illystre's chair, and in his grey gloved hands was a Starheart crown. "To the Prince, then. I suppose our conversation is overdue."

Illystre's smoke and ice eyes gave a long look through the Hunter's mask, as the Fox and the Dragonfly dressed and cleaned Isolde's wounds. *Brave, stupid girl. Stronger than you are smart, my bullmoose of a sister,* Illystre let himself have that last feeling before slipping the rest of the way into the Grey Hunter and dashing out the door into the orange torchlight.

Swiftness came to The Hunter as naturally as the breath in his chest. The flights of stairs in this twisting warren gave him no challenge as he hurled himself up the grey stone. *Stone like this, stairs like this broke Curr.* Again, The Hunter forced himself to put Illystre aside, though he knew he may yet need to send his Sister-Witch and her Hanging Hemlock on the matter of Lady Lilah Stagg.

The winding stair led to an iron gate, dust-covered in a forgotten armory basement below the dome. The Hunter wound between helms, dry and cracked with age, never to be worn. Beside them, swords whose edges had dulled only to rust. Another stair led to a small hall and the yard above. Legs like steel launched him into the starry night of Honeyhome, and he raced through low fogs and an empty midnight to his Prince.

As he approached the tower, The Hunter saw a great ebon bird clutching the bust of some old lord above the door. An owl of significant size and a menacing bearing locked its great eyes of aurelion on him and gave a screech that stopped him in his stride.

There was a tumble of smoke and fog and feather, black and grey and umber. The menacing owl was a bird and a man and more all at once. It swung a face full with that same hateful burning aurelion gaze on him, and The Coronox spoke, a voice a rattling thunder, "...The Hunter returns with his prize." Leathery hands reached out, as if the great creature could feel the light of the crown at The Hunter's belt.

The Hunter fell to a knee, and slid his mask off. It was Illystre who said, "Your Grace." He lifted the twisting spikes of the Starheart crown in his hands, a bit of the celestial gold that had fallen from the stars themselves and lived below the Isle of Avalar, in its deep tunneling mines. *A mark of power stolen,* Illystre thought to himself. *Light of the stars devoured by golden eyes.*

Those hands of black leather, tipped in those talons like iron, gripped one another, like a scavenger readying to feast. The Coronox, *The Crown of Night,* peeled away leather flesh and iron talon, revealing the five fingered hands of a man. Strong and fine fingers, pale as moonlight. The man's hands took the Starheart, and a deep exhale of satisfaction rumbled from the Coronox. "My hunter, my grey fox, my spy... The light you bring today will change the course of history. You have done well."

Marble white and marble strong, the Prince's hand stroked the silver locks atop Illystre's head, a gesture of blessing, a gesture of graciousness, "The opportunity to serve again is all I ask, my Prince." Illystre would stand on tradition here, and he would do it without irony. "My life is yours to command."

"This I know, Coldhearth. Old debts are being paid, anchors gathered. We may yet still have a chance, because of you." The Coronox's man hands slid back into their leather and iron sheaths. A cloud crossed the moon in its soft blue, and the tones of the Coronox echoed again, "My time here grows short, and I have great distances before I sleep." There was something youthful about the toss of the Owl Prince's head. "I shall not forget your service here. Rest, feast, you have earned it, spy." Striding away, the prince called over his great feathered mantle, "There will be little time for either in the coming months, enjoy them now."

And he was gone. Another tumble of smoke and shadow and feather, and the great black owl was gliding. Blue moonlight shimmered on feathers of the deepest void, as owl, prince and crown swooped skyward. Illystre watched his prince make four lazy circles around the tower, before settling on the ledge of a window.

Illystre Coldhearth knew a broken boy slept under that window. The Spymaster knew better than to wait. He would rest, he would feast, he would gather his allies and sharpen his daggers.

Illystre Coldhearth knew that day cannot stay, and night is only safe when you are a shadow.

VANDRE VI

"No matter the shape a life takes, the ends all look the same. Black, nothing fades like the light."

It was just before dawn on the third day when Vandre rolled out of the woman's bed. He took soft steps, before crossing into Clan Saddler's common room. It had been a few decades since the last time he'd silently crept from a maiden's chamber, he was no young man any more, but she was no maiden, either. He managed to dress silently, pulling his breeches on, lacing those fine new boots. He crept, silent as the slivers of silver sunlight that crossed the floor through the window.

Despite his old bones, and the full rooms around him Vandre had managed to both gain his pleasure, give her her own, and escape back to his little white chamber. The tired old man would wash, and look his face over in the little round mirror he had been given.

Who is this old man, and what happened to me?

Brown eyes, grey stubble, scars and wrinkles. The tall smiling boy from Hammerdale was still somewhere under all the years. His morose, angry lover had found him for long stretches last night, but this was as foolish an endeavor he had ever undertaken and vowed not to do it again.

Unless asked. He smirked to himself. Self preservation had never been one of Vandre's strong suits.

The soft feather bed allowed him a few long, precious minutes of stolen sleep, before duty would demand he rise again. New wools, new leathers, a sharp sword he had yet to swing, he was a worn soldier in new dress, and it was a notion he might grow fond of. He was riding an unbroken stallion, he knew, it was as likely to buck him as anything, but it was a beautiful opportunity.

His reunion with his newly sworn lord was pleasant enough, Hartwin, *Lord Hartwin,* he forced himself, had been especially palatable since his pink pearl had accepted his proposal. The tall boy had even paid him a compliment when he strode through the door. "You look fierce enough to rival Birse himself today, old man."

"I'm feeling it, my lord. Shame I'm not in the tourney." Vandre smirked.

There was a snorting laugh as Hartwin Saddler's younger brother chided him, "Maybe thirty years ago, friend. But you're too stiff and too slow today." Hugo Saddler had been the soul Vandre had originally held the least concern for, as another swordsman, another soldier, he was sure common ground could come quickly. He had not anticipated that the younger Saddler would seem instantly so dead-set on killing him for reasons he could not yet fathom.

"I'm not that much older than Axe, Ser Hugo." Vandre set his jaw, taking in the broad knight, "And he's got as much chance as anyone to knock you in the dirt."

Hugo gave a cruel, braying little laugh, "Of course you'd think another crippled old man is like to beat me." He took a long draw of his horn of his morning ale, before rising. He turned to his older brother as he made his way out of the Saddler's borrowed apartment, "When this one is too feeble to hold his sword, you oughta toss him into motley, he's a born fool."

Once his brother had gone, Hartwin beckoned Vandre to sit, "Don't mind him. He's got a hard fight ahead of him. He is always petulant and disagreeable before a tourney."

Vandre gave an unbelieving stare, "That is his idea of petulance?"

Hartwin shrugged, "You ought to see him upset, a few of my Young Stallions still limp." Hartwin chuckled, "I have a little cousin, Leland. The boy squires for him, absolutely terrified of Hugo. It's hilarious."

Vandre frowned, "I've never known a good knight to mistreat his squire, m'lord."

"Hugo is a terrible knight." Again, the admission was almost casual. "He's a fantastic fighter, a better killer, but vows and chivalry mean less than horse leavings to my brother." Saddler looked over the tensing Vandre, "Does that bother you? Do you need a squire, too? I have other cousins. Joelle has little second cousin–"

"I don't need a squire." Vandre cut in, "I'm not a knight."

"Your rules, not mine." The lordling loved his airy japes. He was pouring over a bound little ledger, and only occasionally raised his glance to meet his bodyguard. A little mug of steaming brown bitter bean tea sat before Saddler, with a kettle of the stuff beside it. "When the tournament ends, we're riding south."

Vandre nodded, "I expected as much, my Lord."

"I will be riding into the Lowlands with Lady Joelle." Those sharp little chips of jade and moss that made up Saddler's gaze were locked on him.

The old sword did everything he could to not show fear, but clearly he was failing, "As you wish, Lord Hartwin."

As his unease was as plain on his face as his scars, Saddler pounced, "Riding isn't an issue to you, I am well aware. So, what makes you uncomfortable, my lady or her city?"

Vandre was tired and he was bored of pretext, "Both, my lord. Your lady has made it clear that in the event something happens to you, I'll be held personally responsible." He paused, pouring his own mug of the steaming bitter bean tea, "And, well, m'lord, Cobalt Bridge is mighty close to home, and, well, home ain't exactly a friendly place to me." He sipped the hot brew, "Not too many men with happy homes live under another's name, m'lord."

"Too true." Hartwin said, "Lady Joelle and I will be riding south to Rain Tower Hall and Cobalt Bridge, but *you* will not."

The exhale Vandre gave rustled a few of the Young Colt's papers on the table, it was so deep, "Thank you, my lord."

"You should not thank me yet." Saddler finished his brew, with a self satisfied little sigh. "You are going to The Far Fort, Vandre."

"I'm sorry, my lord, I thought my crimes were forgiven." The Far Fort was the most notorious prison camp used by the crown. A man went there to toil in a mine, field or orchard and to be forgotten. Vandre would rather die.

Hartwin gave his rumbling laugh, "No, no, I need you to act as a messenger. Lord Morsk Selach has been exiled there after his failures as Lord Executor." He slid a small sealed envelope across the table toward his bodyguard, "Can you read, Vandre?"

"No, my Lord." The shame was clear on his face, "I was never taught."

"Good." Saddler was smug, smirking. "Then you won't bother opening the letter." Vandre dragged the parchment across the little table, before stuffing it into a pouch on his belt. "Finish your coffee, it's time to watch my brother win this farce and leave Honeyhome in our pasts."

He nodded, "Couldn't agree more, Lord Hartwin."

"Don't start getting respectful, if I grow fond of you, I'll be upset when you die." Saddler slithered from the room.

Yesterday's cool rains had turned hot and muggy once more as the sun blazed overhead. Under his layers of cotton, leather, wool and metal, Vandre sweltered. There was no place under the shade today, as temperatures soared, the old man baked in the sun. The Saddler stand was full, as none of them had gone to the royal box. Vandre had not been informed as to whether this was an intentional choice to support Ser Hugo, or if the Royal Family had simply deigned not to invite them.

It did not appear that Ser Hugo especially needed the aid, however. In the arena, Lord Lukas Axe had been a fearsome force through the previous rounds, battering his opponents with the heavy maul that had been affixed to the stump of his right hand. Against Hugo and the heavy oak-and-gold shield *Hoofbeat,* the hammer was nearly as effective as a feather duster.

Axe would smash the maul with all the force such a big bull of a brawler might muster, but *Hoofbeat* could take it all. That was the point of the shield. No matter how damn hard you struck it, the shield felt it. *Hoofbeat* remembered every shot pummeled into it, and the magic shield could hand them all back. He'd done it to Coldhearth, Hugo had done it to Vellen, and it appeared Axe was about to make the same sort of mistake.

The Brute of Stonestall had planted his feet, readying himself to unleash the hell his shield carried, but Vandre thrilled as the older knight feinted. Lord Lukas raised his maul, as if to swing, and when Saddler went to block with it, Axe seized the shield in left hand and sent it whorling to the ground. When it struck, it flared and flashed like green flame, and bounced nearly twenty feet into the air. It sputtered and sparked and glowed, clanging to the gravel and sand with a sound like thunder.

A lesser killer may have become disheartened, given in to thoughts of defeat. But Ser Hugo Saddler was the deadliest sword alive, he did not need magic. Under his high peaked helm, with its horsehair plume, Hugo grimaced. He shifted his grip, with the shield gone, there was little reason to not shift to a two-handed stance. It was the very same logic Vandre used when it came to his longsword; Hand-and-a-half. It takes a strong right arm, but you can transform yourself into a whole new fighter, simply by tossing your shield aside.

It stands that a one-handed man might not think that way, Vandre thought to himself.

Vandre of Hammerdale had killed plenty of men in his time, more than he cared to reflect on. Even in his sunsetting days, here, he imagined he could whip most of the men in this tourney. Hell, days ago, he killed four bandits, himself at the age of two-and-fifty. Suffice to say, Vandre was comfortable around a blade.

The way Hugo Saddler's gilded blade danced was art, no, it was more than that, it was death in a dance. Thrusts, parries, slashes, and jabs rained down on the Lord of Brimstone, as the Brute of the Goldengrass decided to end his practice session. First, Saddler lopped the shaft of Axe's maul, leaving only an inch. *Nothing to parry with,* Vandre watched and comprehended. The next slash cut the leather belts that bound Axe's shield to his left forearm. The kiss of Hugo's blade was so light that the scrollwork on Axe's glove was unmarred, but still the shield fell.

One handed and unarmed, a lesser knight may have become disheartened, but the Old Bull of Brimstone was too stubborn, too proud to quit. Rather than reach for his shield, he tried to headbutt Hugo.

Vandre would later swear he saw Ser Hugo Saddler smile before what came next. The Brute took a juke-step, spun and slashed with both hands, right at the throat and gorget of Lord Axe.

There was an eerie, reverent silence as every breath in the stands, every breath in the arena stopped, as the tip of Ser Hugo's blade parted another belt, the leather strap holding the devil-horned helm of Lord Axe. As Axe stumbled forward, the helm took to the sky much as *Hoofbeat* had, though without the arcane fireworks. Unhelmed and unnerved, Axe fell to the ground, a heaving heap. As he rolled to his back, the older knight gave a laughing submission, "I cannot hope to beat *that.*"

Though there was mirth in his loss, Hugo kept his sword point at the southern lord's throat for just a few seconds longer than was appropriate. To a practiced blade like Axe or Vandre, the message was clear: *I could have.*

The cheer from the Saddler stand seemed to ignore the fact that their champion was a monster. Raucous, mead soaked cries filled the air as this handsome young brute moved to the finals of the tourney. There was a creak from above, as someone was descending the stairs, slowly and deliberately. Heeled boots of cinnamon leather announced the arrival of the stately Lady Kalistah. A cruel haught hung on her pinched face, though she seemed pleased enough by her son's victory. "You there." She said, like it was his name. "I have a need for air after such a thrilling contest. You will escort me."

"I suppose I will, m'lady." He took a sharp little inhale through his nose, and hoisted himself from the wooden fencepost he had placed his back against.

His initial intent was to follow the old woman at a step, a shadow, but she chided him, "Get up here, you're not guarding a wagon of oats. Make a presentation of escorting the High Lady of your Clan, Ser."

"I ain't a knight." He stepped quickly, coming to her side.

"You're not?" She sourly snorted, "Of course you're not." She took his arm in her bony grasp, "We'll need to have my husband or one of his knights tend to that."

He bristled a little, "I'd prefer not, m'lady."

As they moved amongst the smoke and mud, little vendors selling folded parchment cups of wine, hot sausages spiced with nutmeg and sage, and other such common delicacies, Lady Kalistah practically groaned, "And why on the gods' great ground might that be?"

"Knights are supposed to be good men." He said with a dirge, "I ain't."

"Romantic." It was a reply devoid of romance. "This entire tournament has spiraled out of control." The shift in topic was sudden, as if something angry inside her could no longer be contained, a wild mare free of the stall. There was no anger in her tone, but the rage was apparent merely from the seconds-long loss of control, a single hairline crack in her mask.

"How do you mean, m'lady?" Vandre was astutely aware of what she meant, but goading her into yelling about the youth may keep her from chiding him, for a few moments longer at least. "Ser Hugo is likely to win the whole thing."

Shouts behind them signaled the beginning of the other semi-final, a match between the Prince Talor and the Snapping Turtle that Vandre had hoped to witness. Twenty or so years back, at another tourney, Vandre had crossed swords with the Snapping Turtle during a melee, and disarmed him. Until the Turtle had knocked him unconscious with his off-hand, it had been the proudest moment of Vandre's life to that point. *Duty before pleasure, I suppose.*

"Hugo is the one member of my accursed family doing his part." She sulked. "And the Selach boy, I suppose. None expected Ser Doyle to rise so high, and a blessing that." Urgency and ceremony coated her words, as if she knew she must say them, and hurried through them. "But my own brood is rebellious, despite all I have done for them. My sacrifices go unseen, because they think they know better. Do you have children, m'goodman?"

"That's a complicated question, m'lady." Vandre smirked and despite herself, a tinge of blush filled the Lady's cheeks, "At least for a man of my stripe."

"Squalling little Vandres from the Lowlands to the Wylde?"

He nodded, "Something not unlike that, yes."

"Perhaps I should have left my own babes to their own devices." She grumbled, rounding them back toward the stand, "You commons have the right of it, I think. Feed yourself or starve." She chuckled, placing her foot on the bottom stair of the rising stand, ready to return to her family, "You did well this morning." Her voice was a strange blend of firm coldness and warm, wet lust. "You will return to my chambers tomorrow morning, before dawn, and you will bathe before you do so."

Vandre nodded, "I will smell of rosewater and ambergris if it so pleases you."

She ascended out of his sight as Vandre shuddered himself against his fence post.

The old sword leaned up a bit, hoping to catch the final moments of the match between Ser Tullus and Prince Talor. In the wet heat, Tullus was soaked. Even this Lowland man was struggling as the

500

match had begun to drag on. He carried sword and board. The pauldrons of Mirebreaker's armor rose and dipped with the sheer effort of breathing.

The prince across the simple ring of sand and gravel didn't sweat, there was only a light glow of the dew of battle on his cheeks, bare and fresh and young. Though he was winded, he was not breathless, a clear advantage over Mirebreaker.

The Prince was clearly relishing the challenge, a grin on his face, as he chuckled with each strike. The tired old knight continued blocking, parrying and side-stepping, but each motion came slower and took more effort. The Prince's speed was steady as the waves on the shore. *Clang-clang-clang.*

Skill and experience were turning to ash and loam in the face of time and youth. Just watching made Vandre feel every single one of his years. Sheer grit urged the Snapping Turtle forward, and the boy prince chopped, the sword crunching the hard old cottonwood of the shield on Mirebreaker's arm.

Canny and a little pissed off, Mirebreaker cursed under his breath, trying to slash at an ankle or a knee, a wild, low sweep of the sword. The younger man deftly leapt, clearing the sluggish cut with ease. Artus gave a spinning, sweeping cut of his own, splitting the breastplate of Mirebreaker. Golden sparks flew as bronze and steel clashed. The old man roared, "Not fuckin' today, *boy!*" He smashed his little round wooden shield into Artus's gut, "I am not spent!"

Sweat and spittle flew, as this prizefighter swung his sword with aching muscles and a blazing heart. But no matter his words, he *was* spent. Pathetic was not a word Vandre wanted to use to describe the greatest knight he'd ever seen, but carried on the passing of days, it crept into the edges of his thoughts. When the Snapping Turtle stumbled and fell to a knee, the roars of the crowd fell to a sad, concerned rumble.

A black cloud crossed the silver sun, a shadow passed over the two men in the arena. The Prince held his sword, still as a stone, level as the ground itself with a smile plastered to his cheeks. His expression was joy, but his gold eyes flared fury and competition, "Ser, it is done. It is time to lay your sword down. You sparred with honor, Ser Tullus."

The Snapping Turtle placed his sword in the dirt, and lifted his helm. Rivers of sweat mixed with tears on the burly blonde knight's cheeks. He panted with effort and held back his sobs, "I… s'pose… it is, yer Grace…" He bowed his head and a rain of sweat and tears dappled the dirt he stared at, "I submit."

The picture of grace, the Prince would not gloat, he would help this honorable old knight to his feet while they both basked in an outpouring of love from the commons. As Vandre watched Tullus, he knew there would be no more tournaments for Ser Snapping Turtle, his time was over, and Vandre's was tailing it. *Not yet. I have more. I am not spent.* Another black cloud over the sun.

A Saddler serving girl rounded into sight. Vandre had seen her in the common room: bronze skin, black hair like a crow's wing, sharp little eyes of the coolest blue, like a winter sky. *Snake's eyes,* thought Vandre as she smoldered by, but he said nothing. Noting his sword and his posture, the serving girl rounded back, smiling as she poured ale from a pitcher slick with dew into his horn. He was thankful for the cold drink in the face of the overwhelming heat, though more clouds had begun to chase each other across the sun and the sky. By the time the girl was heading up the stairs, Vandre was already shaking the last drops of the ale onto his tongue.

In the yard, that young prince, the little shitsack that he was, strode. Prince Vernus was attended by his father, grim and gallant as always, and the ponderously wide Lord Executor Grigori Bridge. Bridge looked to be roasting; nearly as wide as he was tall, wrapped in pink furs and even wearing an enormous white tangle of a beard. His cheeks were cherries and his bald pate blazed red in the heat. In his hands, the old man carried a small pillow of violet velvet. On that pillow sat the twisting golden crown that had gotten the old man in so goddamn deep.

More black clouds dappled the sky, shadows swooping over the arena and those gathered in it, like raptors over shivering vermin. The air lost the edge of heat it had previously held. The Prince Vernus raised a willowy arm, calling for the silence of the commons. Once gained, Vernus filled the silence, "Thank you, thank you. Your kindness overwhelms me as always." He lowered his hand, rounding in a princely turn, "For the past three days, I have feasted on your gifts, enjoyed your hospitality, and I have had the dearest pleasure of your company." A whooping cheer went up from the Fisher stand. The Prince continued, "I have had the honor of watching thirty-two brave souls fight for glory, and I have mourned two of the bravest of those souls lost."

The grim king placed a hand on his son's shoulder and called out to his people, "My Vernus, your Prince, today begins his journey into manhood." The clouds above had grown thicker, steel grey and sworling blue, the speed of the storm notable. In the far distance, the wind rustled and rambled, a whisper of motion. Vandre felt the hairs on his neck rise, as gooseflesh prickled across his arms. *Something ain't right,* he could feel it, crackling like static.

The hardened old sword tried to lift himself from his fencepost, and found his legs jelly. He took a stumbling step, one hand on the hilt of his sword, the other on the fence beside him, as he willed himself toward the stair. He remembered the serving girl, with her snake's eyes, "S-something in…" he slurred and huffed, "the ale…"

He had to get up the stairs.

In the darkening arena, Vernus spoke as the wind rose, "And as I become a man, I shall raise a woman to royalty. I shall make a lord's daughter a Princess, and my bride." His words hung on the wind, oily and proud. Oily and proud described the pallid and fleshy Lord Amund Selach as he wound down the stair, his lovely twin daughters flanking him on each side. Vandre could not have told which girl was Elise nor which was Amelie, but he could feel those girls walking into doom.

He lurched as the distant rustle grew closer, louder, clearer. He could feel gusts whipping and ripping through the silks of the stand. The rough-hewn wooden stairs trembled and shuddered hard as the sudden storm swelled. The sun had disappeared behind a blanket of hard grey clouds. The pink puffball of a Lord raised the little cushion of violet velvet, and Vernus snatched the crown with greedy fingers. "Though every maiden I was blessed enough to meet held unique charms." He stepped behind one of the twins, lifting the crown above her black haired head.

Vandre took two stumbling steps into the box and found Clan Saddler in various states. Hellendre seemed to be as incapacitated as Vandre himself, if not more. The horned witch was fighting to stand from her chair. Lady Harlow was nowhere to be seen. Lady Joelle clung to her betrothed, and to his credit, Lord Hartwin had pulled his dagger. Ser Doyle roared fiercely in front of the High Lord and Lady who had backed themselves into a corner, feeling the same ill atmosphere creeping through Honeyhome.

Vernus leisurely crowned Lady Elise, slowly bringing the crown toward her fine black hair. "But only one lady held my heart the instant I lay my eye–"

The crown touched the girl's skull and Vernus Artus would never finish that statement, a noise came, like a splitting glacier or a crack of a great cliff about to collapse. Unsteady, it rocked Vandre's chest and set his ears to ringing. He'd like to have collapsed, if his limp body had allowed to fall. Instead he dangled, from a collar of black shadow and cold iron, hard around his neck. He would find his feet fast enough to stop from choking, but a collar of some shadow stuff had locked itself around his throat. As he raised his gaze, his guts turned to ice: every last living soul; man, woman and child, lord, king and peasant alike, was bound with a similar, ethereal black collar, and everyone of those collars was bound by a network of smoldering black iron chains.

Each one of those chains was tethered to the hole in the world where Elise Selach had stood but seconds ago. It was a hole in nothing, a hovering doorway of black, and its shadow chains had gripped the Empire by the throat.

The King himself raged in the arena, his voice a scream of fury as his gold eyes burned. His hands gripped the collar, a king's hands, wreathed in the holiest of magic flame. King Gallus burned the collar, flares like the sun itself as his hands themselves sparked and sputtered. The sputters grew greater, the glow fainter and the King's eyes lost their gold. He slouched into his collar, impotent.

Thundering rumble grew overwhelming as a thousand thousand wing beats overtook the sky. A cluttering cacophony of feathers and talons, a squall of birds, and at the head swooped a huge black screech owl. The owl took a low swoop at King Gallus, a threat with no intent of harm, a feint. It tumbled and rolled to the ground, bursting forth fierce, into a thing that was both man and bird. Vandre watched as its hard yellow eyes swept over the commons. Beside him, a great black hound stalked, though Vandre could not say where it had come from.

The black bird beast in the arena dragged its long fingers down the face of the incapacitated King Gallus, relishing victory. He spun to Prince Vernus, and did the same. Vandre watched the creature savor fear like men savor the scent of a meal.

The creature placed its hands on its temples, and with a deft little flourish, the bird man thing removed its head in one fell pull. Vandre saw the pale face of a handsome young lord peer up from the owl shaped helm he had worn.

Smoke and shadow radiated from his great black feathered mantle, his noble bearing clear in his pitiless violet eyes. He threw the helm down, and his leather gloves, tipped with hard black iron talons to the dirt. Thrilled on victory, this black bird of a prince called out, "Do not fear, I bring grand, grand tidings!"

He stroked the slathering black dog at his side, raising his arm in a great grand display, "I am Dunkan, and I am the last scion of Clan Mertens." Vandre felt his chest tighten as he strained at his own collar. This Dunkan's voice rang through the arena, "I am your Prince, and I will be your king."

From his mantle, motes of feathers floated upward, "For centuries, my line has lived in the shadows. Princess Lyra disappeared into the Unseelie Hells, and I am her get. I am the blood of your lost King Rast. The Owl Kings are near, we should never have left you." He raised a sword, a blunt ancient thing of black, shining iron. Black as the steel chain he wore. "These usurpers have failed to protect you. I will take what is mine." He pressed the sword to Gallus's throat, "My time will come soon, our apotheosis as an empire, but preparations must be made." He pulled the falchion away, "But I am not unmerciful, I am not unchivalrous."

The pale wraith of a prince called to the crowd, "Lords and ladies, you have feasted on my kingdom. You have sucked her spirit dry at the cost of her people. Good men starve while you feast full bellies." His voice was choked with sadness and rage and defiance, "You drain the very life from land and man, drive those you deem monsters into the dark, and..." Dunkan Mertens glowered, "Until you submit to your *true king*. None of you are safe."

Gallus raised his face, murmuring defiance, but it was too faint to hear. Dunkan the Coronox leaned to the Grim King's straining face, "When I kill you, aberration, it will be on the field of battle, like that man you imitate."

Vandre choked, his collar had grown tight, and the chain taut, it pulled him forward, and the cries around him indicated he was not alone in this. As suddenly as this pull had bid him forward, yanked him toward the hole in the world, it ceased.

"I am not unmerciful." He repeated, "I could have claimed every soul in this place, but I will only take nine, as penance for blood given. I will take nine of you bandits-who-call-yourselves-Lords." Black flame coated motes of feather and shadow and smoke, these bits of puff grew. They grew heads and torsos. They grew black wings and hard talons. Nine little puffs of feather had become nine twisted man-bird-beasts, and they circled their prince, in want of command. "Those of you that remain will be granted mercy as long as you kneel."

He bid his dog step into the black doorway in the air, and shortly strode toward it himself, "I will return and I will return in force, for my throne. I will come to shatter this empire of glutton-lords and I will free you all from such *bondage*." He gave his command, "You may each have *one.*"

The screech may have come from shattering shadow steel as the chain and collars shattered like glass. The screech may have come from the hole in the world knitting itself shut, healing like a wound in the air. The screech may have come from the owl-beasts, but it didn't matter. Dunkan the Coronox was gone. Vandre was free and two of those awful fucking birds were swooping for Clan Saddler's box.

The sword he had not swung came clean from its scabbard, and before another thought could cross the old man's mind, he had shoved himself to the front of the little gazebo, and gave this bird a taste of hate. *I am not spent.*

The creature was leaner than it had looked initially and one snapping slash had opened most of its torso. Vandre managed to finish it with his boot crushing its temple with a squelch, and turned to survey the scene around him. Hartwin and Joelle were drenched in gouts of black blood. The Young Colt had managed to open the creature's throat when it lunged for them, "Some fucking bodyguard you are, Vandre."

"Sorry, boss." he heaved, "I was otherwise engaged."

Vandre shuffled to the railing, he needed to see where the rest of these black raptors had gone:

The Big Bronze Kraken, Rolof Deepreach, stood over the broken body of one, though it clutched some bloody corpse in its sharp talons.

Another one lay battered at the feet of a pretty girl in red, lips trembling under big buck teeth. Two children huddled behind her. The dead bird's skull was crushed, and the young mother held a shattered pitcher of ale.

At the base of the Curr stand, one of the birds had been shoved over the rail and now lay shattered in the dirt. Ellari Curr sobbed over the rail.

The Little Mirebreaker boy held a dagger in his shaking left hand, doused in black blood as one of these feathered fiends shuddered and bled at his feet. Beside Slade Mirebreaker, an old southern lord had been cleaved in half.

A furious Illystre Coldhearth had one dying at his feet as well. He had thrown daggers into each of its eyes, and it had fallen inches from his sister. The Lord of Spies raged under his breath.

In the royal box, Queen Natasha bled profusely from a wound to the shoulder, but the bird who touched her had been slashed to ribbons by that young Grey Duck. The queen winced and moaned, but looked like she lived.

From the low area where the men prepared to enter the arena, both Ser Hugo and Prince Talor fumbled, both boys covered in deep cuts. They drug a dead or dying owlman between them.

I am not spent, but perhaps I ought to be.

Behind him, Vandre heard the dead bird shift. Vandre rounded as the thing wheezed. His sword was in his off-hand. He was too old, too slow. The owl shrieked, and Vandre felt talons on his face; black and the fading of the light.

TALOR III

"Laugh, goddamn you, don't you see the joke? Don't you see how funny it is?"

The Crown Prince, Talor Artus, sat in the dark hold of his personal schooner, *Zeal,* as the little brown boat bobbed northward on choppy seas and under grey skies heavy with omen. It had been four days since the Faefall, since the first recorded Unseelie incursion in centuries, and Talor had only managed to grab fleeting moments of sleep at all. He has kept to himself these last days, a sullen, dour phantom where a charming young prince had been.

He had kept alone, taken meager meals alone, kept no counsel, save for his companion in the shadows. *Zeal* shifted in the wind, and Talor gripped his sword in his hand, and leaned hard on it, gouging the floor at his feet.

He had not swung it since Mertens had threatened his kingdom.

The Owl Prince had taken four souls from the stands, though he wanted nine, which was a small blessing. Four of his citizens were dead, and he had failed. He drank in the darkness, and tried to break his chest free into breath.

"You are near as grim as the old man." His companion's voice rang out, "Heh, yer even starting to look like him."

Talor refused to respond to the jab, though his confidante had heard it all over the previous few days. Mocking, and cruel, the voice had been needling him constantly for days, droning ever on.

"Heh, did I finally get to you?"

Talor spoke, his voice raw with disuse, "You are a joke."

"The *joke*," came a rattling wheeze of laughter, "...is that you think the structures and rituals you hide behind might be your savior." Talor lifted his head, hearing his companion lurch to his feet and shuffle in the shadows. "The joke is that those things nearly killed you and Saddler. Two big bad knights barely escaped alive, but a mother and a cripple managed to kill them big, black turkeys and walk away without a scratch."

"We are lucky that Lady Stagg and the Mirebreaker boy are unharmed, Tymm." He gave his tormentor its name, and it laughed again, burbling and low.

"They are, sure." Light from the porthole caught the companion's eyes and flashed like an animal in the twilight, a hunter pouncing. "Nothing fiercer than someone who knows they're about to die." Its cackle was rising, holding nothing but scorn, "I'm lucky enough to know all about that, Talor."

He would not answer.

He would not take the bait or fall into the trap.

The thing feasted on his despair and the Prince would feed it no further, "Fuck you."

The glint in the eyes grew gold, a gold that matched Talor's, "Language, language. Hahah." More mocking cackles, "You don't sound like a prince, do you?"

Talor leaned on his gold sword, "I am enough." The words came through cracked, dry lips, they came from a voice worn thin from pain and regret, "I will be more." The boy prince stood on trembling legs, "And you will be another unpleasant nightmare. You will leave me now." He raised his sword to the darkness, "I would be alone."

There came a heavy step, squelching wet. Then another. And another, Talor felt the sword shake in his grasp, his arms feeble. He would not show fear.

A shock of red hair, brown freckles splashed over his pale skin, green eyes filled with hate.

A bone white smile.

Smilin' Jack Tymm lurched from the shadows, a corpse suspended on oily strands, glinting with golden light, "You will never be alone again, heheh. You and me, we are in this together, Your Grace."

Talor retched on an empty stomach, bile flooded his mouth as there was nothing else, "Please…"

Something black and aberrant and eldritch hulked and slumped behind this revenant, something black and blue and gold pulled at Tymm's strings, "Save your prayers, Prince." It leaned low, dripping wet with seawater, " Save them for your owl, your Dunkan." The strands writhed, black worms working through Tymm's flesh. They pulled, lifting Tymm's dead green eyes to Talor's face, "You are wasting them on me. I'm inside your head, boy."

There's someone in my head, and it's not me.

The strings of black abominable death twisted the Jester's face into a rictus grin, hooks of ebony pulling the corners of his mouth tight over gums going moldering with rot, "Unless of course, you can murder me again."

The breath from his maw stank of death, but fouler still was the rank stench of doom and despair clinging to his words.

Fly, Crown of Night, fly.

APPENDIX

THE HIGH CLANS AND THEIR NATIONS

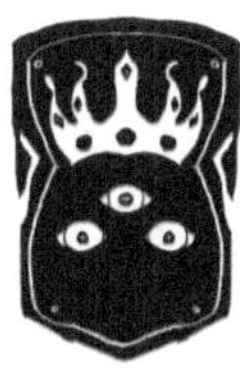

THE HIGH CLAN OF AVALAR, DANEAU, OZWYK AND HER NATIONS

CLAN ARTUS OF AVALAR

High Emperors, sorcerers. Able to enchant man, beast and monster alike. The Artus family claims descent from the stars and their good looks, flashing gold eyes, dark hair and otherworldly charisma speak to that. They were once humble stewards and advisors to the old Unicorn Kings of Avalar, but through marriage and other means, have united Avalar, Daneau and Ozwyk under a single Imperial Throne. They gained the Isles of Avalar in 387 AU, when the last Unicorn King of Clan Avalar killed himself. They became sovereigns of Daneau in 500 AU, when the last Owl King of Clan Mertens disappeared. Ozwyk would eventually fall under their purview in 772 AU, when the Chimera Kings knelt.

KING GALLUS ARTUS III, In his 13th year of rule, GALLUS ARTUS is a popular king with the lords and smallfolk alike. A mercurial man, most of the actual ruling of his empire is accomplished by his LORDS ASCENDANT. Artus spends most of his time in meditations or meetings with his sorcerers.

HIS HOUSEHOLD

-QUEEN NATASHA HARLOCK, *his wife, known as 'The Witch Queen.'*

-CROWN PRINCE TALOR ARTUS, *his heir, wed to* **KIARA REAVE** *of Ozwyk.*

-HOBAR *and* **SELORA,** *their wee children*

-PRINCE VERNUS ARTUS *is coming to manhood at this event.*

-PRINCESS BARA, *a precocious girl of eight.*

-THE DOWAGER QUEEN TARA MIREBREAKER, *the king's widowed mother*

HIS COUNCIL OF LORDS ASCENDANT

-LORD GRIGORI BRIDGE *of Cobalt Bridge, THE LORD EXECUTOR, the King's right hand.*

-LORD VARYON CLEARCALL *of Dawnhorn, THE LORD OF DEFENSE*

-LADY CARELIN MARLE *of Old Salt, THE LADY ADMIRAL*

-LORD ILLYSTRE COLDHEARTH *of Three Tall Towers, THE LORD OF SPIES*

-LORD HINRIC SADDLER *of Stonestall, THE LORD OF TRADE AND FINANCE*

-LORD CLIFTON TORCHBEARER *of Lake Light Beacon, THE LORD OF JUDGMENT*

-**HIGH LEARNER FRANZ,** *The Grand Pedagogue and Greatest Theriac*

HIS SWORN SWORDS

THE GREY GUARD OF THE SHINING COMMAND

-**SER COLE CANDEN** *of Sheepsvale*

-**SER AUBERON SOZEN** *of Black Pearl Bay*

-**SER JURGEN SHORESHRIKE** *of Galder's Net*

-**SER GNASH SELACH** *of Brinegate*

-**SER DARWYN TYMM** *of Leaper's Ledge*

-**SER DRAKE CANAR** *of San Canar*

Brothers of the Grey Guard serve for life. When one is killed, the high emperor and the Liege Lord of the Kingdom represented by the deceased knight submit candidates to the remaining brothers, who elect a new member of their order from among them.

HIS SWORN FOLK ON THE ISLE OF AVALAR

-**LORD LUCIUS CUTFREY** *of Sharpshore*

-**LORD VIRGIL MARIANOS** *of Sunset Rock*

    -**DANTE,** *his son and heir*

        -**HOMER,** *his son, squire to ILLYSTRE COLDHEARTH*

-**LADY DARCIE AQUILA** *of Tidefall*

-**LORD ERRON REDSTAR** *of Ruby Beach*

-**THE SOJOURNED LEARNER VAUGHN,** *a wandering wiseman, a guest of the Crown*

THE HIGH CLAN OF THE WYLDE
CLAN CURR OF RIME RIVER

Stern lords of a frozen steppe, coursed with icy rivers, The Curr never submitted to rule from Avalar, joining The Empire only through marriage and gifts. The tall, stern Currs tend toward a lean frame and smoky features. Icy eyed, the Curr family members often go prematurely grey.

HIGH LORD HULLEN CURR III is a precise, ordered man. He is a just ruler and avid hunter, loving nothing more than the woods and his trained pack of hounds. He has ruled over a peaceful period in the Wylde, only riding with his men to deal with up-jumped bandit lords, not open rebellion. He's ruled capably for fifteen years with his wife by his side.

HIS HOUSEHOLD

-LADY GAIL WOODBJORN, *his Lady Wife*

-HULLEN CURR IV, *his son and heir*

> **-ELLARI CURR,** *his wife, and LADY EXECUTOR to the HIGH LORD HULLEN CURR III*

> **-SER HALE TORCHBEARER, SER CHADDAR GOLDENLOCK, AND SER ESBEN HORNBLOWER,** *HULLEN IV's sworn swords*

-MASHA CURR, *His Maiden Daughter*

-DEVLIN CURR, *His second son, currently serving as a squire at Korpiklaani.*

-ERON CURR, *His third son, pudgy and stoop shouldered*

-JASMINE MIREBREAKER and **DARYON CURR,** *the widow of the Liege Lord's youngest brother, and her son.*

-LEARNER MAESH, *a healer and teacher*

-MISS MAEVE, *the Head Stewardess*

HIS SWORN WYLDEFOLK

-LORD CLIFTON TORCHBEARER *of Lake Light Beacon*

> **-SER CARLIN TORCHBEARER,** *his son who rules as lord, while the Lord serves on Council.*

-LORD CALDER GREENEYE *of Korpiklaani*

> **-LADY VELDA CURR,** *his wife, sister to the liege lord*

-**LORD GYLES HORNBLOWER** *of Port O' Plenty, a boy of six, and* **LADY FICKE TALLMAN***, his mother and regent*

-**LORD IVAN HELM** *of Frostfruit*

-**LADY BARNA LUDNA** *of Jasperfelt*

-**LORD CZELAW SHORESHRIKE** *of Galder's Net*

-**LORD STOFFEL JYTTE** *of Grey Pine*

-**LORD LEOPOLD JYTTE** *of Seawatch-on-the-Ice*

-**LORD HERLIEF MORS***, of Mors Point*

-**LORD REINHELT GODDAR** *of The Whorl*

-**LORD RED RONNIE TALLMAN** *of The Ivory Longhall*

-**LADY DANIKA SNOBJORN** *of The Hollow HIll*

THE HIGH CLAN OF THE GOLDENGRASS

CLAN SADDLER OF STONESTALL

The Horse Lords first gained wealth and power from breeding the finest horses in Daneau. "From war to plough, from reins to bridle to saddle, no finer friend than a horse or a Saddler." The genial Saddlers are hardworking, honest and well beloved and they've turned that reputation into a merchant empire. Though they've expanded far beyond the pasture, the studs and stallions of Stonestall are never far from the heart of the Saddler business empire. The Saddlers tend to be plain looking, strong bodied and good hearted.

Few expect **HIGH LORD BYRONY SADDLER** to be eloquent, intelligent, kind and fair, but the big beast of man certainly is. He is one of the finest economic minds in the realm, and has an enormous heart. Gentle, without giving up his pride, Saddler is well loved by both his lords bannerman and his smallfolk. He is unconcerned with the trappings of heraldry, often holding court in his horse paddock to the horror of his lady wife. Saddler cares for the well being of his people and the health of his herd, above all. His old black warhorse, *Agro*, is his dearest companion of decades.

HIS HOUSEHOLD

-LADY KALISTAH MALBES, *his wife*

-HARTWIN SADDLER, *his eldest son and heir, the first triplet*

-SER HUGO SADDLER, *his second son, the middle triplet*

-HARLOW SADDLER, *his maiden daughter, the third triplet*

-HELLENDRE, *the personal attendant to Lady Kalistah, an ifre'croi and a sorceress*

-EUNA SADDLER, *sister to the high Lord*

    -BASTIEN SELACH, *her husband*

        -BYRELLE SELACH *their daughter and her husband,* **SER BARIN REDSTAR**

        -SER DOYLE SELACH, *their son, a knight*

-SER ISSAC SADDLER, *brother to the high lord*

    -ORYLIA ALBIN, *his wife*

-LORD HINRIC SADDLER, *brother to the high lord, Lord of Trade and Finance*

-LEARNER POWELL, *a teacher and healer*

HIS SWORN LORDS OF THE GOLDENGRASS

-LORD DOBSON MALBES *of Honeyhome.*

-LORD EZRA CANDEN *of Sheepsvale*

-LORD MORTIMER OSPREY *of Talon Bay*

-LADY ZAKARIA LAVICA *of The Leonmont*

-LORD MABIN ALBIN *of Hope's Hill*

-LORD GENO DOLAN *of Codd Stone*

-LORD POE VELLEN *of Spring o' Blue*

HIGH CLAN OF THE LOWLANDS

CLAN MIREBREAKER OF OKOBOJI

The moormen are bombastic, loud and powerful, men who dine on spicy peppers and wrestle the scaly beasts of the swamp. Short and hirsute, some claim dwarven blood flows in the Mirebreaker hearts. The Mirebreakers were raised to the high seat at Okoboji after Clan Niles rose with six other Clans in rebellion. Clan Niles was extinguished and the Mirebreakers were given their lands, rights, duties and honors.

At the tender age of fifteen, **HIGH LORD MARTEN MIREBREAKER** became the Liege Lord of Okoboji, after losing his parents (**Gellen Mirebreaker and Burana Haymaker**) to a fiery fever that ripped through the province. Marten is a smart, charming boy, skilled with a spear and bow. His Uncle, **Tullus**, serves as castellan and his most trusted advisor. As he is now eighteen, his uncle pressures him to marry.

HIS HOUSEHOLD

   -**SLADE MIREBREAKER,** *brother to the high lord, a scholar*

   -**JAMEN MIREBREAKER,** *brother to the high lord, a boy of nine*

   -**SER TULLUS MIREBREAKER,** *uncle to the high lord*

      -**LADY CARMINE LILY,** *his wife*

   -**GAR THE SMITHEE,** *a hulking smith*

-LEARNER GRACEL, *a teacher and healer*

HIS SWORN SWAMP LORDS

-LORD FALANT LILY *of Frog Pond*

-LORD JAKUB CORALSPEAR *of Coralspear Cape*

-LADY JOELLE BRIDGE *of Cobalt Bridge*

    -LORD GRIGORI BRIDGE, *her uncle*

-LORD ARONST BLACKCART *of Horek's Hill*

-LORD AMUND SELACH *of Brinegate*

-LADY MORNA PLOVER *of Hammerdale*

-LADY PRYMM HAYMAKER *of Sweet Orchard*

-LADY LILITH SAGE *of Mistwatch*

-LORD LUKAS AXE *of Brimstone*

-LADY MELAUGH "GREENFINGERS" FEVERFEW *of the Witchwood.*

HIGH CLAN OF THE GREATWOOD, MOUNTAINS OF ORRE AND COLDWATER LAKES

CLAN IRONARM OF DEEPSTEEL

The Ironarms are traditionally tall, hirsute and broad chested. These are men and women who earned their place through ferocity in battle and hard work.

Unlike most of the men of his family, **HIGH LORD TORVALD IRONARM** is tall, pale and sickly. He's an intelligent and well-educated man, with a deep interest in magic and the elements, possibly explaining his marriage to a witch of Coldhearth.

HIS HOUSEHOLD

-**LADY ISOLDE COLDHEARTH,** *his wife*

-**LADY GRETE IRONARM,** *sister to the high lord*

-**SER MANDEL STAGG,** *her husband*

-**SER REUBEN STAGG,** *their son and heir to the high lord*

-**LADY LILAH RASK,** *his wife*

-**OALLA STAGG,** *their daughter*

-**SER JOSIAH TYMM,** *her husband*

-**LADY RELE IRONARM,** *sister to the high lord*

-SER RUDOLF FURROW, *her husband*

-LEARNER SEPTUMBUS, *a teacher and healer*

-TOTHO, *a strange halfling attendant to the High Lady*

HIS SWORN BANNERMEN OF THE MOUNTAINS, WOOD AND LAKES

-LORD PAI'DRAIG WOODBJORN *of Starlight Shore*

-LORD WILMAR BRAZTON *of Steamsong*

-LORD VARYON CLEARCALL *of Dawnhorn*

> **-SER VASANT CLEARCALL,** *brother to the lord, rules in his place as the lord serves on the Council.*

-LORD ARDAL COLDHEARTH *of Three Tall Towers*

> **-LORD ILLYSTRE COLDHEARTH,** *his son, the Lord of Spies.*

-LADY DONLA RASK *of Nuttley*

> **-SER SABBAT OF THE ACORN CLUTCH,** *her husband*

> **-LADY DOREEN RASK,** *her sister*

-LORD SHARMAN STAGG *of Bronzebough*

-LORD KIER SOZEN *of Black Pearl Bay*

*HIGH CLAN OF THE WETLAND FISHER KINGDOMS AND THE
SCATTERED RAIDER ISLES*

CLAN FISHER OF ROGUE'S REST

Never the biggest or the strongest, the men of Clan Fisher rose to
prominence through social climbing and seizing every opportunity.
When the feuding wetland kingdoms were forged into a single realm,
the Fishers scrapped their way to high lordship. When the Scattered
Islands were deemed too wild and dangerous to remain a
semi-sovereign state, Clan Marle was forced to kneel before the wild
little racoon kings. They may be down, but this scrappy house is never
out.

Once a sly politician, trader, and smuggler, no one can accuse **HIGH
LORD LUDO FISHER** of leaving his life half lived. Possibly owing
to some blood of Cuddy Cutfrey, Ludo Fisher was much the same
manner of men, though less well regarded. He sailed far and wide on
his tall, three masted *Masked Bandit.* As a matter of fact, he's outlived
two wives, three sons and a grandson, leaving his inheritance a house
of cards that has left the Racoon house divided.

His household has divided itself into three clans locked into a cold war
for the inheritance, The Ducks, The Bears, and the Vultures, named for
the matriarch of each faction.

HIS HOUSEHOLD

THE DUCKS

-LADY ROSALYN CANAR, *the widow of the Lord's eldest son*

-LADY CECILY FISHER, *her daughter, the Lord's eldest grandchild*

-SER SANCHO MADAPPLE, *her husband, a knight of brutal renown*

-REMY MADAPPLE, *their son*

-LADY TILDA MARLE, *the widow of his eldest Grandson*

-LELAND FISHER, *her son, a claimant to the Lordship, a boy of thirteen*

THE BEARS

- LADY PETULA DOLAN, *the widow of The Lord's second son*

-LADY THANA FISHER, *her maiden daughter, a tinkerer*

-CALUN FISHER, *the High Lord's oldest living grandson, a claimant to the Lordship. A boy of sixteen*

-LADY WERNJA SWOTT, *the widow of The Lord's fourth son*

-MOSS FISHER, *her son*

THE VULTURES

-LADY LARISSA GORGE, *the young wife of the High Lord*

-KARL FISHER, *their son, The Lord's only living son, a claimant to the Lordship, a boy of nine.*

-SER ROLOF DEEPREACH, *a knight of brutal renown, sworn sword to Lady Larissa*

-LEARNER LIZAN, *a teacher and healer, he serves all three factions and the Lord with no bias*

HIS SWORN LORDS AND LADIES OF THE WETLANDS AND ISLANDS

-LADY AGNES MARLE *of Old Salt*

-LORD VULTON GORGE *of Starving Craig*

-LORD MALCOM CANAR *of San Canar*

-LORD HUBERT POLIS DEEPREACH *of Ryleh*

-LORD SAWYL MADAPPLE *of The Witchwood*

-LORD FERRER BLEAKE *of Bleachbone Beach*

-LORD ERN CORK *of Long Oar*

-LORD MERVYN SWOTT *of The Far Fort*

-LORD SHARGA MOORBJORN *of Honeyvine Swamp*

-LORD ERASMUS GRIMGRIN *of The Dour March*

      -LADY ADELPHA GRIMGRIN, his sister and heir

-LORD LIAM CROWE *of Strawman's Hollow*

-LORD GERARD FURROW *of Harvest Hearth*

THE NOBLE COURT OF OZWYK

THE COURT OF CLAN REAVE

The Reaves still style themselves the "Chimera Kings", but have bent the knee in submission to their old allies and rivals, The Empire of Avalar and its Clan Artus. Decades of blight have been afflicting their island from the east, taking half of the island, The Haunted Wastes of Ayre. The Court of Reave has led the effort to stem this tide, eventually sacrificing their patriarch, house weapon and enormous stores of elemental magic somewhere in the Nine Foggy Hells. This desperate act after decades of struggle has led to a stalemate with the encroaching blight, but has left the Courts of Ozwyk depleted to the point that an alliance with the Empire had to become a submission. The Empire gains the powerful, mysterious and magical lands of Ozwyk, and Ozwyk gains soldiers to guard from the monsters on their borders.

HIGH LORD KARAS REAVE was always an intelligent, careful young man, but after absorbing the full force of the blast that killed his father, he's been left a scarred, burning mass of magic and twisted flesh. He's learned to "see" things unseen with his burned eye and can manifest flame from his burned left hand. He remains intelligent and patient, but now has an air of melancholy. He hides his face behind hoods and masks, only removing them around in the privacy of his personal household. He is a good father and dutiful husband. He's liked well enough by his lords, and his people find him strange and eccentric, but good hearted, calling him "The Burned Prince".

HIS HOUSEHOLD

-**LADY UNA TEMBER,** *his wife, strange and unusual*

    -**VARAGON and KIMBER,** *their children; a boy and girl*

-**ATHENA WEBB,** widowed *mother to the High Lord, Ser Kyne and Lady Kiara*

-**SER KYNE REAVE,** *brother to High Lord, a One-Eyed Warlock Knight*

-**LADY KIARA REAVE,** *sister to the High Lord, wed to the Crown Prince*

-**SER DALAS REAVE,** *Uncle to the High Lord, younger brother to his late Lord Father, a widower and dedicated father*

    -**LANABEL REAVE,** *his daughter*

-**LADY DIANE REAVE,** *Aunt to the High Lord, younger sister to his late Lord Father*

    -**SER CABOT GOLDENLOCKE,** *her husband*

        -**COLBY GOLDENLOCKE,** *their son, a tourney knight who is yet to be knighted*

-**LEARNER PADILLA,** *a teacher and healer*

HIS SWORN COURTS AND CITIES

-**LORD VIN TEMBER** *of Cold Lake, brother to the High Lady*

    -**LADY INEZ TEMBER,** *his youngest sister, a spearwoman*

-**LORD PURVIN WEBB** *of Blackstone*

-**LADY AGATHA HARLOCK** *of Belleden, Aunt to Queen Natasha Harlock*

-**LORD DECIMUS PURESPRING** *of Purespring Deep*

-LORD ARKADY WYRE *of Breakshore*

-LORD IAONE GRANT *of Savagescale Isle*

    -LADY EOSTRE, *his wife, born on the continent. They rule as one.*

-LORD PROVO GOLDENLOCKE *of Borrowhall, father of Ser Chaddar of Rime River*

-LADY VADALI SMITH *of Wildcat Rush*

-LORD "SMILIN' JACK" TYMM *of Leaper's Ledge*

New roads ahead...

The World of Gyent and the Empire of Avalar hold many more adventures and stories, and I cannot wait to discover them alongside you.

The second Faefall novel is well underway as of this printing, and will likely be in the wild before too long.

There are too many people I need to thank. Ben– my reader, my dreamer, my boy, who named our little press. Quinn–my sweet, daring girl, always looking for dragons to ~~slay~~ befriend. To Zac, who's been a better friend than any man deserves, I hope he doesn't mind the broad strokes of him I borrowed, but it's hard not to look to the best people you know when you're trying to build heroes.

This book, this world. This is a dream of mine that you now hold in your hands. Thank you for sharing my dream.

I hope you stay to see how wild it gets.

-Preston Nelson

July '25